Praise for *Murder Under the Bridge*

"Raphael has created a wonderful cast—most especially her Palestinian police-woman, Rania—and a taut, page-turning plot. But the real star here is the setting. When an immigrant is murdered, Rania's investigations take her directly into the treacherous, deadly politics of Israel and Palestine. Authoritatively and vividly rendered, *Murder Under the Bridge* is a compelling read."

—**Karen Joy Fowler**, PEN/Faulkner Prize–winning author of *We Are All Completely Beside Ourselves* and *The Jane Austin Book Club*

"One of the best mysteries I've read in a long time. Kept me from doing ten important things I should have been doing, because I just had to finish it! Kate Raphael writes great women characters and does a fantastic job of portraying the realities of Palestinian life as background to a gripping story."

—**Starhawk**, best-selling author of *The Fifth Sacred Thing* and *The Spiral Dance*

"A stunning mystery novel by a talented new writer. Anyone picking up the book will be drawn in by Rania and Chloe, a dynamic, realistic pair of women sleuths who bridge cultural divide and distrust to investigate a death on the Israeli–Palestinian border. Raphael's experience in the Middle East adds convincing detail to this compassionate and suspenseful tale. An outstanding addition to the global mystery field. More, please!"

—**Sujata Massey**, Agatha Award–winning author of *The Sleeping Dictionary*

"Kate Raphael gives us smart, complex women who challenge the boundaries of states and expand the boundaries of mysteries. This is a great read!"

—**Elana Dykewomon**, Lambda Award–winning author of *Beyond the Pale*

"This riveting story provides a rich portrait of life behind the headlines of the Israeli–Palestinian conflict."

—**Ayelet Waldman**, author of *Love and Treasure*

"Strong and complex female characters, a unique and vividly drawn setting, and an utterly compelling story—Kate Jessica Raphael offers you everything you could possibly want in a page-turning mystery. Let's hope this is the first of many novels to come."

—**Elaine Beale**, author of *Murder in the Castro*

Murder under the bridge

Murder under the bridge

a palestine mystery

Kate Jessica Raphael

SHE WRITES PRESS

Published 2015
Printed in the United States of America
ISBN: 978-1-63152-960-3
Library of Congress Control Number: 2015951294

For information, address:
She Writes Press
1563 Solano Ave #546
Berkeley, CA 94707

She Writes Press is a division of SparkPoint Studio, LLC.

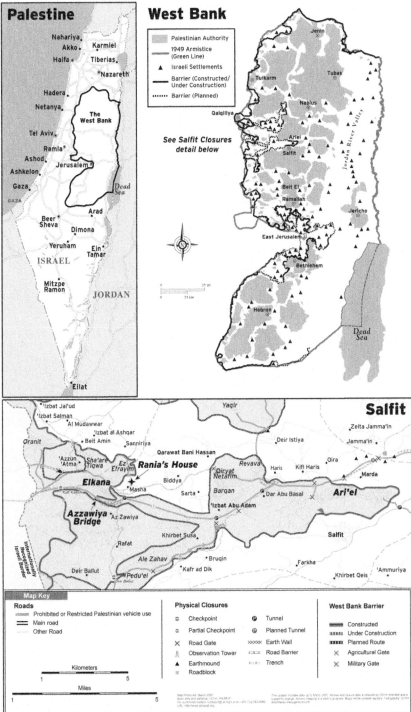

Palestine

Nahariya.
Akko. Karmiel
Haifa. Tiberias.
*Nazareth.

Hadera.
Netanya.
                The
                West Bank
Tel Aviv.

Ramla*
Ashod.
Ashkelon.   Jerusalem*
Gaza.   Dead
GAZA   Sea
                        Arad.
Beer *
Sheva. Dimona.

    Yeruham.   Ein*
                 Tamar
ISRAEL

    Mitzpe
    Ramon.   JORDAN

                        *Eilat

West Bank

▨	Palestinian Authority
-----	1949 Armistice (Green Line)
▲	Israeli Settlements
──	Barrier (Constructed/ Under Construction)
•••••	Barrier (Planned)

See Salfit Closures detail below

Jenin

Tulkarm   Tubas

            Nablus
Qalqiliya
                    Ariel
                    Salfit

            Beit El
        Ramallah   Jericho

    East Jerusalem

                Bethlehem

    Hebron
                            Dead
                            Sea

0   25 mi
0   25 km

Jordan River Valley

Salfit

'Izbat Jai'ud   Yaqir
'Izbat Salman
    Al Mudawwar   Zeita Jamma'in
        'Izbat al Ashqar
Oranit   • Beit Amin   Sanniriya   Deir Istiya   Jamma'in
                    Qarawat Bani Hassan
'Azzun Sha'are Ez   Revava   Qira
'Atma   Tiqwa Efrayim Rania's House Qiryat   Kifl Haris
                                Netafim   Haris
Elkana   Biddya   Barqan   Dar Abu Basal   Ari'el
            •Masha   Sarta •   'Izbat Abu Adam   Marda
Azzawiya   Az Zawiya
Bridge   Khirbet Suša   Salfit
        Rafat
International   Ale Zahav •Bruqin   Farkha
Recognized   •Kafr ad Dik   'Ammuriya
Israeli Border Deir Ballut •Pedu'el   Khirbet Qeis

Map Key

Roads
⬛⬛ Prohibited or Restricted Palestinian vehicle use
═══ Main road
---- Other Road

Kilometers
1   5
Miles
1   5

Physical Closures

⊜	Checkpoint	⊕	Tunnel
⊜	Partial Checkpoint	⊕	Planned Tunnel
✕	Road Gate	⋊⋉	Earth Wall
⌇	Observation Tower	⊏⊐	Road Barrier
▲	Earthmound	⊏⊐	Trench
▨	Roadblock		

West Bank Barrier

▨▨▨	Constructed
▨▨▨	Under Construction
▨▨▨	Planned Route
✕	Agricultural Gate
✕	Military Gate

Map Produced March 2007
Basic data and statistics: OCHA, PA/MOP
For comments or contact: kvidhani@un.org or tel +(972) (02) 5829962
URL: http://www.ochaopt.org

This update includes data up to March 2007. Access and closure data is collected by OCHA field staff and is
subject to change. Access mapping is a work in progress. Maps will be updated regularly. Cartography: OCHA
Information Management Unit

A note about names

Formal Palestinian names have four parts: first name, father's name, grandfather's name and family name. In official situations, a person might be called by two, three or all four names. Once someone has a son, he or she is known as "Abu" (father) or "Um" (mother) and the name of the eldest son. (In some communities, people use the name of the eldest child, son or daughter.) Using the honorific is a sign of both respect and affection. Typically, at least in villages, family members and childhood friends call one another by their first names, and everyone else uses the honorific Abu or Um. In this book, for example, the mayor's brother calls him Thamer but everyone else calls him Abu Jawad. When I was a human rights monitor in Salfit, we spent a fair amount of our time asking, "Which Um Mohammed do you mean," and the person might say, "Nawal Um Mohammed," meaning her first name was Nawal, or they might say, "Um Mohammed who lives near the school."

Israelis generally use first names in every situation. Even Palestinians call Israeli police or army commanders by their first names most of the time. This informality does not connote friendship.

Chapter 1

Rania placed the little brass coffee pot on the flame, resting one hand on the long handle so she could snatch it up before it boiled over. Her mouth tingled in anticipation as she inhaled the cardamom-laced steam.

"The boss wants you," said Abdelhakim at her elbow. The man must wear sheepskin soles, he crept up on her so silently. His cherubic good looks were spoiled by a permanent smirk.

Rania reached for the knob to quench the flame, but he held out a hand to stop her. He grasped the pot's handle as she let it go, taking care that their hands did not touch. She tried not to let the thought of him drinking her coffee gnaw at her, as she went into the captain's office.

"There is a situation in Azzawiya," Captain Mustafa said. His roly-poly frame spilled out of his overstuffed leather chair.

"What kind of situation?" asked Rania.

"One requiring great tact."

Rania knew the captain well enough to take this as a warning, not a compliment. She was not known for her tact.

Captain Mustafa cleared his throat. Suddenly self-conscious, Rania removed her head scarf. The men were still learning to accept her in this job. Traditionally, women were nurses, engineers and teachers, more recently a few were doctors. Women as police detectives was a new concept. Wearing the *hijab* made the men she worked with feel like they were talking to one of their sisters or cousins; taking it off made it possible for them to treat her like a colleague. To her it was not important. Sometimes she told her friends, "I think more clearly without something between my brain and the sun," but in fact she felt the same, whether she was wearing it or not.

"A car is abandoned on top of the bridge," Captain Mustafa said.

1

"A Palestinian car?"

"Yellow plates," he answered.

An Israeli car on an Israeli road. Why should the Palestinian police care about that?

"The Yahud say that the car is stolen," her boss continued. "The jesh have closed the road under the bridge and no one can pass on foot or by car."

Rania understood now why she was being sent on this errand. Mas'ha was her adopted home, her husband's village. If the Israeli army had closed the road between Mas'ha and Azzawiya, it would be necessary to find another way to approach, and she knew the land. She would know many of the people waiting to pass the roadblock and would have a plausible excuse for being there. A woman could surreptitiously gather information, while a Palestinian man moving around an army roadblock asking questions would not last long. The captain hoped she could find out who did what with that stolen car before the army did. She would deliver, if it killed her.

She tied the scarf around her hair again, grabbed her purse and removed a bag of supplies from her desk drawer.

"Tread lightly," Captain Mustafa called after her.

Rania didn't bristle at the caution. It was his job to remind her of things she was likely to forget. On the other hand, she was unlikely to heed his advice.

* * *

She walked out into the street, squinting in the bright spring sunlight. She wondered if she had time to run into the shop for a coffee. Every night, she told herself she would get up early enough to make herself a cup. But every morning when her alarm rang at half past five, she shut it off and did not get up until six. By then she just had time to get Khaled up and ready for school before she had to leave. Since the Israelis put up the roadblocks, she often suggested to Bassam that they rent a little house in Salfit City so she could walk to work. She would love to be away from her mother-in-law's prying eyes, but Bassam did not want to leave his village. He liked being the center of his mother's universe.

She spied a collective taxi, a seven-seat orange Mercedes, at the corner, so she gave up on the coffee and dashed to the car. Two men sat silently in the middle seat, one reading a newspaper, the other talking on his mobile. The one on the phone scooched forward so she could climb awkwardly into the back, gathering her *jilbab* in one hand to ensure she didn't show anything improper. The fiftyish driver stood next to the open front door, smoking and joking with a friend.

"I am in a hurry," she called out the window. "I can pay the rest of the fares." It could take ten minutes or more to fill the three empty seats. She couldn't afford to wait that long. At least, she didn't want to.

"No problem," the driver said. He ground out the cigarette on the side of the car and climbed into the front seat.

The drive was one of her favorites in Palestine, giving a spectacular view of beautifully groomed olive terraces, the stately buildings of the city visible in the distance. The best thing about the view of the hills was that there were no Israeli settlements in sight. For those few kilometers, which took about twenty minutes to pass, she could almost believe that Palestine was as it had always been.

Today, she was too nervous to enjoy the drive. She wanted to justify her boss's confidence in her by finding something to keep him one step ahead of the Israelis. But she hated working so close to home. Mas'ha, where she lived, and neighboring Azzawiya were small villages with a lot of inbreeding. If anyone from Bassam's family were involved in shady activities, she could end up handing someone a weapon against her husband. His family, in turn, would use that against her, to prove once more that she was a bad wife and mother, that she should be home taking care of Khaled and making more babies to work in their olive groves and two dry goods stores.

Eventually, this argument would lead her to make the point no one wanted to hear—that with the Wall enclosing Mas'ha from both sides, their olive groves would soon be theirs no longer, and no one would be able to come from the nearby villages to shop at their stores. When that happened, her income from the police might stand between her family and starvation, and it could be an advantage to have fewer mouths to feed.

The road was thankfully free of the flying checkpoints that dotted the roads at commute hours. She changed to a private cab at the first roadblock and in fifteen minutes, the bridge loomed before her.

Azzawiya Bridge was really an overpass, where the new Israeli highway ran on top of the old Palestinian road. Normally taxi drivers lined the road under the bridge, waiting to ferry people back and forth between Deir Balut checkpoint and Biddia roadblock. Today, though, a row of medium-sized stones fifty meters in front blocked the entrance. Rania wondered what good the boulders would do, if the four jeeps and two Hummers under the bridge did not deter someone from trying to drive through. Eight soldiers patrolled the dark underpass, four facing in each direction. All of them caressed the triggers of their M-16s.

Rania's driver stopped a respectful distance from the command center, where the paved road gave way to a dirt track. The track went both ways around a mound of old tires and car parts, as if people whose cars were damaged by the jutting stones simply ripped off the offending part and drove their crippled cars on until they stopped running altogether.

She paid the driver and walked toward the dozens of taxis and vans jammed together pell-mell, waiting to cross the roadblock. Men sat on the hoods and stood in clusters, smoking and craning their necks for a better view. A young boy moved among the men, pouring coffee into tiny paper cups from a brass coffee urn on leather straps draped over his shoulder. Looking south to the Azzawiya side, Rania saw an equally large crowd assembled. To the west, the Mediterranean was just visible, and rising before it the Tel Aviv skyline, a fifteen-minute drive and a world away. In the no-man's land between the bridge and the people, two young soldiers drank Pepsi out of a bottle and kicked a rock as if it were a soccer ball.

To the right of the throng of cars and men, women perched as comfortably as possible on the stone terrace leading down to the olive groves. As Rania expected, she knew many of them, teachers and nurses on their way to work, students heading to the university. They uniformly wore the long dark jilbab and white headscarf. Some wore sneakers or sandals, while others sported heels as high as any Lebanese supermodel's.

"Sabah al-kheir, ya banat," Rania greeted them. *Good morning, girls.*

"Sabah an-noor, Um Khaled." *Mother of Khaled.* Just hearing his name brought a little smile to her lips.

Her sister-in-law, Maryam, was there, pink pajama bottoms peeking out from under her jilbab. Maryam hated getting up early even more than Rania did. On her way out of the compound every morning, Rania invariably heard Amir yelling at Maryam that she was going to be late.

"Why aren't you at work?" Maryam asked. "You don't have to go this way."

Would she get more information by pretending to be stuck like everyone else, or by claiming inside knowledge? The latter would be titillating to the women. Hopefully they wouldn't find out just how paltry her information was.

"I went all the way to Salfit and had to come back," she said, playing for sympathy. "Captain Mustafa sent me to see what I could learn about the stolen car."

"That car is stolen?" Salma, a thin young woman who always looked like she had just heard a good joke, leaned forward. Rania followed her finger. She could just make out the dark blue car up on the bridge, the open front doors making it look like a square bird. A platoon of blue-clad men, their vests proclaiming "POLICE" in English and Hebrew, ran back and forth, gesticulating and talking into their hands and shoulders.

"That's what the Yahud said," Rania said. "Have you been here a long time?"

"Sea w nos?" *An hour and a half*, Salma said, looking at her friends for confirmation.

"Seateen." *Two hours*, said Um Raad, who worked at the Ministry of Prisoners in Salfit. That probably meant an hour, Rania figured. It matched her guess based on the size of the crowd.

Rania wondered why Um Raad was going this way. It would have made more sense for her to take the same buses as Rania, but she must have her reasons. It didn't matter. Though they were not friends, Rania was glad Um Raad was here. She had been in prison during the First Intifada, and like most former prisoners, spoke fluent Hebrew. If the soldiers had said any-thing, she would have been the most likely to understand it.

"Did the jesh say anything about the car?" she asked.

"Walla kilme." *Not a word*, Um Raad said. "They are not in the mood for talking. I asked that one how long it would be and he threatened to arrest me."

She indicated one of the soccer players. Very tall and very thin with a shock of straw-colored hair, he reminded Rania of a broom. If he was in an arresting mood, she would stay away from him. His partner was short and lumbering and kept scratching at his cheek. She walked slowly towards Itchy until he noticed her.

"What do you want?" he asked. He sounded rude but not aggressive, and she gave him credit for speaking English. Most Palestinian men in this area knew Hebrew, but few women did. Even those who understood a fair amount, like Rania, generally pretended they didn't, in an unspoken pact of resistance.

"Do you know how much longer it will be?" she asked. "We need to get to work."

"Work? What work?" His voice cracked. If he'd spent any time at all at checkpoints, he couldn't be so ignorant as to believe Palestinian women didn't go to work. But she certainly wasn't going to tell him she was a policewoman.

"I'm a teacher," she said.

"Well you might as well go home," he said. He clawed at his cheek, his scraggly nail leaving behind a bloody streak. "School will be out before you can go through."

"Really? Why so long?"

"You see that car?" he pointed in the direction of the blue car. She could see a trace of blood from his cheek on the tip of his finger. "There might be a bomb in it. If it blew up while you were walking under it…" He waved his arms in an exploding motion.

Rania inched closer to him. "What makes you think there could be a bomb in it?"

He shrugged, scratching his jaw again. "They don't tell me that. They just tell me to keep everyone off the road."

She turned away from the soldiers and started to walk toward the taxi drivers, the best source of information in any Palestinian town. A sharp crack made her spin around. She didn't see what had made the sound, but she saw the soldiers tense. The Broom shouldered his rifle, and she heard the clip slide into place. He tore off up the hill, his itchy friend plodding after him.

"Atah tamut hayom," The Broom yelled suddenly, at no one she could see.

Rania jumped into action, moving toward him with no clear goal. *You are going to die today*, he had said.

Young men from the village nearby must be engaging in their favorite pastime: throwing stones at the army.

"Do you really want to kill a child?" she asked, running alongside The Broom and trying not to pant.

He made the gesture with clumped thumb and fingers that meant "Wait," and aimed his gun at the kids. She stayed near him, weighing the options. Standing in between a soldier and the stone-thrower he was bent on murdering would not fall under Captain Mustafa's definition of treading lightly. Plus she didn't want to get shot. But she could not simply move back and let him kill someone.

More stones rained down from the hillside. One passed dangerously close to her head. That would be the most ignominious thing of all, to be trying to protect the kids and get hit with one of their projectiles.

"Haji, go down!" one of the invisible youths called. The respectful appellation was more humiliating yet. She was not haji yet, not by a long shot. In her mind, she was barely out of her stone-throwing teens, when she had been better with a slingshot than half the boys in the refugee camp. She pumped her legs, willing herself to move faster, to get ahead of the soldiers and in a position to reason with the kids. Not that she had a clue what she would say to them.

The soldier fired in the air. The shot was so loud, it made her ears throb.

"Khalas, don't!" she shouted, in Arabic for the kids and English for the soldiers. She hated these games, even as she knew the kids needed the outlet for their rage. Who were they, anyway, and why weren't they in school? She couldn't see if they were youngsters, or young adults. She pushed herself forward, recoiling as another shot rang out. She finally passed The Broom, and could glimpse one of his targets up on the hill. She turned around to plead with him. More stones thudded to the ground at her feet.

"Please," she shouted, targeting her words at the shorter soldier, who had made it to his friend's side. "Go back down, and I will get them to stop throwing stones."

"You go down," The Broom growled. "You are not allowed here, it's a closed military zone. If you don't leave, I will arrest you."

"Fine, if you are arresting me, then you won't be shooting at the children."

He actually stopped and looked at her then. She imagined his thought process. Drop his pursuit of a group of young men armed with stones, to arrest a tiny woman for mouthing off? Still, could he shrug off her disrespect for his supreme authority? He took one step closer to her, his finger still on the trigger of his M-16. She was so close, she could count the tiny whiskers on his cheek. He reached toward her with his left hand, his right still clutching the rifle. She wanted to back up, but she would not allow herself that.

"You know, you're on film," a clear voice carried on the wind.

A foreign woman was striding toward them, video camera pointed straight at The Broom's face. Rania's eyes quickly took in the woman's wild curls, black jeans faded in the knees, and baggy beige polo shirt. The other woman flashed her a smile, showing an appealing gap between her front teeth. The Broom swiveled, his rifle now pointed squarely at the other woman's face. Relief washed over Rania, and she surreptitiously moved out of striking range.

"You're not supposed to leave your post, are you?" the foreigner said to The Broom.

He did not answer, just peered through the sight on his rifle into the lens of the camera. Rania held her breath. If his finger moved on the trigger, the woman's head would explode. How could she just stand there, calmly filming him?

Seconds ticked by, each one feeling like an hour. The rain of stones had stopped. The boys must be transfixed by the scene below them.

"Yalla." *Let's go*, The Broom said to Itchy. He slid the cartridge of bullets out of his rifle and they scrambled down the hillside.

Rania exhaled sharply.

"You're very brave," she said to the other woman.

"Not really," the other woman shrugged. "I really didn't think he'd shoot me. I'm Chloe."

"Rania."

Chloe extended her right hand for Rania to shake, but it felt a little formal for the moment. Rania raised herself on tiptoes and kissed the taller woman first on the left cheek, then the right and the left again. The end of her head scarf caught on something on the other woman's shirt. She extricated it. The offending item was a little silver charm, two interlocked circles with crosses attached.

"Is it something religious?" Rania asked, fingering the little icon.

Chloe hesitated. "Something like that."

"Where are you from?" Rania asked.

"The States," Chloe said.

"Which state?"

"California. San Francisco, to be exact."

"Like Michael Douglas," Rania said.

"Um… sorry?" Chloe cocked her head to one side, cat-like.

"The Streets of San Francisco," Rania said.

Chloe laughed. "That stupid show from the seventies? How do you know about that?"

"It comes on late night satellite television. San Francisco looks very beautiful."

"It is." Chloe's face softened, and she looked off into the distance, as if San Francisco, not Tel Aviv, lay just beyond the trees.

"Let's go down," Rania said. "I need some coffee."

Chapter 2

Abu Anwar picked his way carefully along the rocky path.

"Watch the thorns," he said to the donkey, who whinnied in resigned acknowledgment.

Abu Anwar steered the beast away from the thorny cactus lining the trail. They slowly climbed rock terraces. He walked next to the donkey, one hand on its scraggly mane, the other steadying the mound of tarps, tools, and provisions tied onto the animal's back. The terraces were not a problem for him—he knew them like he knew his own children. They were built by his family and his neighbors' families over the decades, with the rocks they cleared from their olive groves. But he had to pay close attention to the exposed sewage pipe, pouring waste from the settlement of Elkana into Azzawiya's precious soil. He guided the donkey over one shallow pool of sludge, partially covered with branches. Soon though, they came to a raging river of filth, too wide to step across.

"Ya haram." *For shame*, Abu Anwar exclaimed. He looped a rope loosely around the donkey's front legs and tied it to a nearby olive tree. He clambered back over the low stone wall and wandered down the path, looking for a plank of wood big enough to make a bridge for them. He shook his head, muttering at the debris rotting in the fetid earth: plastic soda bottles that had carried water for last year's olive picking, bits of tools long since corroded and cracked, rotting meat, a pair of baby shoes.

More surprising was the adult shoe a hundred meters further down. A woman's shoe, high heeled, shiny leather, in good condition. Abu Anwar mused over the shoe as he continued to scour the litter. Some young women dressed to go to the fields as if they were going to a wedding and changed into picking clothes when they reached the trees. He supposed someone might have gone to the fields in her good party shoes, but at the end of a long day's picking, not bothered to change out of her sneakers. Laden with buckets, picnic supplies, and children, it was plausible that she would not have seen a shoe slip out of one of her bundles. Satisfied with that explanation, he let it go.

He spied a board about a hundred meters away that looked like it would hold the donkey's weight. A thicket of brambles blocked his path. As he bent to clear it, a bit of bright violet caught his eye. He reached cautiously into the tangle of branches and exposed the source of the bright spot—a small circle of cloth, gathered with elastic bands, caught on one of the thorns.

Abu Anwar knew that something was not right. He couldn't have told you how he knew it, but he would bet his house on it. He also knew it was none of his affair. He would leave the bit of cloth where it was, and the shoe, and take the board and go tend his trees and return home to eat his wife's *makluube* and smoke *sheesha* with his brothers in the evening. If something evil was walking their lands, it would no doubt find them in its own time, like the soldiers who came in the night to take their sons and the settlers who set fire to their trees. He would not do anything to hasten it.

He reached the board and pried it loose from the bed of mud and slime. He scraped it on an old tire. A wave of dizziness fell over him as he straightened up. He lost his balance and toppled over in the high grass. He clutched at the long weeds for support, and the sharp prickles tore at his hands. He lay for a few minutes, stunned.

"Shu bisir?" *What is happening?* he asked.

Something was definitely wrong. In his sixty-eight years on earth, he had never had a moment when he did not know where his feet were. Abu Anwar sat up slowly. His old bones ached uncharacteristically. He looked around, shaking his head over his clumsiness. Could he be losing his faculties? He got unsteadily to his feet.

He saw the pair to the girl's shoe a few meters from where he had landed when he fell. That was more unsettling. Two shoes would hardly have been dropped by accident, and no Palestinian girl would intentionally throw away two good shoes like this. Abu Anwar bent to look at the second shoe more closely.

"Haram!" he said aloud again.

This shoe was attached to a girl. *Ajnabiya*—a foreign girl.

"Allah yirhamha." He whispered the prayer for her soul.

Abu Anwar was careful not to touch her, but he thought she had been dead for some hours. Her skin had a bluish cast, and the faint odor which rose from her reminded him of the stench that could hang around your compound after the ritual slaughter of a cow for Eid, if you didn't clean up well enough. She wore a violet blouse with gathered sleeves and black slacks. Her hair was shiny black, her features small and delicate. Abu Anwar thought she must be Japanese. She reminded him of pictures he saw once from the bombing of Hiroshima. At the time he had only thought, "If the Israelis get hold of this weapon, we are truly finished." But now he heard that they had the weapon. Yet he and his family were still there, Allah be praised.

Abu Anwar was quite undecided about what to do. This girl was not a Palestinian, and no Palestinian would have left her in this state. Still, it was Palestinian land, so it was a matter for the Palestinian police. But if Abu Anwar called them, to report this dead girl, the Palestinian police would call the Israeli police. The Israelis would ask the Palestinian police who had found the girl, and then they might decide Abu Anwar had something to do with her getting dead, and he could find himself in a *belagan,* a big mess.

He left the girl where she lay. He took his board and went back to where he had tied up the donkey. It did not seem right to let her rot in the sun, but he could not think right now. He would work on his trees, and when he was done, he would go back to the village and discuss it with his brother, Thamer, the mayor of Azzawiya.

He slowly untied the donkey and headed into the groves.

Chapter 3

Rania sought out one of the coffee kids and bought two small hot cups, *nos hilwe*, half sweet. She handed one to Chloe, and they settled under the shade of an olive tree, a little ways from where the group of women still sat. Rania sipped at the bittersweet liquid, savoring the feel of the tiny grounds in her teeth.

"Are you a journalist?" she asked.

"Not exactly." Chloe had been evasive about the little object around her neck, and now she didn't want to say what her work was. Rania started to wonder if it was wise to be hanging around this woman. Perhaps she was an Israeli spy. But a spy would probably have her story down.

"A student?" Rania persisted, though certainly, Chloe was too old for a student in the conventional sense.

"Sort of… I'm trying to learn about the situation."

"But why here?"

Chloe was quiet for a few seconds, looking into her coffee cup, as if for an answer that would satisfy.

"I grew up in a small town in North Carolina. Do you know where that is?"

Rania thought about lying; she hated to sound ignorant. But if North Carolina was important to the story, she should know exactly what it was. She shook her head.

"It's a state in the southeast, the part that used to have slavery."

Rania instinctively glanced at her watch. She had learned about American slavery in school. That had ended in the 1800s, before the Jews even began to settle in Palestine. If Chloe was going to start that far back, they would be here all day.

"Sorry." Chloe acknowledged her impatience. "The point is, it was very racist there. Especially against Blacks, but there was a lot of prejudice against Jews too. There were only about seventy-five Jews in the whole area, one synagogue for three towns. After regular school, we—the Jewish kids—had to go to Hebrew school, so we would know what it meant to be Jewish. Most of what they taught us about was Israel. About how it was the only place in the world where men and women were completely equal, Golda Meir could be prime minister, and the people were so smart they could grow things in the desert."

Chloe blushed when she said this. She started talking so fast, she sounded like a tape on the wrong speed. Rania almost asked her to slow down *just a little*, but her pride wouldn't let her.

"And then during the Intifada, I saw Palestinian kids dying on television. I mean, they don't report it nearly as much as it happens, not half as much as Palestinian suicide bombings, but they showed that little kid with his father…"

"Mohammed al-Dura," Rania supplied.

"Yes, him. And it was like I could *feel* the terror through my television screen."

Rania liked that. She had felt that way too.

"I started thinking maybe what I'd learned about Israel wasn't the whole truth. When I was little, we used to put quarters in these blue and white cans, to plant trees in Israel. It never occurred to me to wonder what had been there before."

"So just like that, you decided to come here?"

"Not just like that, no. I started reading a lot, people like Edward Said and Tom Segev. I watched movies—this one called *Peace, Propaganda and the Promised Land* is really good. And that one that just came out, *Ford Transit*, about the checkpoints."

"I have not seen it," Rania said.

"Oh, sorry." Chloe blushed again. Rania wondered why she was apologizing. She didn't want to see any movie about checkpoints.

"How long have you been here?" Rania asked.

"About nine months."

"You came here by yourself?"

"Not at first. Have you heard of the International Network in Solidarity with Palestine, the Jamiyat Ittadamon Iddawliya?" Chloe asked.

"Of course." Rania wasn't really sure if she knew about that particular group. There were so many groups, and all of them had similar names, she couldn't keep track.

"I came to work with them," Chloe answered. "But it was... not very good for women."

"Not good how?"

"They didn't respect us. Like in one village there was a tent to honor the prisoners and the Minister of Prisoners had come to speak. We all arrived together, and only men were in the tent. The leaders of the village came and shook hands with the foreign men, and took them to sit in the very front. They completely ignored us women, and the men in our group didn't say anything. So I went to find the women from the village. They were all gathered over on one side of the tent, with the sun beating down and the kids running around, and just one little tree for shade. They were holding pictures of their sons and husbands in prison, and they couldn't even hear the speeches."

Rania thought she might have met her match in the anti-tact department. She liked Chloe's sharp sense of justice, though. Before she could open her mouth to make some sympathetic comment, Chloe started talking again.

"So, are you on your way to work?"

"I am at work. I am a policewoman."

"Really? I didn't know there were women in the police up here."

Rania bristled at the words "up here." As often as she longed for the more cosmopolitan, easygoing culture of Jerusalem and Bethlehem, where she had grown up, she didn't need foreigners making assumptions.

"Well, there are," she said. She drained the remaining coffee in her cup and crumpled it in one hand. "I have to go."

"Go where?" Chloe asked. "The road's still closed."

Rania pointed up at the settler highway.

"To talk to the Israeli police up on the road."

Chloe jumped up. "I'll come with you. Given how jumpy the army is, they might shoot at you."

"Stay here," Rania ordered. "I can handle the jesh."

The waiting around had not improved her mood. She charged off to her right through the olive groves to the dirt path that climbed up to the settler road. The path was well marked, hammered out by the feet of hundreds of men, and a few women, who used it every Saturday night to slip into Israel where they could, if they were lucky, make enough money to feed their families.

She carefully made her ascent. When she neared the top of the embankment, one of the policemen called out, "Diiri baalik, fii jesh honak." *Be careful, the army is there.* Surprised, Rania looked up at him. He was perhaps fifty, with short, bushy, salt-and-pepper hair and a kind, wrinkly face. Despite his blue eyes, she would have known him for a Palestinian even if he had not spoken Arabic. His name tag said "Ali" in Arabic, with Hebrew letters above it. She looked down to where he was pointing.

Two soldiers stood about a hundred meters below, aiming their guns straight at her.

"Atzri!" one of the soldiers called in Hebrew. "Mi at?" *Stop! Who are you?*

She could hear fear in his voice. Improbable as it seemed, these heavily armed men were really afraid of a woman climbing up to the road in broad daylight, in full view of the Israeli police.

"Shorta," she said calmly, then "police," in case he didn't know any Arabic.

"Palestinian police?" he asked in Hebrew. Obviously, she thought. She ordered herself not to be a smartass right now.

"Yes."

"Mi zot?" *Who is that?* She followed his outstretched hand, and saw Chloe huffing up the embankment after her.

"No idea," Rania said. She turned back toward the Israeli policeman, Ali, who reached out a hand to help her over the guard rail. Rania declined the help, gripping the filthy metal rail for support instead, but she smiled into Ali's twinkling blue eyes. Out of the corner of her eye she saw Chloe filming from a few feet away. Fine, as long as she kept her distance.

"Tik alafia, Ali," Rania said, using the Arabic greeting for someone who is working. "I am from the national police in Salfit. What's going on?"

"The car has been here since early morning," Ali told her. "It belongs to an Israeli called Rotem Lehrman, from Rosh HaAyin. He reported it stolen a few hours ago. It was in the parking lot at the industrial park where he works."

"What does he do there?"

"He is a security guard. He was working the night shift, and when he went to go home, the car was gone."

"Are you sure he is telling the truth?"

"He has no criminal record. His employer verified that he works the night shift, and he punched his time card in and out at the usual times. When he came out of work and found the car gone, he called the police immediately."

Rania nodded. It would be too easy, that the owner of the car would be the one who left it here. Lehrman said he never went into the West Bank, Ali told her. He didn't know anyone who went there. It was too dangerous. His car keys were still on his key ring, and he had not given anyone else a key. The car was a late model Citroen, one of the most common cars in Israel, which was probably why it was taken.

Ali handed Rania a gold bracelet with some Cyrillic writing on it.

"We found this on the floor in the front, where the passenger would sit," he said.

Rania turned it over in her hands. It was heavy. That much gold would be worth a lot of money. She was sure there was more information she should get about the car, but really, she was starting to wonder what she was doing here. It didn't seem likely that whatever happened had anything to do with her people. Probably some Israeli teenagers took the car for fun, ran out of petrol, and in their panic at finding themselves stuck near a Palestinian village, ran off without closing the doors.

"Does the car have petrol in it?" she asked Ali.

"It is more than a quarter full," he told her. "No mechanical problem either."

She peered around, asking the land she knew well to share its mysteries with her. She had only lived in Mas'ha seven years, but she had a deeper sense of this countryside than of the hills around Bethlehem, where she had spent seventeen years. Maybe it was because this was where she had learned to be a detective, to sense with every pore in her body.

Some few hundred meters ahead, toward the Israeli checkpoint, she saw a crowd gathered. There were only men there; she saw no headscarves. She spied a few soldiers among them.

"Thank you for the information," she said to Ali. He nodded and watched her move toward the checkpoint.

She walked purposefully, careful not to run, which might cause a bad reaction from the army. Chloe shadowed her, about fifteen meters to her left and a few steps behind. It was ridiculous, Rania thought; two women moving together but pretending to be apart, like a kite with a long tail.

When she got closer, she saw that the people in green uniforms were actually border police, who were like soldiers, but worse. In the border villages they were nicknamed Druze, because many of them were Israeli

Palestinians belonging to that sect. People said the Druze border police were more brutal even than the Russians. Rania didn't know about that. To her, they all seemed equally bad.

Only one of the three border police guarding this spot was actually Druze. The other two were Jewish Israelis. One was very tall and lanky, with a bush of dark hair. The other was pale and wore a skullcap, marking him as an Orthodox Jew.

They had rounded up about two dozen men, nearly all between twenty-five and forty-five, and mostly dressed for construction work. Some wore plaid flannel shirts, even in the heat. A few carried metal lunch pails and tool belts. Most carried nothing, only some cigarettes peeking out of a shirt pocket. Occasionally they passed around a nearly empty water bottle. They were lined up along the guardrail, several layers deep. When one of the older men tried to sit down, the tall Druze waved his gun at the old *haj* and screamed "Kum!" *Stand Up!* in Hebrew. Rania found it especially galling when Druze spoke Hebrew to the people, as if they were too good to speak their native Arabic.

"Why can't they sit down?" she asked in Arabic.

"Usquti," came out of his mouth in a bored snarl. *Shut up*, without even looking at her. She walked straight up to him and looked up into his face. Her head would just fit under his chin.

"Why shut up?" she asked. "What did they do? It is hot, they are old, they want to sit down. Why should you care?"

"Mish shughlik," he snarled. *It's not your business.* At least she had succeeded in getting him to speak Arabic.

"It is my business," she said. "I'm a Palestinian policewoman. It's my job to protect them."

"You are police?" He looked at her now, and the hatred in his face made her want to recoil, but she held herself steady. "Let me see your ID."

"I don't have to show you my ID. You are in my land."

Almost lazily, he hoisted his gun so it touched her heart. Out of the corner of her eye, she saw Chloe jump. The other woman moved quickly to stand behind Rania's left shoulder.

The Druze ignored her, his piercing black eyes fixed on Rania.

"I can make real trouble for you," he said in Arabic. "Get lost, or I will arrest you. I will beat you," he promised, waving his gun slightly to show her how, "even *if* you are a woman."

She was irrationally amused by his emphasis, not sure if he meant to suggest that she might not be a woman. She put all her concentration into not laughing, which would probably really push him to violence. Chloe moved back a little and raised her video camera. He noticed and turned toward her.

"Close the camera," he said in English.

Chloe hesitated.

"CLOSE IT!" he bellowed, starting to lunge toward her.

Chloe snapped the screen shut and lowered the camera, although Rania noticed that the red recording light was still on. As Rania had the thought, Chloe covered the light with her thumb.

The other soldiers were lounging nearby, watching the interaction as if it were a soccer match. The tall one kept up a running commentary, punctuating his words with chuckles. The Orthodox seldom seemed to say anything. Chloe strolled over to stand next to the joker. Rania moved to where she could hear their conversation without being drawn in.

"That man is very violent," Chloe said. "Can't you get him to calm down?"

"He is the commander," the young man responded. "The Arabs call him 'Top Killer.'"

"Why do they call him that?"

"He says he killed three Arabs in one day, for no reason."

"That's terrible," Chloe said. "You know, these men are only trying to feed their families."

"They have to learn that they cannot work in Israel," he said with a shrug.

"Well, you're working in Palestine," Chloe said. He laughed. Chloe pulled a pamphlet out of her backpack and handed it to the soldier.

"What is it?" he asked.

"It's written by soldiers, for other soldiers, to tell them why they should not fight in the Occupied Territories."

To Rania's surprise, he started reading it right away. He didn't speak again until he had read every word.

"Where are you from, America?" he asked when he was done.

"Yes."

"What's the matter," he said. "You don't have enough problems in America, you have to come here? Look what you are doing in Iraq."

"I agree," she said, "that's a problem too."

"Why don't you go there?" he asked.

"It's too dangerous right now. I hope maybe when I am done with my work here, I will be able to go there."

"What is your work here?" he asked.

"I work for peace," Chloe said.

"I am also working for peace," and he rattled the gun that hung by his side. Chloe's pamphlet didn't seem to have had much impact.

"Peace will never be won with guns," Chloe said. "In my country and yours, we all need to understand that."

"Please go to Iraq as soon as possible," he said and walked away.

Top Killer was lecturing the group of men now. Chloe and Rania both made their way back there. Top Killer pointed to the Palestinian road that wound through the fields. "Go to Beit Amin and wait," he ordered them. "Baregel." *On foot.*

It was at least ten miles to Beit Amin.

"Fii sayara." *There's a car,* one of the men said.

"No, you walk." Top Killer motioned with his gun.

"Look, it's enough they have to spend all day waiting, not working," Chloe objected. "At least let them take a car."

He spun around and glared at her. Then, with the concentration of a dance move, he smacked the first man in line in the face with the butt of his gun. Blood spurted from the man's cheek. Chloe moved toward Top Killer, but stopped.

The wounded man's friends were gathered around him, stanching the blood with a handkerchief. One of them offered him the tiny bit of water remaining in his small bottle. Chloe turned to Rania, tears glinting in her eyes.

"I should learn to keep my mouth shut," she said.

Rania shook her head. If this woman was going to live here, she needed to toughen up some.

"You think he did that because of you?" Rania asked. "He did it because he wanted to. He is not a nice man."

"That's all? Not nice?"

"What else is there to say?"

The men walked off in a straggly line in the direction Top Killer had pointed. Chloe and Rania watched them silently.

"I'm going with them," Chloe said.

What did Chloe want? Rania wondered. Permission? Praise? To be talked out of it? It seemed as good a thing for her to do as any, though she didn't exactly look like ten mile hikes were her daily routine.

"Diiri baalik a la haalik." *Take care of yourself*, Rania said, and watched the American make her way into the sad little march.

Chapter 4

Nearly two and a half hours after Rania arrived at the crossroads, the army commander finally kicked away the boulders comprising his makeshift roadblock and gestured to the cars they could pass. The women gathered themselves up from the low walls and rocks where they had sat for so long, brushing the dust from their backsides. Most of them headed back to their home villages. It was already eleven. In most Palestinian offices, the work day ends at two or three in the afternoon, giving everyone several hours to get home before dark. School would be over at half past twelve, so the teachers certainly need not go. Rania wondered uncharitably why they hadn't figured that out several hours ago. She supposed curiosity had kept everyone glued to their positions, not wanting to miss anything exciting that might happen. In their situation, she might have done the same.

She climbed back down the embankment. In the rainy winter season, it would be treacherously muddy, but now it was no problem to scamper down the baked earth. She pondered the mystery of the abandoned car. Why would someone take a car from Israel, drive it to the edge of the West Bank, and then leave it? The most logical explanation was that they needed to move something from one place to another, but couldn't risk being stopped at the checkpoint. Weapons, probably, for who would go to so much trouble for anything else? Someone may have brought something from Israel and buried it here in these fields, or they could have snuck into Israel, taken the car, and driven back to the West Bank to load up some cargo. But in that case, why go get an Israeli car, rather than using a local one? Because an Israeli car would not be stopped on the road at night, while a car with Palestinian plates might.

The army had had dozens of men searching the groves. If they hadn't found anything, they would continue to look for days or weeks, using every unpleasant means at their disposal, mostly informants. They had all kinds of ways of finding informants, willing or unwilling. The people who had the misfortune to live in those tall houses on the edge of the villages would almost certainly be having visits from army units in the next weeks. The open top floors people left so that they could build up made perfect lookout perches. An ugly period was coming.

She glanced around, thinking about where you would hide something in plain sight. She wandered along the sewer pipes, at the bed of the nearly-dry creek. She didn't see anything weird, just detritus from the new throwaway lifestyle of rural Palestinians, combined with the garbage from the settlement. A pile of rotting meat caused her to cover her face in revulsion. She was about to give up when she spotted a fashionable high-heeled shoe in the brush, not the kind of thing that usually gets thrown away. She looked around for its pair, but didn't see it.

She picked it up and walked on, paying closer attention to patches of tall grass that seemed to have been tamped down, as if by something being dragged over them. She climbed a ways up the other hill from the one where she had talked to the police, the one leading toward Elkana, getting enough distance to survey the area below. It was easier now that she knew what she was looking for; the path made by the flattened rushes jumping out at her. She memorized its path before descending again, knowing that it would look less clear up close. She followed it for about two hundred meters and caught a flash of lavender fabric. She fought her way through the brush, snagging her sleeve on a tangle of brambles. She impatiently tore it off. She wondered if she could coax one of her nieces or sisters-in-law to mend it for her. If she did it herself, she'd probably end up sewing the sleeve to the skirt.

Obviously some other woman had been less lucky than she—her flouncy sleeve had shorn straight off on the sharp thorns. But why would anyone have gone this way when there were clear paths from the village to the groves? These bushes were good cover from the border police, but a woman trying to cross illegally would not do it in high heels and a lavender blouse. This would not make a bad hiding place, she supposed, for whatever cargo might have been in that car, but again, no one would let a woman go out to make a drop in party clothes.

She looked down, canvassing the area for footprints that might match this misplaced shoe. She saw none. She could make out one set clearly, but they were made by flat sandals. She stepped into the tracks until she reached a spot where something heavy had been pried loose. From the impressions in the muddy ground, it had been a wide board, probably the soggy remains of someone's cart. A clump of mud on a limp tire drew her eye briefly, but it told her nothing. She straightened up from her examination and caught another glimpse of lavender. Over there, something was hidden in the grass. She couldn't imagine it had anything to do with the stolen car or whatever the army was after, but she was curious and you never knew. She pointed to the bright spot in the distance, and keeping her arm oriented in that direction, sidled carefully through the high grass.

"Wallah!" Her exclamation seemed to ricochet in the quiet valley. She hastily peeked around, imagining soldiers leaping out at her. But nothing moved, least of all the blue-gray corpse of the young foreign woman.

Rania had seen plenty of death. Her first boyfriend had bled out in her arms, as she screamed at the soldiers who refused to let the Red Crescent medics come through. But in her years with the police, she had never been confronted with a dead body. Most deaths in this area were not mysteries. People were killed by the army, or by Israeli settlers, or they were collaborators, or a family feud exploded in unfortunate violence.

Rania squeezed her eyes shut, breathed deeply, opened them again. She needed to think.

There had to be some relationship between this woman and the stolen car, right? But what? Was she the driver, and something had scared her so badly she had left the car and run? Had whatever frightened her chased after her and killed her? Or had she fallen and injured herself? She could not have made it far wearing one high-heeled shoe, and the other had been two hundred meters back. And there would have been tracks.

Rania fished a plastic bag out of her work supplies. She tore it open, spread it on the wet ground and knelt next to the body. Even after she pulled on latex gloves, her hand hovered over the other woman's head, loathe to violate the sanctity of death. But then her police training took over and she clinically parted the matted black hair on the woman's forehead. Her fingers located a wound the size of a baseball, from the temple to just above the ear. The blood was still a little wet. She pulled her hand away and looked at the blood on her glove. Memories of Qais—she pushed that aside. This wasn't a time for sentiment.

Had the girl been clubbed or fallen and hit her head on a rock? Rania walked back to where the drag marks began. Now she saw tiny traces of rust-colored blood on the brown grass, but no obvious instrument that would have caused them. That suggested her death was no accident. If she had fallen and hit her head, the rocks would not have gotten up and walked away. If, on the other hand, someone hit her with something, they could have taken it with them.

She wondered for a moment how she could have found in an hour what the army had missed in twice that time. Was it possible they had found the body but left it? She dismissed the possibility. They had been looking for something very different. They would have concentrated on places where something might be buried and marked so it could be easily found again. They would not have paid attention to Palestinian garbage, or looked in places that might be so easily stumbled over.

She climbed back up to the road, wondering what to do if the Israeli police were still there. She did not want to tell them about the body before she had had a chance to talk to Captain Mustafa about it, but even less did she want to risk them finding it for themselves. Fortunately, they were gone. She returned to the place where the dead woman lay and called the captain.

"I am coming," he said.

While she waited, she examined the area, moving cautiously to avoid disturbing anything. Several people had been near the body, she could tell. There were the sandal tracks she had noticed before, going up and back and up again. That would have been a farmer, and from their unevenness, she thought he was old—she detected a slight limp. There were also donkey tracks.

Donkey droppings under this tree, so the donkey was tied up here. The old man's tracks went this way, then veered off to pick up the shoe, and back onto the so-called path. He stopped here, next to the body's left hand, and crouched down, no doubt to make sure she was really dead. But there, by her head, was another footprint, made by a little-worn running shoe. She found the others that went with it, running up toward the road. The tracks were uneven, the right ones more pronounced than the left. The person—almost certainly a man from the size of the shoe—was carrying something in his right hand as he ran. He was running fast, so probably he was young.

She walked back to the place where she had noticed the drag pattern on the ground, some one hundred meters distant from where the body now lay. There were more tracks leading to and away from that place. She did not think they were from the same shoes that had run from the place where the body was finally left, but she couldn't be sure, because that person had been running, and this person was moving slowly. The area was a bit muddy, so the set of tracks along the creek bed was not as distinct as the other two.

How had the girl gotten from where the drag marks ended to where she was left? Could she have been dragged, left, gotten up and walked, and then fallen down and died? She couldn't be sure. There were many sets of footprints in the area, and no wonder; so many people used this unofficial crossing into Israel, it would be impossible to sort out one young woman's, or those of the person who had caused her to be lying here dead.

The captain did not come by taxi to the bridge as she expected. After half an hour, a Mercedes came bumping along through the fields, stopping just short of where she was working. The captain got out of the passenger's side. She stifled a grimace when she saw the driver, a thin, stooped man whose heavy mustache gave his face an indelible frown.

Why had she assumed the captain would come alone? Of course, in such an unusual situation, he would go immediately to his friend, Abu Ziyad. They had known each other for twenty years. They had fought together and been in prison together.

As District Cooperating Liaison, or DCL, Abu Ziyad was the bridge between the Israeli authorities and the people. People distrusted him because of his job, and because of his personal wealth. His personality didn't help either. But if you really needed something, he was the one man in Salfit with the best chance to get it for you. People said he had known Arafat personally.

The phrase "old boys' network" could have been created for Abu Ziyad. When Captain Mustafa decided to hire her, Abu Ziyad had tried to dissuade him. People even said he went to the governor about it. He was probably the reason that five years later, she was still the only woman investigator in this district. She wasn't going to let him rattle her now. She greeted him politely, then showed the men the body and the drag marks.

"She did not simply fall down the hill," she concluded.

"We must notify the Israelis," Abu Ziyad said. "Whoever this girl is, she is not from one of our villages."

"We should try to find out if anyone in the area knows who she is first," Rania objected. "If we call the Israelis before we know how she came to be dead in this land, they will go charging into the villages and frighten the people."

Captain Mustafa considered the point, but Abu Ziyad shook his head. "If we do not tell them about the body and they find it themselves, they may try to make it a problem for us."

She had to admit that made sense, but she did not want Israeli soldiers and police poking around her land yet. Of course, she did not want them there at all, but since it seemed inevitable, she needed a little time to get organized. She would not give the Israeli police the names of the people she had seen at the roadblock, but if she told them nothing, they would take it as a sign of the Palestinians' complete incompetence and go off on their own fishing expedition. Once she knew what information people might have that was relevant, she could figure out how to protect them.

"Wait a few hours," she insisted. "I know the people here. Let me ask around and perhaps we will find there is no need to involve the Israelis."

Abu Ziyad shook his head. "We cannot leave the body here for people to stumble over, and we cannot remove it without telling the Yahud."

"Why not?" Rania argued. "It is on our land."

Abu Ziyad's usual scowl deepened. He spoke as if to a particularly slow third grader. "What if she belongs to one of the settlements?" he said. "Or was married to an Israeli? What do you think will happen if we call and tell them she is in a Palestinian hospital, dead? If they find out we did not tell them right away, they can make hell for us."

"We," Captain Mustafa made a circle enclosing himself and Abu Ziyad, "will go inform the Israeli DCL in person."

Did Rania want to insist on going with them? She had no interest in talking to any Israeli officials, but she wasn't going to be sent out to play while the grownups did important work.

"I will go talk to the women who were at the roadblock earlier." She looked at Captain Mustafa, avoiding Abu Ziyad's glowering face. "They may know something that would be useful."

"Go back to Salfit," Abu Ziyad said. "We do not want word to spread among the people yet."

Captain Mustafa did not say anything. Rania decided to take that as tacit approval for her disobedience. As soon as she could no longer see the dust from Abu Ziyad's fancy tires, she headed off to find Maryam, Salma, and Um Raad.

Chapter 5

Maryam taught in Deir Balut, Salma worked as a visiting nurse in the three villages in this sector, and Um Raad worked at the Ministry of Prisoners in Salfit. But as Rania had guessed, none of them had gone to work after the checkpoint was finally cleared. She found them all in Biddia, the larger central town for this part of the district. Maryam and Salma were eating lunch together in a restaurant. They were both in their late twenties. Maryam had a sweet, serious, round face. She seemed a little dull to Rania, who always found it a little surprising that she should be a teacher. But she taught first grade, so the children would not notice that she was not the brightest star in the sky. She was very patient with her own three children, and Rania thought she was probably a good teacher for the little ones. Salma was her polar opposite, with a lively, expressive face atop the lithe frame under her jilbab, her hands always moving when she talked. Her career also seemed well chosen, the intellectual challenge of nursing, combined with the variety of moving from town to town, preserving her youthful enthusiasm.

They were making the most of an unexpected day off from work, to socialize and gossip until their children came home from school. They were happier to see her than she expected.

"Did you find out what the jesh were looking for?" Salma asked eagerly, leaning toward her.

"They found a stolen car on the big road," Rania answered.

"Just a car?"

"That's all they told me," she said. She would get further if she could cough up some juicy intelligence, but emphasizing that she wasn't in the confidence of the Israeli authorities would have to suffice.

"You got to the junction at seven o'clock this morning?" she asked

them. They had told her they were there for one and a half hours, she
remembered.

"Seven, seven thirty," Salma replied.

"Did you see anyone in the fields?"

"The fields? Which fields?"

Rania wanted to kick the woman. If she was going to feign ignorance, she
could at least put some feeling into it.

"In any groves next to the road, near where you were waiting. You were
there for such a long time, you must have had a lot of time to look around."

"No," Salma said quickly, giving Maryam a sidelong look. "We weren't
looking there, we were watching the jesh."

Rania looked at Maryam, and she nodded, but a beat too late. Rania
leaned into them. If she had to, she would separate them and Maryam would
be sure to crack, but it shouldn't be necessary.

"Look," she said, "whoever you think you are protecting, they don't need it.
I am not working with the Israelis. I don't believe that any of our people are
guilty of anything. I just need to ask them some questions, about what they
might have seen, just like I am doing with you, and you know that you have
not done anything wrong."

Maryam was clearly reassured by this logic. Salma seemed to be weighing her natural suspicion of Rania as a policewoman and an outsider against
what her good sense told her was the better part of wisdom. Rania's temper
flared. If Salma wanted to be snotty, she could play that game too.

"Don't make trouble for yourselves, my sisters," she said sweetly. "If you
do not want to talk to me, the Israelis will be along soon, and their methods
are more persuasive than mine."

Salma took another minute to consider that before saying, "There were
some men."

"Some men? Which men?"

"I didn't know all of them. Some going up to the trees, and some waiting
near the road."

"Abu Anwar was looking around under the bridge for a while," Maryam
supplied.

"Who is Abu Anwar?" asked Rania.

"The brother of Abu Jawad, the mayor of Azzawiya," Salma told her.

"He fell down," Maryam interjected.

"Fell down?" Both women nodded vigorously.

"I thought maybe he was sick," Salma concurred. "I was going to ask if he needed help, but then he got up again and went back to his donkey."

"Did you see anyone else?" Rania asked.

"Walla wahad." *No one*, the two women said in unison.

Rania was sure they were lying, but she would not pursue it right now. It probably was not even important, and if it was, she knew where to find them and it would be better one on one. She would see Um Raad, and then go to find this Abu Anwar.

Um Raad was home in Biddia, preparing vegetables stuffed with minced meat. She placed a row of hollowed-out squash on a plate and spooned the meat into them as she told Rania a story about seeing an Israeli girl walking through the fields.

"An Israeli woman? Are you sure?" Rania asked. Since the Intifada, even most Israeli men were afraid to walk through Palestinian lands by themselves, unless they had guns.

"She was wearing a scarf like the settlers wear, and a long skirt. And dark glasses."

Um Raad sounded quite sure. Rania couldn't imagine why she would be lying, unless it was to protect someone else. She thanked Um Raad and left.

✳ ✳ ✳

Abu Anwar's house in Azzawiya was quiet, and no one answered her knocks. She found the mayor, Abu Jawad, at his palatial home at the top of the village.

"Yes, I know," he said when Rania told him about the body. "My brother called me from the fields. He said he had discovered an *ajnabiya*, lying dead on the land."

"And you didn't call the police?" She supposed it was possible that he had talked to someone in the police and they had not thought to call her.

"Abu Anwar said he would come when he was done with his work. After that, we would figure out what to do."

"I don't understand," she said, exasperated. "What was there to do besides call us?"

It crossed her mind that the unkind things villagers in Mas'ha said about their Azzawiyan neighbors might not be completely unfounded. To find a dead body and not call the police? These people were very strange indeed.

"We were going to talk to the DCL," he said.

"Why? The DCL is the liaison between our community and the Israelis. Do you have some reason to believe that the Israelis are involved in this girl's death?"

"Abu Ziyad is a friend," he said. There it was again. The secret brotherhood.

"What time will Abu Anwar be back from his fields?" she asked neutrally, as if she were interested in borrowing a tractor from him.

"I don't know, maybe three, maybe four o'clock," the mayor replied.

"Can you call him to come back now?"

"No, he has no mobile."

"But he called you."

"He borrowed a phone from a neighbor."

She literally bit her tongue. Nothing good would come from lecturing this man, who was old enough to be her father or even a youngish grandfather. She needed that tact that she was so short on.

"Where are his fields?" she asked.

"Ba'id." *Far.*

She smiled. Was he trying to keep her away from the old man, or did he seriously believe it wasn't that important, and she wouldn't want to go far?

"I don't mind," she said, "I can walk a long way."

He pointed out the window, indicating trees far across the Israeli bypass highway, up near the big water tower belonging to the settlement, Elkana. "It will take you at least an hour to walk there," he said. "By then, Abu Anwar will be coming down. You may as well wait for him here."

She could see that there was no drivable road into the fields. She did not have a donkey, and it would take her a long time to find someone willing to lend her one, especially if the word was out in the village that people should not give her too much help in her quest. She could try to intercept Abu Anwar on his way down, but she did not know the fields and there was more than one path he might take.

"I am going to call Captain Mustafa," she said, "and we will both come back here at four o'clock to talk with Abu Anwar. Please make sure that he is here."

Chapter 6

Chloe tore up the wide stone stairs and thrust her key into the lock of the red metal door. She headed straight for the bathroom, without even removing the pack from her back. Relieved, she tossed off backpack and shoes before flinging open the refrigerator door. There wasn't a lot to choose from. She grabbed a piece of stale bread and smeared it with Nutella. When in doubt, chocolate was her default position.

Two things she had never been able to really adapt to since she'd been in the country were the absence of opportunities to pee and the Palestinians' apparently complete lack of appetite during the day. She supposed these were natural adaptations to climate and economy, but like the language, they did not seem to be things you could easily acquire later in life.

She was drinking juice from a plastic bottle, her mouth uncomfortably fitting around the large opening, when she heard a small voice behind her.

"Fii wahad taht."

Chloe jumped, sloshing the orange liquid down her t-shirt. No problem, the shirt was already filthy anyway. She faced the sweet-faced ten-year-old, who looked eight, still in her striped school dress and pigtails.

"Miino, habibti?" *Who's downstairs?*

The little girl shrugged extravagantly. "Wahad Israeeeeli."

"Jesh?" Please, she thought, don't let it be the army. She was exhausted, and not ready for another confrontation.

The girl shook her head vigorously. She stroked her chin, indicating the man had a beard.

"What is he doing?"

"Talking to my father."

There was no point standing here playing twenty questions with Alaa.

31

Five minutes later, robbed of a shower but at least having splashed under her arms, wearing a clean blue silk blouse and with her hair neatly pinned back, she knocked on the door of Ahlam and Jaber, her landlords and neighbors. Ahlam welcomed her with kisses on both cheeks and thrust a teapot into her hands.

"Ruhi, habibti. Sobbi shai." *Go, pour the tea, dear.*

The fact that she was given a chore to do marked her as family. It meant that Ahlam didn't have to interrupt her cooking and cover her head to serve the Israeli man, who had so inconveniently turned up near dinner time. Chloe smelled fried cauliflower, her favorite, and hoped she would be invited to eat. She stepped into the living room.

Alaa had mentioned only one guest, so Chloe was surprised to see two men sitting on the couch, opposite Jaber in a matching wing chair. Jaber's handsome, hollow-cheeked face was animated in conversation. Chloe always had to remind herself that Ahlam was younger than she; the effects of bearing and raising six children gave her a matronly air, though she was still attractive. Jaber, on the contrary, looked like he could be fresh out of college, despite his three years in prison preceded by five years in hiding. Jaber tended his olive trees and goats like every other farmer in Azzawiya, but Chloe always assumed he came from money, based on the size of this house, the elegantly tiled floors and expansive courtyard, and the starched, pressed look he always had. Today, he wore a violet open-necked shirt with his clean blue jeans.

The second man didn't really merit the noun, in Chloe's opinion. The mysterious "Israeli" whose presence had summoned her was only twenty. His name was Avi Levav, and she had met him several times at demonstrations around the West Bank. He had short dark hair and a tightly clipped beard, no doubt an attempt to look older. On one forearm he wore a white sock, the bottom cut off and dyed like a Palestinian flag. It could pass for a sweatband, but Chloe knew it was covering the most god-awful collection of tattoos she had ever seen, a relic of his drug-abusing, squatter days in Europe.

The third man could have been 100 years old. His face was like a road map carved in leather. He wore stiff blue jeans with the traditional *keffiya* covering his head, Arafat-style. The cracks in his bare feet carried the dirt of years spent tramping up and down into the hills. Chloe had never seen him before, and Jaber did not interrupt the conversation to introduce her. She put the tea things on the coffee table between them and squatted down to spoon sugar into four glasses, added sprigs of mint, and poured the amber liquid. She could not sort out what they were discussing, though she caught familiar words here and there, and it dawned on her that they were speaking Hebrew, not Arabic. Of course, because Avi didn't speak Arabic.

"Yslamu ideeki," Jaber murmured as she handed him his tea.

"W ideek," she answered clearly, so the old man, whoever he was, would understand that she spoke Arabic. If he noticed, she would never know. He did not glance at her, even when she handed him a glass of tea. He simply took it from her hand and slurped greedily.

Chloe settled into the empty wing chair and nursed her tea while the men continued their animated conversation. She could only make out a few words—*mitnachlim*, settlers; *chayalim*, soldiers; *etzim*, trees. Before she came to Palestine, she had imagined that eight years of Hebrew school had taught her something. After a few minutes, her impatience got the better of her. They had called her, the least they could do was clue her in. It would be highly improper for her to interrupt. The most unobtrusive thing would be to ask Avi to translate for her. She inched her chair closer to the couch.

"What's going on?" she asked him quietly.

"The settlers in Elkana are building on the other side of the Wall."

"I know."

He shook his head.

"No, you don't know about this. You're talking about the houses after the built part of the Wall in Mas'ha."

She nodded.

"But now they're getting ready to build on Azzawiya land, where the Wall isn't built yet. They cut forty trees today, and they plan to uproot them tomorrow. It's his land," gesturing to the old man.

She quickly sucked in breath, making a small whistling sound.

"Who is he?"

"Abu Shaadi."

"Do you know what he wants to do?"

"Well, Jaber called us, so probably he wants to resist."

Chloe tried to contain her excitement. It wasn't seemly to jump up and down on hearing that you were going to have the opportunity to breathe teargas and be shot at. Sitting in front of bulldozers to stop them from uprooting sacred olive trees was the kind of thing that had brought her to Palestine nine months ago, but since then, there had been precious little of it to do.

"What are they talking about?" she asked Avi eagerly.

"Goats," he said with a wry grin. She caught his meaning—he had not defied the customs of his land, bluffed his way through checkpoints, and climbed over fences to hear about goats. They endured a few more minutes of chitchat before the old man turned to Avi.

"Do you think you can stop the bulldozers?"

Avi surprised Chloe by deferring to her.

"It is not we who can stop them," she said carefully. "If you want to try to stop them, we can bring some people to help." Avi nodded approval as Jaber translated for Abu Shaadi. The old man's face fell.

"But you will not stop them?"

Chloe rolled her eyes at Avi. This was a constant struggle. People wanted to believe that the internationals were the answer to their prayers, that you only had to call them and poof! the army and its tanks and bulldozers would disappear. Jaber stepped in to prevent the old man's disappointment from insulting his guests.

"How many people can you bring?" he asked the two foreigners.

They consulted silently. "I can call INSP," Chloe said. "I don't know how many people they have now—they couldn't bring more than four or five, I would think."

"It's short notice," Avi said. "But I can usually find five or six."

"They will bring ten foreigners," Jaber told Abu Shaadi. Chloe cringed. She didn't feel as confident as that sounded.

"Will others from the village come?" Avi wanted to know.

"Perhaps. After we eat, we will go and talk to the mayor."

Alaa appeared in the doorway. "You're invited," she said. That meant dinner was ready. Chloe went to the kitchen to help bring out the food. Ahlam had made all her favorites. In addition to the cauliflower, there was *mjaddara,* rice and lentils; *labneh,* yogurt strained of liquid, and a spicy stewed tomato dish.

Two of Jaber's sons joined them at the table. Ahlam and Alaa did not eat with them. They would eat later, in the kitchen. Now they hovered, making sure no one wanted for anything. Chloe felt guilty eating while they watched, but to decline their hospitality would be even ruder.

Avi ate only tiny amounts. Chloe tried to spoon cauliflower and tomatoes onto his plate, as Ahlam did to hers. He waved her away.

"You're not eating enough," she said. "You'll offend Ahlam."

"I don't eat dairy," he said.

"There's no dairy in tomatoes," she said, too softly for their hosts to hear.

"I hate tomatoes," he pouted.

"That's ridiculous. A vegan has to like vegetables."

"Yeah, well, I don't."

When she was feeling generous, Chloe acknowledged that Avi was an impressive young man. His father, who came from one of Israel's wealthy "First Families," was a news anchor for one of the big television stations. As a teenager, Avi had cofounded a small direct action group called Anarchists Without Borders, traveling to Palestinian villages by himself using a combination of settler buses and Palestinian public transit. His English was flawless and he was starting to teach himself Arabic. She seldom thought about how young he was, but every now and then, something like his eating habits reminded her that she could easily be his mother.

A scant fifteen minutes after the food had appeared on the table, Jaber pushed his chair back.

"Yalla." *Let's go*, he said.

When she had first come to the West Bank, Chloe had been startled by the pace of meals. At her parents' home, meals had been long social affairs, where the events of one's day or the events of the world would be recited and dissected. She had continued this tradition with her friends in adult life. With the love of her life, Alyssa, whose memory still smarted, preparing and consuming meals had played a central role. Palestinians, by contrast, treated meals as if they were about—well, eating. Guests or no guests, they ate solemnly and nearly silently for a few minutes, then abruptly stood up and left the table. If people were going to linger, they did it in the living room or on the porch.

Avi slung a fraying black backpack over his shoulder, his body tilting slightly under its weight.

"You could leave that," Chloe said. "You're spending the night, right?"

"No, I need to get home," he said. "I've gotta find out who can make it tomorrow, and call the press."

"Why not do it from here?" she asked. "We can split up the calls."

He mumbled something about the mobile being expensive, and it would be better to do it from a land line—an obvious lie. Israelis and their cell phones were like peanut butter and jelly. She had rarely seen Avi without his phone glued to his ear.

There was some reason he didn't want to stay. It was probably his girl-friend, Maya, a Ukrainian-born Israeli. Chloe didn't know her well, just that she was gorgeous and studied dance at the university. At demonstrations, she hung onto Avi, as if she didn't trust him more than a few inches from her side. Probably with good reason. If something was going on between Maya and Avi, Chloe had no interest in getting in the middle. She followed Avi into the cooling dusk, where the fragrance of four hundred dinners blended through the open doors.

Chapter 7

Before Rania could call Captain Mustafa about Abu Anwar, he called her. "Meet me under the bridge," he instructed. "The Yahud are coming to take the body."

When she got to the bridge, she was relieved to see that Abu Ziyad wasn't with him. A blue jeep with Hebrew writing on it lurched toward them. A beefy, mostly bald man unfolded himself from behind the wheel. His charcoal eyes seemed to pop out of his head as he surveyed the scene.

"This is Benny Lazar," Captain Mustafa told her, shaking the man's hand enthusiastically. The captain seldom showed pleasure, at least when Rania was around, but he actually smiled when Benny asked in Hebrew about his family.

"Does she speak Hebrew?" Benny asked Captain Mustafa.

"Lo," the captain replied. "Yodaat Anglit." *She speaks English.*

Knowing that Mustafa did not speak English, she could have made it easier by admitting that she knew some Hebrew. Benny would have double work translating everything into Hebrew for the captain, but that was fine with her.

His quick eyes sized her up, and she imagined what he was seeing. A short woman, light on her feet, with strands of dark hair peeking out from under her hijab. She bet he was thinking she would be pretty if her heavy-rimmed glasses did not give her small face a striped look.

"What've we got?" he asked in English. She led him to the spot where the young woman's body lay.

"Sinit," he said. *A Chinese woman.*

"Mumkin," Captain Mustafa mumbled in reply. Rania recognized the captain's habitual skepticism in his "maybe." Apparently unlike his Israeli counterpart, he disliked assumptions. "Tell me what you know, not what you believe," Rania had heard from him over and over.

Benny was circling the body now, much as Rania had done earlier, and talking compulsively about what he observed. He noted the different sets of tracks, just as she had, the girl's clothes, and the fact that she had no possessions near or on her. She pointed out to him the blood-stained grasses, and the indications of her being dragged over the ground.

"So," he said when she was done, "whodunit?"

She tried to assess what he was after. He couldn't think she really knew anything about how the girl ended up here. But whether he was trying to challenge her, or if it was a joke, she couldn't tell. She glanced at Captain Mustafa, but of course, he had not understood their exchange. He stood a little ways from them, smoking. He was leaving it to her to do the show and tell, which she thought meant that he trusted her and didn't want to interfere. Or maybe he was testing her to see how she would relate to this big, arrogant, Israeli cop. Whichever, she was going to make him proud of her and not be goaded into losing her temper.

"No idea," she said. "But it wasn't a Palestinian, so maybe you would know better than me."

"Why do you say it wasn't a Palestinian?" He stood so close, she could feel his breath. She forbade herself to move back.

"The only foreign women living in the villages here are married to Palestinians," she said, realizing as she spoke that it was not quite true. There was the woman she had met that morning, Chloe, who said she was living in Azzawiya. But she was nothing like this girl. "Dressed like this, she could not have set foot in one of these villages. She must have come from one of the settlements, or from the road. Either way, no Palestinian would have a reason to kill her."

"Maybe someone objected to the way she was dressed," he said. "Besides, there's a kid in Azzawiya with a Chinese girlfriend."

"Where did you hear that?" she burst out. That could not be true. She had talked to a number of people in Azzawiya today. None of them had mentioned ever seeing a Chinese woman in the village.

"I have my sources," he said, arching an eyebrow at her. She hoped she was not going to have to spend much more time with this guy. He seemed to enjoy annoying people, and she was easily annoyed. Now she wondered if he was telling the truth or baiting her. Israeli police and soldiers loved to set Palestinians against each other by insinuating that they had informers.

"Who is the boy?"

"I can't tell you that."

No, of course you can't, she wanted to say, because there is no such boy.

"You can't believe everything you hear," she said instead.

He chuckled and made some notes in a little spiral-bound notebook he kept in his breast pocket. He put on glasses to write, she noted, and then immediately took them off when he was done. She waited anxiously for him to ask what she had been doing since she found the body. She and the captain had agreed that they would not say anything about Abu Anwar until they had had a chance to talk to him. But Benny seemed too well-informed. What else did he know? she wondered. Or maybe he didn't really know anything, and it was all a bluff.

Thankfully, the Israeli coroner's people arrived and Benny rushed away to direct them. They strung yellow tape all around the area. Then they put numbers on the ground and took lots of pictures. Benny called her over to tell again how she had come to find the body. He did not ask her anything about what she had observed. These were crime scene experts, she understood, who did not need any help from a Palestinian policewoman to identify evidence.

When they had piled the body onto a stretcher and loaded it into their van, Benny shook hands with Captain Mustafa.

"See you later," he said in Hebrew. He opened the door of his jeep. She didn't like the sound of that. The Israelis had taken over, just as she had feared. She wondered momentarily why she cared. She felt a proprietary interest in the body because she had found it. Plus, if she had noticed the donkey tracks and the shoe prints, the Israelis had too. They would be snooping around in the villages before long, and she intended to be there to protect the people who needed protecting.

"What happens now?" she asked in English.

"We'll get in touch with the embassies, and try to find out who she was."

"And then?"

"We'll find out how they want to handle it."

Could that be it? She supposed so. She had never thought about what it would be like, to die far away from home, with no one to care. But why did she assume that? Maybe the girl had a family in Israel, who would call the police when she didn't come home.

Benny turned again to get into his jeep.

"Keep me informed," she said. He looked at her in surprise and then at Mustafa as if to say, "Rein her in." The captain stayed a little removed, smoking and saying nothing. She was taking advantage of the fact that he didn't speak English, but she guessed he was also happy to let her do the interfering, keeping it semiofficial.

"No problem," Benny said with a shrug. He even fished a business card out of his front pocket and scribbled a number on the back. "My mobile," he said.

✴ ✴ ✴

Captain Mustafa sat ramrod straight on the floral-cushioned couch. It was a little too low for his long legs, which nearly met his chest. Rania tried to emulate him, keeping her hands folded in her lap.

Abu Jawad lit one cigarette from the end of the last. He sucked on the new one, puffing out his cheeks slightly. "Hai mushkele kbiire." *This is a big problem*, he said.

That's the understatement of the century, Rania thought. "Indeed, Abu Jawad," she said. "Why didn't Abu Anwar come to us directly when he found the girl's body?"

"He wanted to talk to me first."

"But he didn't go straight to you either. He worked all day in his fields. Didn't you find that strange?"

"Not really. His groves are an hour's walk from the village. He had already gone half way. If he had to come back, and find me, and talk about the girl, and then go back to the field, it would have been very late when he got to work."

"But the girl was dead."

"Yes, and she did not get any more dead."

"If she had been a Palestinian, don't you think he would have acted right away?"

"She was not a Palestinian." He puffed on his cigarette some more, then put it out in the dregs of his tea. "I think he hoped someone else would have discovered her by the time he got back, and he would not have to say anything."

The door opened and Abu Anwar entered, his cane tapping on the wooden floor.

"Assalamu aleikum," he said. The fact he did not knock meant that this was a second home for him.

"W aleikum assalam," they all murmured.

Rania spooned sugar into a glass and poured tea from the steaming pot in front of her. She slid it before the old man, who had settled in an armchair opposite them. She hoped assuming the traditional female role might set them at ease with her. When he had taken a sip or two of the tea, she began, taking care to speak softly and not to sound aggressive or anxious.

Although it had been she who invited the captain to come to this interview, now that he was here, she felt she was being inspected. She wished he would simply take over, but he seemed to have no interest in doing that. He was trying to act like he had no interest in the proceedings at all; he was just now cleaning under his fingernails with a business card. She knew, however, that he was hearing and remembering every word.

She began by asking Abu Anwar the same questions she had already asked his brother. Why hadn't he come directly to the police when he found the body? Whom had he talked to during the day? Who else did he see in the morning? What did he think when he found the body?

He didn't know what to think, he answered. It's something very unusual, to find a dead person on your land. It unnerved him. He didn't want to be involved. He had not seen anyone else on his way to the land. He seemed embarrassed about his decision, and he also seemed afraid. She supposed it made sense to be afraid, when you found a dead body and didn't tell anyone, and now the police were here questioning you. But she thought that was not quite all.

"If there is anything else you know or observed, you need to tell us right away because the Israelis already know you were there," Rania said sternly.

She felt a twinge about lying to him in this way, knowing that he had been in an Israeli prison, and now had two sons in prison, but it was part of the job. He insisted that he had just wanted to get his work done. He never saw the girl before. He explained how he was looking for a board to put across the river of sewage, and found the shoes and how he fell down and thought he was sick.

"So, you see, Um Khaled," he appealed, "I wasn't right in my mind."

"And?" she encouraged. She stole a look at the captain, but he was still sitting like a statue. Why had he come if he wasn't going to help? she asked herself and then answered her own question. He came to show that she had the backing of someone who mattered, a member of the club. But if he gave them the chance, they would only talk to him. Only by maintaining his silent presence could he bestow on her the authority she needed to conduct the investigation.

She waited Abu Anwar out as he wrestled with himself. At last he slurped a bit of tea and heaved a deep sigh.

"There was a woman," he admitted.

"A woman where?"

"Crossing the fields. An Israeli woman."

The woman had on dark glasses, he said, a long dark skirt and white blouse, and a scarf over her head like the settler women wear. He could see her hair was dark. She was about thirty, maybe a little younger, attractive.

"You observed her very well given your distracted state," she commented.

"I must have been aware of her without realizing it. In my subconscious." Seeing her smile, he added, "My son, Ahmed, studied psychology at the university."

His description exactly matched Um Raad's, so whoever this woman was, she must have been there. But it didn't make sense; what would an Israeli woman dressed for work be doing in Azzawiya's fields?

"Abu Anwar," she said. "Why didn't you want to tell me about the Israeli woman? It will be better for us if we can tell the Israeli police about her."

He looked ashamed. "That is true, Um Khaled, but I did not want to become involved."

She felt some sympathy for the old man. He was right to be wary. Accusing an Israeli of having something to do with a murder was not something a Palestinian could do lightly. But now that he had told them, he seemed glad to have it off his chest.

"What do we do now, Abu Walid?" the mayor asked. Rania was momentarily irritated that he had excluded her so deftly. But if he had asked her, she would have had no idea how to answer him.

"I will talk with Abu Ziyad," the captain said. "And we will speak with you tomorrow."

She heard the muffled ringing of her phone, deep inside her handbag. She managed to dig it out before it stopped ringing.

"Where are you?" Bassam said. "We are ready to go to Dunya's."

She had completely forgotten that they were to eat at his sister's house in Deir Balut. But it was no problem.

"I'm in Azzawiya," she said. "I'll pick up some sweets and catch a car to Deir Balut. I'll probably be there before you."

"No, it won't look right."

"That's ridiculous." It would be fine for him to arrive on his own from work, but for her to do it would raise eyebrows from his brothers. As if they didn't know that she traveled all over by herself for her work. As if Dunya herself did not travel around for her work with the Elections Commission. But not at night, he would say. She wished he would simply tell his brothers, and his mother, where to get off. If it was something important to him, he would, she thought irritably.

"Pick me up by the sweets shop," she relented.

She hung up the phone. She needed to get going, but she didn't want to leave before the captain did. A knock on the door solved her problem. Abu Jawad ushered in a man in a violet shirt, with an old farmer and two foreigners.

"Chiif halach, Abu Fareed?" Mustafa shook hands with the violet-shirted man.

She recognized Jaber Haddad, though she didn't know him well. He was another one of the club of ex-fighters. One of the foreigners was Chloe, the woman she had met in the morning. The other was a young Israeli man she had seen in her village, Mas'ha, during their protests against the Wall, rakishly good looking, despite his abominable clothes.

"What happened at Beit Amin?" she asked Chloe.

"The usual," the American woman said. She turned to her friend. "This is Rania, Um … Um aysh?"

"I prefer Rania," she said. This Israeli man did not need to know the name of her son. Maybe Khaled was only six now, but one day, he would be old enough to be taken out of the house, beaten, tortured… she steered herself away from that train of thought.

"Rania works for the Palestinian police," Chloe told the young man. "And this is…"

"Abe," the boy filled in quickly. Smart boy, not wanting to broadcast his nationality, though she doubted many people would be fooled. He walked like an Israeli. That special arrogance shone in his face.

Captain Mustafa was leaving and that meant she could too. They went their separate ways, he toward the main road and she toward the shops in the village. The spring air was pungent with thyme and sage. Rania felt contented. She had acquitted herself well in front of the captain. She thought she would be able to convince him to let her continue working on the case, no matter what Abu Ziyad said.

Chapter 8

Dunya's courtyard was a pleasant oasis. It reminded Rania of her parents' house in Aida. The tiled terrace was surrounded by a low stucco wall and planted all the way around with fragrant herbs. A lemon tree bloomed in one corner, and brilliant purple hyacinth peeked out from behind the trellis. The coup de grâce was a real fountain that Dunya's husband and his brothers had assembled stone by stone during the curfews of the First Intifada. Their father, an engineer, had rigged it up to use recycled water. When she perched on the wall and gazed at the fountain, Rania could feel the pride with which the young men had polished each stone until it gleamed.

This warm evening, the men were gathered there with their mother. Everyone sat on hard purple plastic chairs, except Um Bassam, who reclined in a cushioned wicker armchair. Surrounded by her sons, her apple-cheeked face held a serenity Rania rarely got to see. The other women, Rania knew, were in the kitchen. Dunya's three sons and two of their boy cousins were playing soccer on the lawn. With them was Dunya's youngest, Hanin, who had just turned eight and insisted on having her hair cropped short. Khaled ran to join them. Bassam shook hands with his brothers and pulled up a chair. Rania dutifully kissed her mother-in-law on both cheeks.

"Why are you late?" the older woman grunted.

"I had work."

"Hmmph," came the reply.

"You found the body of the *ajnabiya* in Azzawiya's fields?" asked Amir. Rania had expected this. Word traveled quickly in the villages.

"That's right," she said.

"Do you know who she is?" Marwan inquired.

"Not yet," she said. "The Israelis are trying to find out."

"What is this?" her mother-in-law asked.

Rania left the men to fill their mother in on the news and went to help her sisters-in-law.

"You've put too much salt again," Marwan's wife, Jalila, was saying. Seeing Rania, she held out a spoonful of whitish broth.

"Taste this," she said. Rania took a sip.

"Perfect," she said.

"I can always count on Rania," Dunya said, laughing. She kissed Rania's left cheek, then her right and then the left again.

"What does she know about food?" said Maryam. "She's from Bethlehem." She was peeling cucumbers at the sink.

"True, they don't know good food in Bethlehem," said Jalila.

Rania found a knife and busied herself chopping the cucumbers into tiny cubes. Jalila went to work on the tomatoes.

"What about the girl they found in Azzawiya's fields?" asked Maryam.

Rania supposed she had better get used to repeating herself. The incident would be the talk of the area for a while.

"What is there to tell?" she said. "We don't know anything about her yet."

"I heard she was Chinese," said Jalila.

"We don't know that," Rania said. She felt annoyance welling up and tried to quell it. Naturally, her husband's family would feel they should have inside information to show for their connection to her. If there were a scandal around the elections, she would expect Dunya to share some juicy details with her. Police work is different, she told herself. But was it, or was it arrogance that made her assume that? She tried to think of some tidbit she could release to her sisters-in-law without compromising her investigation.

"The Israelis are trying to take the investigation over," she said. "They sent a big, bald Israeli cop to take the body away." She launched into a description of Benny that had the other women doubled over laughing by the time the chicken came out of the oven.

"How is your work?" she asked Dunya, as she carefully upended the mound of rice into a perfect pyramid. Dunya was the one member of Bassam's family she truly liked. She ran workshops for women in all the villages on how to participate in the electoral process, both as candidates and informed voters.

"It is good," Dunya replied. "I think more women will register than men."

"That is good," Rania said. "Especially if they vote for Fatah," she added, laughing.

"No, no, no," said Dunya. She and her husband belonged to the People's Party, the post-Soviet reconstitution of the Palestinian Communist Party.

"I heard that Hamas will win," said Jalila.

"If Hamas wins, Rania will have to leave her job," said Dunya.

"Where did you hear that?" Rania asked.

"A colleague at work."

Why me and not you? Rania started to ask, but then she answered her own question. Because Dunya's work was with women, and Hamas supported that. They wanted women to participate in civil society, but not alongside men, and not in ways that gave them authority over men.

"Hamas will never win," she said.

Rania had been active in Fatah since she was thirteen. Her best friends had joined the Popular Front for the Liberation of Palestine because they had the cutest boys, but she didn't care about that. Fatah was the party of Abu Amaar, Yasser Arafat, who had created the Palestinian nation, and no one else was going to lead the nation into freedom. If you wanted to make a difference, you had to be with Fatah. It had paid off for her. She was a little troubled by the stories of corruption, but every political movement has its corruption. There are no pure leaders in the world; anyone alive who has nothing, if you say *here, here is a nice house, here is a new car*, he will take it.

Now, with Abu Ammar recently dead, everything was up in the air. There were rumors among the police about what would happen to their jobs if Hamas gained power. She wasn't worried. Hamas might look good to the poor people when they gave away food at Eid and built kindergartens for the children, but Palestinians didn't want a government of religionists. They wanted freedom. And Fatah was the party of freedom.

"Why don't you run for council?" Jalila asked her.

"I don't have time," she said. "Why don't you?" Jalila was the only one of her sisters-in-law who didn't work. Of course, she didn't need to. In addition to his share of the family stores, Marwan had a thriving business in mobile phones. No matter how poor the people got, they would not let go of their phones.

"Maybe I will," Jalila shrugged. "I think I would be good, don't you?"

"What is your platform?" Dunya asked.

"Dishwashers for every woman. And internet in every house."

"I will vote for you," Rania said. She loaded dishes onto a huge metal tray.

"Then I will get one vote," her sister-in-law said with a grin. Balancing dishes on her forearm like an experienced waiter, she pushed the swinging door open with her backside. Rania followed her with the tray. They placed the dishes on a huge sheet of plastic on the floor and set cushions all around it for everyone to sit on.

They ate in silence, with al Jazeera in the background. Rania watched bombs explode in Baghdad, saw the half-burned bodies carted away, their family members wailing and tearing at their hair. Who would wail for the young woman she had found in the grass? How long would it be before they knew what explosion had taken her from them?

Chapter 9

Early the next morning, fortified by a good cup of American coffee and a crust of bread dipped in olive oil and the gritty herb mixture called *zaatar*, Chloe went downstairs to meet Jaber. They walked in companionable silence to Abu Shaadi's.

A white minibus was disgorging its passengers in Abu Shaadi's front yard. Avi stood next to the bus, talking to the driver, a Palestinian Israeli with a heavy handlebar mustache. Since he was occupied, Chloe studied the people getting off the bus.

Rabbi Shimon Dreyer was a forty-something American who talked so fast that he often stumbled over his words. He was clearly the leader of the group of ten or so Israelis, which included the effervescent Maya. The dancer's long-sleeved yellow shirt was a tad sheer for propriety, camisole straps clearly visible underneath. Chloe bit the inside of her cheek to avoid starting the day off with trouble. A rabbinical student named Itai, the leader-in-training, hustled the group into the house, looking nervously over his shoulder as if terrorists might burst out from the trees. It took Chloe exactly three minutes to decide that Itai was one of those annoying men who try to take over every action and tell the Palestinians what to do.

There were five other internationals too. Chloe was relieved to see none of the men she had known during her brief stint with INSP. The average lifespan of an international activist in Palestine was a month or two. Four of the activists here today were an "affinity group"—INSP jargon for a group that had been trained together—comprising two French women chicly attired all in black, a huge Italian guy with long stringy hair, and a tiny Swedish woman who spoke British-accented English. Though affinity groups were in principle rigidly egalitarian, the Italian guy seemed to have appointed himself their leader, no doubt by virtue of his ability to speak both broken French and broken English very loudly. The four of them stood together in a tight group, while the other woman stood by herself. She was extremely tall with caramel skin and a model's posture. Henna-tinged dark hair was caught into a knot at the nape of her endless neck.

The woman saw Chloe looking—or gawking—at her and made her way to where she stood.

"Six-one," she said.

Chloe didn't need a mirror to know her face had turned an unpleasant salmon color.

"Five-seven," she stammered. "But you can call me Chloe."

The tall woman's wide-set, gray-green eyes danced, and Chloe felt her cheeks cool to medium rare.

"Tina," sticking out her hand. The brief contact hit Chloe like an electric shock. She followed Tina into the house, where Abu Shaadi's wife was busy plying the foreigners with tea and crescent-shaped date cookies.

"Maamoul?" Chloe took the plate and offered it to Tina.

"Love them," Tina said, helping herself. Good, Chloe thought, not a dieter. So many of the foreign women who turned up talked on and on about how much weight they were gaining from all the carbs Palestinians served.

"You're from Australia?" Chloe guessed. She took a cookie and tried to nibble it rather than swallow it whole.

"Melbourne," Tina said. Chloe gave herself a point, wondering if Tina would think identifying the accent was such a great feat.

"So, are you working with INSP?"

"No, no, I'm volunteering at a counseling center in Ramallah. Maria," indicating the Swedish woman with the long blonde braid, "came the other day to see about volunteering with us. I gather she finds INSP a little male dominated."

"Gee, I can't imagine that," Chloe said, winning a smile from Tina.

"Anyway, I told her I would like to participate in demonstrations, and so here I am."

"Do you counsel in Arabic?" Chloe said, accepting a tiny cup of sweet coffee from one of the children.

"Yes, of course."

"Where did you learn?"

"From my parents. We speak it at home."

Chloe felt heat rise in her face again. She really had wanted to make a good impression on this woman, and her foot was stuck so deep in her throat, she couldn't even swallow her coffee. She started coughing, and Tina rapped her smartly on the back. It was so absurd, thinking about choking on her foot had actually made her choke, that Chloe started laughing and Tina good-naturedly joined in.

"I was born here in Palestine," Tina said. "We moved to Australia when I was three. This is my first time back."

"That must be intense for you. Do you still have family here?"

"Sure, a lot. That's why I wanted to come."

"Where do they live?" Chloe hoped she didn't sound like an airport interrogator.

"All over. Jerusalem, Ramallah, some in the Galil. I'm staying with my aunt in Beit Sefafa."

"How long are you here?"

"I've been here just over two weeks, and I'm staying… I don't know. As long as I can, I guess. What about you?"

"I've been here nine months and I'm staying until my money runs out— which will probably be pretty soon."

"What are you doing?"

"I'm living here in Azzawiya."

"Alone?"

"I came with INSP when they started building the Wall here. There were demonstrations every day then, and at first the women were amazing, sitting in front of the bulldozers, but then the army started coming deeper into the village every day, shooting more gas than I ever saw, and after a few days, it was only young men and us. I don't know what would have happened, if the high court hadn't made them change the route of the Wall to take less land from the village."

"So why did you stay here, once the demonstrations were over?"

"Jaber and the mayor were worried that the army would retaliate against the village for their resistance, so they didn't want the internationals to leave right away. But the guys and the younger women didn't want to stay, once it was calm. I stayed with one other woman who was even older than me—"

Tina acknowledged the self-deprecation with a half-smile.

"—but she was only here for a few weeks. I got involved in doing some stuff with Ahlam, Jaber's wife, who runs the women's club here. I'm helping her write grant proposals to some western foundations, and teaching the girls computers."

"Do they pay you?"

"Oh, no, I couldn't take money from the people here, that would be all wrong."

"So how can you afford to be here so long?"

"At home I'm a software engineer. I worked for a startup that made a lot of money for a little while, and everyone who worked there got stock in the company. I managed to sell off some of my stock before the company went broke. I didn't get rich, but I can live for a year or so, if I'm frugal. Which I am."

The front door opened and two youngish Palestinian women entered, followed by a brood of children who looked between eight and twelve. The noise level in the house skyrocketed as the young boys tore around, greeting the men and talking excitedly in Arabic. The young women disappeared into the kitchen.

"Are you staying with a family?" Tina was asking.

Chloe turned her attention back to their conversation.

"I wanted to, so I'd have to speak Arabic all the time, but Jaber said people wouldn't accept a single woman living in a household that included men. He has an empty apartment upstairs in his house, so I stay there by myself. Sometimes when women get sick of the sexism in INSP, they come and stay there for a while. I call it our refugee camp."

She suddenly worried that a Palestinian would think the jocular reference to refugee camps was in bad taste. Thankfully, Tina chuckled.

"People don't think it's weird, you being here alone?"

"I'm sure some of them do, but Jaber has a lot of clout in the village. When the army raids people's houses at night, usually someone calls me to come and take pictures of the damage and help find whoever's been arrested. So I guess they are glad enough I'm here."

Engrossed in the conversation, Chloe had not realized everyone was standing up. The Israelis followed Shimon and Abu Shaadi out of the house. Three of Abu Shaadi's sons joined them, as well as the two young women Chloe presumed were his daughters-in-law, and their children. Chloe was disappointed but not surprised that no media had shown up. She had called every contact she had the night before, and some of them had said they would try to make it, but uprooting trees was not news any more. One TV reporter had told her to call him if there was violence.

When they reached the land, the trunks of olive trees with lopped-off branches greeted them like ghostly gargoyles. There was no sign of bulldozers or soldiers. Chloe hoped they would come soon. Even in the early morning, the sun was beginning to beat down. By noon it would be unbearable. The Israelis seated themselves in one group, shading under a tree that had not been cut. A few of them had spoken briefly to Abu Shaadi in the house, but now they seemed content to talk among themselves. Rabbi Shimon and Avi sat with Abu Shaadi and Jaber, talking rapidly in Hebrew.

With her limited Hebrew, Chloe saw no point in joining them. She sat with the women for a while, not really talking. She didn't know them, and they didn't seem interested in making conversation with her. She ambled over to where the small children were playing, and asked them to help her with her Arabic. Kids were always good teachers for her, since she was closer to their level. They taught her the word for slingshot, and some sports-related words like "net" and "basket." She promptly forgot them all.

Tina was sitting among the women now, and they were all talking animatedly in Arabic. The women were touching her hair, making big gestures. One of the women was pulling a scarf out of a picnic basket—doubtless it had been covering bread or something—and wrapping it around Tina's head. Tina didn't look happy. Chloe couldn't help her. Palestinian women would never try to tell *her* how she should dress or pray, but diaspora Palestinians were another story. Tina could take care of herself, Chloe figured.

Chloe wandered over and sat down in the circle of Israelis. Itai turned to her.

"So, you are living here?"

"Yes, in Azzawiya."

"What do you do here?"

The dreaded question. What did she do, indeed?

"Mostly I take pictures and video of human rights violations in the area and support Palestinian nonviolent resistance to the occupation."

"Nonviolent resistance, yes. That is what the Palestinians need to do. If they could get everyone in their communities to commit to nonviolence, give up armed resistance, they would win."

"Well, if the Israelis would commit to nonviolence, maybe the Palestinians would follow suit."

He shook his head fiercely, his beard a waving exclamation point. "It never works like that. The occupier will not disarm first. The occupied people always have to take the risk. It's not fair, but it's reality."

"But the Palestinians have been using nonviolence for years and years, and where has it gotten them? All during Oslo, there were no bombings in Israel. The number of Israeli settlements doubled, and so did the number of checkpoints. There was a nonviolent movement then. People would plant trees, and the next day the army would come and dig them up."

"No one said it would be easy," said the young man. She was about to retort that his life seemed easy enough, but a hand on her arm stopped her. Tina, her head dutifully covered, was perched next to her, waiting for what Itai would say next.

"But," he went on, "ultimately, the settlements will benefit the Palestinians, because now it is not practical any more to talk about two states. Right now, the suicide bombings allow our government to justify harsh measures, to destroy the Palestinian resistance. But if the Palestinians used only nonviolent pressure, eventually, our government would have to grant Israeli citizenship to everyone who lives between the Jordan River and the sea."

"Well," Chloe said, "I'm not sure you are right, but even if you are, who says the Palestinians want to be Israeli citizens?"

"As long as everyone is equal," a man named Gil chimed in, "what's the problem?"

"There's no problem," Chloe said, "as long as you think it's okay to annex territory by occupying it."

"Exactly," Tina said. Chloe turned to glance at her. Her expression was controlled, but a muscle in her face twitched.

Itai said, "You have to be pragmatic. Israel has already annexed the territory, the point now is for everyone to have equal rights."

"What about the right to our nationality?" asked Tina.

"Nationality is a luxury," said Itai.

"Fine," Chloe said, "why don't you give up being Israeli? That's a nationality that has not existed for even sixty years, no one has had much time to get so attached to it, right?"

Gil turned to Tina. "What do you really want?" he asked. She flinched. Chloe thought she understood why. With one short statement, she had become the spokesperson for the entire Palestinian population.

"What do I want? I want the Jewish settlers to get out of my grandfather's house in Jerusalem so my family can move back in. I want the Israelis to pay my family for the land you took away from us, and the houses you knocked down in my mother's village. I want you to admit that you killed my cousin in cold blood, and I want to hunt down the men who deliberately shot her on her front porch in broad daylight, and put them on trial for war crimes, and I want to see them go to prison for the rest of their lives."

Chloe watched the shock settle on the faces of Itai and his friends. In the space of a minute, or maybe half of one, she saw them go from relaxed and conversational, to wary and combative, to frightened and angry, and they had not even gotten in a word. She observed Tina with a mixture of awe and tension, wondering if she knew how dangerous it could be to be so honest with Israelis. Probably, these men would never report her or her family to the army or the secret police, but they could. Some of them might even *be* in the army.

Tina wiped something from her cheek, that could have been sweat or the beginning of tears. Chloe thought it would be very hard to be the only Palestinian involved in a conversation like this. The Israelis were just passing time; they could have been talking about anything. She wished the bulldozers would hurry up and come.

The sun was approaching its zenith. Chloe's water bottle was empty. She strolled over to where Avi sat alone, writing in a notebook.

"They won't come today," Chloe said. "They'll wait a day or two, to catch him unawares."

"You don't know that, they could just be late."

"They could also come at six p.m. If we wait all day, and they don't come, people will be demoralized and not come next time."

"If we leave and they come in an hour, people will be more demoralized."

He had a point. No one was very interested in her opinion anyway. The Israelis would pay no attention to her because she didn't speak Hebrew. The Palestinians wouldn't pay attention to her because she was a woman. They would rather talk to Avi, even though *he* realized she knew more than he did. He would listen to what she had to say, and if he agreed, represent it to the Palestinians as his idea.

He turned back to whatever he was writing, and she snuck a glance over his shoulder. He was not writing after all, but sketching. He had done a creditable job of capturing the scene, giving it a liveliness her photos couldn't match. She was in the center of his drawing, arguing with Itai.

"I didn't know you drew," she said. One more thing to hold against him—she couldn't draw a stick figure.

"It's my job," he said. "I'm an animator." Funny, she had never imagined him having to work at all.

"One of my best friends is an animator," she said. "For Pixar. She works at night."

"So do I," he said. "That way I can have my days free for this. But I only work three nights a week."

A distant clanking brought him to his feet. Two bulldozers were chugging up the hillside, a yellow Caterpillar with a wide iron blade in front for moving and leveling piles of earth, and an orange Volvo with a serrated bucket for digging up trees by the roots. A blue border police jeep led them and another brought up the rear. Top Killer's head poked out of the top of the lead jeep. The soldier who told Chloe to go to Iraq aimed his rifle out the passenger's window, straight at Abu Shaadi's grandsons.

The boys had slingshots in their hands, and now they scrambled around, looking for stones. Chloe hoped this wasn't going to disintegrate into a slingshots versus automatic weapons competition. Jaber said something to the boys and they moved aside. They didn't drop their stones, but they relaxed their arms. The Palestinians arranged themselves in two ragged rows, men and boys in front, the women behind. The internationals ran to the front. Some of the Israelis went forward toward the jeeps, yelling things in Hebrew.

Chloe stood off to one side, near the boys with the slingshots. She switched her video camera to standby and slung it over her shoulder, then took a small still camera out of her backpack and snapped a few pictures of the soldiers and the protesters. Wordlessly, Tina came and stood next to her.

The jeep stopped about ten meters from the group. Top Killer and Iraq took their time dismounting. They gathered their weapons, clad themselves in bulletproof vests and helmets, checked the readiness of their long sticks, and walked forward with their hands cradling the triggers of their rifles. Immediately, Itai and two other Israelis, a man and a woman, walked forward to intercept them. Abu Shaadi hung back with Jaber.

Chloe sprang into action, moving in between the two little bands of Israelis.

"Come talk to the soldiers," she called to Abu Shaadi in Arabic. "This is your land. It's for you to decide what will happen."

The older man looked to Jaber for concurrence. Jaber urged him forward, one hand on his arm. The mayor and Rabbi Shimon went too. They spoke quietly, too quietly for Chloe to hear what they were saying. Top Killer kept fondling his gun. The bulldozers loomed behind, occasionally revving their engines.

"This is our land," Chloe heard Abu Shaadi repeat over and over in Hebrew.

"Shetach sagur." *A closed area*, Top Killer kept replying.

It didn't sound like they were making much progress. Shimon remonstrated with the armed men, who waved papers at him. He tried to take them, but Top Killer lifted them over his head. Then they all went over to the jeep together and spread the papers on the hood. Shimon pointed to the paper and then to a clump of trees, and Top Killer shook his head and tapped his finger forcefully against the paper and swept his arm out, indicating all the land they could see.

"Eser dakot," Top Killer said finally, loud enough for everyone to hear. He was giving them ten minutes to leave or his troops would use force, possibly arrests, to disperse them. The Israelis erupted in a din of Hebrew, arguing about what to do. Shimon seemed to be saying they should leave, because there was no media present, and Avi was arguing they should stay and be arrested if necessary, so the Palestinians would see that they were serious about their solidarity. Abu Shaadi and Jaber stayed out of it, pacing and smoking.

Their ten minutes were almost up. Shimon was talking on his cell phone. Top Killer, Iraq, and two other guys were fiddling with the orange bulbs Chloe recognized as sound grenades. Once upon a time, the sight of those grenades would have scared her. Now she was relieved to see them, because as long as they had these "non-lethal weapons," they would probably not resort to live ammunition. Of course, their choice of weapons was partly based on the presence of Israeli civilians. If the Israelis really left, or were arrested, the strategy might change in a hurry.

Chloe went forward until there was no one between her and the army vehicles. She crouched down, aiming her camera, trying to capture the soldiers, the jeep, the bulldozers and the land behind them, in the same shot. She snapped a couple pictures, then moved across to the other side to see if she could get a better angle. She was thinking of trying to get behind the bulldozers to get a shot with the bulldozers and the Palestinians in it, when suddenly she heard, "America. Boi."

Iraq was pointing to her, but it was Top Killer who was commanding her presence. She ignored him, but backed away slowly, getting closer to the rest of the internationals.

"Why do you take pictures of us?" Top Killer demanded.

"Documentation."

"What?"

She cursed herself for using an English word he wouldn't know. Iraq translated the word into Hebrew for him.

"Let me see your camera." Top Killer reached out his hand for it. Chloe hesitated. She didn't want to be the center of a confrontation, but her camera was her prize possession.

"I'll show you the pictures." She turned the camera to playback and held the image in front of his face. "See, it's nothing, you're not doing anything wrong."

"Give me the camera."

She quickly shoved the camera into her backpack. Top Killer started to lunge for her. Avi and the others blocked his path. He snarled, reaching for his baton. Iraq touched his arm, speaking urgently in Hebrew. Chloe signaled to the others to take the moment's distraction to move back a little, not so much that they would seem to be running away, but just to give them a little more space. Top Killer seemed undeterred. He had the baton in his hand now, and was swinging it over his head the way he had the day Chloe first saw him, at the checkpoint. She imagined how it would feel, coming down on her head.

She heard a car approaching. A cloud of dust appeared in the road, and then a white jeep swept around the other vehicles and pulled up in front of where they stood. Top Killer turned around, as a Druze officer climbed out of the jeep. Chloe let out a deep breath.

The officer was short and swarthy, his pressed tan uniform carrying the insignia of a captain. He did not speak to Top Killer and the others—they simply melted into formation behind him, as if in a dance performed so many times that the dancers' feet knew the steps without the music. The officer shook hands with Shimon, and then with Abu Shaadi and the mayor.

"I know this is your land and your father's land and his father's," Chloe heard him say in Arabic. Compassion oozed from his expressive face. "It's a shame, but there is nothing I can do."

"But you yourself told me, when you came to tell us about the Wall, that nothing would happen to my land," Abu Shaadi argued.

"I know, I am sorry about that. I didn't know," said the captain. "If you tell everyone to move away, we will uproot the trees properly, and replant them for you somewhere else. But if you make it hard for us, then we will have to come back with lots of troops and maybe even declare a curfew, and you and your sons might be arrested, and the trees could be damaged."

Abu Shaadi was wavering, Chloe could see. His heart said one thing, but his mind knew he would not win this battle. Shimon stepped forward then.

"Wait a minute," he said. "You are obligated to give a three-day notice of confiscation of land, so that the owner has time to go to court. But Abu Shaadi only heard about this yesterday."

"I gave the notice to Abu Ziyad three days ago," the captain said.

"Who is Abu Ziyad?" Chloe whispered to Avi.

"The Palestinian DCL," Avi whispered back.

"I've never met him," she said.

"You didn't miss anything," he said. "He's a jerk."

She didn't have time to ask what made Abu Ziyad a jerk. The captain was getting in his jeep, and so were the soldiers. A slow cheer rose from the collected body, as the bulldozers swung around in a huge circle and headed back toward the settlement. Top Killer's jeep was now at the back. As it sped off, kicking up dust, Top Killer leaned down from his perch and yelled to Chloe, "Next time I see you, I am going to arrest you."

"I'll have to make sure he doesn't see me," Chloe said to Tina, who had materialized at her elbow. She hoped her performance here had piqued the other woman's interest. Tina did seem to prefer her company to any of the other internationals, but that wasn't saying much. The two French women didn't even speak English.

When the jeeps and bulldozers were gone, Abu Shaadi's sons-in-law turned to give high fives to each other, and then to some of the Israeli men. Abu Shaadi seized Shimon's hand in both his own and shook until Chloe thought the rabbi risked a dislocated shoulder. He went through the same ritual with Avi and then with Jaber. None of them said anything to Chloe. It was like she hadn't even been there when the action was planned, like she hadn't spent three solid hours on the phone to the press, not to mention having just been threatened by a crazed border policeman. She joined the women and helped them gather up their belongings.

"The bus is here to take us back to Jerusalem," Shimon announced in Hebrew, and then it was like a vacuum cleaner sucked all the Israelis out of the area. Chloe tapped Tina's shoulder as the other woman was about to climb into the van.

"Hope I see you again sometime," Chloe said.

"Right-o," Tina responded and then she was gone. The adrenaline draining from her body, Chloe suddenly realized she was exhausted and hungry. She promised herself to stop for a falafel on the way to her flat, a hot shower, and a nap.

Chapter 10

Rania got to work early on Tuesday. She had heard nothing from Benny or Captain Mustafa since leaving Abu Anwar's house the previous evening and she was eager for news. She peeked into the captain's office even before she got coffee, but he was not there. Abdelhakim was the only one in ahead of her, reading over some files. He was just out of school, and she figured he was trying to make a good impression. She made herself a coffee and brought him one too.

"Has Abu Walid been in?" she asked.

"He is with Abu Ziyad," he responded.

Abu Ziyad's office was a block away, in the Baladiya, the municipal office building. She was tempted to walk over there, but it wouldn't be appropriate. She sat down at her desk, but immediately popped back up, too restless to sit still. She had no open cases, nothing to distract herself with. Her hand went into her pocket almost of its own accord and pulled out the business card Benny had given her. She shouldn't call him without talking to the captain, but he wouldn't know that. She dialed the number, and held her breath while it rang.

"It is Rania Bakara from the Palestinian police," she announced. "Have you identified the dead girl?"

She was almost sure he was going to say, "I just told your bosses all about it," and hang up, but he didn't.

"We're working on it," he said cheerfully. "The Chinese consulate doesn't think she is from China, but if she is, they won't be able to ID her. Nearly all of the Chinese women come here illegally from Egypt, so there's no record of them."

"Why don't they think she is Chinese?" she asked.

"Her clothes and haircut," he said. "The consul suggested she could be Filipina or Malaysian. We've sent a picture to the Philippine Consulate as well. The Malaysians don't have a consulate—it's a Muslim country."

"I know that." She hadn't, actually. She just didn't like the way he stressed the word "Muslim."

"She might not be a worker," he said. "She could be one of those peace activists. A lot of them are hanging around this area now because of the Fence."

"It's not a fence," she said. "It's an apartheid wall." Abdulhakim set down the file he was reading and made a note on a small yellow pad. Her desk was behind his, so she couldn't tell if he was eavesdropping.

"Let's not get into politics," Benny said. He sounded amused, though. "Our medical examiner says she was six weeks pregnant," he added.

"Is that why you say she was an activist? Because only loose women care about Palestinians?"

"I didn't say she was loose. She could have been married to a Palestinian."

"Not dressed like that. Besides, there was no ring on her finger." Of course, the killer could have taken the ring. But if the girl was married to a Palestinian, a Palestinian might have killed her, and Rania didn't want to consider that. "Have you canvassed the settlements?"

"We are getting ready to," he said. "Some boys from the immigration police are on their way to Elkana now. They think there are some illegal domestic workers employed there."

"I want to go with them," she announced. She had never before wanted to set foot in any of the colonies built on her people's stolen land. She looked down on the Palestinians who took jobs there. But this was her case, and she wasn't going to sit around waiting for the Israeli police to find out who this girl was and why she was killed.

"No problem," he said, forestalling all the arguments she had been preparing. "Be at the entrance to Ariel in half an hour."

As she raced down the steps, Captain Mustafa was clumping up them. Over his shoulder, she saw a service taxi on the street and waved to it frantically.

"Weyn rayha?" he asked. *Where are you going?*

"I spoke to Benny," she answered. "I am going with him to Elkana." Not strictly true, but close enough.

He frowned more than usual. "There will be trouble," he said. "The DCL wants to handle the case. It's Area C."

"Area C," she scoffed. The Oslo accords had divided Palestinian land into a complex web of Areas A, B, and C, ostensibly governing who had responsibility for civil affairs and security in each area. The larger Palestinian cities were classified as "Area A," and theoretically under total control of the Palestinian Authority; most villages were areas of shared control, "Area B," but lands nearer to Israeli settlements and roads, including border villages and most agricultural lands, were "Area C," under complete control of the Israeli occupiers. The Israelis never worried about whether they were breaking the agreements. Since the Second Intifada began, their tanks were in and out of Bethlehem, Jenin, Ramallah, all the cities, almost daily. Under Oslo, the Palestinians were supposed to have their own country by this time.

"What is Abu Ziyad doing?" she asked.

"He is in touch with the Israeli DCL," the captain responded.

"No, no, no," Rania said, then stopped herself abruptly. The captain always treated her like a daughter, but even daughters had to observe certain protocols. Her sense of injustice reared up—how dared they give away her case without even consulting her? But of course, no one had ever said it was her case. She had found a body, that was all.

"Benny invited me to go with him," she said. "What will it hurt?"

The captain stroked his mustache, thinking it over. "Tamam," he said. *Okay.* "Perhaps it will not hurt." He might be glad to have her as a mole with the Israeli police. Abu Ziyad was his friend, but she didn't think he trusted the man completely either. She would have today to convince Benny she could be valuable to him.

* * *

She caught a shared taxi to Yasouf and then another to Kifl Hares, and crossed the highway to the long entrance to Ariel. She wasn't sure if she should wait near the bus stop, or go up to the gate. She would rather not speak to the soldier at the gate, who was already staring at her as if he thought she had a bomb under her jilbab, just ready to blow herself up along with him and the teenagers waiting for buses. She was about to call Benny on her mobile when a jeep screeched to a halt next to where she stood.

"You are the policewoman?" one of the young men inside called loudly in English.

"Yes."

He gestured for her to get in. It was an enormous step up, and she nearly didn't make it. She felt a little pull in her groin muscle as she hoisted herself onto a half-seat covered with guns and flak jackets. Once she was as settled as she could get, she inspected the company.

Two of the young men looked like they were doing their compulsory military service; they could not have been more than nineteen. The third was a little older. They were full of jokes and at the end of a joke, they would punch each other in the arms, like ten-year-olds.

They reminded her of the soldiers who used to come into the camp when she was in high school, driving slowly, baiting the young men to come out and throw stones so they could shoot at them. That was the First Intifada, and Rania was heavily involved with the Fatah youth movement, organizing among students, and sneaking off to meetings at night. Her parents didn't want her involved. Two of her brothers were already in prison.

She threw stones at the jeeps too, when they did their constant sweeps through the camp. She was good with a slingshot. The boys would praise her aim, better than most of theirs, but when the soldiers got out of the jeeps and started running after them, looking for kids to arrest and beat, two older boys whose houses were near hers would grab her arms and run with her to her house and throw her inside, telling her, "Stay here, you have another role to play. You will not serve your country from prison." She never understood it, they were out there, they would probably end up in prison, if they were not killed first. But she accepted it, because their caring was obviously genuine. They were not trying to exclude her. They saw in her something special and part of their job was to protect certain leaders. So she would stay in the house and peek out of the windows and see which boys got snatched up, who was shot or beaten until he was bloody.

"I am Nimrod," said the tall man sitting next to her. She restrained a grin. One of the soldiers who used to terrorize Aida had that name, and then she read something like it in an American novel, but there it wasn't a name, it was a word that she gathered meant "idiot." She loved thinking of that evil soldier as "Stupidhead." Nimrod introduced the driver as Dani.

The third guy's name she didn't catch, but he was talking to her now, asking in Hebrew if she wanted a cookie. She hesitated, trying to decide if it was advantageous to let them know that she knew some Hebrew. They would accept her more readily if she spoke Hebrew with them, but she didn't know if she wanted to be accepted by them. If they didn't think she understood them, they would talk more freely and she might learn more.

"Sorry, I don't speak Hebrew," she said in English.

The guy whose name she didn't know said to Nimrod, "Ask her if she wants a cookie."

Nimrod held out the package of cookies to her, and said in English, "Are you hungry?"

"No," she said, but she took a cookie. She should take anything she could get from the Israelis. They got her land, at least she should get a cookie.

They ignored her now and talked to one another in Hebrew. They didn't say anything interesting, but she gathered they were excited to be on this mission because they might get to beat people up. As they sped down the highway, Nimrod and Dani told the other guy about some Nigerians they arrested yesterday, who had tried to run.

"We beat the shit out of them," Nimrod said, and they all laughed.

One of them had to go to the hospital, Dani said, but they held him in an ice-cold cell for a few hours with his bleeding head first, to punish him for giving them so much trouble. Nimrod said the Nigerian women always lied and claimed to have kids.

Just when she thought she might explode and say something she would regret, the car screeched to a halt before the yellow gate that led to the settlement of Elkana. The soldier in the guard booth pressed the button that lifted the gate. Rania took a long look around her as they drove into the settlement. She had only seen the identical rows of red roofs from the hills above it. She had always wondered what it would look like inside. She had never seen anything like it, a town seemingly cut out with a cutter, like the handbags in her aunt's factory in Aida. Every house was exactly like every other, with identical small yards of green grass and a few flowers. All the streets seemed to go around in circles, each leading to another circle that looked exactly the same. She figured the policemen would never leave her alone in here, but they better not because she would never ever find her way out. She would wander in Elkana for the rest of her life.

Behind some of the houses, she glimpsed oblong swimming pools, filled with still turquoise water. There were no chickens or sheep, like you found in the yards in Mas'ha, nor fragrant patches of mint and sage for tea. Every house had a terrace, and on the terraces there would be a wooden table and two big wooden chairs, not the stacking plastic ones many Palestinians kept in a corner in case a host of family or friends decided to drop by. There seemed to be water spurting out of the ground, drenching the lawns and keeping them bright green.

"What is making that water?" she asked Nimrod.

"What water?"

"Coming out of the ground like that."

He followed her outstretched hand. "Oh, sprinkler systems."

"Do they go like that all time?"

"Most of them are on a timer, so they start and stop every so many minutes."

She considered that. All this water. In Aida in the summer, there was never enough water for everyone in the camp. You got it on a rotating basis, but sometimes there was not enough pressure to pump it up to the houses at the top, even when it was their turn. You were lucky if you got to take a bath twice a week.

They split into pairs. She was paired with Nimrod, because he spoke English. He handed her a picture of the dead girl, printed on a color printer. It had been digitally cleaned up so she did not look dead. They went house to house. Most people were at work, and the first ten people who were home did not recognize the girl. At a grocery store with signs in English, Hebrew, and Russian, the woman said yes, she came in sometimes, but no, she didn't know her name or where she lived, who she worked for or where she came from.

"Sorry," the woman said, looking curiously at Rania, "I didn't pay that much attention. We're very busy during the days." Rania looked around the empty store and wondered.

"Are there other stores?" Rania asked.

"Not ones with vegetables like mine," the woman said firmly.

"Is that what she usually came for?"

"Not just. She bought everything from me, milk, toilet paper, everything."

"Then it makes sense that she lived in this area of the settlement?"

"I guess so," the woman acknowledged.

They concentrated in the neighborhood around the store. They were approaching a house where there were four small children playing in the front yard with a young Asian woman. She saw them and vanished into the house, slamming the door after her. The children started crying. While Nimrod struggled with the locked front door, the nanny burst through the back door and headed for a series of fences. Nimrod took off after her. Rania hesitated. Her clothing was not designed for jumping over fences. Maybe she should stay with the kids. She looked around. She saw no one on the street. Surely a religious Israeli settlement would be safe for its children for a few minutes alone. She tore off after the woman and the policeman.

By the time she caught up to them, Nimrod had pinned the young woman against the wall of another housing complex. The young woman was out of breath and crying.

"No, no, please don't take me away," she begged in Hebrew.

Rania gestured to Nimrod to let go. She ushered the young woman to a picnic table in the middle of a courtyard and they sat down close together. Nimrod stood nearby, clearly annoyed at being dismissed but not interfering.

"It's okay," Rania said in English.

"No, not okay. I don't want to go back to the Philippines," the young woman said in English.

"What's your name?"

"Delmarie," the young woman sobbed out.

"Delmarie, I am not with immigration," Rania said, thinking that that should be self-evident. Although there were many Palestinian Israelis in the police, she highly doubted there were any hijab-wearing women in the immigration police. "But," she said in a warning voice, "that man over there is an immigration policeman. If you cooperate with us, nothing will happen to you, but if you don't, you could find yourself going home very quickly."

She pulled out the picture of the dead girl, and asked Delmarie if she knew her. Delmarie barely looked at it and shook her head.

"I don't know her."

"Please look more closely."

"I don't know her."

"I think you do know her. Tell me what you know, or these police will take you away and you'll be deported."

She hated herself for bullying a terrified girl, but she was sick of people lying to her. It was not usually so hard to get to the truth; just another reason not to get involved with Israelis.

Delmarie said, "I know her a little, but I don't know anything about the trouble she is in."

"What trouble is she in?"

Delmarie looked away. Rania pointed to Nimrod, who was standing nearby, fingering his handcuffs.

"Maybe you'd rather talk to him?"

Delmarie shook her head vigorously.

Rania said, exasperated, "Delmarie, I am very busy. What is her name?" She tapped the picture.

"Nadya."

"Nadya is dead, and we need to find out who killed her. If you know something, tell me now."

At the word "dead," Delmarie made a small *uss* sound and crossed herself. "She had a problem with a man," she said.

"What kind of problem?"

"I don't know. But I saw them arguing, and he said he would call the police on her, and she said she would call them on him."

"When was this?"

"One week ago."

"Did you know this man?"

Delmarie shook her head again.

"Describe him."

"Big," she said, lifting a palm high above her head. "Hair short, and a beard. Religious." She drew a circle on her head, where a skullcap would sit.

"Was he the man she worked for?" Rania pressed.

"No."

"How do you know?"

"I know who she worked for. Sometimes she brought the children to play here."

"Where do they live?"

Delmarie started to explain it, but Rania couldn't keep track of the lefts and the rights, and looking around here, with all the houses looking alike, she would never be able to give them a landmark.

"Show me," Rania said, getting to her feet and indicating for Delmarie to do the same.

"But the children are by themselves," Delmarie objected.

"You already left them by themselves," Rania said. She realized Delmarie had left in a panic, and now that she was calmer, she was worried about the kids, or maybe about what their parents would do if they got home and found them alone.

"We will go back to the house now, and you can go ask a neighbor to look after the kids for a few minutes."

Delmarie agreed, since she had no choice. Once the children were safely ensconced with a cartoon on television and a neighbor to keep them company while they watched it, she showed them to a house about two blocks away. En route, Rania asked her more questions about Nadya.

"Was she also from the Philippines?"

"No."

"Where was she from?"

"I don't know. She didn't want to say."

"Then how do you know she wasn't from the Philippines?"

"She didn't speak my language."

"How did you communicate?"

"We spoke Hebrew."

"What language was she arguing with the man in?"

"Hebrew."

"Did she speak English?"

"No. But I think she spoke Russian."

"Why do you think so?"

"I heard her speaking to the woman in the store, in a language I didn't know."

Delmarie showed them the house, and then ran away. Nimrod was about to bang on the door, but Rania stepped in front of him and knocked politely. A young teenage girl, maybe thirteen, answered the door, still in her school clothes. She had thick, wavy brown hair, bobbed nearly to her shoulders and a sweet face with gaps between her front teeth. She looked uncomfortable in her slightly chunky body. When she saw Rania and Nimrod, she said immediately in Hebrew, "My parents aren't home."

Rania asked her, "Do you speak English?"

The girl nodded. "My father's American."

"Are you here by yourself?" she asked, trying to sound motherly.

"With my little brother and sister."

"When will your mom be home?"

"Probably in an hour." The girl was shifting from one foot to the other. Rania could hear the same cartoon playing that they left the other children watching. She considered whether it was a good idea, but she showed the girl the dead woman's photo.

"Does this woman work for your family?"

The girl looked very scared, but she nodded. "That's Nadya."

"Do you know her last name?"

"No. Where is she? Where did you get that picture?"

Rania tried to deflect her questions with one of her own.

"Where does Nadya come from?"

"I'm not sure I should be talking to you. Why are you asking about Nadya? Is she all right?"

"Has she worked for your family for long?"

"No, only four months."

"Do you know where she lived before this?"

"I think she said… Eilat."

"Was she working for a family there too?"

"I don't know. I don't think I should be talking to you. You better come back when my parents are home."

The girl tried to close the door. Rania caught it with her foot. "What's your name?" she asked.

"Malkah."

Queen, Rania thought. "That's a pretty name."

"It doesn't really fit me."

"It will." Rania was annoyed by her compassion for this girl, who had no idea what a hard life for a teenager is. She sure didn't have to clean out chicken coops like girls her age in Mas'ha, or climb a ladder and jump from roof to roof to avoid being shot on her way to school like students in Hebron. But when you are thirteen, a pimple can ruin your life faster than a missile, or at least you feel like it can. She wanted to reassure Malkah that some day she would have the stature and confidence to give her name credibility, but that wasn't her job here.

"Malkah, I am trying to help Nadya. If you want to help her too, you must tell me everything you know about her life before she came here."

"She wasn't working for a family. She lived in a house with a bunch of other girls, and men would come… and there was a man who told them what to do. He said he would hurt her little girl if she ran away, but she did anyway."

Pimps and brothels? Rania had heard rumors about such things in Israel, but she hadn't necessarily believed them. Most Palestinians would believe the Israelis capable of anything. She always prided herself on being more discriminating. Now she thought maybe she had sold them short in the evil department. Maybe the stories about generals keeping the heads of children they killed on their mantels were true too.

One thing that was clear was that this was a bigger problem than she had anticipated. It didn't seem like something to be discussing with a thirteen-year-old girl.

"Malkah, where do your parents work?" she asked.

"My mom's a teacher at the elementary school," she said, glad to be asked something she could answer without hesitating. "My dad works in Tel Aviv. At the Kirya," she added.

Rania's heart did a somersault. The man worked at the Ministry of Defense? The case was getting more sensitive by the minute. If she was on her way out of it before, she would truly be history when the two DCLs heard about this. Unless, she thought, they already knew. Nimrod's ears had also pricked up, and he decided that this was the moment when an Israeli man should step in and stop letting a Palestinian woman call the shots.

"What's his name?" he demanded.

"Nir Gelenter," she answered.

Nimrod started. Rania looked at him. He was digesting this piece of information, which seemed important. She had no idea why.

"The deputy defense minister?" Nimrod said.

Malkah nodded, a little proudly. Her father would be back at six p.m., she told them.

Elation mixed with frustration in Rania's soul. If this were a normal case, now that she knew who she was looking for, she would go off and find him. But she could not even get to Tel Aviv, let alone waltz into the Ministry of Defense. She would need to call Benny and see what he wanted to do. She didn't want to do that, especially in front of Nimrod, or even Malkah. She made a snap decision.

"We will return at six thirty," she told Malkah, who quickly closed the door.

She looked at her watch. It was two thirty, too late to go back to Salfit. She was so close to Mas'ha, she could almost see her house. Two years ago, she could simply have walked from the gate of the settlement over the road-block at the entrance to her village and been home in ten minutes. But now there was the Wall, and the Israeli highway was completely separate from the Palestinian roads. She would have to ride back all the way to Ariel and catch a taxi to the Qarawa blocks, cross over and catch another taxi to Mas'ha. She would arrive home too late to make Khaled's favorite okra stew for dinner. Of course, if she were a *good mother* like her mother-in-law wanted her to be, she would have prepared the stew last night, and it would be ready to heat up. She would have to stop at the falafel stand and buy falafel and hummus and red cabbage salad for dinner. Khaled wouldn't mind. She would fry some potatoes to eat with the falafel and it would be like a picnic.

On the way back to Ariel, she called Benny with the news. She feared he would say he would go to Tel Aviv by himself to talk to Nir Gelenter, but he merely grunted assent to the six thirty assignation. He had other things on his mind.

"Mustafa said you interviewed a farmer in Azzawiya, who discovered the body yesterday."

"Abu Anwar," she replied warily.

"I want to talk to him."

"Why? I'm sure the captain told you what he said."

"I want to hear it for myself." Naturally, the Israelis were not going to take the word of Palestinian police about a key witness—even Palestinian police they acted all chummy with.

"I will call him and tell him we will come tomorrow morning," she said.

"No, I want to go now." Again with "I want."

"I need to get my son's dinner," she said.

"No problem, I can go by myself. Give me his telephone number."

She would not be able to stop him from going to Abu Anwar's without her. Her responsibility was to protect the people. That meant she must go with him. *What about your responsibility to your family?* her inner mother-in-law challenged. *Two days in a row, you are not there to make dinner for your son?*

"I will meet you there," she told Benny. It wouldn't look good for her to arrive with the Israeli police. She needed to get there first. But he could drive straight on good roads, and she would need to take two taxis on bad ones. There was only one way she was going to get there before him. She tapped Dani on the shoulder.

"Turn around," she said in Hebrew.

She prayed he wouldn't argue with her. There was no way she could explain to these young men why they should go out of their way to protect her reputation. Fortunately, Dani looked at Nimrod, who seemed to be the man in charge here. Nimrod shrugged, and Dani spun the jeep around with as much squealing of rubber as humanly possible.

She would absolutely make it up to Khaled on the weekend. He would be proud of her, because she would make sure nothing bad happened to his people.

Chapter 11

Avi had not gone back to Jerusalem with the others. He was walking with Jaber at the front of the little parade back to the village. They were conversing in Hebrew when Chloe caught up with them, but Jaber finished his sentence and switched to English when he saw her. She smiled at him gratefully. Just then his phone rang. When he hung up, he told her, "Ajat shorta la beet Abu Anwar." *The police have come to Abu Anwar's house.* He quickened his already frenetic pace.

"Ana maak," she puffed. *I am coming with you.*

"Very good," he nodded. Then he turned to Avi and explained to him in Hebrew. "You must come with us," he told the young man. Chloe felt her chest tighten. Why did Jaber suddenly think she couldn't handle the police? Avi didn't seem thrilled either. She wondered why. He usually seemed anxious enough to stick his nose into every crisis.

Abu Anwar's house was at the top of a hill. Chloe had to pause for breath before entering the house, or she wouldn't even be able to say hello to anyone. She noticed with irritation that the men were not breathing hard. Rania was there, leaning forward on the sofa, a cup of coffee untouched in front her. A big, bald Israeli policeman sat in an armchair that was clearly not as comfortable as he had thought it would be. Chloe observed that there were only grounds in his coffee cup. Ali, the Palestinian Israeli policeman she had seen on the road the day before, was standing a little behind the other policeman and saying nothing. Rania was showing Abu Anwar some photos, and the old man was shaking his head a lot.

"What's going on?" Jaber asked, when they had all been introduced and served coffee.

"They found a dead girl on our land," Abu Anwar said succinctly.

"Really?" Jaber didn't sound very surprised. "Was she from the village?"

"No, she was *ajnabiya*."

"So why are they here?" Jaber asked him. Abu Anwar shrugged, as if to say, who knew why the Israeli authorities did anything.

Whatever they wanted, they appeared to be done with it. The big Israeli cop was staring at Avi now.

"What are you doing here?" he asked him. Avi said he had come to visit friends, and to see what was happening with the work they were preparing to do on the land near Elkana. He did not mention the confrontation with the army and the bulldozers.

"Do you come here often?" asked the big policeman. According to the tag he wore, his name was Benny Lazar.

"Sometimes," Avi said.

"Did you ever see this girl here?" Benny thrust a photo under Avi's nose. "No."

Avi covered well, but Chloe was sure he knew something. Probably the policeman could tell too, but he did not push it. She thought he wouldn't want to threaten an Israeli in front of Palestinians. Rania had definitely noticed Avi's discomfort. Chloe wondered why she didn't say anything.

Benny asked Avi for his ID. Chloe was surprised that the young man handed it over without a protest. She wouldn't have. Benny pulled out his telephone and gestured to Ali to follow him outside. Again, Chloe was surprised that Avi just sat there and let these policemen walk away with his ID. There was a lot she didn't understand about Israelis. Rania made no move to follow her colleagues. Chloe wondered if that was her way of showing she was not interested in their business, or if they had somehow signaled her it was none of hers, or maybe they had already agreed that if they had some reason to leave the room, she would stay to keep an eye on the locals.

"Do you know who the dead woman is?" Chloe asked her.

"Not exactly, but she was working in Elkana," Rania said.

How awful, Chloe thought, to die in a foreign country, and have no one who cares for you back home even know! The thought sent a shiver through her. It would never happen to her, of course, she had valid ID, but even so, she suddenly pictured herself lying forever on a slab in an Israeli morgue.

"Benny," Rania gestured in the direction of the Israeli policeman outside, "thinks she might have been involved with a young man here in the village. Can you think of anyone who might have been seeing her?"

"A girl like that? Impossible. Why would he think that?"

"I'm not completely sure. But she was *hamel*," Rania said, using the Arabic word for pregnant.

"And they think a Palestinian was the father? That makes no sense."

After a full fifteen minutes, the Israeli police came back (not bothering to knock at the door, Chloe noticed), and handed Avi his ID. Benny wrote a telephone number on the back of a business card and gave it to Avi as well.

"Whenever you are coming to this village, I want you to call and let me know," he instructed. To Chloe's surprise, Avi agreed.

"Are you really going to call him whenever you come?" she asked him after they left the house.

"I don't know, maybe," he answered.

"Why? It's none of their business."

"Yes, but if I don't, they might start coming into the village to look for me."

"You think they'd really do that?"

"They have. They went house to house in Deir Balut once, because some of us went in through the checkpoint and then left another way."

"At home, we would never agree to tell the police anything. They're the enemy," she said.

"They're mine too," he said, "but they seriously worry about us here. They're afraid we will be kidnapped and they'll have to come in and rescue us."

"That's ridiculous," she said.

"Well, it has happened," he surprised her by saying. She was about to ask him to elaborate, but as they reached the main village road, he turned to Jaber. "I need to talk to you," he said quietly in Hebrew.

"Come to my house," Jaber said to him. At the house, Jaber shook her hand in polite dismissal. She nodded goodbye to Avi and headed upstairs. She hoped he would feel the slight that she did not shake his hand, but she doubted he was well mannered enough to notice. She was unlocking the door to her flat when she heard footsteps behind her. She swung around.

"Take my number," Avi said. "If there are any problems in the village, call me."

"Why? What will you do about it?" she asked.

She had not meant the question seriously, but he actually thought about it. "I don't know," he admitted. "Get people to come… If there's an incursion, I can call the army and find out what they want… I just want to help."

He sounded sincere, not as arrogant as usual. She put the number in her phone and called it right away, so he would have hers. He went down to Jaber's and she entered her flat.

She showered, changed, and ate, but was too keyed up to sleep or read. It was rare that she felt lonely or bored in her flat. Living among Palestinians involved a lot of togetherness—big families often sleeping and eating in close quarters, and so many group activities. She enjoyed it, but she was always happy to return to her quiet oasis. But today the high ceilings echoed with her discontent.

At home she had lived alone for ten years, minus the two when she lived with Alyssa. She hadn't longed for the companionship of a group house since the day she moved out of her last one. She cherished her friends and community, but she cherished being able to get away from them too. But at home she could go out if she wanted to be around people, to the movies, out to dinner, or just aimlessly wandering the streets, stopping in for groceries or coffee or whatever. Here a woman could not wander around without purpose, and anyway, there was nowhere she wanted to go.

Thinking about friends brought Tina to mind. Had she imagined the spark, or was it real? She was assuming Tina was a lesbian because of her height. Alyssa was also tall, nearly six feet. Of course, Maria Sharapova, the tennis player who had just won Wimbledon, was over six feet and no one thought she was a lesbian. But there was something else; Tina had looked her in the eye. Her first girlfriend had told her that if a woman looks you directly in the eye, she's a dyke.

It's wishful thinking, she told herself sternly, *and anyway, it's irrelevant*. It would be nice, though, to hang out with a woman she liked, to be able to be open about her feelings. These months of having to hide part of her identity were starting to wear on her. She missed her friends. She missed Alyssa.

No, she was *not* going to think about Alyssa. Getting far away from the woman who had broken her heart had been one of the attractions of this place. She made herself think of Jill and Diane, her two best friends in San Francisco. What were they doing now? she wondered. It had been almost a month since she had talked to them. When she first got to Palestine, she had been on the phone to them every other day, but the longer she stayed here, the more able she was to talk to people here, the less rooted she felt back home.

She thought about calling Jill or Diane now, but it would be too early in

California. For lack of anything else to do, she started to cook. She chopped onions and garlic, and fried them with rice and cauliflower, adding some cinnamon and cumin. She ate a few spoonfuls, but she was still full from her recent lunch. She put some of the food in a dish and took it downstairs to Ahlam. Ahlam didn't need her food, but it was an excuse to go down. Maybe now, they would tell her what was going on. Ahlam invited her in, and Jaber asked what she thought of the action at Abu Shaadi's.

"Well, it's good we stopped the bulldozers," she shrugged. "But those Israeli activists are so irritating."

His look made her ashamed.

"They are our friends," he said. "They want to help."

What right did she have to be so intolerant, when he, a Palestinian, was so forgiving of their bossiness and wishy-washy politics? Of course, he hadn't heard Itai and the others saying that the Palestinians should accept Israeli citizenship. She told him about the conversation.

Jaber surprised her by saying, "They are right. That is what must happen."

"But what about your identity as a Palestinian?" she asked.

"We will always be Palestinians," he said.

"That Israeli policeman who was there today, Ali," she said. "Do you think he considers himself a Palestinian?"

"It doesn't matter," he insisted. "I'll always be a Palestinian, my children will always be Palestinians. If they are Israeli citizens, they can live anywhere they want, have Israeli passports and go where they want in the world. They can work, and the Israeli government won't be able to uproot their trees and tear down their houses."

"The government demolished twenty houses in Kufr Qasem last year because they didn't have permits," she said. "They do that in Palestinian towns all over Israel. When's the last time they demolished houses in Tel Aviv?"

"But if all the Palestinians can vote," he said, "we will be the majority, and we can change the government."

She sat quietly for a little while, trying to envision such a peaceful transition. If Jaber, who had grown up amid the tanks and nighttime raids, and had gone away to become a military man himself, could imagine a different future, she should be able to. But it seemed light years away.

This afternoon seemed light years away, too. She remembered a question she had wanted to ask him.

"When Abu Anwar told you they had found a woman's body, it seemed like you already knew."

"The mayor mentioned something about it yesterday."

That made sense. She felt a little hurt that no one had told her. Not even the little kids, who usually couldn't keep quiet about anything.

"Did Avi know?" she asked. "Is that what he wanted to talk to you about?"

"No," he said at once. "It was something else."

He had more information, she was sure, but she wasn't going to get it, at least not now. She couldn't take it personally. She might be almost family, but she was still *ajnabiya*.

Even so, talking with Jaber had soothed her. Much of her time here was spent with women who were interested in things she knew nothing about, children and crafts and family gossip. Even Ahlam, who was always bristling with industry and ideas for women's development projects, had no interest in politics. Chloe had asked her once why she never came to the living room when Jaber met with other leaders of the village. Ahlam had stretched her arms and mouth in an exaggerated yawn.

"It's too boring," she said. "During the First Intifada, when Jaber was in prison, I had no choice. Now he is here, so I don't need to be involved in that nonsense."

Sometimes Chloe felt like she wasn't a "real woman." She thought momentarily of Rania. There was someone she could relate to more naturally, who also had work she was passionate about. If she could make Rania like her, she was sure the policewoman could tell her fascinating things. She took the tea things into the kitchen and kissed Ahlam goodnight, and went upstairs.

She was fast asleep when Avi called. She strained to read the clock: 11:45 p.m. What was wrong with him? He had been up as early as she, why wasn't he crashed out too? He was twenty years younger, she reminded herself. She was entitled to her lack of stamina. But she felt old old old. As she adjusted to being awake, she realized he sounded upset.

"What's wrong?" she asked.

"I wondered if Fareed was at home."

Fareed was Jaber's oldest son. He was studying in Nablus, and because of the difficulty of getting through the checkpoints, he shared an apartment there with some other students, only coming home on weekends.

"I didn't see him," she said. "I assume he's at school. But why are you asking me? Why not call him yourself, or ask Jaber?"

"His phone is closed." *Jaber's or Fareed's?* she wondered. But she wasn't really interested enough to ask.

"I haven't seen him," she repeated.

"Call me if you do," he said. She bristled at the order.

"I'll tell him to call you," she said. "Now I'm going back to sleep. Good night."

Chapter 12

Rania had just enough time, after they left Abu Anwar's house, to make the falafel shop before closing. The good cabbage salad was all gone, and she had to settle for eggplant instead. Khaled did not like eggplant. She made him extra fries to atone.

Benny had offered to pick her up at her house to go to the Gelenters'. She couldn't tell if he was really an idiot, or if he was joking. He must know she was never going to let an Israeli policeman pick her up inside her village.

"Meet me on the road," she instructed. Bassam drove her to the bridge, where she had found the girl's body the day before. Khaled sat wedged between them on the front seat. Bassam would take him for an ice cream on the way home. She climbed up to the road and found the blue and white car there waiting.

The soldier at the gate of Elkana was unhappy about letting a Palestinian into the settlement at night, even with Benny vouching for her. The soldier called his commander for permission to allow her through the hallowed gates. She took off her hijab before she got out of the car.

"I'll ask the questions," Benny said. "Don't say anything. If you do, it will only provoke him and he won't give us any information."

"I will ask questions if I have them," she said.

Nir Gelenter was expecting them. He did not try to shake Rania's hand, and he asked for her police ID and not for Benny's, but he was courteous, gave the ID the once-over and then said, "Todah rabah," *thanks very much,* when he handed it back to her.

"Can we speak English?" she said at once. "I don't speak Hebrew."

"No problem at all," he said, looking only at Benny.

"My daughter said you were looking for Nadya," Gelenter said, again to Benny alone. "We have not seen her since the night before last."

"I'm afraid she's dead," Benny said.

"Dead? Are you sure?" Gelenter managed a stricken look, even took out a handkerchief and acted like he was wiping away tears. Or maybe he really was.

"Weren't you surprised, when she didn't return for two days?" Benny asked.

"I thought she just went into Tel Aviv for a break," Gelenter answered.

"Would she have gone on a break without telling you?" Benny queried. Telling? Asking would be more like it, Rania thought.

"Who knows what she would do?" the military man said with a sigh. "She was a bit wild."

"Wild? Wild how?"

The man heaved another big sigh. "She was brought to Israel from Uzbekistan, by terrible people, to work in a pardon-the-expression whore-house." He looked at her for the first time when he said "pardon." "These people threatened to harm her family if she left the brothel, or told anyone who they were."

"But she did leave," Rania said.

"Yes, she was mortally afraid, but she could not take being a prostitute any more. She was forced to see ten clients a day sometimes, and she was not paid anything. She came to Israel because she could not support her young daughter at home, but now she was not making any money at all. So she had to go."

"You don't know who the people were who brought her here?" Benny asked him, his pen poised over his notepad to take down the names Rania doubted would be forthcoming. She was right.

"No, I have no idea," the man said, shaking his head for emphasis.

It was a lie. Rania could see that in his face. She looked at Benny, whose face was impassive, his stance unchanged. He wasn't going to press this guy, just because he was some mucky-muck in the Ministry of Defense—the Ministry of Offense, where her people were concerned. Well, Rania wasn't going to let him get away with it.

"How did she end up here?" she asked.

Gelenter glanced at Benny as if for permission to answer her questions. Benny waited, his pen still in the ready-to-write position.

"I hired her through an agency in Tel Aviv," Nir said. "Here, I have the card right here." He had obviously prepared well for their visit. He pulled the card from his shirt pocket and handed it to Benny, who copied the information into his notebook. Rania craned to read over his shoulder, but both the card and his writing were in Hebrew. She should have studied Hebrew at university, as Bassam had. She had disdained learning to read and write the occupier's language.

"Did she have her passport?" She continued asking the questions, and Benny scribbling the answers, or she assumed that was what his hieroglyphics represented.

"No."

"Did she show you any kind of ID?"

"No."

"So you don't know for sure that she was from Uzbekistan, or even that her name was Nadya?"

"Well, now that you say it like that, I guess not."

She asked about Nadya's duties, her schedule, if she had friends here. He said she got every Friday night and Saturday off, but she rarely went anywhere, because she was afraid of being seen and captured by the men who had brought her to Israel. He said he didn't know how she got from Eilat to Tel Aviv or how she came to the agency where he hired her.

"How did she get from Tel Aviv to Elkana?" Rania asked.

"I picked her up after work and drove her. The agency is near the Kirya, where I work."

"Why did you hire someone to take care of your children?" Benny asked suddenly. Rania looked at him in surprise. A few minutes ago, he had seemed happy to accept whatever story the big man spun. Now he was leaning forward, his protruding brown eyes wide open and trained on Nir's face, giving him somewhat the appearance of a bald eagle.

"My wife isn't too well," Nir said, clearly uncomfortable with the line of conversation.

"Oh?" Benny invested the syllable with a host of meanings.

"No, she had a... traumatic episode a few years ago," Nir said.

"Her illness isn't physical." Benny made it a statement, not a question.

"No."

"I see. But why an immigrant girl? Surely, there's a child care center in the settlement." He used the word *yishuv*, the soft word for settlement, the same word used for communities in Israel. Rania would have called it *hitnachlut*, colony, but then she would not have succeeded in making Gelenter squirm like he was now doing. She caught herself feeling a drop of admiration for Benny's technique.

"Yes, but it is not so near here. I need to leave very early in the morning for work, and my wife doesn't drive."

"You weren't worried about the effect someone who had been a prostitute might have on your children's values?" Rania almost gasped. Benny's forward posture made this a full-fledged challenge to Nir's qualifications as both a religious man and a father. She almost felt for the man as he struggled to control his rage and embarrassment. Instead of lashing out, he chuckled.

"My children have a very strong moral foundation. Nadya didn't even speak that much Hebrew. She certainly could not discuss her former life with my children."

"Did she ever bring friends to the house?" Benny asked.

"She didn't have any friends here," he said. "She called home once a week, on my phone. I allowed her to do that." He looked at them as if expecting praise.

"Then you must have a phone number for them," Benny said.

Nir's left eyelid twitched slightly. He did not want them talking to Nadya's family, Rania thought.

"I suppose it would be on a bill, but I don't keep them," he said. He made a big show of giving Benny the number of his mobile.

"Last week a woman named Delmarie, who works for another family, saw Nadya arguing with a man," Rania said. She repeated the description she was given. He contemplated it before shaking his head sadly.

"No, that doesn't sound like anyone I know. It must have been someone connected with the traffickers. They must have tracked her down and killed her."

"Traffickers would wear a kippa?" she asked.

"They would if they were trying to fit in here. We are a very religious community."

"You seem to have pretty good security here," Rania observed.

"Criminals have a lot of ways to get what they want. Besides," he suddenly switched gears. "This girl Delmarie, she could have made up the story."

"Do you know her?" Rania asked innocently.

"Not personally, no. I know Nadya sometimes took my children to play with the children she watches."

"Do you know if Nadya had any friends in Eilat?"

"She did have one friend, who she sometimes called. I think her name was Vicki."

"Did you know that Nadya was pregnant?" she asked.

"What? No, that's impossible."

"It's true." She held her ground.

"Well, of course," he recovered quickly, "she was a prostitute, she had sex all the time before she came here. It could have been any one of hundreds of men."

"She was only about six weeks pregnant, not four months. You say she never went away after she came to live here, so it must have been someone she slept with right here, right? In this house?"

He puffed out his chest. "I tell you, that's impossible. There are no men here except me."

She let the statement hang in the air.

"We need to look in Nadya's room," she said, rising and turning as if to go find the room for herself. She was overreaching her position, she knew, and he knew it too, but Benny's silence backed her up.

"Of course," he said, "but could you possibly do it tomorrow? My wife and I need to get dinner on the table and get the kids to bed."

She was about to say no, but Benny preempted her.

"We will come tomorrow morning," he said, removing a small appointment book from his breast pocket. "Would half past seven be convenient?"

Nir nodded assent. Benny stood up and thanked Nir for his time.

"Would you be willing to take a blood test?" Rania asked. "Just to make sure you are not the father of Nadya's baby?"

His dark red face spoke for itself. He said something she did not understand in Hebrew to Benny. She filled in the blanks for herself. She was sure he was already plotting to have her investigated by the SHABAK, if not to have her entire family locked up summarily. Benny steered her out the door.

"With someone like him," Benny scolded on their way out of the settlement, "a soft touch is more likely to get what you want."

"I'm not good at the soft touch," she told him ruefully. "You might as well get used to it."

"Why do I need to get used to it?" he challenged. "You're not working this case any more."

She felt the disappointment swelling her throat. Obviously, between leaving Abu Anwar's house and now he had talked to the captain or Abu Ziyad or the Israeli DCL. Why had he let her come to the house? she wondered. And why had he said "we" would come back in the morning?

"Come on," she said, trying to strike a light note. "You know you like having me here. It rattles people like Gelenter to have a Palestinian policewoman in his house."

She had guessed right. He gave her a goofy half-smile. "I'm a good guy," he told her. "I take guns away from the settlers, when they fire in the air to frighten people. They hate me. Ask Mustafa. We used to eat lunch together, during the Oslo years. I ate at his house. I know his wife."

"You want a prize for that?" she asked.

Chapter 13

A chorus of loud voices outside woke Chloe from the soundest sleep she had had in weeks. She popped up, startled, and then realized it was only the neighborhood kids, passing under her window on their way to school. She snuggled back into her pillow, and reached for the dregs of the dream she had left. Alyssa was in it, but she had looked like Tina. How embarrassing.

She tried to go back to sleep, but she heard the roosters crowing erratically and the donkeys braying as their farmers loaded them up for the trip into the fields. The light was already streaming in through the sheer curtain, foretelling the heat that would soon descend on her sanctuary. The bright space created by the big plate glass windows was a blessing, if a little foolhardy in a place where most people have bars on their windows to deflect stray bullets and gas canisters. But in the summer, these big windows could turn the pleasant little house into a furnace. It was just May, so the early mornings and late evenings were bearable, but by nine a.m., no one who didn't have to would want to be in the sun.

She was past the great divide between sleeping and waking, too awake for sleep, too sleepy to do anything very productive. She got up and reached for the gold coffee filter she had brought from California. At the last minute, she reached for the Arabic coffee pot instead. She half-filled the little long-handled pot with water and a spoonful of sugar. When it boiled, she added a heaping spoonful of finely ground coffee and cardamom and watched it bubble up, snatching it from the burner before it overflowed. She put it back to the flame twice more, letting the flavor deepen, then poured off barely more than three thimbles full of steaming dark liquid into a tiny cup.

Now clear-headed, she took her camera and headed out to the crossroads to see what the situation was like. She passed a group of men hunkered down in the weeds, snacking. One of them was talking on a cellphone and she heard him saying in Hebrew, "Yesh po mishmar hagvul." *There are border police here,* so obviously he was calling his Israeli employer to explain he couldn't get in right now. Hopefully, the man would wait for him, rather than pick up someone else. Cell phones were a gift in this situation, she thought. Five years ago, he would have lost the job.

The man with the phone saw her and motioned her over. He was about her age, hefty, with bushy graying hair and sideburns. She approached the group of men, hoping she wasn't about to get another marriage request. She had had at least ten since she had been in Palestine. Even understanding it was her passport, not her appearance, that men found so attractive, there was something disconcerting about being proposed to within five minutes of meeting someone.

"Assalaamu aleikum," she greeted the men.

"Aleikum salaam," replied one of them, not the one who had summoned her. That guy didn't waste time on pleasantries.

"Fii jesh fok." *The army is up there,* pointing toward the road.

"What are they doing?"

"Watching."

"How long have they been there?"

"A long time."

That was typical for this time of morning. The border police knew that men crossed into Israel here every morning, and they made it their business to hang around and wait.

"Inshalla," *hopefully,* "they will leave soon." She strolled away toward the road. She would park herself at a safe distance and watch the watchers.

"Hey," the man called after her.

She turned.

"Can't you make them go away?"

She smiled, though from the distance they probably couldn't see. "Laa, asfi." *No, I'm sorry.* She started walking again.

"Then what can you do?" The man's scornful voice rang out across the fields. The other men with him laughed.

"Not much," she muttered. Her eyes burned, and she was glad they couldn't see her blushing.

She reached the border police jeep. Top Killer was there, with two of the others, including the one who told her to go to Iraq. They were lounging by the side of their jeep, smoking. They seemed relaxed. She didn't even see the young man kneeling behind the jeep until Top Killer sauntered over and kicked him in the head. The young man flopped over on his side from the force of the kick. His hands were cuffed behind him so he couldn't right himself. Top Killer walked away, leaving the prisoner writhing on the ground.

Chloe's fury got the better of her good sense. She walked quickly to the young man and helped him sit up.

"Thank you," he said softly in English.

Chloe was relieved. Ordinarily she would ask a Palestinian man before touching him, but she had reacted on instinct.

"It's nothing," she replied. "What are they holding you for?"

"They say I am wanted."

She wondered if he was. She wasn't sure how to ask without being completely inappropriate. If he was, she would definitely not be able to help him. If not, she probably still was unlikely to have any influence over these border police, but one of her Israeli friends might be able to call a higher-up to have him released. She took a few pictures, close up enough to show his bruises.

"You didn't go to Iraq yet?" She looked up to see Iraq and Top Killer coming toward her.

"What is your name?" she asked the young man. At least if she knew his name, she could try to find out what happened to him.

"Mohammed."

Before she could ask his last name, Top Killer had grabbed her by the hair.

"You don't speak to him!" He was dragging her by her hair. She tried to remember what she had learned in her long-ago nonviolence training. Lean into him. She did so, and the pain in her head lessened. He threw her against the jeep.

"Give me your ID," he ordered.

"Why? You know who I am," she said.

"Give me the ID now."

Chloe figured she was damned no matter what she did. She reached into her back pocket and brought forth a green plastic folder. She held it out to him, trying not to show her trepidation.

"What is this?" He almost spat the words.

Chloe concentrated on keeping her voice quiet and even. "Open it and you will see."

Top Killer stared down at the little plastic folder as if he suspected if he opened it, it might blow up in his hand. Finally he opened it and ripped the copy of her passport out from between the flaps.

"This is shit!" He threw the paper down on the ground. Chloe quickly bent and retrieved it. She tucked it back into her pocket before he could tear it up. It might be only a copy, but it was all she had right now.

"Give me your passport!" Top Killer screamed in her ear.

"I'm sorry, that's all I have," indicating the empty green folder he was twisting between white-knuckled hands.

"It's shit," he said again. "Where is your passport?"

"I don't carry it with me. It might get lost or stolen." That wasn't the whole reason she didn't bring it with her, but it was a good enough one.

"If you don't have your ID, you know what that means?"

"No, what?"

"It means I have to treat you like a terrorist. Only wanted terrorists don't carry ID. And do you know why?"

"Why?"

"Because they are going to blow themselves up anyway."

That didn't make much sense to her. If they were going to blow themselves up, why would they care who saw their ID? But she had a more immediate problem.

"You know I'm not a terrorist."

"How do I know?"

"Has there ever been an attack by a middle-aged foreign woman?"

Iraq laughed, which made Top Killer angrier.

"I don't know," he said. "But you have to come with me now."

"Come with you where?"

"To the police."

He grabbed her arm in a vise-like grip. She tried to break free, but Iraq grabbed her other arm. She thought about sitting down, but the ground was rocky and pocked with thorns. Iraq twisted her arm behind her back, not too hard, but hard enough to prevent her from struggling.

Top Killer snapped the handcuffs from his belt—metal ones, not the plastic ones Mohammed wore—and jangled them in her face.

"Give me your hands," he said.

When she didn't hold out her hands, he grabbed both her wrists in one hand and cuffed them in front, to her surprise not too tightly. Iraq prodded her into the back of the jeep and got in next to her, while Top Killer jumped in front with the driver. The driver gunned the engine fiercely before taking off. They seemed to have completely forgotten about Mohammed. As they drove into Israel, she peeked out between the doors and saw the men who were waiting starting to trickle up onto the road. At least her arrest did two good things. Hopefully someone would have a knife to cut Mohammed's cuffs off.

She watched the road signs fly by, excited in spite of herself. She should be beside herself with worry; what if they deported her? She was not ready to go home yet. But this was a new experience, and she couldn't help wondering what it would be like. Would she be interrogated? What would they ask? What should she say?

They would probably take her phone away when she got to the police station. She better try to let someone know she where was. She wondered who she could tell. She didn't want to bother any Palestinians, and she didn't know any Israelis well. She flashed on Tina, even the fleeting thought making her pulse rise. What would Tina do, if a woman she had just met once suddenly sent her a message saying, "I'm in jail, you have to get me out"? Tina had only been here a short while. Would she have any idea who to call? Would she have any interest in calling them if she did? Better not chance it.

She took out her phone surreptitiously, cradling it in one nearly closed hand and shielding it with the other. She must look like she was petting an egg, but fortunately neither of the police were looking at her. She flipped through phone numbers with the barest flick of a fingernail. Avi's was the second number. They weren't friends, but he respected her and she was starting to think she had underestimated him. Plus he had been arrested a million times. He'd know what to do. She spelled out "I arrested need lawy," before Iraq saw her and grabbed for the phone. She just managed to hit send before he got it out of her hand and stuck it triumphantly in his pocket. A minute later, the jeep screeched to a halt in the parking lot of the Ariel police station.

"Get out," Iraq ordered her when he opened the door. She followed him and Top Killer into the station. He uncuffed her and ordered her not to move from the hard wooden bench next to the door. A woman cop took her into a little room and went through all her things. When she found Chloe's passport copy, she stared at it for a long moment.

"San Francisco," she read.

"Yes. In California."

"I know where it is. I was there once."

"Really? You have family there or something?"

"No. I went with a school trip. To play soccer. It's very beautiful."

"Yes, it is." Chloe tried frantically to think of a way to use this little bonding encounter to her advantage. She couldn't really think of one.

"You live in San Francisco and you came to Israel? You must be nuts."

"Well, I'm not exactly in Israel." Chloe knew as soon as the words were out of her mouth she had blown it.

"Take your things and follow me." Chloe scooped up all her belongings into her jacket and followed the policewoman back to the same wooden bench. Top Killer and Iraq were talking excitedly with the police in Hebrew. She didn't know what they were saying, but she could tell it was about her: "HaAmerikayit. Deportatsia," Top Killer kept saying.

The border police finally left, and she sat around more hours with no one talking to her. She hadn't even brought a book, which was like a religion with her. Here or at home, she almost never left the house without one, but just today, because she wasn't planning to be out long, she had brought nothing to read or to eat. There was nothing in the station with one word of English on it. She had not had breakfast, and was starting to get hungry and cranky.

It was early afternoon when a brusque policeman finally summoned her from the bench to which she had nearly become welded. He showed her into an office that was covered from wall to wall with stacks of manila folders. There were two chairs parked opposite a big desk. Both contained piles of folders. She waited for the man behind the desk to suggest what to do with them, but he was yelling into the phone at someone. Finally, she added the stack from one chair to one on the floor. She doubted there could be much order to this chaos, but if there was, she could only hope to upset it a little. She sat down and studied the guy on the phone.

He was the big, bald policeman she had seen the day before at Abu Anwar's house. The nameplate on his desk reminded her that he was Benny Lazar. His main modus operandi appeared to be yelling at people; Chloe wondered if he had gotten to the top by drowning everyone else out. But when he turned to her, his manner was mild.

"So," he said, eyeing her over the top of his glasses. "You know you're going to be deported, right?"

Her stomach lurched at the words, but she made herself answer calmly. "Am I? Why?"

"You broke Israeli law."

"Well, even if I were in Israel, which I'm not, I don't think I've broken any laws."

"In the first place, you were interfering with the police. And in the second, the law says you have to have ID, and you don't have any."

"I have ID," she said, gesturing to the green folder which sat in front of him, next to her telephone, and the small bag in which the policewoman had put the contents of her pockets.

"That is not valid ID," he said. "I'm going to read you your rights." Her stomach turned over again. The rights he read, translating from a page in Hebrew, were pretty much like what she had heard on *Law & Order*, except that there was a kind of catch-22 that said that if she exercised her right to remain silent, her silence "along with other evidence" could be taken as an admission of guilt.

"Your last name is Rubin. Are you Jewish?" he asked.

"Is that a crime?" she retorted.

"Where are your people from?" he tried again.

"North Carolina," she answered. "What about you?"

"I'm from Duluth, Minnesota."

"I didn't know there were any Jews there," she said.

"That's why I moved to Israel," he said with a wry grin. "Why didn't you?"

"I don't know if I want to live in Israel. I don't even speak the language."

"If you move here, the government will send you to *ulpan*," he said. Ulpan meant the language schools that were free to Jewish immigrants. A minute ago, he was telling her she was going to be deported. Now he was making plans for her indoctrination into Israeli society.

"What were you doing in Azzawiya yesterday?" he asked suddenly. So he had noticed her at Abu Anwar's house.

"I live there," she said.

"Why there?"

"I just ended up there."

Thankfully, his phone rang. Amid a torrent of Hebrew she heard him say "Azzawiya." Was the call about her? Or about events in the village? If only she understood more Hebrew. He covered the telephone mouthpiece with his hand and turned to her.

"I have something to do," he said. "Get out of here."

"You mean I can go?" Had he just been passing time with her, because he had nothing else to do?

"No, the other police want to talk to you about your ID. They are busy now too, so you need to wait."

"Anywhere special you want me to go?" she asked.

He yelled for a dark-skinned man, who came running and showed her into an empty office. "Stay there," the man ordered, pointing to a chair near the door. He left her alone.

She saw no reason to sit in that particular chair. She wandered around the office, where there were two empty desks. One of them held a stack of manila folders, like the ones that covered Benny's office. She glanced at them, for no reason other than boredom, and started puzzling out the Hebrew labels.

Each folder seemed to bear the name of a Palestinian. Marwan Abu Rahma. Salam Hakim Mahmoud Shuafat. None of them meant anything to her. Were these the infamous files of information the Israeli police collected from collaborators in the villages? Would they just leave them lying around where anyone could see them? Of course, they knew she didn't know Hebrew. Well, did they really know? Were they hoping she would read something and repeat it to someone, or was she being paranoid? *Just because I'm paranoid doesn't mean they're not out to get me,* she thought. That old saying had never seemed so relevant.

"Jaber Murad Haddad," she sounded out. She racked her brain, trying to remember if Jaber's long-dead father had been Murad. She didn't think there could be another Jaber Haddad. She eased the door nearly shut before flipping the file folder open. There was a large sheaf of papers inside, some scribbled notes, some official-looking reports. She could not understand anything on any of them, hard as she tried. If she made it out of here, maybe she should take Benny up on the ulpan idea.

Frustrated with herself, she closed the Jaber file and glanced at the one below it. "Fareed Jaber Murad Haddad." This one contained only a few sheets of paper, most of them handwritten. She supposed it made sense that the Israeli police would keep a file on Jaber, who had been a fighter and was in prison. But his son, a student, who was only nineteen and had never been in trouble? She needed to tell Avi. She needed her phone.

She went to the door and stopped the first policeman who happened by.

"What's going on? I've been here for six hours and no one even knows where I am. I demand to make a phone call."

"Wait a minute," he said and walked away. She was sure she wouldn't see him again. She paced the empty office, getting increasingly agitated. She heard a noise and turned around with an angry protest on her lips.

Ali, the policeman who had been at Abu Anwar's house yesterday, stood there with her phone and other possessions in his hand. He handed her everything except the ID folder, which he opened and looked at, she was sure not for the first time.

"Btihki Arabi?" he asked her.

"Schwei." *A little.*

"W ana schwei Inglizi." *And I only speak a little English*, he said, an expression of apology on his wrinkled, friendly face.

"Njarrab bil Arabi." *Let's try in Arabic*, she said.

He held out the ID to her.

"This is not good," he said. "From now on, you need to have the original passport on you."

Then, just like that, she was free to go. He took her downstairs, opened the door for her, and pointed to where she could catch a bus back out of the settlement.

"Azzawiya is dangerous these days," he added. "Maybe you should stay somewhere else, in Israel."

"It's not dangerous for me," she said.

"Maybe, maybe not," he said.

Chapter 14

"Benny wants you to go with him to Elkana," Captain Mustafa said on the phone.

"Okay." Rania hoped she sounded nonchalant.

Perhaps she had convinced the Israeli policeman she could confront the military bigwigs in ways he could not afford to. Or maybe he just found her reactions entertaining. He picked her up at the Qarawa blocks. They sailed through all the checkpoints and arrived at the Gelenters' promptly at seven-thirty. Mrs. Gelenter, dressed for work, admitted them. The children were already at her mother's, she said in answer to Rania's question. As soon as she showed them into Nadya's room, she departed, reminding them to lock the door when they left.

"She's in an awfully big hurry," Rania observed.

"Well, if she teaches at the elementary school, it's about to start," Benny replied.

"She didn't seem as sick as Nir implied." Rania could hazard a guess why Gelenter didn't want them talking to his wife about Nadya. But why was she so anxious to be away from the police? She looked around for evidence of a late-night cleaning spree, but not having seen the room before put her at a disadvantage.

The room was small but pleasant enough. The battered wooden desktop was littered with pictures: Nadya with other young women at the sea in Eilat; people standing in snowdrifts, wrapped in every kind of woolen garment, presumably her family in Uzbekistan. Nadya holding a bundle of blankets that might have been a baby. In a couple, Nadya stood with men, arms entwined. She looked happy enough, Rania reflected. If they were clients, Nadya was a good actress.

The few clothes in the closet were old. They didn't find any of the outfits Nadya was wearing in the photos. No phone book. No official papers, no ID card or passport, but that they didn't expect to find. They also didn't find a suitcase or bag of any kind she would have used to carry her clothes from Eilat. So either she had come with nothing, or she took some things with her when she left the house.

Rania opened the door next to Nadya's, which held a crib and a small bed. The walls were painted with teddy bears. She shut the door and moved back toward the living room. She dredged her memories from the night before, trying to feel if anything was in a different place. She turned over objects on the mantle: a menorah, a misshapen clay an animal. When she touched the framed *ketubah*, the marriage contract between Nir and Chaya Gelenter, Benny spoke at her elbow.

"We don't have permission to search the rest of the house."

"Well, get permission," she said.

"I have no grounds to ask."

"Why are we tiptoeing around this guy?" she fumed. "His maid was found killed in a ditch, and he acts like it's a minor inconvenience. He's not telling us what he knows, and you know it too."

Through an open door off the living room she glimpsed what was plainly Nir's study. She charged in, before Benny could stop her. She looked around the study, taking in the shelves of leather-bound Hebrew books and the well-preserved antique writing desk. It was an Ottoman design she recognized. Probably stolen from some Palestinian family kicked out of their home in 1948. She sat in the deep leather chair and opened drawer after drawer. None of them were locked. Right there, in the middle drawer, underneath a small stack of bills, was what she was looking for. Not one but two passports, one green, one burgundy. One was for a Nadya Kim, born in Tashkent, Uzbekistan, 1986. She flipped through the pages and found no visa stamp for Israel. The other bore the same photo, but was in the name of Alexandra Marininova, born in Odessa, Ukraine, nationality, Jewish. This one contained an A1 visa, permitting her to come and go and work in Israel for five years.

"Put it back," Benny said from the doorway. "We don't have a warrant."

"You're not even going to call Nir and ask why he has two different passports for the same girl and told us he didn't even had one?"

"I can't do that, because we had no right to look for it. You should have waited," he said.

"Waited for what?" she wanted to know. "You're not planning to do any investigation of this guy."

"Don't accuse me of not doing my job," he said, ruffled now. "I told you, I'm one of the good guys."

But he joined her at the desk, and copied down the details from both passports as she did. "I assume this is the real one," he gestured with the green Uzbek passport. "But I'll run them by both consulates just to be sure."

She was deeply afraid he was going to tell her he would take the case from there. She didn't want that. She wanted to solve the case, and not only for her own ego. She felt a connection with Nadya, a need to know who had done what to her. Her job was to protect the Palestinians, not to worry about some dead Eastern European prostitute, she reprimanded herself. True, but the job was not everything. She had come to this work because she cared about justice. She expected that a prostitute who had entered Israel illegally, living in the home of one of the most powerful men in Israel, was no more likely to receive justice from the Israeli authorities than a Palestinian. Though she knew little about Nadya, she felt her spirit in this house. She could almost feel the relief the young woman would have felt, to escape from her dangerous, shameful servitude in Eilat and come to live in this peaceful, prosperous home in a tightly protected enclave. Yet somehow it had been here that the ultimate danger had found her.

"We need to find this man she was arguing with," she said to Benny as they climbed into his car.

"We?" he said with a little smile. "How do you propose to do that?"

Good question. "Talk to more people here," she suggested. She had a sudden thought. "What about the Israeli woman who was in the fields that day? She might know something."

"What woman?"

"The one Abu Anwar and the other women saw."

"What are you talking about?"

They had been joking around, challenging each other without hostility, but now he was angry. She realized that she had never told him about her interviews with the women who were waiting that morning. When she and Benny had gone to talk to Abu Anwar, he hadn't mentioned the young woman either. She had frankly forgotten about that, in all the excitement of discovering where Nadya worked.

"Several witnesses reported seeing an Israeli woman, in work clothes, walking in the area where the body was found," she said.

"Where are these witnesses? I want to see them, now." He started the car. "There's a great falafel place in Azzawiya. We can stop there for lunch."

"When were you there?" she wanted to know.

"Last summer, when they had those demonstrations against the Fence," he said.

"I'm not going there with you."

"Why not?"

Could he really be so dense? First, she could not eat alone in public with a man not her husband and not related to her. And second, she wouldn't be seen in the villages socializing with an Israeli policeman.

"It's haram," she said. *Shameful.* "They must have food in Elkana."

They went into a store and bought some bread, hummus, and cheese and ate it in the car. She and her friends sneered at Palestinians who spent money in Israeli settlements, but it was the lesser of evils right now. And anyway, Benny insisted on paying for all the food, and he spent money in settlements every day, so the tiny bit he spent on her was not going to make a difference. She was rationalizing, but her life was full of contradictions.

✳ ✳ ✳

Benny drove through Deir Balut checkpoint into Azzawiya. As soon as they passed the checkpoint, Rania put on her jilbab and hijab.

Abu Anwar was out at his land, his daughter told them.

"Call him to come back," Benny ordered.

Rania bristled at his tone and his taking command. He should let her take the lead here, with Palestinian women. She would be much more likely than he to get cooperation from them. But as she was thinking this, she heard the daughter on the phone, saying to someone, "Find him and tell him Yahud are here."

Jews. Not police. If she were here by herself, or with another Palestinian officer, what would the daughter have said then? The Palestinian police did not try to instill fear in the people. The people knew they were here to help. A good relationship to have, but not necessarily one that would impress an Israeli policeman.

Abu Anwar's wife made coffee, and they drank it silently in the living room while they waited. Abu Anwar arrived, dirty from the land, and went to wash up and change before coming to sit with them. He was unsure which language to speak, Hebrew or Arabic, and settled for a mind-rattling mixture of the two, switching back and forth sometimes in the middle of a sentence. Rania started to ask him about the woman he saw, but Benny insisted on going back over everything, how he found the body, how he fell down, why he didn't report it right away, and then they got to the Israeli woman he saw. He gave the same description he had given before, straight dark skirt and white blouse, scarf over her dark hair, late twenties to early thirties, attractive. Benny took out his book of photos and pointed out a few of them to Abu Anwar. He asked him to say which looked the most like the woman he saw. He insisted he couldn't really remember. But Benny persisted, and Abu Anwar pointed to one of the photos and said, maybe more like this one. Why that one? Benny wanted to know. Abu Anwar said the shape of her face, it was like this. Was he sure? Benny asked. More like that one than this one? indicating one with a rounder face; the one Abu Anwar had picked was more heart-shaped. No, like this, Abu Anwar said. Could he remember anything else about her? Did she walk fast or slowly? Not fast or slow, Abu Anwar said. Sure about that? Not fast or slow, he repeated. Did the woman look at him? He couldn't tell, she had on dark glasses. He didn't think so.

Rania called Salma and reported to Benny that she was at the health center in Rafat, the next village over from Azzawiya, ten minutes by car.

"But there is no reason to go there," she said. "Salma didn't even mention the woman to me. Only Um Raad did."

"You said the women were together." He beetled his eyes at her, as if daring her to contradict herself now.

"Yes, when I saw them, they were all together."

"So they are sitting there together, bored out of their minds while the army keeps them from crossing, and you think one of them sees something that strikes her as unusual, and doesn't point it out to the others?"

Rania had to admit it was unlikely. They headed into Rafat. On their way into the little town, about half the size of its neighbors, Benny pointed to a massive pile of dirt and rock, the remains of a substantial compound.

"You know what that is?" he demanded.

"Of course," she replied calmly.

"The home of Yahya Ayyash," he continued. "The Engineer."

"Yes," she said. Yahya Ayyash was the most famous son of these parts.

He had used his engineering training to develop low-tech bombs for Hamas, bombs which had killed ninety Israeli citizens from 1991 to 1996, when he himself was assassinated. After he was killed, the Israeli army had come to Rafat, where he had not lived for years, and demolished his family's home.

"Why haven't they rebuilt it?" Benny asked Rania now.

"How should I know? I don't live in Rafat, I live in Mas'ha. There's the health center."

Salma rushed them into the back after only a few seconds in the large waiting room, but it was enough for Benny's presence to send the toddlers burrowing into their mothers' skirts. In the little white examination room, with its shelves sparsely stocked with bandages and analgesics, Benny stood back while Rania asked Salma why she had not said anything about the Israeli woman. Was he testing her, to see if she would be as ruthless in questioning Palestinian women as she had been with Nir Gelenter? Or was he maybe unsure himself about how to question a Palestinian village woman? She decided to believe the latter. She carefully translated Salma's answers into English for him. Salma had forgotten about the Israeli woman, she said. She had been stuck at the roadblock for hours. She had noticed dozens of people. The woman hadn't made a big impression on her.

Rania showed her the photos Benny produced. Salma picked out the same one as Abu Anwar. The only time Benny talked was to ask Salma if she thought the woman was older or younger than her, and if she had seen clothes like she was wearing in any stores in the villages or in Nablus. Salma said yes, in Nablus, you could buy clothes like that.

"The woman's not Israeli, she's Palestinian," Benny announced as they descended the health center steps. Rania was shocked. She had not considered that, but now he said it, it made perfect sense.

"Why do you say that?"

"The woman in the photo that they picked out was Palestinian, not Israeli. Besides, an Israeli woman would have had no reason to be walking through the fields; she would take a bus or get a ride straight out of the settlement. So she must be a Palestinian trying to look like an Israeli in order to go to work in Israel."

"But an Israeli woman who had something to do with killing Nadya might have been in the fields."

"This woman had nothing to do with Nadya," he asserted.

"How do you know?"

"She wasn't walking fast or slow," he said. "She was proceeding normally. People who have just killed someone don't do that."

"Well, that doesn't help us much," she said. He was obviously much more experienced in this kind of investigation than she, and that annoyed her. Why shouldn't he be? Israelis had all kinds of gruesome murders, drugs, crime that Palestinian villages never imagined.

"It helps a lot," he said confidently.

"Oh? We're going to wander into every village in the north asking for women who work in Israel? We will be doing that until we are grandparents."

"Why do you think she is not from around here?"

"She is not from Mas'ha, or I would know her," she said. "If she were from Biddia or Deir Balut, one of the others would have known her. And women in Azzawiya and Rafat, well, they do not go to work in Israel. She is more likely from Qalqilya or Nablus."

"A needle in a haystack," he said softly, more to himself than to her.

"I don't understand."

"It's like looking for a particular cup of oil in Saudi Arabia," he clarified. "We'll start in this area."

Rania didn't want to canvass the Salfit villages with an Israeli policeman, looking for this girl. She tried to suggest that she would have better luck going alone, but he wasn't having it. He didn't trust her, she understood, because she hadn't told him about the woman in the first place. Well, that was fair enough.

"I know what to do," she said finally.

"What might that be?"

"We'll go talk to the taxi drivers at Qarawa. No matter where in the north she is from, someone will know her."

"Good idea," Benny said.

His phone chirped. He turned away from her, talking into his hand.

"Something has come up," he said when he hung up. "I need to go back to Ariel for a little while. Why don't you come with me and have some tea, and then we can go see if we can find this girl coming home from work."

Rania didn't love the idea of hanging out at an Israeli settlement police station, but it would be ridiculous to go to Salfit if he couldn't drive her; by the time she got there, she would have to turn around and leave again.

When she got out of the car, Benny glanced at her and she could tell he expected her to take off her hijab. She didn't. The Israeli policewomen sitting at the desk eyed her suspiciously.

"Mah zeh?" one of them said to Benny. *What is this?* Not who, but what.

"Palestinian police," he shrugged. No name. That was fine. She didn't want to know their names, or for them to know hers.

The two young women—near twins with dark hair, dark circles drawn around their dark eyes, big chests peeking out of their blue uniform shirts—laughed at the idea of a Palestinian policewoman. Or maybe it was something about *her* as a policewoman that struck them as funny, she had no way of knowing. They treated her like something they found on the bottom of their shoes. She wanted to kick mud in their over-made-up faces, but instead she ignored them completely.

"There is an American here," one of the women said to Benny. "The border police arrested her near the Machsom HaChayalim. They said she was interfering with them. This is her ID."

She handed him a green *beit hawwiya*, and Benny opened it and said, "tsilum," *copy*. Rania thought it must be Chloe. She didn't suppose there was another American woman running around here with a copy of her ID in a hawiyya folder.

"I'll talk to her in a few minutes," Benny said. He installed Rania in his office, asked her if she wanted tea, coffee, or soda. She chose tea, and he brought it to her with a bowl of sugar.

"If you need to use the phone, press nine to get an outside line," he said. "But if you're calling a mobile it will cut you off after five minutes and you'll have to call back. Cost savings," he added with a wink.

Captain Mustafa was not in his office. She had to call his mobile phone three separate times before she was done telling him about the passports and the interviews. He grunted when she said that Benny refused to confront Nir Gelenter about why Nadya had two passports. He had more important things on his mind.

"Listen," he said, when she was done. "There is a young man from Azzawiya who is wanted by the SHABAK, and he is missing. His name is Fareed Jaber Murad Haddad. The SHABAK want to talk to him about a terrorism case, and the *muhabarat* is cooperating with them. If you hear anything about him while you are in the villages, bring it to my attention right away."

"Mmmm," Rania said, careful not to agree directly. She didn't know what she would do if she ended up with information like that. She had never had to deal with such a problem.

Benny was gone for about an hour. When he came back, he said he needed to make a few calls, would she mind waiting down the hall? He showed her into another office, where some women were working. They said nothing to her, nor she to them. She called Bassam and told him she would be late so he should feed Khaled. She felt like the Israeli police all stared at her when they heard her speaking Arabic on the phone, but she told herself she was being paranoid. She heard people in the hall speaking Arabic, so she peeked out. Ali was there, talking to Chloe. So she was right about the ID belonging to Chloe, who was now taking it back from Ali and promising to carry her passport on her all the time now. Rania doubted that would happen. She ducked back into the room before Chloe could spot her.

When Chloe was gone, Rania walked out into the hall to say hello to Ali. Benny had a booming voice, and she could hear him talking on the phone. "Fareed Jaber Murad Haddad," she heard him say. She wondered if it could be a coincidence that this young man from Azzawiya was suddenly wanted, after Chloe, who was staying in Azzawiya, was in this police station all day. She thought the man Chloe had accompanied to the mayor's house the other night was named Jaber, and Captain Mustafa had called him Abu Fareed. She didn't like that she was thinking these things about Chloe, but really, what did she know about her? And wasn't it a little strange for a lone American woman to be staying in a small village in the middle of Palestine? She should try to find out more about Chloe.

Benny emerged from his office, pulling on his jacket.

"Yalla." *Let's go*, he said.

He lurched ahead of her, bounding down the steps. She wasn't going to trail after him like some medieval serf. Before he made it through the door, she stopped in her tracks. He stopped half in and half out of the door, turning to stare at her.

"What's the matter?"

"People who are going somewhere together go *together*."

He closed the door and walked back to the step where she stood, approaching with a little bow.

"Forgive me." He matched his stride to hers then, careful not to gain one inch on her. Good. Let him learn.

Once behind the wheel, he was in a hurry again, tearing out of the parking lot in a rubber-scorching blur. It was rush hour, and a line of traffic waited at the junction to turn left onto the main road. Rania glanced idly at the red Dan bus disgorging its passengers across the road. Her eyes slowly focused on a young woman with a heart-shaped face and a halo of frizzy brown hair. Benny perked up at the same instant.

"Got her," he said.

The young woman looked both ways carefully, spotting the police car a fraction of a second after Rania spotted her. She hesitated, telegraphing her thought process. Should she brazenly cross the street to Kifl Hares, knowing they could not prove she had not boarded the bus inside the West Bank? Or walk up into the settlement, where a host of security guards lurked to demand her ID? Or maybe she should just sit here in the bus stop, as if she were meeting someone.

Her decision was made for her, as Rania and Benny did a fast U-turn in the turnaround and squealed up next to her.

"*Marhaba,*" Rania greeted her. "We need to talk."

Her name was Fatima, and she came from the hamlet of Izbet Salman, near the city of Qalqilya. She had studied chemistry at university. She was engaged, and her fiancé had no work, so she needed money and wanted to work in her field, which was impossible in the West Bank. About a year ago, she had taken a job at a chemical company in the industrial town of Rosh HaAyin.

No, she answered Benny's question, the company didn't know she was from the West Bank. They thought she lived in Jaffa. Her voice trembled. Rania knew she was waiting for them to ask for the name of the company, which she would have to give, and that would be the end of her working there. Rania had no intention of asking for that information. She couldn't stop Benny from doing it, but she put in a little prayer that his desire to impress her with his righteousness would mean he wouldn't want to ruin a young woman's life in front of her.

For the moment, he seemed focused on other things. He asked Fatima how she traveled from Izbet Salman to Rosh HaAyin. He was standing very close to Fatima, letting his size intimidate her. Rania saw a throng of men across the street, at the entrance to Kifl Hares where the taxis waited, looking over at them. Among them she saw some of the drivers she knew. It wouldn't be good for her to be seen here, questioning a Palestinian woman on the street in front of the settlement with an Israeli policeman. Better to go across and sit on the roadblock, where everyone could see and hear.

She stepped around Benny to the street side and took Fatima's arm gently.

"You look uncomfortable here," she said in Arabic. "Let's go across the street where we can sit down."

Before Benny could protest she led the way across the intersection and parked them on the remains of an old stone wall. He had no choice but to follow, only stopping to extract a radio from the police car. Rania nodded to the gathered drivers, and Fatima did too. Benny greeted them in Hebrew and a few of them mumbled "shalom" in return. She imagined they knew him too, from many encounters on the road. If he was as good a guy as he said, they would know that.

She asked Fatima again about the route she took to her job.

Each morning, she took a taxi to Azzawiya bridge and climbed up onto the road and walked, or sometimes got a ride to the first bus stop inside Israel. Coming home, it was easier; she could take a bus all the way to Ariel, and then cross the road and take taxis to Izbet Salman. Five mornings a week she left home at four-thirty and returned at almost seven at night.

She changed in the fields near Azzawiya bridge, she told them. She was in the brush for quite a while on Monday morning, because there were a lot of jesh and she had to wait a long time. She saw many people crossing, like herself, she said. She didn't notice any of them in particular. She was only interested in the jesh.

Abruptly, Benny produced the doctored color photo of Nadya's body.

"Did you see this woman dead in the fields?"

Fatima gasped and shook her head vigorously. "Laa laa laa," she said adamantly. *No, no, no.* "Don't you think I would have said, if I had seen such a thing?"

"What time exactly did you arrive?" Benny asked.

"Six-fifteen, maybe six-twenty," she said.

"And you are sure you did not see her body?"

"I am telling you, it's not something you forget."

"No, I guess not."

He was quiet for a few minutes, writing on a notepad. They were the first minutes she had spent in his presence when he wasn't talking, Rania reflected.

"Okay," he said to Fatima, sounding slightly apologetic. "We're going to need you to come show us where you were exactly."

Rania knew that Fatima was terrified of getting in the police car. She didn't blame her; she was still frightened too. But Benny's plan made sense. If Fatima walked right by where the body was at six-fifteen, when the abandoned car was already up above the bridge, and the body was not there, then the relationship between the girl, her killer, and the car was not what they had been assuming.

Fatima was quiet on the drive through the Deir Balut checkpoint into the Azzawiya lands. She directed them to a tree that looked like any olive tree, but when they got close revealed a hollow in its trunk.

"This is where I always put my clothes," Fatima said. She reached into the hollow and removed jilbab, hijab, and a battered pair of sneakers.

"So on Monday morning, you changed here, and then where did you go?" Benny asked.

Fatima showed them a spot where the reeds were well tamped down by years of feet and behinds, crossing and sitting, just as she had done. From there she would have had a good view of the goings-on on both roads, the Palestinian one below and the Israeli one up above, but she would not have been visible from either. When she got there, she explained, the jesh were all along the road above, but after an hour or so, they moved down to just where the car was stopped. Then she had been able to climb up to the road and catch a ride across the Green Line.

Benny had her go through the motions of changing her clothes, waiting, and climbing. He mirrored her, to get her perspective.

"What are you doing to her?"

Rania looked up to see Chloe standing there, hands on hips. Her brush with the police had apparently not dampened her desire to butt into every situation.

"We're getting ready to beat a confession out of her with a rubber hose, so scram," Benny said.

"You think that's funny?" Chloe asked hotly.

"I think you've been in enough trouble today, so unless you really do want to be deported, you'll get out of here."

Chloe looked to Rania.

"Ruhi," Rania said, jerking her head toward the Azzawiya road. "Kul ishi tamam hon." *Go, everything's fine here.*

Chloe looked at Fatima for a cue. The young woman was impassive, just watching with interest. Chloe walked about fifty meters and sat down on a rock. The other three continued what they were doing and ignored her.

Fatima continued to insist she had not seen anything unusual that day except for the army —but that wasn't unusual, she said with a sly look at Rania.

"There must have been lots of people in the fields, more than usual," Benny observed. "Did you speak to any of them?"

"No," she said firmly. "They were all men, and I don't like to speak to them."

"But you must have noticed them," he pressed. "What were they doing?"

"Waiting," she said. "Eating breakfast, talking, like always."

"Nothing else?" Rania interrupted. Fatima was not revealing something. If she could tell, Benny could tell. She hoped the girl would not be stupid enough to think she could hide whatever it was. It would only make trouble for her.

"There was one man," Fatima said finally, "who was running through the fields. He wasn't dressed for work, he looked like a student."

"Can you describe him?" Benny perked up, reaching for his notepad.

"He was ordinary looking," Fatima evaded. "Young, Palestinian, nice pants, and a light colored cotton shirt."

"You say he was running? From where? To where?"

"I don't know where from. He was going toward Azzawiya, and he had something in his hand, a bag like you would take to go away for the weekend."

She could not, or would not, tell them anything more about the young man. Rania declined Benny's offer of a ride, and called Bassam to come pick her and Fatima up at Mas'ha Junction. She would persuade him to drive Fatima to Izbet Salman, so at least the young woman wouldn't arrive home much later than usual. Rania watched as Chloe rose from her perch and headed off toward Azzawiya. She wondered if she should warn Chloe not to tell anyone in the village that she had seen Fatima talking to them. But she wasn't so eager to answer the woman's questions about what *she* was doing here, and didn't imagine her advice would make much difference. She would have to rely on Chloe's discretion, if she had any, and the good judgment of the Azzawiyans, which she wasn't sure existed.

Chapter 15

When Chloe got back to Azzawiya, the story of her arrest had preceded her. Some of the men who were waiting to cross to Israel were from the village, and had seen her taken away. A few people stopped her as she walked home, asking "Shu sar?" *What happened?* She just shrugged. She was too tired to chat, and anyway, she wasn't really sure what to tell them.

Before she turned off the main road, she ducked into her favorite store to buy some bread and hummus.

"Do you have bread?" she asked Dilal, who lived above his store. He and his brothers were sitting around in green plastic chairs, watching al Jazeera. He rose and went over to the cooler where he kept bread, and she breathed a sigh of relief. Often all the stores in the village were out of bread by evening. She didn't want to have to make rice. She wanted to plow into some comfort food.

As he counted out her bread rounds, two men walked in. Maher and his brother Samer were her least favorite people in the village. They were both tall, with light hair and blue eyes, and would have been handsome if they didn't wear permanent sneers. Maher in particular had seemed to resent her presence in the village from day one. His children often threw stones at her, and while she never heard him actually encourage them, he would watch them without objecting.

Now he cast a cold look up and down her body, and said something she did not understand to Samer. The brothers were close in age and pretty much inseparable. They were also close friends with Dilal and his brothers, which she tried not to hold against the shopkeeper. In villages, you didn't necessarily pick your friends, at least not the way westerners did. They were a product of complex family relationships, neighborhoods, political affiliations, and probably more things that she didn't know about. Dilal never appeared to share Maher and Samer's hostility toward her, but he also never tried to protect her from them. She guessed she couldn't hold that against him—after all, he had known these people most of his life and her only a few months, and he would continue to know them long after she was gone. Still, it always disappointed her when he didn't stand up for her. She knew he would never allow Maher to speak to or look at a Palestinian woman the way he did her, but then, Maher would not treat a Palestinian woman that way.

You're not a Palestinian woman, get over it, she told herself sternly.

"You were at the police station?" Maher asked her.

She nodded. She put a five shekel coin on the counter, took the plastic bag with her purchases and turned to go. She was out the door when Maher's voice caught up with her. "Why did they release you?"

She knew what he was implying. When Palestinians were picked up by the Israeli army or police and returned quickly, it often meant that they had given information to help themselves. This was not the first time that Maher had suggested to people in the village that she was a collaborator. People whispered that accusation against him; she figured that was why he was so anxious to cast suspicion onto someone else.

"They didn't have anything to hold me for," she said.

She knew that in their experience, that often didn't make a difference, but what else could she say? It was the truth, and they could believe her or not. She walked home quickly, imagining that she was getting suspicious looks from others she passed on the road. Or was she imagining it? There were plenty who said that the Foreigners were all traitors, giving information about the villagers to the Israelis. Well, there was nothing she could do about it now. She hadn't asked to be arrested, and she hadn't done anything wrong. They would just have to see that no one got in trouble because of her, and then whatever buzz there might be would quiet down.

When she got to her house, Avi was sitting on the porch with Jaber. Had he come because she was arrested? The thought cheered her.

"Hamdilila assalam," Jaber said.

"Allah ysalmak," she responded. It was comforting, that he gave her the traditional Arabic greeting for someone who has returned from a trip—or from jail.

"What happened?" he asked.

Was it paranoia, or was there a hint of guardedness in his voice? She told them the story as simply as possible, but left out the part about the folders she had seen. She didn't know if that was the right decision. She didn't want to worry Jaber, but she did want to warn him. She would try to get Avi alone before he left.

"What are you doing here?" she asked him. "You didn't come because of my text message?"

"No," he said. Of course not. How could she have thought what happened to her was so important—and besides, anything he might have done to help her could as easily be done from home. Still, it cut into her joy at being home.

"Well, why then? Did something happen with Abu Shaadi's land?"

"No, not that either. Fareed's missing."

"What do you mean, missing?"

"No one has heard from him since Monday, and we can't reach him by phone," Jaber supplied.

"Well, you know how unreliable mobile phone service is in Nablus."

"His phone is closed," Jaber said shortly.

"Maybe he forgot to charge the battery."

Neither of the men looked convinced. They did look at each other. Chloe felt resentment welling up. They were hiding something from her. Jaber hadn't invited her to join them. She should go inside her house and leave them to whatever it was. But she was tired of being out of the loop.

"Do you think he could have been arrested?" she asked, hoping a bold question would shake loose some information.

They both looked startled.

"Why do you say that?" Jaber demanded.

Now she regretted her self-absorbed ploy. She had not meant to increase his concern about his son.

"Well, you know, the checkpoints going to Nablus are so bad," she stammered. "I just wondered, because you seemed so worried."

"A friend of mine works in the muhabarat," Jaber said. "He told me the SHABAK is looking for Fareed."

That could explain the files she had seen in the police station. "Did he say why?"

"No," Jaber said. He stubbed out his cigarette and immediately lit another. Avi spoke up.

"We think it could have to do with the girl who died."

"What girl? The foreigner? What would she have to do with Fareed?"

"Fareed knew her," Avi said. "Her name was Nadya, she was from Uzbekistan, and she worked in Elkana. She wanted to run away, but her employer had her passport. Fareed asked me to help her get it, so she could go free."

"I still don't understand," she said. "How did Fareed know a woman who was working in Elkana?"

"He found her crying in the groves one day, when he was on his way back from Nablus. He told me something bad had been done to her. I think she'd been raped."

"Raped? How do you know? Who raped her?"

"I don't know. I don't even know she was raped. But Fareed fell in love with her."

"Fareed? Seriously?" Chloe tried to imagine the shy young man falling in love with a foreign woman. She had never seen him talking to a girl except his sisters. All of his friends were young men, mostly other students. She didn't know why she was so shocked. She had met women from a number of Russian-speaking countries in the area. They were married to Palestinian men who had studied in the Soviet Union. Nadya would have had no trouble finding people to talk to.

"Did you know?" she asked Jaber. He shook his head.

"How were you helping them?" she asked Avi.

"I hadn't really figured that out yet," Avi said. "The day they found her, I was supposed to meet them at the checkpoint. They didn't show up. Since then I've been trying to call Fareed, but he doesn't answer."

"So maybe he doesn't even know," she suggested.

"Maybe." Avi sounded doubtful. He rose and shook hands with Jaber. "If I hear anything, I'll call you," he said in Hebrew. Jaber said he would do the same.

"See you," Avi said to Chloe.

"Wait," she took off after him. "Where are you going?"

"I have to get back. Maya has a gig tonight, and I'm doing the door." Maya sang in a punk band called the AK-47s.

"Wait. There's something I need to tell you." Quickly, she told him about the folders.

"You couldn't tell what was in them?"

"No, I don't read much Hebrew. But I'd texted you I was there. If you'd called me, maybe we could have figured it out."

If he'd called her, she wouldn't have answered because her phone was in Benny's office, but he didn't know that.

"What are we going to do about Fareed?" she asked. "He could have been arrested already, or he could be hurt."

"I don't think so."

"How do you know?"

"I don't know, but I'm pretty sure."

"You have reasons?"

"Yeah."

"Well, are you going to tell me what they are?"

"I can't right now."

Supercilious asshole! How dare he treat her like a prying nobody? She lived here, this was her family, and he knew something and was acting like she had no right to know it. But she could see that she was not going to get it out of him.

Chapter 16

"What's our next move?" Rania asked Benny on the phone. It was seven thirty in the morning, and she could tell from how he talked that he was driving.

"I'm heading to the agency where Nir said he met Nadya," he said. "Hopefully they can tell me which is the real passport, if either of them is."

"I want to come," she said.

"I'm going on my way in." Of course—he had told her he lived in Herzliya, just north of Tel Aviv. He wouldn't want to drive into the West Bank and then back out. But she wasn't in the mood to care what he wanted. She hadn't been in Tel Aviv since before the Intifada. There should be some benefit to hanging around Israeli police.

"You owe me," she said. "If it weren't for me, you wouldn't even know about the passports."

"Do you have a permit to go to Tel Aviv?" he asked.

Of course she didn't. "Why do I need a permit? They're going to stop you at the checkpoint?"

"It could happen. The police are not that popular with the army."

"Well, if they stop you, tell them you're arresting me."

"Be at Mas'ha Gate in half an hour," he said. There was no point in arguing with him that she didn't want her neighbors to see the army opening the gate specially so that she could go through and get into an Israeli police car. She would just have to hope that by this time of the morning everyone would be far from there.

* * *

The small internet café was full of teenage boys playing violent video games. They sat together in bunches in front of the four aged computers, giving out grunts and yelps as they killed off their targets. Chloe could barely see through the haze of cigarette smoke. She walked over to the register, where a young man only slightly older than the players was reading a newspaper.

"It's time for the girls," she said.

"Mmm," he said. When she didn't move, he looked up from his paper. "Ya shabab," he called out. "Il banat ajau."

Two of the boys swiveled around in their chairs to see that indeed "the girls had come." One winked at Chloe and said something that brought riotous laughter from the others. These were sons of Maher, who had taunted her in the store the night before. They turned back to their game.

Chloe glanced at the eight girls in the doorway. They would not come in while the boys were there, and they would not want to be seen standing around on the street. She needed to get the place cleared out quickly.

"Yalla shabab," she said loudly. "Doorna." *It's our turn.* Most of the boys slowly gathered up their headphones and went to pay for their time. Maher's sons remained stubbornly parked in front of their computer. Chloe walked over and eased herself in between them and the screen.

"Respect your sisters," she said in Arabic.

The young man behind the counter made a small *ssss* sound and the boys reluctantly got up. Just before walking away, one of them slammed his cup down hard on the table where the computer sat. The dregs of the coffee leapt up and splattered on Chloe's shirt.

"Jasoosia," he said as he passed her. *Traitor.*

She stood fuming, wondering what she should do. Her impulse was to convene her girls and act like nothing had happened, to show she was above it. But would she lose face in their eyes? She really didn't know. The café's proprietor saved her from having to decide. He came over and handed her a damp paper towel. While she daubed at her shirt, he cleaned up the mess around the terminal. By the time he was done, the boys were all gone and the girls had clustered around the other three computers, waiting expectantly.

"Did you bring the cameras?" she asked them. Three of them held up small digital cameras, a donation from her former employers. She gave each group a USB connector and showed them how to upload the photos from the memory cards.

"What did you photograph?" she asked a shy ten year old named Huda.

"My cousin's henna party."

"Can I see?"

The girl pointed out one of the women painting henna on the palms of the bride. "Imi," *my mother*, Huda said. "And this is my sister, Noura. She studies at Bir Zeit."

"She must be very smart," Chloe said. At Bir Zeit University, near Ramallah, all classes were taught in English. It was one of the most exclusive Palestinian colleges.

"Are you a traitor?" Huda asked suddenly.

Chloe bit back an angry reply. The girl was just repeating what she had heard.

"What do you think?"

"I don't know," the little girl said. "I never met a traitor."

There was logic in that, Chloe acknowledged. "Who says I'm a traitor?"

"My father says you are Yahudia."

"Well, it's true that I'm Jewish, but I am not an Israeli. I'm a Jew from America." All activity in the room had ceased, as the group focused on this all-important conversation.

"You were in the police yesterday, weren't you?" said a girl named Wafa. She was the granddaughter of Dilal, the storekeeper. Remembering the unpleasant interaction with Maher in Dilal's store, Chloe wondered what the girl had been told. She had always thought Dilal liked her, but maybe he was just polite.

"I am not *in* the police," she said, deliberately misinterpreting the Arabic expression. "The police arrested me."

"Why did they take you?" asked Huda.

"They had arrested another man, a Palestinian, and they were beating him. I tried to help him."

Chloe hoped she didn't sound like she thought she was a hero. She remembered how the men in the fields yesterday had taunted her with how little she could do to ease their suffering.

"Did you help him?" Wafa wanted to know.

"Not exactly. But when they took me away, they left him."

The girls looked impressed at that. It seemed like a good note to change the topic on.

"Let's get back to your pictures, shall we?" Chloe said. "We only have this room for an hour."

The girls obediently turned back to their screens. She heard them talking quietly among themselves. She was sure they were not through with the subject, but that was okay. Nothing she could say would convince people to trust her. Her actions would have to do that.

* * *

"Yes, of course," said Galit, the owner of the Tel Aviv employment agency. "Nadya had her passport, everything was legal."

Galit was forty-something and well groomed, with too-black hair cinched in a tight knot behind her head.

"Did she take the passport with her?" Benny asked.

"I gave it to her employer, Mr. Gelenter."

"He told us he never saw it." Benny kept his voice casual.

Galit hesitated. Rania wondered why she didn't simply say, "He's mistaken." It would make things much easier for her, but she guessed lowly employment agency proprietors couldn't just accuse powerful officials of lying. The two police waited patiently for her to make up her mind.

"I'm sure I gave it to him," she said finally. Her voice squeaked on the word "gave."

"Did you make a copy?" Benny wanted to know.

"Well, usually I do."

She didn't move to pick up the file from where it sat on top of the cabinet. Benny gestured toward it. "Could you check?"

She had no choice. "Here it is," she announced.

Benny took the file from her. "What about the visa?" he asked with his trademark eyebrow arch.

"Isn't it here?" Galit took the file and pretended to search its contents. Now Rania understood the woman's dilemma. If she accused Gelenter of lying about the passport, he could counter that he did it to protect her, because the passport contained no visa.

"I felt sorry for her," Galit said, shifting her eyes from Benny's face to Rania's. Maybe her neck was just tired from looking up, Rania thought. Or she hoped another woman would share her soft heart. Rania kept her expression neutral. "She looked very frightened. So many of these girls escape from desperate situations. If I didn't help her, where could she go?"

"How did she find you?" Rania queried. How likely was it that Nadya simply wandered into an agency where someone would overlook her status out of compassion? But perhaps she had gone door-to-door until she found one.

"She had a recommendation from another girl I placed," Galit responded. "Mr. Gelenter happened to come in that afternoon. He took a liking to her."

"Is it common for employers to come into the office?" Benny asked. "I would have thought they would place the order over the phone."

"Well, yes, most do, but he said he worked nearby and wanted a walk," Galit said with a shrug. She was trying to be cool, Rania saw, and act like the discussion about her business practices was over. Benny let her sweat, keeping the file in his hands while they talked about other things.

"I trust this was a rare exception," he said at last, putting the file down on the desk. Galit replaced it in the file cabinet immediately, as if hoping she could make it disappear. If she was smart, Rania thought, she would indeed misplace the papers soon.

The agency was on Ibn Gvirol, not far from the fashionable shopping center at Dizengoff Square. Cafés with outdoor tables lined the sidewalk. Benny pointed to one which looked particularly inviting, with umbrellas providing shade over the spacious tables.

"Let's eat," Benny said.

He was a man who liked to be comfortable, Rania reflected. He seemed to think about food almost obsessively, yet he wasn't fat, just big and strong. Palestinians seldom ate between eight in the morning and four or five in the afternoon. But she looked at the scantily dressed women sitting in high-backed metal chairs with sunglasses on, eating sandwiches and sipping mint lemonades, and thought it might be nice to be one of them for a change. She did not protest when he chose a table right on the sidewalk, and even let him order for her in Hebrew. Here, she didn't need to worry about being seen with an Israeli man or eating in public. She didn't know anyone in Tel Aviv.

She removed her hijab and stuffed it into her purse. It was hot, and the sun felt good on her face and hair. Benny raised his eyebrows and that made her regret the gesture, but she wasn't going to let him see her embarrassed. She hoped she wasn't blushing. Her face felt a little hot. It got hotter as she had a terrible thought—what if he imagined she was flirting with him?

She pushed her untouched lemonade away and jumped up. "Let's go," she said.

He gawked at her in disbelief, which embarrassed her even more.

"Come on!" she said. "It's late. I have barely seen my son and my husband all week."

"It's not even twelve," he protested. "You'll have the whole afternoon with them."

"I don't like it here," she said. "It's bourgeois."

He laughed, making her wish she could kick him with the high heels on that girl seated over there.

"Sit down," he said. "Eat your sandwich."

She stood by the table, feeling foolish, seeing people looking at her, trying to figure out what her problem was. She supposed a Palestinian woman with a Jewish Israeli man was noteworthy enough, and now her raised voice had aroused people's curiosity. Slowly she sat back down. He was eating with gusto. She had lost whatever appetite she had come with, but she nibbled a little just so he wouldn't dwell on it.

Chapter 17

Chloe bolted awake. Someone was pounding on her door. She sat up, rubbing her eyes. It was pitch dark outside, but she could see bright lights too. The banging on the door grew more insistent. She got up and threw it open.

"Jesh," Alaa's small mouth said soundlessly.

The young girl stood there in her pajamas, clutching her teddy bear, soft brown hair sticking out in every direction. She was visibly shaking. Chloe slipped her feet into sandals, feeling momentarily bad when she looked at Alaa's bare feet. But Alaa could stay inside if she wanted to, and she could not.

"Jesh where?" she asked. "Here? Hon?" She couldn't remember how to speak Arabic when she was half asleep.

"Barra." *Outside.*

She could hear them now, yelling. She heard a shot and went running downstairs.

Jaber stood in the doorway in his long sleeping robe, talking to a soldier who had guns all over his body. One, of course, was in his hands, both hands on the trigger, the barrel more or less under Jaber's chin. Jaber appeared cool and composed. Chloe didn't understand the Hebrew words he was using, but from his gestures, she gathered he was asking to see a warrant. His sons crowded behind him.

She saw five jeeps forming a semi-circle around the house. She could count thirty soldiers, posted every ten feet or so. All of them looked ready to shoot at anything that moved. As she watched, one of them called something to the one next to him. She tensed. The other guy reached into his pocket and pulled out a lighter and threw it to his friend, who had to take his hand off his gun to catch it, fumble in his own pocket for a cigarette, and light it.

Chloe stood on the porch, just behind the commander and facing Jaber and his sons. She saw Ahlam come into the room, wearing a loose robe and her hijab, carrying her smallest daughter. The little girl was crying. Ahlam shushed her gently, but that only made her cry louder.

The commander was ordering all the men to come out of the house. "The women and children can stay in this room," he said.

Jaber disappeared inside, and one of the soldiers charged in after him. They emerged together, Jaber refusing to be hurried, acting like he didn't even notice the gun prodding his back. Mohammed went with his father immediately, without a word, his chin defiantly jutting out, his chiseled face showing anger mingled with pride. Naeem, at fourteen, wasn't sure if he qualified as a man, or if he wanted to. He was small for his age, and he could probably have stayed with the women and children if he wanted. Chloe saw him hesitating and said softly in Arabic, "You can stay here if you want." She thought maybe her saying that pushed him over the edge, certainly not her intent, but he strode out, a little wobbly at first but composing himself so that by the time he reached the other men, he was standing straight and not trembling so anyone could see.

The commander pointed to a spot on the ground, and indicated with his gun that the men should make a single file line. Chloe seethed as he adjusted their positions, just so much space between them. She hesitated, not sure what to do. She wanted to go with them, both to show solidarity—if they must stand out in the chill night air, so would she—and to be there in case the army guys were inclined to violence, but she thought maybe Ahlam and the children needed her more. They certainly looked more frightened than Jaber and the boys, who stood rigidly.

As a compromise, she stood in the doorway and watched the commander examine the male members of the family, asking a question or two, ordering each of the boys to lift the thin t-shirt in which he slept. When he came to Jaber, she feared he would do something horrible, like tell him to lift up his long robe. He hesitated, and she was sure he was considering it. She moved closer, so that she could hear what he was saying. She felt goosebumps covering her forearms, a combination of fear, the cool night air, and the discombobulation of being woken so abruptly from her sleep. She could see the neighbors gathering on their porches, discreetly watching, trying not to miss any details without drawing any attention to themselves.

The commander decided to presume Jaber did not have a bomb under his night clothes, and simply asked him and Mohammed for their IDs. He took for granted that Naeem didn't have one, so he must have known how young he was, but he did not suggest he go back into the house. Chloe didn't know what she thought about that. It would have been humiliating for the boy to be sent back to stand with the children, and the commander would know that, so maybe he was actually trying to be nice. It might have just happened, that what he wanted and what the boy wanted coincided at this moment, or he just had bigger things on his mind than playing king of the mountain with a teenager.

Jaber explained that Mohammed, who was tall for his age, was only fifteen also, still too young for ID. Give me yours, the man said, holding out his hand impatiently. His other hand was resting on his gun, finger inches from the trigger.

"Babayit," Jaber said, gesturing to the house.

"Tavi et hateudot shelo." *Bring his ID*, the commander yelled toward Chloe.

"Shu biddo?" *What does he want?* Ahlam asked tensely.

Chloe whispered to her, and Ahlam turned around and went back to the bedroom. She came back with the ID, along with three sweaters. Chloe took them and went outside. The captain immediately held out his hand for the ID. Chloe ignored him, handing the men the sweaters first. Jaber seemed to approve of her stuntsmanship. He and the boys took their time putting the sweaters on before he reached for the ID and passed it on to the captain.

The commander called another soldier to come and guard the men while he took the ID and went over to one of the jeeps. He took out a cellphone and called in the ID number. While he was on the phone, another man strode over to him. He was not in army uniform, but wearing slacks and a blue shirt. When he moved into the headlights, Chloe saw that it was Benny, the guy who had questioned her at Ariel. Almost at the same moment, he turned and saw her. His eyes popped and he strode over to where she stood.

"What are you doing here?" he hissed.

"Just watching," she said.

"Who told you we were coming here?"

"No one," she said. "I live here."

His eyebrow shot up. "You live *here*?"

He marched over to Jaber. She followed. "How long has the tourist lived here?" he demanded in Hebrew. The Israelis used the word *tayeret*, tourist, for a foreigner who was not clearly a worker, but the word always made

Chloe bristle. If she was a tourist, why wasn't she getting to sit around on the beach, drinking piña coladas, and reading novels?

"A few months," Jaber answered.

"Why does she live here?"

"She wanted a place to stay, and I have the apartment."

A tight knot formed in Chloe's stomach. Was Jaber going to feel he had to kick her out now?

Benny was apparently satisfied that there was nothing more to know about her relationship to the family, and moved on to the business at hand.

"Where is your son Fareed?"

Jaber shrugged. "Lo po." *Not here*, he said. Chloe drew in a sharp breath and held it. That was the kind of answer that could send someone flying to the ground. She didn't know if her presence had anything to do with Benny's controlled response.

"I need to talk to him," he said mildly.

"What about?" Jaber asked, his eyes betraying no fear.

"About the murder of a young woman near here."

"What could my son have to do with that?"

"People say that he knew her."

"Who says that? Who was she?"

"A foreign woman."

"My son doesn't know any foreign women."

"He knows *her*," he said pointing to Chloe.

"She is not a foreign woman. She is one of us."

Warmth coursed through Chloe's body at this. But of course, Jaber was just making points with the Israeli policeman. He might feel different in the harsh light of his neighbors' stares.

"More than one person told us they saw her with him," Benny told him. "And besides, there is something else."

"What else?"

"We believe he might have been involved with the terrorist that we arrested a few months ago."

"He is not involved in anything like that."

"Someone gave us his name."

"I ask you to tell me who."

"You know that I can't do that."

"Well, then, why should I believe you? If someone is implicating my son for a terrorist, I have the right to know who it is."

"It is impossible for me to tell you. But if it is a mistake, I'm sure we can clear it up very quickly. If you want to call Fareed to come home, we will wait out here for him to come. Otherwise, we will need to search the house."

Jaber said nothing.

"I'm a fair guy," Benny said suddenly. "Just ask her," pointing at Chloe. "Didn't I get them to free her when she didn't have her passport?"

Now people were sure to think she was a collaborator. Did he do that on purpose? She couldn't be sure. It seemed to her his pointing at her was unnecessarily expansive, so that anyone watching would be certain not to miss it. Now he turned to the army commander, and made a sweeping gesture toward the house.

"Let's go," Benny said.

Fifteen soldiers stormed into the house. Chloe followed them. They were thorough and violent. One soldier pulled the cushions from the sofa, and another sliced them open with a bayonet. They ripped the curtains from the windows, yanking the curtain rods from the walls. They tossed food from the refrigerator, emptied the garbage on the floor, smashed Ahlam's lovely china plates. They didn't seem interested in anything. Obviously their orders were to do a certain amount of damage, to show the family the price of noncooperation.

They were searching, or ransacking, in several groups. Chloe wasn't sure who was best to follow. She heard glass being broken in the back, so she went toward the sound. The mirror in the master bedroom was shattered, and the soldiers were in the process of throwing Ahlam's lingerie on the floor and stepping on it. At least they weren't peeing on it, like the ones who had searched the home of a friend of hers in Jenin. Chloe followed behind them and picked the things up, aware that it was a futile gesture. Somewhat to her surprise, they paid no attention to her. But she supposed if they were putting on a show, it helped to have someone to witness it.

They finished in the master bedroom and moved on to the room that Fareed shared with his two brothers. The soccer posters they simply tore off the walls, but the one "martyr poster," of a young man from the village who had been shot in the back by Israeli soldiers in the first year of the Intifada, they ripped into a hundred tiny pieces. One of them turned to face Chloe after they did that.

"That is what we do to terrorists," he said.

She wasn't sure what he meant. Was he talking about the boy in the picture, or making a threat against Fareed? Or possibly, remembering how Top Killer said he was going to "treat her like a terrorist," the threat was meant for her. Regardless, there was no benefit to answering him. She simply stared back.

Jaber's kids did not sleep on mats on the floor like most of their neighbors did. They had real twin beds on wooden frames, so the soldiers had plenty to do, cutting into the mattresses, pulling out handfuls of cotton rag stuffing, smashing at the wood frames with the butts of their guns. After they shattered the first one, Chloe couldn't restrain herself. She went and sat on the second one before they could destroy it.

"Enough!" she screamed in English. "You've made your point."

One of the soldiers aimed the butt of his M-16 at her, as if about to smash her along with the bed frame. But one of the others tapped him on the shoulder, and they turned to the desk instead. The one who had stopped his friend from hitting her yanked open the desk drawers, two at a time, pulling them all the way out until they thudded to the floor. His more violent friend turned them over, strewing the contents on the floor, and then poked at it with his gun. There were the usual mementos of teenage boys' lives—papers with high marks written at the top in red Arabic numbers, a few marbles, a Rubik's cube, a pocket Koran. Some crude drawings, including one of an Israeli soldier beating a young boy. The more aggressive soldier picked that one up and handed it to the other, who studied it for a second, wadded it into a ball, and tossed it to the ground.

They were most interested in the photographs, of which there were quite a few. Photos of boys playing soccer, family members at weddings and on the beach. Chloe glimpsed one of Ahlam, looking young and beautiful, in capri pants and a tank top, shading her eyes with one hand. Her other hand was on the shoulder of Fareed, who must have been about twelve at the time, and he in turn held Mohammed and Naeem in front of him. The tiny Alaa was wedged in between the feet of the two younger boys. Chloe hadn't known that only seven years ago or so, Ahlam had not covered herself in public. She would have to ask her about that.

Something shiny gleamed up from the pile of papers and trinkets. The soldiers noticed it at the same moment Chloe did. One of them picked it up and they both turned it over in their hands, talking quietly between themselves. Chloe could see it was a thick gold bracelet. She didn't recall ever seeing Fareed wearing it. From where she sat, it didn't really look like the kind of thing Palestinians wore at all. They tended toward silver or copper, and if they wore gold, it would be thinner, hammered or filigreed, not a simple gold band like this. But she didn't really know. Maybe it was some kind of heirloom given to Fareed by one of his parents or grandparents on some special occasion.

The quieter soldier, who seemed to be in charge, put the object in his pocket. Chloe started to say something, but stopped herself. She didn't have any way of knowing what standard practice was, or what the man intended to do with the bracelet. So far, she had gotten to observe this operation much more closely than she would have predicted. No need to draw attention to that fact, and to herself, over something that might not be irregular at all. She would watch and see.

They found nothing more to interest them in the boys' room. They surprised her by not going through the girls' room at all. They peeked in, surveyed the beds, with their tumbled covers and menageries of stuffed animals, and left again, even turning off the light as they did.

Chloe followed them back to the living room. Although she had watched them vandalize the room, a survey of the mess stunned her anew. It would take hours, maybe days to restore any order here. She could not meet Ahlam's eyes. She had failed to protect them. No matter what anyone said to or about her, she would know that in their hearts, they were all thinking, "What good is she?"

The two soldiers who had searched Fareed's room handed the commander the things they had taken. Benny came and joined them, and they talked quietly among themselves. Benny took the gold bracelet and showed it to Jaber.

"Is this your son Fareed's?"

"I don't recognize it," Jaber responded placidly.

"It's very important that your son come and talk to me at once," Benny repeated.

"If he does not," the army commander threw in, "we will come back in two days and arrest all the males in the family over fourteen." She thought Benny looked uncomfortable with this line of attack, but he didn't say anything. He wrote his mobile phone number down on the back of a business card and gave it to Jaber. Jaber stared at it for a long moment, as if willing it to tell him what he should do. It was an impossible situation he had just been put in, Chloe thought. If the army had threatened to take only him if Fareed did not turn himself in, he would not have given it another thought, but of course, they knew that.

When the police and army left, some of the men from neighboring houses came over to talk. Jaber ushered them into the living room, and Chloe went to help Ahlam make tea.

"Do you think I should move out?" she asked, her heart pounding.

"Ya haram," Ahlam said. "Why are you talking like that?"

"But the policeman said—" Chloe said.

"Who wants to listen to him?" Ahlam handed her the tea pot and sent her into the living room to serve it.

Chloe quietly poured ten cups of tea. "Yslamu ideeki," murmured one man after another. She tried to take comfort from that. They would not bless the hands of someone they thought was a collaborator, would they? She took a cup and sat down in the loveseat, even though she was not completely sure she was welcome. Alaa came and snuggled next to her. Her presence was incredibly comforting to Chloe in that moment, and she soaked in her warm child smell, buried her nose in the frizzy mop which smelled faintly of shampoo.

"Jesh bifattash ala Fareed." *The army is looking for Fareed*, the little girl whispered in Chloe's ear.

"I know," Chloe said. "Maalesh, kulishi bisir tamaam." *Don't worry, every-thing will be okay*. Guiltily, she realized she had no reason to think this was true. Fareed might well end up imprisoned for years, no matter whether he did or didn't have anything to do with any explosives or Nadya's death. But Alaa knew she had no magic powers. Right now she was a frightened little girl and she needed to be told that her brother would not be kidnapped by the jesh in the middle of the night and taken off to be tortured. If that hap-pened later, which it almost surely would, would Alaa be angry at Chloe and feel she lied?

"Mush tawbaane?" *You're not tired?* she said softly to the little girl.

"Khaife min jesh." *I'm afraid of the army*.

"I know, habibti, but they will not come back tonight," Chloe said. Of this, at least, she was sure. The two-day deadline loomed like a mushroom cloud on the family's horizon, but in that moment, it was a reprieve.

Chapter 18

Friday Rania did not have to work. She slept until eight, woke up slowly, and went to the kitchen to make coffee and eggs cooked in lots of olive oil for breakfast. She and Bassam sat out on the patio drinking their coffee, while Khaled tooled around on his tricycle. The specter of summer's oppressive heat hovered ever closer, but this morning the air was still a little cool, and the dew carried the scent of jasmine to them from their neighbor's yard. The wall around the compound was high enough that she could sit outside in a light robe, enjoying the stillness of the Sabbath morning. She asked Bassam about his week. She realized she had barely talked to him since finding Nadya's body on Monday afternoon.

Before the Intifada, he had worked full-time in the Ministry of Interior, helping new organizations get licensed by the Palestinian Authority. In the financial crisis of the last four years, his job had been cut to less than half-time. He still went to his office in Ramallah three or four days each week, but he was paid for only fifteen hours, and often even that was theoretical. The shortfall had made them both more grateful for her salary from the police, but it had also made things more awkward between them. He never said, "My wife should not make more money than I do," but he became more upset if she did not come home on time, or was called to work on a holiday.

He was starting to tell her about an interesting new women's cooperative that had applied for a permit when the phone jangled in the house. She snatched it up on the fourth ring. The voice on the other end made her wish she had ignored it.

"We found a bracelet in the home of a boy in Azzawiya last night," Benny's voice said. "It matches the one we found in the abandoned car. I thought you would want to know."

She felt a heavy tingling in her head, as her blood rushed in. "What were you doing in Azzawiya last night?" she half-shouted.

"We were looking for someone," he said tersely.

"If you were working on the Nadya case, you should have let me know," she said hotly.

"Mustafa and Abu Ziyad knew we were going there to search."

And the captain hadn't told her. But she had no time to brood on that now, because Benny was still talking.

"Nadya was definitely from Uzbekistan," he said. "But remember the Ukrainian passport you found, in the name of Alexandra Marininova? It belongs to a woman who lives in Eilat. I'm going to go talk to her, see if she knows how her passport came to be in Nir Gelenter's house with Nadya Kim's photo on it. She might be able to lead us to the people who brought Nadya from Uzbekistan. You want to come?"

"Today? Can't it wait until tomorrow?" Tomorrow was his Sabbath, but he was disrupting hers so why not return the favor?

"No, it's better to go today. We might need to spend the night," he added.

She guessed he was only asking because he expected her to decline. She wanted to disappoint him, but she couldn't see herself leaving Khaled. She had never spent a night away from him in six years.

"Could I bring my son along?" she asked. "He has never seen the sea."

"Are you kidding?"

She couldn't possibly explain that Palestinian men would not think anything of a woman they worked with bringing her child to work. She had gone back to work when Khaled was just over a year old, and had often carted him around with her in those early days. He had slept under her desk and the policemen had competed to see who could bring him the best sweets.

If she could take him along to Eilat, it would serve two purposes. It would assuage her guilt over wanting to go, and allay anyone's disapproval of her going off for a whole day or more with an Israeli man. She couldn't imagine Bassam, or his mother, being very understanding of her need to travel to the distant seaport.

"Our insurance won't cover it," he said. "I'll call Mustafa, see if he wants to send someone else."

"When are we going?"

If that surprised him, he didn't show it. "I'll pick you up in an hour."

Bassam definitely wasn't thrilled.

"You sometimes spend the night in Ramallah for your work," she reminded him.

"But that's Ramallah," he said. "Eilat is in Israel, and it is dangerous. There are men there who do not respect Muslim women. And I do not spend the night with an Israeli woman."

"I will not be *spending the night* with Benny!" she exploded. "If we have to sleep in Eilat, I will make sure my room is very far from his."

"It is not right," he said, thrusting a spoon into the bowl of labneh.

"It is my job," she said, tearing into a round of bread with equal force. "I do not tell you how to do your job, and I will not give mine over to one of the men, so they can whisper about how my husband will never allow me to succeed."

"They will whisper about you more if you go off for days with this Israeli man," he growled. They finished their meal in silence, and he stomped off to dress. Khaled watched his father walk away, tears starting to trickle down his chubby cheek. She lifted him out of his high chair and cuddled him close.

"I'm sorry," she told him. "We didn't mean to frighten you."

"Are you going away?" he asked.

"I will be back tonight or tomorrow," she said. "Your grandmother will spoil you with so many treats, you won't even miss me."

"Bring me a present," he said.

✳ ✳ ✳

It grew hotter and hotter as they drove south. Benny turned on the air conditioning in the car, though she would rather have had the breeze. But she was feeling kind toward him, for some reason, probably because he had not been put off by her outburst in the café. She let him ramble on about his trips to Eilat when he was a conscript in the army, how he would go there with his friends to pick up girls and get drunk.

"What did you do in the army?" she asked him.

He looked at her then, taking his eyes off the road for several seconds, and she thought that only then did he remember he was talking to a Palestinian woman.

"I was in Lebanon," he evaded.

Was he trying to reassure her that he wasn't in the Palestinian Territories? What difference did he think that made? Nearly all Israeli men his age would have fought in Lebanon. It was the war then, same as what they were doing to her land now. Maybe he was one of those who slaughtered the women and children in the Sabra and Shatila refugee camps. Maybe she should ask him. She chose not to. He was quiet after that, and fiddled with the radio until he found a music station he liked and he sang along in Hebrew.

She had imagined the Red Sea would be like the Dead Sea or the Mediterranean. She was unprepared for the intense blue-green and white-white sand, drawing her eyes to them like a laser. Though the city behind her was as unspeakably ugly as she had heard, while she stared at the water she thought she had never been anywhere more beautiful.

Benny was watching the road with one eye and handling the wheel with one hand, simultaneously checking a map. They veered away from the water, and before long were in a section of town where all you could see were tenement complexes, dirty children, and trash. He stopped the car in front of a nondescript housing bloc that looked exactly like all the others on the street. He rang the doorbell. Nothing happened. He rang again, this time leaning on the bell for a long time. Rania was about to suggest that Alexandra wasn't home when the door opened a crack. A thin face peeked out from behind a chain lock.

"Da?" the woman asked. Apparently Russian was the lingua franca in these parts.

"Politsia," Benny knew at least one word of Russian. He held his badge up to the slight opening in the door. The woman closed the door and then opened it wide, admitting them.

Alexandra Marininova was in her late twenties, Rania estimated. She was attractive in an amply endowed, bleached blonde sort of way. She spoke no English and her Hebrew sounded like none Rania had ever heard. She had to struggle to understand her, but as the woman spoke very slowly, she made out most of what she had to say.

"Have you ever seen this girl?" Benny produced one of the photos they had taken from Nir Gelenter's house. Alexandra looked closely and shook her head.

"Or any of these other people?" He brought out the pictures of Nadya with friends in Eilat. The woman looked at one after another, shaking her head, but her gaze lingered on one of them.

"You know someone?" The eagerness in Benny's voice was palpable. Clearly, he had not believed this errand would lead them anywhere, any more than she had. But now he was practically falling off the couch, leaning forward to scrutinize the photo along with Ms. Marininova.

"Him," she said, pointing to a portly man in dark glasses. He looked about fifty, with thinning brown hair. He had one arm around Nadya and one around another young woman. They were standing in front of a beachfront hotel, with palm trees rising behind them.

"Who is he? Where do you know him from?"

"I don't know who he is. But he comes into the restaurant where I work sometimes."

"You are sure you do not know his name, or where he lives?"

"No. He orders a sandwich with chips, I bring it to him. That's all."

"Does he come often?"

"Not often. From time to time." It wasn't much to go on. They could be here for days, waiting for him to get a craving for that particular sandwich.

"Do you know how this girl"—Benny pointed to Nadya's photo—"got your passport, with her picture on it?"

Alexandra was genuinely shocked. No, she insisted. She had no idea. She never saw Nadya before. She never gave anyone her passport.

"Was your purse ever stolen, did you lose your passport?" Benny suggested.

"Only years ago, in Russia. But that passport would be no good by now."

Benny's cellphone played its stupid little song. He answered it on the second go-round.

"Beemet?" he sounded excited. "Matai?" *Really? When?* He hung up after a few more terse questions.

"Thank you," he said to Alexandra. "We'll go now." By the time Rania had grabbed her purse and flown out the door, he was unlocking the car.

"They found the Azzawiya kid," he said. "We need to go back."

"But what about this man? Shouldn't we try to find him?"

"There may be no need," he said. "If there is, we'll have to come back."

Her stomach churned. *Please, please, don't let it be this kid,* she begged the cosmos. *Make it be the man in the sunglasses.*

"Wait," she said, as he pulled away from the curb.

He turned to her, head inclined, waiting.

"I need to get a present for my son," she said. He looked pointedly at his watch. She stared back at him, not giving an inch.

"We need to make it fast," he said. "Where do you want to go?"

"How should I know? I've never been here before. You tell me."

"What kind of thing would he want?"

"I don't know—something special to this part of the land."

"You know Eilat stones?"

"Yes, well, we have another name for them, but I know what you mean."

"I know a place—but jewelry would be more for a girl."

"Let's go."

He drove maniacally, weaving in and out of the buzzing traffic, and turned onto the street that went along the sea. Rania gazed out at the white sails bobbing along on the gentle green waves, wondering what it would be like to be on one of them, with nothing but water around her for kilometers. He pulled up in front of a shop which had a huge picture of a ring on the sign that hung perpendicular to its window. "Top Quality—Low Prices," read the sign in English. The Hebrew one she couldn't read, but she imagined it said the same. Or maybe it said, "Stay Away—This Place Is Only for Sucker Tourists." No way to know. She would have to trust Benny.

The clerk, a dark-skinned Israeli in his early twenties, with curly hair very like her husband's, was helping two skinny American women in short shorts with blonde hair and leathery brown wrinkly faces. The two women haggled with the man for a while, then walked out without buying anything. Rania picked up a bracelet. The stones were okay, but from close up, she could see the settings were sloppy. The sterling was new and made to look old, probably with bleach.

"I don't see anything good here," she told Benny.

"Wait a second," he told her. He explained to the young man in rapid Hebrew what she wanted. The shopkeeper nodded and disappeared into the back.

He came out with a black velvet rack, holding several rows of silver bracelets inlaid with the copper-based turquoise-malachite stone unique to the Red Sea port of ancient Palestine. This was the good stuff, she could see, real antique silver. She picked up one and studied it, the thin metal bands framing the stone. It would be much too big for Khaled now, but he would treasure it… She looked into the eyes of the young Arab Jew, trying to work out if he was someone she could trust, but how could she really trust any of them, these enemies of her people?

"Qaddesh?" she asked him softly in Arabic.

"Miit shekel," he answered her. "Really, madam, this is the best place in the land for these stones."

One hundred shekels was a lot of money. The piece was probably worth it, but she didn't like the idea of giving so much to this Israeli. She glanced out at the sea, which looked so much like the stone she held. On the beach, tourists played volleyball in bathing suits, and a group of young boys ran back and forth trailing a kite. They ran and ran and the kite finally got airborne, soaring in and out of the palm trees like a crazed bird. Abruptly, she put the bracelet down on the counter.

"Laa, shukran." *No thanks*, she said to the young man, leaving him and Benny staring at her in shock. Quickly, she walked two shops to her left, and saw what she was looking for. It was a generic beach store, with lots of tourist kitsch, hats, sunglasses, those little license plates with people's names on them in Hebrew, Arabic, and English. The kites were standing in a big barrel, and she went through them quickly, picking a fanciful orange and blue dragon-bird. She didn't know if Khaled and his friends would really use it, but she hoped so. She liked the idea of them running fast and thrusting their winged creature into the air to careen above the clouds.

Chapter 19

Benny drove fast on the northbound superhighway. On the way, he shared what scant information he had gotten from his colleague on the phone. There was no great drama involved in Fareed's capture. He had come home and an informer in the village had gotten word of his return to the army commander for the area. The captain had called Jaber Haddad and told him that they knew his son was in the village. They told him they had men at every exit from the village, and gave Fareed ten minutes to come to a house on the main road. If he did not turn himself in, they warned, they would come to the house and make a scene that would be unpleasant for Fareed's little brothers and sisters.

He had arrived at the designated place, accompanied by his father and the American woman, Chloe. The American woman, Benny reported, had tried to get into the jeep with Fareed. Benny seemed to find this very amusing. Rania found it endearing, if quixotic. She wondered if Chloe really had any idea what happened at SHABAK interrogation centers. If so, she was brave even to want to be nearby when it was going on.

She remembered that she wanted to find out more about what Chloe was doing here. Would Benny tell her what he knew? Probably not, but she couldn't see any downside in asking.

"What was Chloe doing in the police station the other day?" she asked.

"Some border police picked her up at a checkpoint. They said she was making problems."

"What kind of problems?"

"Talking to a suspect they were detaining."

"What's so terrible about that?"

"Would you want some random person interfering with a suspect you were holding?"

She hadn't thought about that at all. She couldn't imagine that happening. "It's not the same," she said.

"What's different about it?"

She wondered how to explain. If the Palestinian police arrested someone, which didn't happen often, there were usually lots of people around. They didn't try to hide what they were doing from the people.

"If we take someone away, it's because the community wants that person taken away," she said. "So people wouldn't interfere."

"Well, what if a settler came along and tried to talk to that person?"

"Okay, I see your point."

She had no chance to ask more about his conversation with Chloe because he was pulling into the parking lot at Ariel police station. The station was crawling with so many Israeli men, there were not enough places for them all to sit. They walked around talking on cellphones, some in Hebrew, some in Russian, some in shouting. Six of them occupied the small room where Fareed was handcuffed to a wooden chair. Four of these wore blue uniforms like Benny's. The others wore plain clothes, jeans and baggy t-shirts; one wore a leather jacket despite the heat. Those would be the SHABAK guys. They were not talking to Fareed, and they did not talk to Rania either when she entered with Benny. Benny was immediately drawn into a huddle with the two SHABAK agents and the two Russian policemen. One of the other policemen sat at the table, filling out forms. The only one she knew, besides Benny, was the Arab policeman called Ali. He was simply sitting in a corner, watching everyone. She supposed he would be the interpreter when they got around to talking to Fareed.

Fareed was a nice-looking young man with wavy black hair and the angular cheekbones she recognized as his father's genetic contribution. At twenty, he still had the look of a teenager, attesting to his status as the pampered oldest son of a privileged household. There was a recent gash above his left eyebrow. She assumed that had been a gift from the army unit who transported him here. His hands were cuffed behind him with metal bracelets, the wrists starting to swell.

Rania went over to where he sat.

"Marhaba," she said softly.

"Marhabteen," he responded.

"Kul ishi tamam?" She cringed at herself, asking, *Is everything okay?* Of course it was not okay. But he knew what she meant.

"Tamam."

"Shu sar hon?" she asked, indicating the wound on his forehead.

"Jesh," he said with a shrug, including all the men in the room in a quick sweep of his eyes.

"Do you want something for it?"

He shook his head. "My hands hurt," he told her. She nodded.

Rania went over to the Arab policeman, Ali. "Can't you free his hands now?" she asked. "Where could he go, with so many policemen here?"

"I'll see," he told her.

He went and spoke with the man who was filling out the forms. Then he tapped the tallest man, who was in the huddle with Benny, on the shoulder, and they spoke quietly for a minute. The tall man made a "wait" gesture with his hands and continued his heated conversation with the others. Ali shrugged at her and returned to his corner.

Rania decided that if no one else was interested in questioning Fareed, she might as well seize the opportunity. She sat close to his left shoulder, so they could talk without being overheard.

"I asked him about the cuffs," she told him, "but I guess they are busy."

"Maalesh." *It doesn't matter*, he said.

"How did you know Nadya?" she asked.

He looked at her in surprise. "She was my friend."

"Did you kill her?"

"No! I told you, she was my friend." His eyes started to fill with water. He squinted and looked away. She felt bad for him, that his hands were unavailable to brush away the tears.

"Then why did you run away?"

He turned to fully face her now, studying her face. "Miin inti?" he asked suddenly. *Who are you?*

"Shorta Falastinia." *Palestinian police.*

"Why are you here? With them?"

"I am not with them. I am getting information from them," she said shortly.

The two SHABAK guys swooped down on her. "What are you doing? Who are you? How did you get in here?"

She thought for a moment that they might arrest *her*. One of them put a heavy hand on her arm. She noticed the serpent tattooed along his bulging muscle. Benny intervened before she could do anything rash. He took Snake Tattoo aside in a genial fashion, a hand on his shoulder, and she fumed as she heard them laughing together.

When he turned back to her, Snake Tattoo put his hands deliberately behind his back, as if he couldn't trust himself not to grab her.

"What did he tell you?" he asked, standing just too close to her. She could vaguely smell the stale cigarette smoke on his breath.

"Nothing. We were just chatting." She did not like this man, and he had no right to make her feel she was breaking some law by doing her job.

"What are you doing here?" she shot at him.

"That is not your business. This man is a security prisoner, and you don't talk to him unless we say you can."

"Look," she said to Snake Tattoo, who was about to light his eleventh cigarette since they had entered the room. "I'm not interested in whatever your investigation is. I just want to know about his connection with the dead foreigner whose body was found in our lands. Let us talk to him first—" Belatedly, it occurred to her that maybe she should have consulted Benny before laying out a strategy for them. But now that she had begun, best to plow ahead. "And when we're done, you can take him down to your dungeons and place sacks over his head and give him electric shocks or whatever it is that you specialize in."

Tattoo wouldn't be mollified. "I know how to work a suspect," he told her. "I don't need any suggestions from you."

He went over to talk to Benny, leaving his sidekick between her and Fareed. She decided she was through being bounced around, ignored, bullied, ignored again, like a yo-yo that would stay all the way down until you gave it the right wrist action to yank it back up. She deliberately crossed to stand at Benny's left shoulder. To her chagrin and embarrassment, he turned slightly so that his back was to her. They continued their conspiratorial stage whispering, and she could not make out much of their Hebrew. One of the others said something about sandwiches and two of them left the room. The ones who remained continued whatever they were doing, apparently oblivious of all the drama around them.

She tried to think what a more patient person, like Captain Mustafa or Bassam, would do now. She sat down opposite Fareed. She rummaged in her purse for a nail file, astonishingly found one, and started to buff her strong finger nails with it. When she looked up, she saw Fareed studying her. She smiled at him briefly, then looked back to her task.

Snake Tattoo came over and sat down next to her. He sat a little too close, but she would never let him make her move. She sat stock still and refused to look up from her filing.

"Benny tells me you are from Mas'ha?" She could almost smell his struggle to strike a polite tone.

"I am from Aida camp. My husband is from Mas'ha."

"Forgive me. But you live in Mas'ha now."

It wasn't a question, so she didn't feel any need to answer it.

"You're from Azzawiya, right?" he asked Fareed in a harsher voice.

Fareed might have been following her lead, or his own inclinations, but he did not answer either. He also might not have understood, because the man spoke English, and still no one had ascertained whether Fareed knew English. The agent strode over to Fareed, hauling him with one hand, as far out of the chair as he could go with his hands still cuffed to one of its rungs. She felt the punch he delivered to Fareed's chin as if it had hit her own skin.

"I'm talking to you!" he said to punctuate his physical communication. But just in case it was a language problem, he asked this time in Arabic, "Min Azzawiya, inta?"

"Atah kevar yodea et zeh." *You already know that,* Fareed said dispassionately in Hebrew.

The man jerked him once more before letting go and letting him thud back into the chair. He returned to sit next to her again.

"Do you know him?"

"Do you think I would tell you if I did?"

"Look, lady, if you don't want to talk to me nicely, as a *colleague,* I can arrange for us to talk somewhere less pleasant."

"It's unnecessary for you to explain to me how your kind operate," she said evenly. "I have heard a lot about your organization from *colleagues* of mine. It is also unnecessary for you to make threats. I am not hiding anything from you. I don't know this boy or his family, and until a few minutes ago, I believed I wanted the same thing as you—to find out the truth about a young woman's murder. Now I wonder if you have some other agenda I should know about."

"Yes, well, we believe the girl's death was just an unfortunate byproduct of a much larger conspiracy. There is a major terror ring operating in your area, did you know that?"

"A major terror ring? Run by some twenty-year-old boys? Please."

"I have seen twelve-year-old boys with bombs strapped to their chests."

What did he expect her to say? That that never happened? That she supported such senseless acts of desperation? That she was sorry? There was no answer that made any sense to her. Once more, she said nothing.

He had another word with Benny and then announced that they were going to take their prisoner to Petah Tikva. They would let Benny—he was careful to say it that way, not her and Benny—know if they found out anything relevant to their case.

The smaller SHABAK agent, the one who hadn't said a word, folded a strip of black cloth over Fareed's eyes, rather gently brushing his hair off his forehead. He readjusted the handcuffs and asked him in Hebrew if they were too tight.

"Mush khaif," she found herself saying to him as they guided him out, "inta qawi." *Don't be afraid, you are strong.* She breathed a prayer into the words, to give them truth.

Chapter 20

Chloe had been pleased when Fareed asked her to accompany him and his father to the place where the army was waiting for him. She had fulfilled her role with fervor, arguing when they blindfolded and shackled him, even attempting to climb into the jeep with him. In the end, it had all been as futile as she knew it would be. As she returned home with Jaber, she found herself wishing Avi had been there too. At least then people would have seen that he couldn't do anything more than she could. Now, she felt they would always wonder. Even she wondered if an Israeli man might have been able to do more. It was unlikely. When they came for someone with twelve jeeps, they were pretty determined to get him.

It was just dusk. The scent of fire filled the air as families gathered around the evening bonfires, which would provide light, an unnecessary added warmth, tea, and bug repellent. She heard the lively chatter of storytellers young and old, mixed with frequent laughter. She felt a pang, hearing the happy voices. Would anyone be happy to see her in this village again? Or would they always be thinking, "She is the one who let them take Fareed away to the SHABAK"?

Abu Ziyad, the DCL, was waiting on the porch when they got home. Jaber said a hasty goodbye to her and went to sit with his friend. Chloe sensed from the big man's demeanor that it was not a social visit. She kept an ear to the open window, and when she heard them saying goodbye, she ran downstairs to catch Jaber before he went inside.

"Was he here about Fareed?" she asked, hoping she wasn't overstepping her rights.

"Yes."

He sat down in one of the plastic chairs scattered around. The ashtrays on the little plastic stool that served as a table were overflowing with butts.

"Tfaddali," he said.

She paused. She heard "tfaddali" a hundred times in a normal day, and it could mean so many things. It always made her think about growing up in the South and hearing "y'all come," knowing that the people saying that would fall over where they stood if you ever showed up. Tfaddali was often like that. Did Jaber mean it that way, or did he really want to talk to her? She couldn't read him. But she didn't want to be alone, so she sat down.

He lit a cigarette, unaware that he already had one half-smoked in his other hand. His hand shook a little as he held the lighter. She imagined he had not been this upset since his own arrest. He smoked in silence for a while.

"Did you know Fareed was going to come back?" she asked.

More silence, then he shook his head. "No, but I thought so. I sent him a text message that they were looking for him."

"You wanted him to be arrested?" That could not be what he meant. She must have misunderstood.

"Many of our young men are in prison," he said. "Maybe Fareed has to take his turn."

She could not believe what she was hearing. Jaber had talked to her more than once about his arrest and imprisonment, the torture he endured from the SHABAK and the army interrogators. She knew he would never want his son to experience one second of that horror.

When the army drove into the village at night and left with other people's kids, every parent simultaneously ached for their neighbors and thanked Allah that their own children were safe. Jaber could only mean one thing: that he thought Fareed might be guilty of something. But guilty of what? Killing Nadya? Involvement in the plot with the explosives, whatever it was? Would Jaber think the former worse than the latter, because it would have been a crime of passion, not an act of war? Or would he be more upset about the latter, because it could harm his reputation as a leader of nonviolent resistance in the area?

She thought about how to ask, and even if she had a right to ask. She decided to wait. Jaber sat for a long time, smoking and cradling his chin in one cupped hand. Then he started to talk, more to himself than her.

"Fareed was not even two years old when I was arrested," he began. She knew this, but she listened intently anyway. "They came here in the middle of the night. He woke up and cried, but the soldiers would not allow my wife to go take him from his crib."

He went over the familiar ground: how they had pulled him from his bed, not even giving him time to put on regular clothes, only letting Ahlam throw a coat over his pajamas before they cuffed him so tightly that he cried out, causing Fareed to cry louder. How they had driven him around for hours, just so that he would have lots of time to worry about where they were going and what would happen to him, and how they told him that when they got where they were going, they would kill him. How they beat him with their guns when he tried to sit up, how they kept him in a room for days, refusing him a bathroom, screaming at him, standing on his neck until he thought it would break, kicking him in the area of his kidneys and laughing at him when he finally lost control of his bladder. He pointed out the long scar on his arm where the captain had grazed his skin with a knife and then literally poured salt in the wound.

Suddenly he changed direction, talking about the first time that Ahlam brought Fareed to visit him in Ansar III, the biggest prison, in the desert. Always before Ahlam had come alone, he said, and had told Fareed that his father was in Jordan, working. But Fareed had begun asking for him relentlessly, so she decided it was better to let him see his father, even in prison. She tried telling him that they were going to meet Jaber at the checkpoint between Palestine and Jordan, which was why there would be so many soldiers and wire fences around. They never knew if Fareed believed her, but he did not question it. Jaber held Fareed on his lap, he said, and told him how much he loved his country and that he must always put Palestine first, even before his family.

"Always I told him, never do anything that might hurt your people."

When he said nothing more for more than five minutes, she decided to try asking what she wanted to know.

"Do you think there's some connection between this Nadya and the explosives they found?" she finally asked.

"I don't know," he said. "I can't think… but it seems strange, that this girl dies, and suddenly they are saying Fareed is involved with guns."

She tried to piece together where his mind was going, and forbade herself to point out that they were saying he was connected with explosives, not guns.

"You think she could have been working for the Israelis?"

"Abu Ziyad said that she was," he answered.

"How does he know?"

"The Israeli DCL told him."

"Do you believe him?"

"Why would he lie?"

She pondered this. Why would the Israeli DCL lie to his Palestinian counterpart? But then again, why would he tell him the truth? It seemed like dangerous knowledge to spread around in the villages, that the Israeli government was sending foreign spies. Unless…

Don't be absurd, she told herself sternly. The Israeli government wouldn't have made up a story like that just to alienate *her* from the villagers.

It was more logical that Nadya was sent by the Israelis to get information from Fareed and that's why she was killed, than that the Israeli army just happened to be looking for Fareed at the same time a girl he was involved with just happened to be killed. But if that was the case, then that meant… She couldn't imagine Fareed killing a woman, even if she turned out to be a collaborator. She couldn't imagine Fareed being involved in a plot to blow anything up either, though he had been growing more depressed and nihilistic in the last months.

"If she was a spy and Fareed found out, do you think he could have…?" she asked Jaber, holding her breath for the answer. She willed him to say no, *mustahil*, impossible. But he said nothing, just sat puffing on yet another cigarette.

* * *

Rania was tired and took a private taxi from Qarawa. She had never seen the SHABAK in action before. It was a name that got whispered when people didn't show up where they were supposed to be. In the days after her brothers were arrested, she heard her parents and neighbors say that they were with the SHABAK, and everyone would get silent for a few seconds, knowing what that meant. Seeing them in person had unsettled her. On one hand, they were no longer a ghostly presence, they were just big, distasteful men with short tempers. On the other, they knew her name now, and that made them a bigger threat to her. She didn't want to think about what Fareed was enduring now. She wanted to hold Khaled and help him put the kite together.

She thought uneasily about Bassam. When she had left in the morning, he didn't even say goodbye. He would be relieved that she wasn't spending the night in Eilat, but his suspicions would still lie between them. She was not going to apologize for wanting to do her job well. If he thought hanging out with an Israeli policeman was her idea of a good time, he didn't know her at all.

She had been walking quickly up the walkway of her house, anxious to see Khaled. Now, anticipating a chilly reception from Bassam, she slowed. She heard a distant whistle, and seconds later, the street was full of children and young men, running to throw stones at the army. Many of them clutched slingshots, some crafted out of carved wood and leather, others assembled from branches and rubber bands. She watched them idly, recalling her own slingshot-wielding days, but then she glimpsed a familiar, slightly bowlegged figure among them.

She started toward her son, meaning to scoop him up in her arms and carry him into the house and slam the door. But then she stopped, the image of Fareed blindfolded and in chains warring with the image of herself at eight, standing right in front of the jeeps and waving a forbidden Palestinian flag. Khaled is too young for this, she thought. No Palestinian child is too young, her dead brother's voice responded. She trotted along behind the youths, straining a little for breath. She was not used to this. Other women were drifting out of their houses as well. Most simply stood in their doorways, but a few fell into step with her. If it became a genuine melee, even some of them might be gathering stones and passing them to the young men. Fortunately, today was not the day when she would need to choose. A double whistle announced that the jeeps had gone, or maybe it was a false alarm. The youths strolled back in small groups, laughing, teasing each other about who had been in front and who behind. Khaled spotted her and ran to be picked up, not yet self-conscious about wanting his mother.

"Atini shantatik." *Give me your bag*, he demanded, reaching for her purse. She handed it to him, and he quickly found the brightly colored kite.

"What is it?" he asked. His little face revealed some disappointment. She wondered what he had hoped for.

"I will show you," she said. "It is something that flies." She made a flying motion with her hand.

She carried him into the house, where Bassam was waiting just inside the door. Probably he had been looking out the kitchen window, which faced the street. She hoped that meant he had made something for dinner. She didn't feel like cooking.

"Aja jesh?" he asked. *Did the army come?*

"No." She kissed him on the cheek and passed Khaled into his arms.

"What do you have here?" he asked his son.

"Something to fly with," Khaled answered.

"Nice," Bassam said. "We can fly together."

He unwrapped the kite and showed Khaled how to fit the pieces together. "Mama, it's a bird!" Khaled cried when he saw the toy assembled.

He was already running for the door, trailing the kite string behind him. Rania worried that he would let it go and they would spend the next week chasing it around the hills of western Salfit.

"I'm with him," Bassam assured her, dashing after his son. They spent the next half hour taking the kite around to show Khaled's various cousins and playmates, while she scrambled eggs and potatoes for their dinner. Bassam had, apparently, been *thinking* about dinner because a cucumber and two tomatoes sat out on the counter with a knife, but that was as far as he had gotten.

While she cooked, she thought about what she would tell him about her day, especially the encounter with the SHABAK, and that poor boy from Azzawiya. But when Khaled was finally asleep and she was alone with her husband, she found herself only telling funny stories about Benny, and describing the blue blue sea in Eilat. She told him all about the jewelry store and how she had decided on the kite.

"Why didn't you stay the night?" he asked.

She wondered if she should say that she had insisted on coming back. That would make him happy, but omission was one thing, and lying another. She couldn't stand to tell him that she had sat in an Israeli police station—inside Ariel, where both of them righteously refused to go—and watched the SHABAK brutalize a boy from the next village. No doubt he would hear about the arrest tomorrow, and the village grapevine being what it was, he might even hear that she had been there. He would be angry that she had not told him, but she would deal with that when and if it came.

"Benny needed to get back," she said.

Chapter 21

Up ahead, Fareed saw the barbed wire fence looming. He ran toward it. He glanced behind him, trying not to look like he was looking. The soldiers were very far behind him. He pushed his legs a little faster, he was almost there. If he could stretch his legs a little farther, go a little quicker, he would be free. He wasn't sure how he would get out, there was no gate that he could see, but somehow he knew that once he got to the fence it would open for him. He ran and ran, but the fence didn't seem to get any closer. Every time he looked up, it was the same distance ahead, just out of his reach. He leapt over terrace after terrace, and tripped on a loose stone. He was falling, the ground rising quickly to meet his nose.

Someone was pulling him up. He looked up, confused. Two men were raising him from the cot where he was lying, half on, half off, one leg shackled to the cot's iron frame, one arm cuffed to a metal ring far above his head. One of the policemen reached up and unlocked the handcuff. Fareed rotated his shoulder, massaging his neck with his free hand. The relief was brief. They put a heavy burlap sack over his head, cuffed both hands tightly behind him, unshackled his leg and yelled at him in Hebrew to stand up, "Kum!" He tried to obey, but his body would not cooperate. He had not slept more than one hour at a time in four days. His head swam, and his legs buckled. The two men's strong hands kept him from sinking back onto the cot. His legs still would not move. One of the policemen stood behind him and placed one knee behind Fareed's, forcing him to walk. Slowly, he remembered how to do it.

They had not asked him any questions. They had only kept him in these uncomfortable positions, and when he started to fall asleep anyway from exhaustion, they beat on the bars of his cell with heavy metal instruments.

Once when that didn't keep him awake, they threw cold water on his body and left him shivering in his freezing wet clothes for many hours.

Now they led him through a door. "Hinei hu," one said. *Here he is.* So someone in that room was waiting for him. They shoved him into a hard wooden chair. He lost his balance and tipped sideways, his head nearly hitting the ground before they righted him. One of his captors snickered.

"Shush," said a voice across the table. "Remove the bag," said the voice and suddenly he could see the man sitting there, looking relaxed and cheerful, with a cup of coffee in front of him, next to a pile of manila folders. The coffee was fresh, Fareed could tell. A bit of steam rose from the cup, and he could smell it. It wasn't Arabic coffee, it was the bitter type the Israelis called *caffe shachor*, black coffee, but he would gladly take it right now.

"The handcuffs also are unnecessary," the coffee drinker said and his hands were freed. He rubbed the red welts on his wrists.

"Would you like coffee, Fareed?" the man asked in Arabic. His Arabic was not like what the Palestinians spoke, but it was not the fractured Arabic you usually heard from Israelis. It sounded like the Arabic you heard on television. The man must have grown up speaking Arabic—probably an Iraqi Jew. That didn't make Fareed like him any better, but at least if he was going to have an unpleasant conversation, he wouldn't have to struggle to understand what his torturer wanted to know.

This man wasn't acting like a torturer. He was rummaging in the corner, where there were an electric kettle and some ceramic mugs. In a minute, he brought Fareed the coffee, with a sugar bowl and a spoon, so he could sweeten it himself. Fareed added two sugars and gulped the hot liquid until it burned his throat. It felt so good. He tried not to hate himself for his weakness. He had grown up on the stories of his father's interrogations, and those of his father's friends. You didn't take anything they offered, because that let them know you were weak, gave them desires they could use to get what they wanted from you. But he had not chosen this life. He was not an activist. He didn't even know what the interrogators wanted. No one would suffer because he drank their coffee.

"So, Fareed," the man began. "How are you? Everything okay?"

"I want to go home."

"Yes, I'm sure you do," the man answered, nodding sagely. "Perhaps I can help you with that."

Whatever he meant by that, Fareed was sure it was not as simple as it sounded.

"If you help me, I can help you," the man continued. "Does that sound like a good plan?"

"I don't think I can help you."

"I think you can." The interrogator's benevolent expression never changed, his eyes never traveling from Fareed's. He did not seem to need to blink. Fareed did. He looked away first. Another shame. The two soldiers who had brought Fareed here were no longer in the room. He had not noticed them leaving, he had been too intent on the questioner and the coffee. There was another person there, though, a woman. She was seated off to the side, while the man sat directly opposite him. She had raven black hair, and wore a very short dress. Her long legs were crossed one on top of the other. She had a notepad and pen in her hand. She didn't make any sounds.

"I just need you to tell me what happened," the man said. He picked up a pen and put it to the yellow pad in front of him, waiting to write down Fareed's statement.

"What happened when?"

"When you killed Nadya Kim."

"I didn't kill her."

The man sighed, tapping his pen on the notepad.

"You see, Fareed, we won't get anywhere if you insist on doing it this way. We know you killed her."

"But that's impossible because I didn't."

"Someone saw you. You didn't know that, did you?"

"No."

The man gave him a "got you" look, just as he realized what he had said. It made no difference, but he hated himself once again. How could he fall for their tricks so easily? He glanced at the black-haired woman. She was furiously writing on her pad.

"So now that you know, perhaps you would like to save us all a lot of trouble and just explain what happened."

"I didn't mean... I didn't kill Nadya."

The look of gentle disappointment from the interrogator was surprisingly similar to the one he was used to getting from his father when he didn't study hard for his *tawjihi* and got mediocre scores, or when he slept late and his mother had to go gather the eggs from the chicken coop by herself.

Now the man said nothing. He just sat there, looking down at the notes he had made on his pad, clicking his pen open and shut, open and shut.

Fareed didn't say anything either. He told himself to look at the man, but he was afraid if he did, he would blink again, and that would be worse than not looking in the first place. So he looked at the woman instead, and then down at his shoes, then around the room, taking in the spiderwebs lining the bars on the windows, the plastic trash can overflowing with debris and half-eaten sandwiches.

"Okay," the man said suddenly to the guards, who had rematerialized in the doorway. "Take him back."

They lifted him to his feet and cuffed him again, put the bag over his head and roughly turned him around.

"Get some rest," the man said as they led him away. "We will try again tomorrow."

* * *

He was dreaming of Nadya when they woke him. They were sitting under their tree, near the Azzawiya bridge, and she was telling him something about a baby. He kept wondering which baby she meant. He heard a baby in the distance, but it didn't really sound like a baby, it sounded like a group of men babbling. He stared at the men who were shaking him, saying to each other, "He's not going to come. Get the water."

He quickly snapped back to reality. "No, I'm coming," he nearly shouted.

The Iraqi's exhortation to get some rest had been, as he had known it was, a cruel joke. It had been two days since the last encounter, and he had been allowed to sleep only two hours at a time, twice each day. He could not really tell what was night and what was day here, as there were no windows, but there was a tiny crack in the wall through which light from outside trickled in, and he could tell if it was light or dark. At the times he was allowed to sleep, it was always light.

The man didn't offer any coffee this time. Without ceremony, he shoved two pieces of paper in front of Fareed, side by side. Fareed looked at them but couldn't tell what they said. They were in Hebrew.

"Mah zeh?" he asked the man, thinking maybe if he was willing to speak Hebrew, the man would be willing to believe him.

"There are two statements here," the man told him in Arabic. "Both are true, but we are going to give you the chance to sign just one of them."

"I'm not going to sign anything," Fareed said firmly. Of that he was sure. He might look away, he might drink their coffee, he might even get tangled up in their words and say something he didn't mean to, but signing his name was something he could only do very deliberately, and he would not do it.

"Not so fast," the man said. "Just hear me out."

His caramel voice told a tale of great reason. "This one," he said, tapping his pen on the one to the left, "just says what you already admitted here the other day, that you *accidentally* killed Nadya Kim, your sweetheart."

"I never admitted that," Fareed protested. The man held up a hand to silence him.

"This one," the man went on, "is a much more serious affair."

What could be more serious than murder? Fareed wondered. He knew he didn't need to ask. The man was going to tell him. He just had to be patient.

"Do you know Radwan Toufiq?" the man asked suddenly.

Fareed sat still. He willed himself to make no movement that could be construed as an answer. He knew that his face was giving him away, but they could not use his face in court.

"You see, this is bad. This is not going to help you."

He didn't even see the man make his gesture. In less time than it would take you to flick a cigarette lighter, he and the chair he sat on were both on the floor, the two guards on top of him. One was kneeling directly on his penis. The other was kicking him rhythmically in the ribs. The abuse was methodical and without passion. It didn't last long. It didn't need to. It wasn't meant to extract the confession by itself. It was a message, about what his future might look like, if he kept insisting on his innocence. Their task finished, the two guards melted back into whatever woodwork they had materialized from.

They left Fareed to gather himself, and his chair, up from the floor. It took him longer than it should have. It wasn't the physical effort that was difficult for him to muster so much as the will. He had to convince himself he wanted to right himself and pick up the chair and sit again opposite the Iraqi, implacable in the V-necked sweater that made him look like a college professor. The Iraqi was talking on a mobile phone. He said a few final sentences and then, "Okay, *bseder, yalla*. Bye," and put the phone in his pocket.

He shook his head slightly and opened the folder in front of him and began to talk again.

"You see, Fareed, we know that you know Radwan." He drew out a picture of the two of them, Fareed and Radwan, in the detention area at Huwwara checkpoint, outside of Nablus. Their faces were turned towards one another. Radwan's lips were parted, and Fareed was grinning.

"That means nothing," Fareed said sullenly.

It didn't. Hundreds of young men, especially students, were detained there every day. If two guys both lived on the other side of the checkpoint and went to school in Nablus, it was inevitable that sometimes they were going to run into each other there. Even the fact that they were talking, obviously joking about something, didn't prove anything. You talked and joked with whomever you ended up in that pen with. It was something to do, to pass the time. You weren't going to ignore each other.

"No, I suppose by itself it does not mean anything," the man said. He seemed to consider it. "But that is not all we have," he said.

He took out a heavy gold bracelet, and put it on the table between them.

"Where did you get this bracelet?" he asked Fareed.

Fareed's hand reached out for the bracelet and he couldn't stop it. His fingers closed around it. He loved the feel of the gold, because it felt to him like touching her skin. His thumb caressed the tiny indentations on the inside, where the inscription was.

"Where did *you* get it?" he retorted, though he knew the answer. His father had told him that the army had taken it from his room.

"You know where I got it," the man responded. "I need to know where you got it."

"Why do you need to know?" Fareed asked, reasonably enough. Even if he told them, it wouldn't help them establish that he killed or didn't kill Nadya. But the man was not impressed.

"Fareed, do not play with me," he said, pushing the glasses up on his nose. "You know what can happen to you if you do that."

"Nadya gave it to me," Fareed said. This piece of information was not worth suffering for.

"When?"

"Some weeks ago."

"Can you be more specific?"

"I don't know—three weeks, a month ago. Why does it matter?"

"Why did she give it to you?" The man did not need to say that he was asking the questions here.

"To show our love."

"Show it to whom?"

"To each other."

"Who else knew that you loved each other?"

"No one."

"No one?" What was the guy getting at? It was almost true. Avi had known, but no one else. Even if they had some way of knowing that, it made no difference.

"No one."

"Why did you move her body?"

"What?"

Fareed tried to prevent his face from registering his surprise. The disappointed look was back.

"Please, Fareed, stop wasting my time. You must know that we have ways of telling when and how someone is carried from one place to another. And we could tell, from the tracks you made in the earth, that you carried her body very carefully from where you killed her, to where we found her. From that we can tell you didn't mean to hurt her. So we know that it was an accident."

A muscle in Fareed's cheek was pulsing. He couldn't stop it. He bit his tongue, deliberately, and hoped that the pain would disguise what else he was feeling. They knew much more than he realized. Well, whatever they knew, they knew. There was nothing he could do about that. He would not tell them anything else. The man was silent and wrote on his papers for a long time. Fareed sat and twitched in his chair. His ribs ached. He needed to pee, but he could tell it was going to hurt terribly when he did.

The man finally looked up. He cleared his throat before he spoke. "How do you know Radwan Toufiq?"

"He is from my village."

"Do you know everyone in your village?"

"No. But I know everyone there who is a student at An Najah University. There are not so many of us."

"I understand. Did you know that Radwan was going to blow up a shopping center in Israel?"

"No."

"But you knew that he was going to blow up something."

"No."

The tapered fingers drummed on the table. The man looked toward the door, as if he were weighing whether to make the secret signal that would call the soldiers to come abuse him some more.

The policeman's mobile phone vibrated, causing the table to shake. He answered it, spoke for a second, then got up and walked across the room, to a place where Fareed could not hear him or see his lips move. He talked for more than five minutes. When he hung up, he went to the door and said something to someone in the hall, and then he came back and gathered up all his papers. The two guards materialized and fastened the shackles to Fareed's feet and wrists, put the bag over his head, and hustled him to the door.

"Oh," the voice said suddenly.

Fareed instinctively tried to turn toward the voice, even though he wouldn't be able to see the speaker. He could not turn, because the two men were holding his arms. They simply stood stock still, like robots programmed to go and stop on voice command.

"What happened to the bag?"

"Sorry?" His voice came out muffled through the sack.

"The bag that you took from Nadya, when you killed her. You had it with you in Tel Aviv. Where is it now?"

Fareed was stunned. He couldn't possibly sort out what that meant, or what he should or should not say. Not like this, standing here, with a sack over his head. He shook his head. He didn't know if the guy could even see his head shake inside the burlap sack. His ribs hurt when he shook his head. His ribs hurt when he moved at all.

"Okay," the voice said. "We will talk about it another time."

Chapter 22

Captain Mustafa called Rania into his office and gave her the bad news. The boy from Azzawiya had confessed to the murder.

"I don't believe it," she said. "You know what these confessions are worth."

He took a sip of tea, his broad face yielding no hint of his own feelings.

"It's out of our hands," he said. "The boy made his choice."

"What choice!" she exploded. "It makes no sense. We still know nothing about this girl's life. Who was the man she was arguing with in the settlement? What about the people who brought her here? And the baby, are they at least going to do a blood test to see if Fareed was the father?"

"It doesn't matter," said the captain. "He confessed to killing her."

"Please give me just one more week, maybe two," she implored.

He shook his head. "It is over. I should not have let you get so involved."

She bit back an argument and went back to her desk. She couldn't believe he was satisfied with the boy's confession either. He and the rest of the old guard had gotten used to saying, "What can we do?" and letting the Israelis get their way. That was why people were so disenchanted with the Fatah leadership.

Abdelhakim, the young eager beaver, was watching her as she sat restlessly, pushing things around on her desk. She didn't trust him. He was a clean-cut snappy dresser, and she had seen him several times out in the town, each time with a different young woman from the college, Al Quds Open University. She had heard, though, that he was affiliated with Hamas.

"Can I do something for you?" she asked.

"Nothing," he answered and looked away.

"Tell the captain I went to speak to someone." It wasn't much of an excuse, but she couldn't think of a better one. She needed to satisfy herself that

Fareed was really guilty, or find the person who was. She should stay away from Benny if she didn't want the captain to find out she had disobeyed him, but there was no other way to get the information she needed. She went straight to Ariel.

"Convince me that this boy is the killer," she said.

"Does Mustafa know you're here?" Benny asked with that arched eyebrow she was coming to loathe.

She wished he hadn't asked her directly. It occurred to her to wonder if the captain had called Benny himself to enlist his help in controlling her.

"He knows I am following up on some loose ends," she evaded. "He doesn't need to know exactly where I go." Hopefully he would get the message. If not, she would deal with it later.

"What about the passport?" she asked him. "Aren't you at least going to ask Nir why he lied?"

"What's the point?" he asked. "We have the killer."

"Tell him you need it for the files. The woman from the agency told you she gave it to him. You thought he might have forgotten where he put it."

He shook his head vigorously. "That's not going to happen," he said. "This case is finished. It's nothing but a dead Uzbek hooker, forget about it."

"It's also a live Palestinian boy," she reminded him.

"That's not my problem. If the boy didn't kill her, he should have kept his mouth shut. Besides," and now his wide eyes grew serious, "he is probably guilty on the explosives charges, and for that he would have gotten in much more trouble. He is better off being charged as a criminal."

She should have realized this would be a waste of time. She stormed out.

Her next stop was Elkana. Funny, she thought, until a couple weeks ago, she had never been inside a settlement, and now she was breezing in and out of them as if they were her home. Before walking up to the Elkana gate, she put her headscarf in her purse. The jilbab would be more trouble, so she kept it on. The soldier couldn't see her whole body very well from his little windowed cabin anyway. She flashed her police ID at him and walked by without waiting for his okay.

"Hey," he yelled after her, but when she kept walking, he didn't pursue. She thought Palestinian women could probably get away with a lot more than they ever tried.

It was early afternoon, and the streets were filled with youngsters walking home from school. In a small park, not far from the entrance, she spied what she was looking for. Malkah was standing with a group of other girls, kicking at stones and looking at magazines. She seemed to be with and not with the other girls, on the edge of the circle, looking over the shoulder of a taller girl at whatever they were giggling about.

Rania couldn't interrupt them without attracting the kind of attention she had been warned to avoid. But she also couldn't hang around here for hours; someone loitering on this quiet street would doubtless be observed and reported. She located a large-ish stone at the edge of the park and took aim at a big iron dumpster across the street. Calling on her younger sling-shot-wielding self, she heaved the stone at the dumpster and was rewarded with a satisfying crash.

It worked.

The girls turned to see what the noise was, and she walked by slowly, catching Malkah's eye and nodding almost imperceptibly toward the next intersection. When she turned back, Malkah was telling her friends she would see them tomorrow and trotting down the street to meet her.

Malkah was both afraid and excited to be talking to her, Rania thought. Go easy, said Benny's voice in her head. Don't charge in like a herd of goats.

"How are things at home?" she asked.

The girl shrugged. "Okay, I guess."

"Has your dad found someone to take Nadya's place?"

"I don't think so. My grandma's still taking care of my sister and brother."

At that, Malkah looked at her watch as if realizing she was supposed to go home after school. Rania had better get to the point.

"Malkah, do you know why I'm here?" she asked.

Malkah shook her head. Okay, Rania asked herself. Why are you here? To get the girl to say her father murdered her nanny? She hadn't thought this out very well. Malkah was waiting less than patiently for her explanation.

"A Palestinian boy was arrested for killing Nadya, did you know that?" she asked.

"No," Malkah said.

"Your father didn't tell you?"

Why was she asking her about this? What difference did it make?

"No. He hasn't talked about Nadya at all since the day you came to our house."

"A boy was arrested for killing her. He was her boyfriend. You know about boyfriends, don't you?"

"I don't have one," the girl blurted out.

Rania was thrown for a loop. She had been trying to strike a rapport, yes, but she hadn't expected Malkah to take her up on it. The girl was very lonely, she thought. She needed a woman to have heart-to-hearts with. Well, she was the wrong woman. Most Muslim Palestinian women didn't talk about boys with their own daughters. She wasn't about to try it with a settler girl.

"Did you used to talk about boyfriends with Nadya?" she guessed.

"Sometimes." Malkah seemed disappointed. Whatever reaction she had expected to her admission, this wasn't it.

A spate of giggling from the road made both of them look toward the main street. The group of girls from the park was passing by. One of them glanced in the direction of where Rania stood with Malkah. She gave no indication of having seen them, but the look seemed to awaken Malkah's jitters.

"I'm not allowed to talk to you," she said suddenly. "I have to go."

"Malkah, wait," Rania called uselessly. The small figure was already dashing to catch up with her friends.

What a mess I made of that, Rania berated herself as she made her way home to Mas'ha. *So much for my quiet investigation to prove Fareed's innocence.*

When she arrived at work the next morning, Captain Mustafa reamed her. Benny had called him and said he had a call from someone named Gelenter, who said she was harassing his daughter.

"I wasn't harassing her," Rania defended herself. "She wanted to talk to me."

That was sort of true, she thought. She wondered, though, if Malkah had told her father about her visit, or if he had spies all over the settlement. She would have no right to feel betrayed if it was the former. Maybe if she had shown more interest in Malkah's problems, the girl would have felt more loyalty to her.

"This settler is very angry and very powerful," the captain was saying. "He told Benny he was giving your name to the SHABAK. You need to leave this investigation alone, or you will soon be in prison yourself."

"But I haven't broken any laws," she protested, realizing that fact was irrelevant.

"This is no joke," Captain Mustafa told her. "You know how many Palestinian policemen are sitting in Israeli jails right now. This is not a safe profession."

"I know," she acknowledged.

"He did not only threaten to arrest you," the captain said. "Do you want to know what else he said?"

She didn't, but she knew he would tell her anyway. She guessed Nir had threatened to arrest Bassam too, maybe even his brothers. The captain stood up behind his desk, to give extra punch to his warning.

"He said they would take your son too," he thundered.

Her heart caught an express train to her feet.

"But Khaled's only six."

"He said to tell you he has broken boys younger than that," Captain Mustafa enunciated each word.

She didn't believe even such a big military man could be so cruel. But she wasn't going to find out.

"Go home," the captain told her. "You can take tomorrow off as well."

The next day was Thursday, so he was giving her a long weekend. Was it a favor, or a punishment? He would never say. She would just have to come in on Saturday and see how he acted, what new tasks he assigned her. She had two more days to figure out how to help Fareed. She wasn't going to just let him be railroaded, but she couldn't think what to do, with her hands tied like this. She would start by visiting Fareed's family in Azzawiya.

* * *

Chloe was sitting in the garden, writing on her laptop. Rania recalled her suspicions that Chloe had had something to do with Fareed's arrest. She didn't really want to talk to her until she felt sure which side she was on, but she wasn't sure how she was going to get that information except by talking to her.

"Abu Fareed mawjood?" Rania asked. *Is Fareed's father here?*

"Mush mawjood," Chloe said. *Not here.* She looked back at her laptop. Why so standoffish? Rania wondered. Every other time she'd seen this woman, she wouldn't shut up.

"Do you know when he will return?" Rania asked.

"No, they all went to Nablus." Chloe gestured toward the house as if to say, Look for yourself, there's no one home.

Rania sat down next to her on the porch.

"Fareed confessed," Chloe said.

"I heard," said Rania. "That's why I'm here."

"Do you think you can do something?" The hope in Chloe's voice put Rania on edge and made her want to snap. Why was this American pinning her hopes on a Palestinian policewoman? She must have resources in her back pocket no Palestinian could even dream of. The portable computer she was using probably cost more than Rania's annual salary. She cut off these unhelpful thoughts before they became an outburst she would regret.

"Not really," she said. Chloe's face registered disappointment.

"I'm sorry I couldn't stop them from taking him," the American said.

"Did you expect you could?" Rania asked.

Chloe took time to think before answering. "Pretty much no," she said, "but I think many people here think I can do a lot more than I can. They think the Americans run everything, and I'm American. They don't realize I don't know one person in the government."

Rania smiled because Chloe had come so close to verbalizing her own thoughts. "I'd like to help Fareed," she said.

"Isn't it too late now?"

"He hasn't been sentenced, has he?"

"No. That's why his parents went to Nablus, to talk to a lawyer."

"Then it is not too late."

"Well, what can you do?"

"I'm not sure, especially because I'm not even supposed to be working on it any more. I just can't let it go."

"His mother's really freaked out," Chloe told her. "She's been getting strange phone calls."

"What kind of calls?"

"One guy called and said he was a friend of Jaber's from prison. He described Ahlam and said he remembered Fareed as a baby. But Jaber says he never heard of the guy. It's giving her nightmares," Chloe said. "She has flashbacks to the time when Jaber was in prison, and she had to raise Fareed by herself."

"I know," Rania murmured. "We all have nightmares like that." She shook her head to banish the flash forwards of Khaled, led away in shackles, ineffectually calling her name. "I wish I had been able to make friends with Nir Gelenter's daughter," she went on. "She knows something that would help us, I can tell. But I messed up, and now I cannot even talk to her."

"I could try," Chloe said.

Rania was on the verge of saying, "Forget it," but something stopped her. A few minutes ago, she was thinking about her distrust of the woman, and now she was going to send her to Elkana as her proxy? But she couldn't think of an alternative, and this might give her a chance to observe Chloe's motives more carefully.

"You would need to move gently," Rania said. "The girl is really scared of something."

"What would she be afraid of?" Chloe wanted to know.

"Her father, probably. But Delmarie, a foreign woman who works in the settlement, told us she saw Nadya arguing with a man, perhaps one of the people who brought her to Israel. Maybe he came to the house, and Malkah saw him. Or, I don't know," she trailed off. She wished she had the photo of the man Alexandra Marininova had identified, for Chloe to show Malkah, but Benny had kept all the photos. She couldn't ask him for them now. She would have to hope Chloe could get some information out of Malkah. It went against her grain to have to sit on her hands and wait.

Chapter 23

Chloe could easily have walked to Elkana from Azzawiya; there was even a hole in the fence by the water tower, which she could slip through and be right near the girls' school. But she thought she would be less conspicuous on the bus. She got off by the market Rania had told her was near the Gelenters'. She wandered along their street, hoping she had picked out the right house, wondering how to be sure.

A stroke of good luck came her way in the shape of a young Ethiopian woman delivering mail. When she was out of sight, Chloe ran to check the addresses on the newspaper and catalogues she had placed in the box she thought was the Gelenters'. The Hebrew address confirmed it. Okay, she told herself. Well done, so far.

Now where would be a good place to watch? The pristine, silent street was not a place a stranger could stand around unnoticed for more than a few minutes. There was no view of the house from where the store sat, and the street curved around at the end of the block, so she couldn't walk down a few blocks and then seem to be ambling back up. A house across the street had a tallish tree with sufficient foliage to secrete someone. She studied its branches. She was never much of a tree climber, even as a child, and as an adult she nurtured a healthy fear of heights. A burst of young female voices forced her to act quickly.

The driveway of the house where she stood pondering the tree held two vehicles. The front one was a red van, the kind you cursed on the freeway because it kept you from seeing what was going on ahead of you. She supposed it was perfect for transporting the broods of children many religious families boasted. The one behind it was a little Citroen, like eighty percent of the cars on Israeli roads. They made a great contrast, an automotive Mutt and Jeff. They also made a great little shelter. She wedged herself onto the hood of the Citroen, hidden from sight by the Econoline but afforded a great view of the street via its massive windshield and twin side mirrors. Even better, she was comfortable. As long as none of the girls coming home belonged to the family with the fleet, she was in good shape.

She imagined she might not have to wait long, as the Hebrew chatter drew closer. The Econoline's passenger side mirror showed a pair of girls, with matching glossy ponytails and long appliquéd denim skirts, dawdling near the Gelenters' house. But neither of them turned into the house. They continued down the block and turned the corner. Less than five minutes later, a slightly younger girl in a navy school skirt and knee socks made her way up the street, balancing her bookbag on one hip. Chloe recognized Malkah more by the attitude than the physical description Rania had given her. One of Israel's top military muckety-mucks could have only two types of daughter: the kind who thought she was all that or the kind who dreamed every day that she would wake up someone else, somewhere else. Malkah clearly fit the latter profile.

After Malkah unlocked the door and disappeared behind it, Chloe racked her brain for an excuse to knock on the door. She could be a lost American visitor, and ask for directions, but whom was she visiting, and where could she be going? And once Malkah gave her the information, on what basis would she engage her in conversation? She couldn't be selling anything; she had no idea if there were door-to-door salespeople in high-tech Israel, but if there were, presumably they all knew Hebrew.

Looking for work? She toyed with the idea. Maybe she was staying with a relative in Elkana who mentioned that the Gelenters had lost their house-keeper. She might be able to pull that one off, but then Malkah would pre-sumably say she had to come back when one of the grownups was home. For all she knew, one of them was home now. She was thinking she had better take the plunge and find out, when the door opened again and Malkah emerged. Chloe followed her to the school playground. Malkah sat in one of the low swings, swinging slowly back and forth and writing in a notebook. Chloe strolled up, trying for nonchalance, and settled into the swing next to Malkah's. Malkah looked up, so startled she dropped her pen in the sand.

"What are you writing?" she asked.

Malkah dropped down to collect her pen. "Who are you?" she asked.

Chloe decided it was best to stay close to the truth.

"I live in that village there, Azzawiya," she said pointing toward the minaret peeking over the tops of the trees. "I have never been in a settlement before, so I just came here to look around."

"Are you an Arab?" Malkah asked, a little fear creeping into her face.

Don't be so judgmental, Chloe instructed herself. When you were thirteen, you thought what your parents thought too. "No, I'm Jewish."

"You are living with Arabs?" Malkah was aghast.

"Yes," Chloe said. "I'm Jewish, and I live with Palestinians. They are very nice to me. Is that a journal?" indicating the notepad.

"No. I'm writing a story."

"What's it about?"

"Why do you want to know?"

"I'm a writer too." This was half-true. Years ago, Chloe had been a freelance writer for a local gay newspaper. It had been ages since she'd written anything other than an email, but once a writer, always a writer.

"What do you write?"

"Articles, mostly."

"You write about true things."

"I try to. Are you writing about made-up things?"

"I write about things I wish were true."

"Like what?"

"This story is about a girl from Elkana who is driving with her family one night and their car breaks down. They have to get out and fix it. They are next to a Palestinian village, and the girls' parents are all freaked out and afraid. But the girl gets out of the car and goes up to the edge of the road, right by one of the houses. There is a girl her age there, with ragged clothing and no shoes on, and they make eye contact. It's like a silent communication."

Chloe was flabbergasted to be having such a profound conversation with a teen she had just met. Malkah must be an extremely lonely girl.

"And then what?"

"Her father finishes fixing the car and they get back in and drive away."

"That's it?"

"Yes. But it changes the girl's life."

"How do you think it would change her life?" Chloe probed.

"I don't know… it just would."

"Why are you here by yourself?" Chloe asked. "Instead of playing with your friends?"

"I don't really have friends," Malkah said.

"That must be hard."

"I don't care. The other girls just walk around and around the settlement in circles trying to get the cutest boys to like them. It's a waste of time."

"Don't you like boys?"

"They are all stupid, too," Malkah asserted. "Look what some of them did," and she pointed to the wall of the school. *ARAVIM HACHUTZAH!* ARABS OUT! was spray-painted in Hebrew.

"Why does that upset you?" Chloe asked. "Do you know any Palestinians?"

"No," Malkah said slowly. "But it's bad to be against a whole people. We should all live together in peace."

"If you want to meet Arabs, you could come with me to Azzawiya sometime," Chloe suggested. "A lot of the men who live there speak Hebrew."

"I couldn't do that." Malkah sounded frightened. She was moving too fast, Chloe realized.

"I could bring you some information about the villages in this area, if you would like."

"Yes," Malkah said. "I would like that very much."

"Can you meet me here tomorrow after school?" Chloe asked. Malkah agreed.

✶ ✶ ✶

The next day, Chloe was at the playground right at three o'clock. Malkah's round face lit up when she saw her.

"I brought you some things to read," Chloe said, handing the girl several brochures in Hebrew. "These are from the Israeli human rights group Btselem," she said. She added the brochure she always gave to soldiers. "This one is from another group, called Yesh Gvul."

"Thank you," Malkah said. Chloe had imagined Malkah would want to look at the literature right away, but she scarcely glanced at the brochures before tucking them into her school bag. "See you." She started to walk away.

"Wait!" Chloe was so afraid her contact with Malkah was ending precipitously, she nearly yelled. The girl hovered, poised for flight.

"Let me buy you an ice cream," Chloe suggested.

She had hit the right note. Malkah was tempted. "I should get home," she waffled. "My grandmother will be bringing my sister and brother home."

"Is there a shop on the way to your house?" Chloe asked. Malkah nodded and Chloe fell in beside her. "Do you take care of your brother and sister every day after school?" she asked.

"Now I do," Malkah said. "Except Wednesday when I go ice skating in Tel Aviv. Nadya cared for them before, but she is dead."

Here was the opening Chloe had prayed for. Don't blow it, she told herself.

"Who is Nadya?"

"She worked for my family."

"How did she die?"

"Someone killed her."

"Really? How awful."

"I guess." Malkah didn't sound that upset, talking about death. Either she was totally cut off from her feelings, or she didn't care for Nadya. Chloe needed to know which.

"That must be scary for you," she said.

"It had nothing to do with me." Malkah sounded petulant. "I think my father is afraid."

They had reached the little shop where Chloe had gotten off the bus. Malkah picked out two of the sugar cones filled with vanilla ice cream and covered with chocolate.

"These are my favorite," Chloe said. She paid for them and they sat on a bench outside the shop to eat them.

"Why would your father be afraid?" Chloe asked. She tried to make it sound totally unimportant.

"I don't know. But I heard him tell my Uncle Israel on the telephone that the police took something out of our house."

"Who is your Uncle Israel?"

"Israel Wilensky. He is not my real uncle, he is my father's friend. He is a very famous war hero."

"Does he live here in Elkana?" Hopefully Malkah wouldn't wonder why she was so interested in people she didn't know.

"He lives in Tel Aviv. And he has a big company in Rosh HaAyin."

Malkah's eyes shifted to something in the distance. Chloe couldn't tell what had caught her attention, but the girl wolfed down the rest of her ice cream cone and stood up.

"They had a fight," she said. She threw her wrapping in the garbage can.

"Who?" Chloe asked. Her half-eaten cone was melting on her hand, but it didn't seem appropriate to lick it off. "Your uncle and your father?"

Malkah shook her head violently. "My uncle and Nadya," she said. "I have to go."

She took off before Chloe could even say goodbye.

✶ ✶ ✶

There was no internet at Jaber's house, so Chloe went to the internet café to find out about Wilensky. Amid the smoke and noise of young men playing computer games, she learned that *Colonel* Israel Wilensky was indeed a famous air force commander. Three years ago, he had been involved in an incident involving a missile attack in Jenin Camp, which killed three leading members of Hamas and five members of their families. Dozens of Palestinians had been injured. Wilensky and his men said that the militants had shot at them, and that the civilians had been killed by Palestinians in the crossfire. Palestinians said that they had all been civilians, blown up while coming back from the store with groceries. There were pictures, taken by a Palestinian photographer for one of the wire services, of the groceries scattered all over the ground, interlaced with blood and body parts.

It was a well-known incident, because it had occurred during what was known as the "Jenin Camp Massacre" of 2002 (official Israeli documents called it "The Battle of Jenin"). Over fifty people, mostly civilians, had been killed during the invasion of the refugee camp, and there was a small-scale international outcry about that. In response, the Israeli Knesset had convened a commission. That commission had investigated Colonel Wilensky and his troops and concluded that there had been no wrongdoing. A few months after the investigation concluded, Wilensky had resigned his position at the defense ministry, but Chloe couldn't tell if the two things were connected. Officially, the resignation was because he had a share in a corporation that sold construction materials, and he decided to take a lucrative, hands-on role in the company. Online scuttlebutt was that he had had a fight with the defense minister, over his interest in the man's daughter. That was interesting to Chloe, because the daughter, Lilith, was nineteen, as was Nadya. Colonel Wilensky was forty-nine. She called Avi.

"What do you know about someone named Israel Wilensky?" she asked without prelude.

"Why are you asking?"

"He was arguing with Nadya a few days before she was killed. He might have killed her."

"He didn't," Avi said shortly.

"How do you know?"

"He's out of the country."

"How do you know that?"

"He's more or less my uncle."

"What do you mean, more or less?"

"He's one of my father's best friends. They were in the air force together, and they are in the same reserve unit."

Wilensky seemed to have a lot of pseudo-nieces and nephews. But if there was some significance to that, Chloe couldn't think what it was.

"Sorry," she said. "I didn't mean to say your uncle's a murderer."

"It's okay. He's a pig. But he's been in Italy for two weeks. I got a postcard from him."

"Well, I still think he has something to do with Nadya getting killed."

She hung up. She was almost uncontrollably happy, to have things to do, to have Rania and Avi and Jaber talking to her about the case, instead of sneaking around hiding things from her. At the same time, all the cloak-and-dagger stuff was making her tense. Ahlam's scary phone calls, Avi's evasiveness. She wished she could have a glass of wine, but alcohol was forbidden in Muslim villages. She called Rania to report on what she had learned.

"Do you have the internet at home?" she asked. Few Palestinians did, but she was not surprised when Rania said yes.

"Look up Israel Wilensky," Chloe told her. "He's a colonel in the air force. Find a picture of him."

A few minutes later, Rania returned the call. "That's him," she said. "The guy with Nadya in the picture we found."

"So a friend of Gelenter's knew Nadya before she came to Elkana," Chloe mused.

"And Gelenter told us he didn't know anyone matching Wilensky's description," Rania added. "Which means he lied. Again."

Chapter 24

"Jenin, Jenin," chorused the drivers at Anabta Gate, just outside Tulkarem. Good, Rania thought. She would not have to wait for a car. She climbed into a service taxi along with two other women and two little girls. Both women were laden with packages, so after they had filled the trunk, there were still plastic bags covering every inch of the interior. The crowning grace was the live chickens one woman held on her lap. It was going to be a noisy, smelly trip.

Twenty minutes later, they were still sitting in the parking lot. A service held seven, and they were five. At this rate, they might need to wait for the next bus from Ramallah to deliver two more passengers. Rania looked anxiously at her watch. She had not been to work since Wednesday, when Captain Mustafa had taken her off the Nadya case. This morning she had called the station and told the young woman who answered the phone that *zuruf*, circumstances, detained her. She hoped she would be in the office by noon. The woman with the chickens took out a large round of *taboun* bread and tore off a piece for her little daughter. She held out the folded slab to Rania, who politely declined. If the woman really wanted to share with her, she would tear off a piece herself and thrust it into Rania's hand. She didn't. That was fine, Rania wasn't hungry. She just wanted to get to Jenin.

Their driver was sitting with several other drivers on upturned milk crates under one of the shade trees. One of them had made coffee on a small camp stove.

"Haj," she called, and the driver of the car she sat in turned around. "Let's go," she said. "I will pay the extra fares."

He threw back the remains of his coffee, said goodbye to his buddies and climbed into the cab. It was a lot of money, forty-five shekels in all, and she could not afford it, but she couldn't afford to sit here all morning either. The car jounced along the rough roads, making good time. The windows were wide open to the warm air, pungent with the smell of the garlic that grew in the fields along the road. Rania realized she had nodded off when the car made a sudden stop. She sat up straight and looked around, hoping to see the shops and traffic of central Jenin. But no, they were still on the empty road.

"What is it?" she asked the woman with the chickens.

"Roadblock."

Now Rania saw the soldiers, their olive garb blending in with the surrounding foliage. There were five of them. She didn't see a vehicle. She didn't envy them, dropped here in the middle of nowhere, outside the city with the most organized resistance forces in Palestine. Three of them were guarding the road, and two searching a car in the middle of the road. There was one more car between theirs and the one being searched.

Rania fidgeted, craning her neck to see over the driver's head. The car they were searching had been filled with luggage—a family coming back from a trip. The soldiers had made them empty the trunk and the luggage rack and open every bag. They were pawing through the clothes now, asking questions she couldn't hear. After what seemed a very long time, the occupants of the car were left to repack their bags and reload the car—agonizingly slowly, in Rania's opinion. The soldiers could have started on the next car during the repacking, but chose instead to take a break, standing around chatting and idly pointing their guns at the family. Rania was nearly jumping out of her seat with impatience, the driver gently tapping out a fugue on the steering wheel, but the women in her car sat implacably, gazing out the windows as if they had nothing to do but sit on this road until some post-pubescent brats decided they could go. What was wrong with them? she wondered. Or was it something wrong with her?

The soldiers were finally moving toward the second car, the one right in front of them. It was a private car, not a taxi. Two men got out and the driver opened the trunk. They did not have a lot of baggage, so it should go much faster. One of the soldiers reached into a plastic bag and pulled out a handful of strawberries. He tasted one, then put the others back. *Sure,* Rania thought, *you needed to make sure there weren't little bomblets hidden in the berries.* It was almost enough to make her wish there were. Now one of the Palestinians was bending over something on the ground she couldn't quite see. He rose holding a violin by the neck, the way the woman next to her was holding the chickens. That was unusual here. Most Palestinians who played instruments played tabla drums or oud, and more recently guitars and electric keyboards had come into vogue. She wouldn't have a clue where to get a violin.

"Play it," Rania heard the soldier say in English. The man tucked the violin under his chin and drew the bow across the strings twice before lowering it to his side.

"Do you know a sonata?" the stocky soldier asked. "Maybe one by Beethoven?"

"No!" Rania's involuntary shout echoed through the open windows. The man with the violin, the soldiers, and the driver of the other car turned as one to see where the noise had come from. Two of the soldiers who were standing off to the side ran toward their car. Rania decided the best thing would be to climb out, so that any punishment for her instinctive rebellion would be directed at her alone and not the others in her car. She had to climb over the woman with the chickens to reach the door. The two little girls, who had been sleeping in the back seat, were awake now and watching her with saucer-eyes, the littlest one sucking her thumb.

"You have a problem?" one of the soldiers asked when she stood in front of him.

"Your friend has a problem," she said, gesturing to the music-loving soldier. "He needs to abuse his power."

"Who says it is abuse? You?" He looked like he was contemplating spitting in her face. She hoped he would decide against it. His mate stood silently, looking around, his finger on the trigger of his gun. He probably didn't understand enough English to know what was going on.

"Yes, I say so," she said. She walked deliberately to the place where the violinist and the soldier stood as if frozen. She was thankful for the long jilbab so they couldn't see her legs shaking.

The violinist looked in his early forties, dapper, perfectly dressed with full, waving black hair. He was probably a teacher at the Arab American University in Jenin, an expensive private college in the nearby town of Zbabde. He put the violin to his shoulder.

"Khalas." *Enough*, Rania urged softly. "Put it away. Don't humiliate yourself."

The tall man smiled down at her, his dark eyes twinkling, and then drew the bow across the strings with a feather-light touch. The air filled with unspeakable beauty. Rania had never heard anything like the piece he played—she was no fan of Western music—but the emotion it evoked was overpowering. He played and played, the notes carrying across the still countryside.

When the last sweet notes had died away, the man made a slight flourish with his bow, saluting an imaginary audience. He stooped and carefully placed the violin in its case, covering it with a soft red cloth. He snapped the car's trunk shut, without waiting for an okay from the soldiers, but the violin he carried with him to the passenger's side.

"Shukran." *Thanks*, he said to Rania, opening the car door.

"Tik alafia," she replied. *Bless your work.*

The startled driver climbed into the car and started the engine. None of the soldiers had said a word since the music began, but now they bustled around, reclaiming the territory. With the spell broken, Rania realized she was now in the line of fire. The soldiers realized it, too. As usual, she had not thought before jumping into a situation. Here she was, hours from where she was supposed to be, already late, and they could hold her at this checkpoint all day if they wanted.

"Hawiyya," the soldier who had eaten the strawberry said to her. She fumbled inside her large purse for her ID, surreptitiously removing her police identification from the green folder before handing it to him. He took it and went to talk to one of the others, who took out a mobile phone and called someone. Rania wasn't worried. She was not wanted. She just hoped they didn't take too long finding that out. She had seen men waiting hours sometimes to get clearance. The soldiers would often say the computers were down. If they did not give her ID back in ten minutes, she would start to make a fuss. The soldiers were searching the car now, telling the women and kids to get out and stand on one side. They said something to the woman with the chickens and she got back into the car. Rania guessed they were worried about getting pecked.

She heard a giant roar. An armored personnel carrier, APC, was making its way toward them, kicking up massive amounts of dust in its wake. The driver yelled something to the soldiers, who ran to climb aboard, the cars completely forgotten.

"Wait, wait!" Rania ran after the small tank. "What about my ID?"

The taxi sped past her. "Hey!" she called ineffectually. Just what she needed, to lose her ride as well as her ID. Then she realized what the driver was attempting to do. He tried to edge the taxi around the APC, but the road was too wide and surrounded by deep ditches. As the APC sped off, Rania saw a hand poking through the hole in the top, making an obscene gesture.

She climbed into the taxi. The women were laughing and the girls giggling. *I'm glad I'm such a source of amusement for you,* she thought grumpily. Then she imagined what she must have looked like, a tiny woman running after a tank, and she began to laugh with them.

✳ ✳ ✳

Once inside Jenin, Rania realized she had no idea how to go about finding information about what Colonel Wilensky's unit had done. She had only been in the city a few times in her life. She didn't know anyone there. She looked around the busy central market. It was like any other Palestinian city, crammed with stalls full of spices, clothing, meat, luggage, and live animals, carts piled high with vegetables, little street-side stands making falafel and sweets. She looked hungrily at the pancakes spread with apricot marmalade, a treat unique to Jenin. She had not eaten breakfast, and thanks to the flying checkpoint, it was now mid-morning. She had to ask someone where to go, she might as well start with the pancake vendor.

"Were you here during the siege?" she asked him as he rolled up her cake and dusted it with powdered sugar.

"Yes, of course," he responded. "My house was destroyed."

"Haram." *For shame,* she commiserated. In her eagerness for information, she had forgotten that the people here would still be raw from trauma. "Have you been able to rebuild?" she asked, conscious of the minutes ticking away.

"No, we are staying with my wife's family. No money," he said.

"Inshalla, soon," she said. Perhaps she should order another pancake. But then, she didn't even know if he would be able to help her. If she had to ask other merchants, they too would have tragic stories. Best to spread her few shekels around.

"I am looking for people who witnessed a particular incident," she told him. "The family of Hassan Rashid was killed by a missile."

"Yes, I remember," he said. "Many people were injured."

"Do you know where I might find any of them? I am with the police, and I need to ask what they remember."

"The police are investigating this?" he asked skeptically. "After so much time?"

"Not exactly that," she said. "It might be related to something we are investigating."

"The son of my neighbor," he said. "He lost his leg." He motioned to a man drinking coffee at a nearby stall. "This is Abu Saif," he said. "He has a taxi. He can take you to the house."

"Shouldn't we call and make sure he is home? If it is too far to walk, I wouldn't want to go there for nothing."

"He will be home."

She didn't know how he could be so sure. She would just have to hope that he was right, that Abu Saif was honest and knew the way, and that the young man who lost his leg had something useful to tell her. She thanked the vendor and followed Abu Saif to his cab, which was an ordinary, beat-up white car.

"How far is it?" she asked, mainly for something to say. He didn't answer. That wasn't a good sign. Or maybe he didn't believe in talking to women he didn't know. He wove in and out of traffic, making quick turns down increasingly narrow streets. Soon they were driving into Jenin Camp, the largest refugee camp in the West Bank. It reminded her of Aida in the way the shops and houses were crammed together in the dirt roads, but she saw none of the beautiful tiled houses or bright murals that made Aida look so lively. This was a dingy expanse of misery.

"This is the place," the driver said. She followed his outstretched arm. It was an empty square about two blocks long and wide, with only a few half-demolished structures around the edges. "The place" meant the area that had been leveled by the tanks during that fateful week. The story was that the army commander wanted to clear a football field with his tank. At that time, she knew, this area had been filled with the remains of people and houses. She had seen the photos of heartbroken people picking through the rubble, looking for prize possessions or family members. Now, a few small children ran around the lot shrieking with laughter as they rolled hoops with sticks.

After a number of sharp turns, Abu Saif stopped the car and gestured to a house. "Here is where he lives," he said.

He waited for her to get out. "Aren't you going with me?" she asked.

"If you like," he said. He got out of the car and rang the bell. After what seemed like an age, an old man in a tattered dressing gown opened the door a crack. Abu Saif explained what Rania wanted.

"Huwwa hon." *He is here*, the old man said. He opened the door just wide enough for the two of them to slip inside, then closed it again. There were no lights on in the house. The dirty white walls were pocked with bullet marks. In the center of the dim living room, a man in his early twenties sat in a wheelchair. A blanket across his lap covered the stump where his leg used to be. Where the blanket ended, she could see the limp shin of his one good leg, atrophied from disuse. He sipped something from a plastic cup with a straw, like the ones Khaled used to drink from. He stared blankly at a huge television screen where a white-gowned cleric pontificated in high Arabic. An ancient woman sat in the room's only chair, also staring at the television. Sensing strangers in the room, the woman suddenly started and turned toward the man Rania presumed was her husband.

"Yahud?" she asked him, a note of terror in her voice.

"Laa," he assured her. "Palestinian police."

How could the old woman mistake her for an Israeli? Rania wondered. Then she solved her own mystery, realizing the woman must be blind. This house seemed like a highly unpromising source of information. But she was here, so she might as well continue. The old man settled himself on a cushion on the floor, so Rania followed suit. The driver remained standing. She wondered if she had violated some little-known custom of the Jenini, or if he had some reason to know they would not be staying long. Since no one had bothered to introduce her to the young man, she did the honors herself.

"I am Rania Bakara, with the police in the Salfit District," she told him. "You are Mohammed?"

He nodded, and took a sip from his cup.

"I am sorry for your injuries," she told him. "How are you doing?"

"Hamdililah," he responded. The generic and expected response—*praise God*. She knew not to take it literally.

"Can you tell me what happened the day you were shot?"

He looked around at the others, as if hoping someone would save him from answering. Receiving no help, he spoke.

"I was in the street with my mother," he said. "The plane flew down very low. They started shooting. The people ran away, but my mother could not move quickly, so we did not get away in time." He looked toward the old woman when he said that, and Rania realized that she was his mother. She would have put the woman in her late seventies, but that wasn't possible. She identified the sudden throbbing in her skull as rage. The harshness of this life had sapped the life out of these people, made them old before their time. There but for the grace of God, she thought. In some moods she could judge people like this family for not being as motivated as she was, but today, her encounter with the soldiers at the checkpoint fresh in her mind, her emotions were equal parts pity and gratitude. She wondered if there was something she could do for them that would not hurt their pride. She couldn't just hand them fifty shekels. Could she tuck a bill under the cushion she was sitting on without being seen?

Thinking about money, a question popped into her mind.

"How did you get the wheelchair?" she asked the young man. She knew there were organizations that helped disabled people, but there was often a waiting list for wheelchairs. This one, as far as she could tell, was state-of-the-art, not handed down.

"Yahud," he said.

"Israelis? Which Israelis?"

"Jesh." She looked at his father, wondering if the boy's mind had been affected too. The father nodded.

"The army paid for the wheelchair?"

"They paid all his medical expenses," the father explained.

"Why did they do that?" This was highly unusual. She had heard of no one else who had been injured in the siege who was compensated.

"We can't tell you," the father said.

"What do you mean, you can't? You mean you won't?" Could he mean that they had given information? That was the only reason she could imagine the army giving someone money that they couldn't talk about. But in that case, they would not have told her the money came from the army in the first place. Collaborating with the occupation forces was a crime in the Palestinian Authority. They could go to prison in Jericho—if they were not killed first.

The father left the room abruptly. The young man went back to watching the television screen. Had her thoughts been so obvious that she had offended them? Now she became conscious of the incongruity of the big television in this empty house. Before she could decide whether to make another attempt at deciphering this mystery or call it a failed mission, the father returned. His trembling hand extended a business card with writing in Arabic, English, and Hebrew. "Shira Zohari, Attorney," she read in Arabic. It gave a telephone number with an 02 exchange—Jerusalem. She copied the number and handed him back the card.

"You sued the army?" she guessed.

"Talk to the attorney," the father said.

She rose from the floor and thanked them for their time. They were clearly relieved to see her go. Once in the cab, she handed the driver a fifty shekel note. "For the family," she told him. He nodded appreciation and tucked the bill into his front pocket.

"Do you know," she asked, "if any other families got money from the army too?"

"Five," he responded.

"Only five? Out of all the people injured in the siege?"

"Five," he repeated.

"Do you know any of the others?"

"Two are dead," he said.

"They got money and then they died?"

"Their families got money after they died." That was even more unusual than the army paying for people's medical care.

"Do you know if they all had the same lawyer?"

"I think so. I took her to their houses."

"All five?"

"Yes."

This must be why the crepe seller had called this man to drive her. Or else it was a hell of a coincidence. "Did you know this lawyer? How did she contact you?" she asked him.

"My cousin works for Btselem," he said. "He arranged for her to come here and he asked me to take her to meet the families."

Btselem, the Israeli Center for Human Rights in the Occupied Territories, hired some Palestinians to investigate complaints.

"Does this lawyer work for Btselem?" she asked.

"I don't think so. I think she works for herself. But you should ask her," he said.

"I intend to," she said.

It was already eleven. If she went to meet the other families who were paid by the army, she would not make it to Salfit today at all. And probably, they would not tell her anything either. Better to call the lawyer from the road. She asked Abu Saif to take her to the cars for Tulkarem. Once she had settled into one, she fished the lawyer's phone number out of her pocket.

"Ken?" Shira Zohari's greeting was all business. Rania identified herself and told the woman what she wanted.

"There is nothing to tell," the woman replied in heavily accented English. "The army paid the medical expenses on humanitarian grounds, that's all."

"On humanitarian grounds?"

"That's right. They denied responsibility for the deaths and injuries, but paid the medical expenses on humanitarian grounds."

"Why only for these five cases? There were hundreds injured and dozens killed in the siege."

"I cannot discuss the case with you. That is all I have to say." The lawyer hung up.

Rania fretted. There was more to this. She had occasionally heard of the army paying medical expenses of people they shot, but she had never once heard of them paying it to the families after people had died. She called the lawyer back. "Answer," she ordered it on the fourth ring. The woman recognized her number, of course, and she would never answer a call from her again. Rania could try again when she got to Salfit. The 09 exchange was shared by both Palestinian and Israeli cities.

"Yes?" the voice said on the fourth ring. Startled, it took Rania a second to react. "Hello? Are you there?"

"Yes, yes, I'm here. Please, don't hang up."

"I'm sorry, I really can't discuss the case with you on the phone."

On the phone. That meant she might discuss it in person? "Can I meet you?" Rania asked.

"I guess so. Where are you?"

"Right now I am just outside of Jenin, but I am going to Tulkarem and then Salfit."

"Oh." Shira Zohari sounded disappointed. "You are not near Jerusalem."

Obviously, Rania wanted to say. Since Zohari had visited Jenin, she knew very well it was not near Jerusalem. "I cannot go to Jerusalem," she said instead. "But I can meet you in Ramallah."

"And I cannot go to Ramallah," Zohari replied. "It is illegal for Israelis." That was true, but so was Jenin, where she had apparently been willing to go.

"I can meet you in Beit Hanina," Zohari suggested. "We have an office in between the checkpoints." That was possible, barely. Technically, Beit Hanina was Jerusalem and off limits to West Bank Palestinians, but there were still ways around the checkpoint. It would not be easy. Rania would have to go first to Abu Dis, then Ar-Ram and then walk around the checkpoint into Beit Hanina.

"I can be there in three hours," she said, praying that was true. It would be if the roads were open. If there were roadblocks, it would take much much longer, and she could be stuck in the south overnight. In that case, she would have to go to Bethlehem to spend the night with her parents. Only after she hung up did she remember that she did not have her ID. The roads around Jerusalem were littered with checkpoints. She would need a lot of luck to avoid them.

Chapter 25

When Malkah got home from her rendezvous with Chloe, she closed her bedroom door and locked it, just for good measure. She climbed onto her bed and took out the brochures Chloe had brought. She was shocked by some of the stories they told, especially the ones about kids who had to wait at a locked gate every day, sometimes an hour or more, for soldiers to come let them through to go to school, and then they had to do the same thing to go home in the afternoon. Sometimes, the booklet said, they had a half-day at school, but the soldiers wouldn't open the gate early, so they had to wait until evening to go home.

Malkah heard the downstairs door slam and a woman's voice saying, "Shalom? Malkah, at po?" That meant that her grandmother was bringing her little brother and sister home. She quickly shoved the pamphlets back into her schoolbag. She could hide in the bathroom and look at them during recess.

The next day after Torah class there was an assembly where a woman from the Ministry of Absorption told them about some families from Russia, who after spending all their lives living in terrible misery under the Communists, finally had gotten their chance to come to Israel to be Jews and be happy. But, said the woman, these people now did not have enough money to take good care of all their children, and even though the government was helping them, they needed more money to buy their children's school clothes. They brought one of the children to the stage, a girl about Malkah's age, and she talked in Hebrew about how much she loved being in Israel and learning Hebrew and Israeli dancing.

When they went back to class, the teacher passed around a basket and asked all the children to contribute whatever money they had to help these poor families. They should think about what they planned to buy with the money in their pockets, the teacher said, and ask themselves if they really needed it, or if it would not make them happier to help the poor family. Malkah thought about what she had wanted to buy with the fifty shekels she had gotten from her mother for babysitting her sister and brother all week. The last time she went to Tel Aviv for her ice skating lesson, she had gone into a bookstore and seen a pretty cloth-bound journal and a fancy purple pen. She felt that if she could have that book and that pen to write with, she would be able to write something wonderful, like the *Diary of Anne Frank*. But she could keep writing in her school notebooks for a little longer. She gave forty shekels for the poor family, keeping just ten in case she wanted a chocolate bar or some chips.

Recess was cut short because of the assembly. Malkah went out into the yard with her class, and when no one was looking, she slipped back into the school building and headed for the bathroom. She tucked her feet up onto the toilet seat so no one would see that she was in there, and opened one of the pamphlets, the one about a village called Sawahre, in East Jerusalem, which was split down the middle. Half the people were now residents of Jerusalem; they had blue ID cards like hers and could go wherever they wanted. The other half were stuck on the other side of the giant concrete wall, and they had green West Bank ID cards so they couldn't go to pray at the mosque or sell things in the Old City. Some of them even had shops in Jerusalem but they couldn't go there.

She was deep in the story of a young boy from Sawahre when the bell rang, calling the students back into class. The boy, whose name was Ali, lived in a house with two entrances, one on the Israeli side and one on the Palestinian side. When the Wall was built, to keep the suicide bombers from going to Jerusalem to blow up Israelis in the shopping malls, the army wanted to tear down Ali's house, but his family went to court and the court said they couldn't, so they built the Wall right next to the house and put the family in a cage, with a gate going to the Palestinian side. Ali's family had a key to the gate that led to the Palestinian side, and they could go in and out any time, except after eight at night, unless the soldiers decided to keep the gate locked for a few days. But the door that used to lead to Jerusalem now led only to the high Wall, which even blocked out their view of the city. Ali had to change to a different school and leave all his friends, while all his cousins lived on the other side and he almost never got to see them.

Even though Malkah had never seen anything like Ali's house, she felt like she could see exactly what it looked like. She looked at the pictures of Ali walking by the army jeeps, and she felt afraid. When the bell rang for class, at first it sounded to her like a siren, like the jeeps sometimes made. She didn't remember to get up and go to class until the second bell had rung and she noticed suddenly that it was quiet in the bathroom.

Malkah's classroom had two doors, a front one which was next to where the teacher stood, and a back door, and suddenly she thought, oh, it is just like Ali's house. She closed the door very quietly, and moved toward her seat, which was pretty near the back anyway. But the principal was standing in the front of the room, and he stared at her and demanded, "Why are you late?"

What could she say? *I was reading about a Palestinian boy and when the bell rang, I thought it was the police?*

"I was in the bathroom," she stammered, and all the other girls laughed.

"Are you sick?" the principal asked. Why didn't he just let it go? He knew she wasn't sick, and he had already embarrassed her for being late. She shook her head.

"Next time, be on time to class," he said, and he continued to stare at her as he explained that during the recess, someone in her class had taken the money that had been collected for the poor families. The principal said he understood that sometimes people had an impulse to do something wrong, and when they had time to think about it, they realized they were wrong and they wanted to make it right. He was sure that whoever had taken the money now regretted it and wanted to give it back. So he was going to give them a chance to do that. He was still staring at Malkah as he said that, and she realized that because she was late coming back from recess, he thought she was a likely suspect to have taken the money. She wasn't sure how those two things were supposed to fit together.

The room next door, the principal said, was empty. He was going to put a box on the desk in the empty room. Each girl would walk into the empty room, one at a time, and whoever took the money could place it in the box on the desk, and then no one would ask any questions and the incident would be forgotten. But, if they did not, then he would have no choice but to search everyone's things until he found the money. Did everyone understand? he asked. All the heads in the room nodded soberly.

When it was Malkah's turn to walk into the empty room, she couldn't resist looking in the box. There was nothing in it. She didn't put anything in it either; how could she? No one else put anything in it, so the principal announced that he was going to go through everyone's pockets, desk, and school bags. He started at the back, and Malkah was sure, from the way he kept glancing at her, that it was because he believed she had taken the money and so he didn't want to waste too much time until he got to her.

Because the principal kept looking at her, she had no opportunity to hide the literature in her bag, not that she could think of anywhere to put it where it wouldn't be found anyway. When they were searching the girl two desks before her, her stomach started to ache and she started to feel wet between her legs. Oh no, she thought, could she possibly be getting her monthly troubles? It would be more than a week early, but she had read in a book that stress can cause early menstruation. She certainly felt stress. She thought that she shouldn't be so afraid, because they were only interested in the money, and she hadn't taken it, but as they searched the girl next to her, she started to shiver all over, as if she had the flu. She was sure she would not even be able to stand up, or that she would pee all over the floor. But somehow, when it was actually her turn, she calmed down.

The principal told her to empty her pockets. She turned them inside out, so he could see that there was nothing there but ten shekels, a bobby pin, and the fortune from a bubble gum wrapper. He told her to open the top of her desk, and she did, and he looked through all her books and notebooks, and then he told her to open her school bag. She did.

He told her to take everything out of her bag. She put a textbook on the desk, and then the four pamphlets from Btselem, and then immediately put another textbook on top, and her notebooks on top of that. The principal picked up the empty bag, turned it over, unbuckled the outside pocket, where she kept pencils and a hairbrush, and for a minute she hoped that he would ignore the books. But when he was done with the bag, he picked up the notebooks and flipped through them, even stopping for a minute to read a little of the story she was working on, and then he flipped through the textbook and then he picked up the first pamphlet.

From the look on his face, you would have thought that she had had the money folded up in the pamphlet. He curled his fist around the pages, brandishing it at her like a club. "Where did you get this?" he thundered.

She looked down at the floor, willing herself not to cry. All the other students were staring at her. She saw the girls with desks nearest to hers craning their necks to see what it was that the principal held in his hands, but they couldn't make it out. She bet they thought it was dirty magazines. She wasn't sure what to say—"a strange woman gave them to me"?—and anyway, she didn't see why she had to tell him. She thought it might be one of those questions you really didn't have to answer, so she stayed quiet, to see if he would forget about it.

He didn't. He put down the pamphlet he had crumpled up, and picked up the others. He seemed particularly upset about the little one with the triangle on it, the one Chloe had said was for soldiers. The principal leaned into her face.

"Do you know what this is?" he yelled.

She wasn't sure how to answer. She didn't exactly know what it was, because she hadn't read it yet, but she didn't necessarily want to admit that. But if she said yes, he might ask her about it, and she wouldn't really be able to answer him. So she again said nothing. It was a mistake, because he thought she was being smart. He grabbed her arm. "Come!" he snapped.

"Bring these," he ordered, indicating that she should put all the books back into her bag and bring it with her. They walked out to the office, her, the principal, and the teacher. Apparently, he had forgotten all about the missing money. She didn't think she should remind him. If she was going to get in so much trouble anyway, then someone else might as well not.

In the school office, he told her to sit in a chair near the secretary, while he and her teacher, Dvora, went through another door, into his office. She waited a long time. She could hear them talking in the office, but couldn't make out what they were saying. Then Dvora came out and put a hand on Malkah's shoulder and told her not to worry, everything would be all right. Dvora was in her early thirties, pretty, with wavy light-brown hair covered by a black net and eyes that sparkled when she talked about certain books she liked. She was going to have a baby in about five months, and that made her face rounder and shinier. She liked Malkah because she was smart and paid attention in class. Dvora left to go back to the class, and the principal came out and called Malkah to come into his office.

He told her that he had called her father, who was coming from work. Dvora had told him she was a good student, he said, trying to look benevolent but failing.

"Give me the pamphlets," he said. She handed them to him, and he put them to the side, without even looking at them. It was a good thing she had nearly finished reading all of them, because she didn't think she would get them back.

"Tell me," he said, "who gave you these?"

"Just someone I met," she said.

"What do you mean?" he asked. "Someone you met where?"

"In the schoolyard," she said truthfully.

He looked concerned at that, and demanded to know exactly when and where she had met Chloe. He asked her to describe the person, and she was too afraid to think of describing a whole different kind of person. She tried to modify a few details, but she thought that if Chloe showed up in the settlement again, she would probably get in trouble. She had better warn Chloe not to come. She couldn't, though, because she had no way to reach her.

"Why did you want to read something like this?" he asked her.

"Because I want to know more about our country," she said. She was proud of that answer. Who could argue with wanting to know more about your own country?

He sighed. "I understand," he said, but he didn't look like he did. "But this is not information. This is propaganda."

"Well, that's how you see it," she said. "Some people would say that this is propaganda"—indicating a flier posted on his wall announcing a big settler demonstration in Jerusalem, protesting the government's planned evacuation of settlements in Gaza. Elkana was chartering buses so everyone in the settlement could go.

"Maybe this is propaganda," she said, waving her history textbook at him.

She couldn't believe that she was talking like this to the principal, but she was on a roll.

"Even this is propaganda," she said lifting her Tanach, a small copy of the three sections of the Jewish Bible, the Torah, the Prophets, and the Writings.

Her timing was unfortunate. The principal's mouth dropped slightly open, and the door also opened. Her father was standing there, just in time to hear his daughter call the holiest book in Judaism "propaganda."

Her father took two giant steps from the door to where she stood. He grabbed her shoulders and shook her so hard that when he let go, she fell onto the desk.

"How dare you," he hissed at her.

Grabbing her bookbag, she turned and ran out of the office and out of the school.

Outside, she squinted in the sunlight. School was over for the day, and students were pouring out the doors. There were many doors, doors on both sides, just like Ali's house, she reflected. She walked a few hundred meters, then stopped, wondering where to go. She didn't want to go home. Even her mother would probably know about what had happened. Maybe even her grandmother, who adored her and brought her her favorite lemon short-bread every day, would find out and be angry at her.

With everyone so angry at her, it was hard not to feel she had done something wrong. But in her heart, she didn't feel she had. Even if the Btselem material was propaganda, she had a right to decide for herself what to believe.

She wandered around aimlessly for a while, but she didn't want to run into any of the kids from her class, who would either tease her, or would want to know what happened in the principal's office, and how much trouble she was in. After a while, she went home. Her father was already there. He called her into his study. The principal, he told her, thought this incident could jeopardize her chances to get into the best religious boarding school.

"And that could have an effect on your entire future," her father pronounced somberly.

For some reason, instead of feeling afraid, Malkah felt a little ripple of excitement in her chest, like maybe that would lead to some kind of adventure. But that in turn made her uneasy. Was she turning into a "bad kid," in front of her own eyes and without any choice in the matter?

"Who is the woman who gave you these books?" her father asked her.

"I don't really know her. I just met her one day, and she asked if I wanted something to read."

He didn't look like he believed her, even though it was not very far from the truth. But he didn't press it.

"If you see her again, do not talk to her. Tell her that if she comes near you again, she will be arrested," he instructed. He leaned forward. "You know, Malkah, I am very progressive with you."

"I guess," she said, because it was expected.

"Some people think I shouldn't let you go to Tel Aviv for ice skating lessons," he said. She took ice skating lessons every Wednesday, at the big rink in Tel Aviv where the Olympic ice skaters practiced. She went there on the bus by herself, and afterwards, her father picked her up and drove her home. It was their special time together, because she was the oldest.

"The policeman who came here last week asked why I allowed a gentile to take care of my children. He suggested that Nadya might have had a corrupting influence on you all. I told him it was ridiculous, because we are a family of very strong Jewish values. But now, I wonder if I was wrong."

"Dad, Nadya didn't change my values. I didn't spend that much time with her. Not like you did."

Her father looked down. He blew air into his cheeks and the space behind his lips. He opened the desk drawer and shoved it closed with the heel of his hand. When he spoke, he sounded like he did when she heard him talking on the phone to someone at work.

"I don't want you talking to anyone you don't know. If anyone comes around here trying to talk to you, I expect you to let me know right away. If I hear about any more trouble at school, you won't be allowed to go ice skating any more. Do you understand?"

"Yes," she said. For some reason, the fact that he was mad cheered her.

"Good. We won't talk about it any more."

She got up to leave. "Wait a second," he said.

She turned around. He was holding out to her the Btselem booklets, even the crumpled up one. "How …?" she asked.

"I told the principal I would discuss them with you after you finish reading them."

She smiled a small smile at him, and took them from his hand. She went into her room and lay on her bed and finished reading the one about Ali. Someday, she decided, she would find him and tell him about today, and they would become friends.

Chapter 26

Rania was lucky with the roads. Beit Hanina was a bustling town nestled between the Ar-Ram and Qalandia checkpoints, the one marking the edge of Jerusalem and the other sealing off Ramallah. Shira Zohari had told her to look for the Dalla Rent-A-Car. She easily found it, and next to it was a building that housed a dozen nongovernmental organizations. Shira Zohari was waiting inside a little office where faded posters covered the peeling walls.

She was a short, plump woman, about Rania's age. She tapped the eraser of a pencil compulsively on the desk as she talked.

"I'm sorry to make you travel so far," she said, as Rania gratefully accepted a cup of tea. The cookies she offered were stale, but Rania ate one anyway. She had eaten nothing all day except the little sweet in Jenin, and she was very hungry. "I couldn't be sure you were really who you said you were," Zohari continued.

"Who did you think I might be?" Rania asked.

"Who knows?" the lawyer responded with a wave of her hand. "The families who received settlements from the army signed confidentiality agreements. And so did I. If any of us violate the agreement, everyone has to return the money. So you see, I can tell you nothing about the settlement. Only what I said on the phone."

"What I'm trying to understand is why only those five families were compensated, out of all the people hurt in the siege," Rania said.

"I don't know that they were the only ones," Zohari said. "They were the only ones I represented, but there could have been other cases."

"How did you get in touch with those families?" she asked.

"Through Btselem. One of their investigators made a report on the incident. He contacted me." The cousin of Abu Saif. The incident, she had said, not the *incidents*.

"Were they all hit by the missile attack on April 7?" Rania asked.

"I have told you, I cannot talk about this case," Zohari answered. Rania was stupefied. Surely the woman had not brought her all this way to tell her nothing. But she couldn't think of another question to ask. She sipped her tea and made small talk for a few minutes, asking the woman where she lived (the West Jerusalem neighborhood of German Colony), how many children she had (one boy, one girl, both in grade school), where she came from (a kibbutz outside of Haifa). She finished the tea and got up to go.

"Have you ever heard of Yuri Shabtai?" Zohari asked suddenly.

"No, who is that?" Rania sat back down.

"No one. I was just curious."

"He must be someone or you wouldn't have asked."

"Perhaps you want to look him up," was all the lawyer would say. Rania thanked her and left.

∗ ∗ ∗

Bassam was home when she arrived, playing "guess which hand the shekel is in" with Khaled at the dining table. She kissed them both on the cheeks before going into the kitchen to start dinner.

"I got mlochia," she called to Bassam. The soup made from *mlochia*, Egyptian spinach, was his favorite. She dumped the dark-green, pointy leaves into a big pot and filled it with water, then laid out a cloth to dry it on.

"Did you get it in Jenin?" Bassam asked from the kitchen doorway.

"No, Beit Hanina."

"You went to Al Quds?"

"Not Al Quds, Beit Hanina." It was the same thing, but she knew what he was getting at. It was dangerous for Palestinians with West Bank ID to sneak into Jerusalem. Beit Hanina was easy, so it didn't count.

"I thought you were going to Jenin," he said.

"I did. But after that, I had to go to Beit Hanina, to meet a lawyer." She hoped mentioning a lawyer would satisfy him that she really was working.

"What were you doing in Jenin?"

"I needed some information about the massacre."

"Why?"

She looked uneasily at Khaled, rummaging through his toys in the living room. In a low tone, she explained quickly about Colonel Wilensky and his connection to the foreign woman who died.

"Is it true you are supposed to be done with that investigation?" he asked.

She stiffened. "Where did you hear that?"

"From Abu Ziyad."

"What were you doing speaking to Abu Ziyad?" He detested the man, she knew. There had been some bad blood between his father and Abu Ziyad. A little while ago, Bassam had repeated rumors about Abu Ziyad using his position to get business deals for members of his family.

"He spoke to me. On the bus."

"It is not his business," she said. Khaled ran over to stand between them, clutching a toy gun.

"Play with me," he demanded. She made a face. Who had given him a toy gun? Probably his grandparents. All the boys in the village had them, but she hated them—ironically, since most of her coworkers carried guns.

"In a little while," she said. "I need to make dinner."

"Stop making dinner and play with me," he said. She turned around to yell at him that she was busy, but his face stopped her in her tracks. She had been so distracted since stumbling on Nadya's body, she couldn't remember the last time she had really played with him.

"What do you want to play?" she asked.

"Jesh and shabab." *Army and boys*, he said, pointing the gun at her. "I'm the jesh. Bang, you're dead!"

He took off running. She chased after him. He turned and shot at her again.

"It will be a short game if you kill me right away," she said. That seemed to end his interest in the gun. He tossed it aside and picked up a big rubber ball instead.

"Not in the house," she told him. "Bassam!" she called. "Take Khaled outside to play while I make dinner."

He obeyed, but she sensed something was on his mind. When she called them inside, they ate quickly in silence. The mlochia was rich and creamy.

"Go watch television at your grandmother's," Bassam told Khaled. Rania looked at him in surprise.

"What is going on?" she asked when they no longer heard little feet on the steps. She stacked the dishes in the sink and filled a small pot with warm water from the stove.

"Did the Israelis threaten our son?" he asked.

She turned from the sink, pale. "Abu Ziyad told you that?"

"Is it true?"

"I don't know," she said. "Abu Walid told me they did. But he might have made it up. Or Abu Ziyad might have. For some reason, they don't want me looking into the ajnabiya's death."

"You care so much about this foreigner that you are willing to endanger your own son?"

"A Palestinian boy was arrested," she said. "He confessed after a week of interrogation."

"Well, maybe he is guilty," Bassam said.

"I don't think so. I met him. He seemed like a sweet boy."

"You met him? When?"

"The day they arrested him. The day Benny and I went to Eilat."

"You didn't tell me." The statement hung between them. She could read the betrayal in his eyes. They had a closer relationship than any husband and wife she knew. Usually they bored one another with every little detail about their work. Now it must seem to him that she had cut him out of her life.

"I couldn't," she said. "It was so hard, sitting there, watching them beat him. I felt you would judge me. I judged myself."

"And so you are risking your own son to punish yourself?"

"That's not fair," she said, close to tears. "They are just trying to scare me."

"Well, *I'm* scared."

"What do you want me to do?" she asked. "Sacrifice someone else's son to save my own? Isn't that what collaborators do?"

She knew that would get him. He hated collaborators more than anything.

"You wouldn't be collaborating," he said. "Mustafa is a good man."

"Yes, but Abu Ziyad isn't, and he is the one who told the captain there was a threat to Khaled. I need to find out why he wants me off the case."

"So you will disobey Mustafa?"

She nodded. "But I think he will not object." She hoped she was right about that. She thought she had picked up subtle indications that Captain Mustafa was unhappy with the limitations imposed by his old friend. She could be seeing what she wanted to see, she realized.

in Ramallah to the police station in Salfit was a long and winding grapevine. The news could not have traveled here so far.

"Hamdililah," she said finally.

"Good," he said. "Please go to see Um Nader in Hares. Her husband is beating her again."

She groaned inwardly. Her least favorite type of interview in her least favorite village. The woman would show off her injuries and complain, but not want to do anything that Rania might suggest. She would flatly refuse to go to the shelter in Jericho. A good thing nearly everyone refused, or the little shelter would be overflowing. The thought of Jericho brought the vision of the car speeding its way there, taking her son from her. She put it out of her head.

She had one thing to do before she headed to Hares. Unfortunately, Abdelhakim was using the computer. She should have done her research last night at home, but she'd been too upset.

"I am sorry," she said to him. "I need to go out now. Is it possible I could look up something very quickly?"

"No problem," he mumbled. He stood behind her shoulder as she settled her hands on the keyboard. She pushed the wheeled chair back a little, nearly knocking into him. He shifted a bit, but stayed where he was. She couldn't ask him not to look. The computer was there for police business, and one detective's business was everyone's. Let him look, she decided. She was trying to keep a Palestinian boy from going to prison for a crime he didn't commit, and if no one else cared, so be it.

She quickly called up Google and typed in the name Yuri Shabtai, hoping she was spelling it correctly in English. There were three hits, two from the *Jerusalem Post* and one from *Haaretz*. She clicked on the first link.

"The article you have requested is no longer available," she read. She tried the next one and got the same result. *Come on!* she said under her breath. She clicked on the third link, the *Haaretz* one. After what seemed like an age the story came up. "Soldier Suicides Soar" the headline read. Suicides? She skimmed the article, looking for the name. There it was, in the next to last paragraph. "The most recent death was Air Force Reservist Yuri Shabtai, 25, of Kibbutz Ets Or, who was found dead in his barracks last month." The article was almost a year old.

Why had Shira Zohari mentioned this Shabtai to her? What connection could there be between a soldier who killed himself and Nadya's death? Of course, she didn't know there was any. Nadya's death might be—probably was—unrelated to whatever happened in Jenin, and this might not even be the right Yuri Shabtai. She had no idea if it was a common Israeli name or not.

On a whim, she switched to Google in Arabic and searched several phonetic spellings of the name. Nothing. She bet there would be more in the Hebrew press, but she couldn't read it. She looked again at the first two links. If only she could get to those articles. Whom could she ask for help? Not Abdelhakim, who was still looking intently over her shoulder. Not Benny, who was satisfied Fareed was as good a scapegoat as any. She thought of Chloe and her Israeli friend. Chloe had gotten the information from Malkah that led her to Zohari and Shabtai in the first place. She surrendered the computer to Abdelhakim and on the way to Hares, called Chloe and invited her over for dinner.

✶ ✶ ✶

She didn't need to cook, because she had the leftover mlochia and rice. She added hummus, labneh, and a salad of chopped cucumber and tomato. Chloe arrived at 5:30 as promised, bearing a box of chocolates and a toy cat that meowed when you pushed its tummy.

"Where's your son?" the American asked, looking around.

"He and his father have gone to Jericho. My husband's sister lives there."

"I'm sorry I won't get to meet them," Chloe said. She settled the stuffed animal in a corner of the sofa. "You can give him this when he returns."

"I'm sure he will love it. I'm sorry I didn't have time to make chicken," Rania said.

"I'm glad you didn't, because I don't eat meat," Chloe said. "I never know if it's more polite to warn people in advance, so they don't go to the trouble, or just eat around it, so they don't worry about making something special."

"I would rather know," Rania said. The house seemed unbearably quiet without Khaled running around, asking a million questions. Over dinner, Chloe talked about her life in California. Rania tried to imagine what it would be like to work in a big software company and go roller skating by the ocean. She found herself liking the American better. She was not as smug and self-righteous as she had seemed at first. After dinner, she made coffee and then worked the conversation around to her meeting with the attorney and what she had found on the internet. As she had expected, Chloe was eager to help. She called her friend Avi right away.

"His father is in television news," she told Rania. "He will be able to find the information in no time." Avi called back after fifteen minutes.

"Shabtai was one of those who testified in the Knesset about the incident in Jenin Camp," Chloe reported. "His testimony matched Wilensky's. The Palestinians fired at them, and they fired in self-defense. They confirmed that their targets were armed. The inquiry found that they followed the rules of engagement. Six months after the hearings, he killed himself, during his month of reserve service. No one knows why. He didn't leave a note. But Colonel Wilensky found the body."

"That is interesting," Rania said. "But I don't understand why this lawyer, Shira, thought it would help me."

"I don't either," Chloe said.

"Wait a minute," Rania said. "What date did you say he killed himself?"

"I didn't," Chloe said. "Is it important?"

"I think it could be."

Chloe took out her phone again, and Rania chewed her lip as she waited for her to finish her conversation. She didn't know what she expected, but she had a feeling this was big.

"April 7," Chloe reported.

"April 7, 2003?"

"That's right. What's the significance?"

"It was the anniversary of the shootings in Jenin."

"That's right," Chloe said. "But what does that tell you?"

"Nothing much."

"What makes you think Nadya's death had anything to do with Jenin?"

"It probably didn't," Rania replied. "Honestly, at first I just went there because it was something I could do. But there are a lot of unanswered questions about it."

"Maybe we can poke around at the Ministry of Defense," Chloe suggested.

"I would love to," Rania said. "But I don't think I would be able to get in."

Chloe looked embarrassed. "I meant me and Avi."

Rania nodded. Even though she knew she couldn't go, it hurt her feelings that she hadn't been invited.

* * *

Rania hoped she would not run into Maryam in the compound or on the road. She didn't need to worry about any of the others; they seldom got up as early as she did. Fortunately, she saw no one as she fed the chickens and took out the garbage. The only others waiting for the bus were people she knew slightly, who greeted her politely enough.

The bus was very late. Rania looked anxiously at her watch. She had left early today, figuring that these days while Khaled and Bassam were gone, she could make up for her unauthorized absences by being early to work. At this rate, she wouldn't even be on time. There must be a problem on the road. That was something Palestinians took for granted, like the weather. If she was late, others would be late as well. She couldn't do anything about it, but still she watched the second hand on her watch go around and around, and looked at the swelling crowd with annoyance. Perhaps when the small bus finally arrived, there would not even be room for all of them on it. She couldn't be one of those who had to wait for the next one. She edged her way to the front, near the road.

Thwack! Something hard and wet struck her arm, nearly knocking her into the man next to her. He helped her steady herself and handed her a handkerchief.

"What happened?" she asked him, checking the damage to her clothes. The yolk of an egg was running down her sleeve, a bit of shell clinging to the mess. She scrubbed at it with the handkerchief.

"Settlers," the man spat, pointing across the street where the Israeli buses stopped. She saw them, three young men with the ritual fringes and skull-caps of religious Jews, pointing and laughing. Whoever their God was, she thought, He could not be very nice. One of the young men held the carton of eggs, and she saw one of the others grab one and pull his arm back to throw.

Without thinking, she ran toward him and knocked him back just as he let go of the egg. It fell harmlessly in the middle of the street. She snatched the carton from the shocked youth and threw it, eggs and all, against the wall of the little stone shelter where they stood. She felt nothing but the pent-up fury of years of humiliation from scenes like this one, like the one two days ago at the checkpoint.

Calm now, she became aware that both the young men at the Israeli bus stop and the crowd at the Palestinian one were staring at her. She walked slowly back across the street. Thank heavens, the young men let her go, only yelling after her a filthy phrase in Arabic—doubtless the only Arabic words they knew. The Palestinian men at the bus stop had warm smiles for her as they slapped one another's palms. "Did you see her?" she heard one of them ask another. She couldn't remember when she had seen a group of people so happy besides at a wedding. She accepted their congratulations quietly. Something was happening to her. She wasn't quite sure what it was, or if she liked it or not. Maybe Chloe's fearlessness was rubbing off on her, or maybe hanging around Israelis like Benny and Nir was making her less in awe of their power.

The bus was coming. By popular unspoken agreement, she got on first and settled herself in the front seat behind the driver. The others piled in and they took off. Now that she had time to think, her mind returned to last night's meeting with Chloe, and what Avi had learned from the Israeli newspapers. The young soldier had waited six months after he testified at the Knesset hearing, then killed himself on the anniversary of the massacre. It seemed unlikely that it was a coincidence, but assuming his suicide had been out of remorse, she was still left with the question of why Shira Zohari had made sure she knew about Shabtai. She had a sudden thought. She dug in her purse for the card Abu Saif had given her, in case she returned to Jenin and needed a driver. He answered on the second ring.

"Abu Saif," she asked, "do you by any chance know when the young man you introduced me to, Mohammed, got his wheelchair?"

"Two years ago," the man responded.

"I meant exactly," she said.

"No, I don't remember exactly. In the spring, I think." Rania sighed. She shouldn't have expected the man to remember the exact date a young man who was not even a relative had gotten a wheelchair. "The spring, yes. I picked the chair up from the store in Tulkarem," Abu Saif added.

"You did? The medical supply store?"

"Yes, of course."

She could barely hang on long enough to say a civil goodbye. But after she hung up, she realized she had no idea where to get the phone number for the store. Once she got to work, someone would know someone who would know the number of the store. She couldn't explain to anyone why she wanted it, though. She quickly signaled the driver to stop and let her off. She crossed the road and waited tensely for a bus going the other way. On a good day, Tulkarem was less than half an hour's ride. Hopefully, this would be a good day.

It was. The blue and white Tanib bus sailed along the settler highway and pulled up opposite the checkpoint at Jbarra. The soldiers at the checkpoint didn't even glance at her as she passed. Once inside Tulkarem, it was easy to get directions to the medical supply store.

"Of course, the young man from Jenin," the owner of the store said. "I remember that chair. They wanted the very best of everything."

"Do you remember when it was ordered?" she asked, holding her breath for the answer.

"I will check for you," the man answered. He brought her a cup of tea before pulling an enormous sheaf of papers from a desk drawer. He went through them one by one, licking his finger between each one. Rania shifted from one foot to the other, wishing the tea were not too hot to drink. It would give her something to do other than concentrate on the time passing.

"Here it is," he said triumphantly. "April 2, 2003."

"You are positive that is the one?"

"Yes, absolutely positive."

"Thank you," she said. She gulped down the tea and raced out of the shop. Yuri Shabtai had killed himself the same week Mohammed had bought his expensive wheelchair. That, she thought, could not be a coincidence.

✶ ✶ ✶

She heard the silence descend when she walked into the police station two hours later. She looked around and guilty eyes shifted away from her. Only Abdelhakim met her gaze.

"Problems on the road?" he asked.

She wiggled a shoulder in a way that could mean yes, or could mean she was trying to work out an itch. She didn't want to lie to their faces. She could tell them about the settler boys, and their sympathies would over-whelm any curiosity about where she had been. She could imply that she had gone home to change her clothes, though the more discerning among them would surely notice the dark spot on her sleeve. Thinking about the egg striking her made her conscious of the sting on her arm.

"I had to do an errand in Tulkarem," she said finally. The recklessness that had made her confront the settler youths seemed to be following her even here. She unpinned her hijab and put it with her purse into the bottom drawer of her desk.

"I thought perhaps you had been in Jericho," he said. "Your husband and son are there, are they not?"

She raised her eyes and caught his in a death stare. "Who told you that?" she asked.

"Abu Ziyad," he said. "Was it supposed to be a secret?"

"Why was Abu Ziyad talking to you about my personal life?"

"He just mentioned it," the young man said. "I didn't mean to upset you." He took a pack of cigarettes and walked out to the street. He didn't need to go outside to smoke; most of the men in the station smoked constantly. She had obviously made him uncomfortable. Good.

She withdrew the hijab from the drawer and covered herself, then followed him outside. She felt her coworkers watching. Abdelhakim was nowhere in sight. He must have stepped into a shop for a coffee. That was fine; she wasn't looking for him. She crossed the street and took the marble stairs of the city hall two at a time. Abu Ziyad was sitting behind his big wooden desk, leaning back in his big leather chair. He stroked his heavy mustache as he talked on the phone. She barged in without knocking, ignoring the secretary who was objecting that she had no appointment.

"I will speak with you later," Abu Ziyad said into the telephone.

"How did you know my husband and son are in Jericho?" she demanded. "And why are you talking about it to my coworkers?"

"Bring Um Khaled some tea," he said to the secretary. A minute later, the woman returned with a tray and two cups.

"I don't want to drink tea with you." Keep your voice down, Rania instructed herself. She was trying to stop people gossiping about her, not give them more to talk about. "I want to know why you are spying on me, and talking about me to my husband and my coworkers."

"Please sit," he said and she perched on the edge of the armchair facing his desk.

"Why did you go to Jenin?" he asked.

She sat silently, weighing possible answers. Should she ask how he knew she had gone, or tell him it was none of his business? Or would anything she said make her look weaker? Perhaps she should simply walk out.

"You met Abu Saif and Mohammed Omar el-Khatib," he said. "Who asked you to talk with them? Did Captain Mustafa tell you to go there?"

Now she was really in a pickle. Technically, he was Captain Mustafa's boss. If he knew whom she had spoken to in Jenin, certainly he knew that it had to do with the Nadya case. He had told Mustafa to keep her out of the case. If she told him the captain knew what she was doing, she would make trouble for him. If she said he did not, she would make trouble for herself. If she said nothing, he might assume she was trying to protect the captain.

"No," she said.

"And Tulkarem?" he said. "You were in Tulkarem this morning, were you not? Did Mustafa know that you went there?"

"No," she said.

"Then why did you go?" he asked.

"I needed some information," she said.

"Information having to do with the foreign woman's death," he said.

"Yes."

"Didn't Captain Mustafa tell you to leave the girl's death to the Israelis?" he asked.

"Yes."

His phone rang. "Excuse me," he said to her. She found his politeness somewhat absurd, given the conversation they had been having. He swiveled his chair to face the window as he talked, and she took the opportunity to duck out. She dashed down the stairs and crossed back to the station. She snuck into the small bathroom and locked the door. When she emerged she was breathing normally. Abdelhakim was back at his desk. He looked up with a little smirk as Rania once again tucked away her purse and hijab.

"Um Khaled." Captain Mustafa was calling to her from his office door. She made herself cross the room slowly, but not too slowly. He held the door for her and closed it behind her. She didn't sit down. Whatever was coming, she wanted to take it on her feet. The captain settled himself behind the desk.

"Abu Ziyad told me about your conversation with him," he said.

"I'm sorry," she said.

"He said you told him I did not authorize you to go to Jenin. I explained to him that you didn't want him to know I had disregarded his orders."

"But..."

"He understands that I gave you permission to look into the foreign girl's death," he said.

"Thank you," she said.

"Your husband and son," he said. "Will they come home soon?"

"I hope so."

Chapter 28

Chloe put on her tightest jeans and a skimpy tank top. She gathered up her hair into a ponytail, taking care to tuck the gray hairs inside. With shades concealing the lines around her eyes, she thought she could pass for a graduate student. She covered the outfit with a baggy sweatshirt until she got to the road. Glancing around first to make sure no one from the village was in the area, she stripped off the hot sweatshirt and stuffed it into her backpack. She hitched to the Green Line and then caught a bus straight to the Kirya. The entire trip took her only forty-five minutes, but she was in another world.

The Kirya building dominates the Tel Aviv skyscape. It was built to look like a ship, and rises above the trendy town of Ramat Gan, home to the Diamond Exchange and stock market. Chloe sat on the steps to wait for Avi. It felt strange to be here. She rarely went into Israel. When she wanted to get away from Azzawiya, she went to Palestinian East Jerusalem or Ramallah. The streets here were full of fashionably dressed women and men with briefcases, virtually indistinguishable from the people in San Francisco. They bustled by on their way to and from business appointments and shopping lunches, or rushed to pick up their kids from well-regarded schools.

Avi bounded up the steps, his gangly arms and legs making her think of an orangutan. She got up as he neared her, but he gestured to her to sit and plopped down next to her.

"I have something to tell you," he said. "It's about Fareed."

"What about him?"

"The night before Nadya died, Fareed called and said she had found something in her employer's house that she thought they could use to get him to turn over her passport. He asked me to help. I was supposed to meet them in the morning, in the fields near the Green Line, and see what it was."

"So what was it?" Chloe asked.

"I don't know. I got to the meeting place, and they weren't there. I waited almost an hour, and then Fareed called. He told me Nadya was dead."

"He didn't kill her." She held her breath waiting for the answer.

"He said he didn't. I'm sure he didn't." He didn't sound so sure. "He told me he got to where they were supposed to meet, and found her body there. He was standing there trying to figure out what to do, and he saw the Israeli soldiers setting up the roadblock. He was afraid they would think he killed her, so he left her body there and ran. I took him to my house and we agreed that he would stay there, not go out, not talk to anyone, and I would go to Azzawiya and try to find out what was going on."

"That's why you came to the village that day," she said. He nodded.

"And then there was the whole thing with Abu Shaadi's land, and I got stuck there for hours."

She recalled how impatient he had been during dinner and how quickly he had taken off when they left Abu Shaadi's.

"When I got back, Fareed was gone. Maya hadn't seen him at all. He never got in touch with me, or with his dad or any of his friends. He just vanished, until he came back to turn himself in."

She contemplated all this. "If he was in love with Nadya, it must have been a big blow to find her dead. He might just have wigged out and needed to be by himself."

"But he doesn't know anyone else in Tel Aviv. Where did he go?"

"So what do you think it means?" she asked, not sure she wanted to hear the answer.

He shook his head. "I don't know—I felt like there were things he wasn't telling me."

"Like?"

"Like maybe he knows who killed her—or thinks he might…"

"Gelenter," she insisted.

"It's possible," he said slowly. "He could have seen something, and be afraid to tell anyone, but it doesn't seem that likely. I thought maybe one of his friends did something to her, because she was Muslim but not practicing, the way she was dressed …"

"Like an honor killing? But no one in Azzawiya would have had any reason to care about Nadya's virtue."

"They might if they thought Fareed was going to marry her. Especially if they found out somehow that she was pregnant."

"I don't see how they would have found that out," she objected. "It's much more likely the father of the baby, Gelenter or this Wilensky or whoever, killed her to keep her from destroying his pious reputation."

"But why would they need to kill her? They could just fire her, or have her arrested and sent back to Uzbekistan."

She told him what Abu Ziyad had told Jaber about Nadya being a spy. He considered it, absently stroking his small beard.

"Do you think it could be true?" she asked. She realized that if he had something to say, he would say it, but she was nervous and unable to stand silence.

"I guess so," he said. "It would make sense."

"But if she was a spy..."

"People in Azzawiya would have had more reason to want her dead than people in Elkana," he finished.

She didn't like where this conversation was going. If Nadya was a spy, and she was hanging around with Fareed, pretending to be in love with him, that suggested Fareed was involved in something the Israeli authorities were really interested in. Unless, she supposed, the girl had just been told to get close to someone in Azzawiya, and Fareed had been the unlucky, soft-hearted guy to fall for her setup.

"Wait." She stopped her own train of thought. "If anyone from Azzawiya had killed Nadya, surely they wouldn't have dumped her body on their own land."

"Probably not if they had a choice," he said. "But remember the army was there. If they planned to move her body, the blockade would have stopped them."

"Well, I don't believe it," she said, more to herself than him. "This Gelenter and his friend Wilensky had a lot more to lose. We're here to find out what it was. So let's go."

She was doing research in Israel for her dissertation in international relations, she explained to the guard at the door. She was focusing on the international reaction to the Jenin Camp battle—she was careful not to say "massacre," and she had read about the incident in which Colonel Wilensky and his unit had killed several militants. She really wanted to get his perspective on that incident; none of what she had read had quoted him directly. She was very disappointed to hear that he no longer worked at the ministry.

The guard didn't even want to let them through the metal detectors, but Avi did some fast talking. He followed a young woman in a very short skirt into an inner sanctum and returned with two temporary badges in his hand.

Could anyone tell her how to get in touch with the colonel? Chloe asked upstairs.

No one could, but they were surprisingly unsuspicious about why she was asking.

"Do you know why he left the ministry?" she asked the gum-chewing woman who said she had been Colonel Wilensky's assistant.

"I'm not allowed to talk about that," said the young woman. Chloe silently sounded out the Hebrew letters on her left breast to discern that her name was Hilla.

"But you know?" Chloe made it sound like she doubted it.

She had guessed right. Hilla stuck her chin up in the air. "Of course I know."

Hilla spoke English, so Chloe thought she could establish a rapport. She leaned toward her conspiratorially. "I heard," she said, "that Mr. Gelenter had something to do with getting rid of Colonel Wilensky."

Hilla's chest heaved. "Who told you that?" she demanded.

"A confidential source," Chloe threw her own game back at her. "What do you know about his relationship with Mr. Gelenter?"

"They are friends since the army," Hilla said. "They were like David and Jonathan around here. There's Nir now, why don't you talk to him?" and before Chloe could say, no, no, I'm sure he's busy, she was showing them into Gelenter's office.

Chloe kicked herself. They were underprepared for a face-to-face with Gelenter. She had wanted to build up the case against him before confronting him. Avi seemed unhappy too, and in a second, she realized why. Gelenter clapped the young man on the shoulder.

"Avi," he said jovially in Hebrew. "What brings you here?"

Avi looked at Chloe. She should have realized that he and Gelenter would know each other. He had said his father and Wilensky had done their military service together, and Hilla had just said that Gelenter and Wilensky were friends from the army. She must have really meant the air force, Israelis generally called all the forces "the army." Gelenter must have also served with Avi's father.

Given their relationship, she hoped Avi would make up a story that would satisfy Gelenter, but he was waiting for her to do it.

"I'm doing some research about what happened in Jenin during Operation Defensive Shield," she began. "Avi told me his uncle was out of the country, so I thought you would be the next best person to talk to."

"I don't know anything about it," he said. "I wasn't there."

"But Colonel Wilensky is your friend," she objected. "He must have talked to you about it."

"Why are you so interested?" he asked her.

"I want to write about it."

"Why that incident in particular?"

"I'm comparing reports in the international press to the perception of the incident in Israel. I read about the Knesset hearings, but didn't find much information about what was said. The panel concluded that there was no wrongdoing, but Colonel Wilensky resigned immediately afterward. It seems like there must be more to the story."

"What more? What do you mean?"

He narrowed his eyes at her, as if trying to figure out where he had seen her before. She was sure she had never met him before, but she supposed she could have hitched a ride with him, on her travels around the West Bank.

"Well, there is the matter of Yuri Shabtai," she said. "He testified in the hearings, and the next time he went on reserve duty, he killed himself."

His face did a series of contortions and he jumped to his feet. He was well over six feet. She felt every inch of him towering over her.

"I know who you are!" he exploded. "You're the one who has been harassing my daughter. Do you know how much trouble you've caused her?"

"What are you talking about?" she asked ingenuously.

He jabbed a button on his phone and barked something into the speaker. Chloe wanted to run, but she also wanted to know how Gelenter knew she had given Malkah the Btselem information, and what kind of trouble it had gotten her into. And now she couldn't run because he was standing in front of her, blocking her path.

"She described the person who gave her that subversive literature," he growled. "I know it was you. Now they found it in the school and she won't get into ulpena and her life will be ruined."

"What do you mean?" Chloe asked.

"I don't know who you are, but I won't let you make my daughter into an Israel hater."

Chloe was a jumble of emotions. Fear was at the top, because he was still standing very close and so worked up, she thought he might hit her. Her better judgment said she should continue denying his accusations, but pride in Malkah's desire to move beyond the narrow settlement world won out.

"Malkah's a special, beautiful girl," she said. "You support her independence. It will make her a better citizen, and a better Jew."

"Don't tell me how to raise my family!" he shouted, and then the room was full of men shouting in Hebrew, grabbing at her and Avi.

She expected the SHABAK, for certainly that was who these unpleasant people were, to march them to some dank cell for questioning, or beating, or both. But they all stood around in the hall, just outside Gelenter's office, with bureaucrat bees zooming past them, as the men demanded their IDs. Chloe gave them her passport copy, which brought the expected "Mah zeh?" and remonstrations, but eventually they settled for it and stepped aside to call in the numbers to someone they presumably expected to spit back information about what terrorist cell she was working for.

Not for the first time, she marveled that once the Israeli authorities had her ID, they seemed to believe they didn't have to watch her. She was free to wander the hall, and did, watching them from a small distance, one eye always on the open door that led to the stairwell. At one point the men got anxious when they didn't see her, but once they caught sight of her, they immediately turned away again.

They were more interested in Avi than in her. They kept going back and forth between asking him questions and huddling in a big group around his ID. The guy who had taken hers had put it in his pocket after making his phone call, and was now standing in the doorway to one of the offices, chatting with a young woman he found more compelling than Chloe. She wondered that Gelenter wasn't doing anything to protect the son of one of his friends. But of course, Avi hadn't said his father was friends with Gelenter. Gelenter had seemed pleased to see him, but that didn't mean anything. Avi had also said his parents were liberals, and Gelenter was religious and a settler. Maybe he saw this as a way to settle some old score with Avi's father, the famous newscaster.

Two of the SHABAK were talking to Avi now. She heard them say that he was "wanted." They were insisting on something, voices climbing, and now he was sitting down and one of the agents was taking out handcuffs while two others yanked his arms back and up over his head. Chloe thought about going to his aid, but self-interest got the better of her. He was the one with good family connections. He would be okay. She would hardly be able to help him, but she might be able to help herself.

She ducked into the stairwell. She didn't really expect to make it. All the way down the six flights of stairs and onto the street, she waited for footsteps in pursuit, voices screaming her name, but none came. She jumped onto the first bus that arrived and realized with amazement that she was safe, and Avi was a prisoner.

Chapter 29

Rania put off going home as long as she could. That morning, she had gotten out of the house even more rapidly than usual, but the emptiness had still overwhelmed her. The small flat had felt cavernous, the walls themselves reproaching her. She roamed around the station straightening things up. She washed all the squat coffee glasses and dried them with a dirty cloth, even though they would be cleaner if she left them to dry overnight. She read through her notes on the Nadya case for the hundredth time, looking for something she might have missed. She wondered why Chloe hadn't called to report on her trip to the Ministry of Defense. It was unlike the American not to want to chat at length about whatever she had learned. Probably they had not gotten in at all, and she didn't want Rania to be disappointed. She called Chloe's number, but only reached the voicemail.

The station was starting to feel oppressive too. She walked out into the street. It was not a busy time. People who lived in the city were having dinner with their families, and people who only came there to work had already left. She strolled into a store piled high with dark purple eggplants and cauliflowers the size of basketballs. She started to pick things up, but then changed her mind. If she bought them, she would need to cook, and that would only remind her that there was no one to eat with.

A small group of women students in matching black jilbabs and white headscarves walked slowly toward her. As she passed them she heard them laughing at some slightly off-color joke. If only she had friends to laugh with like that, she might be looking forward to these days on her own as a time to catch up with them. Growing up in the camp, she had never been alone. There had been her sister Maysoon, one year younger—they had been inseparable. And once she had joined the Fatah movement, she had been part of a

208

tight circle of young women, bonded by danger and ideals. If she had grown up here in the north, no doubt she would have found soul mates here too. But she had come to Mas'ha as a young bride, soon to be a mother, and since Khaled she had been so busy with her work and her family, she had had no time to make friends. The world her husband's family inhabited felt like a tightly closed book to her. She was three times an outsider: she was not from the village, she was a refugee, and she had an unusual career that she loved. Perhaps she could call Maysoon to come for a visit, but then she would have to admit what she had done, and her sister would probably judge her harshly too. Maysoon wanted nothing beyond her husband and four children.

The savory smells of *shawrma* mingled with the sugary aromas of the pastry shop, reminding her that she had not eaten since a hastily grabbed breakfast. She peeked into the shawarma shop. Dared she walk in and sit at a table by herself? There were a few men gathered in front, watching a soccer match on television. They probably wouldn't pay any attention to her if she sat in the back, and she didn't care what they thought. But sitting there would feel even lonelier than being alone in her house.

The man whose dirty white apron marked him as the proprietor was looking quizzically at her, machete poised over the revolving spit of meat.

"Just some hummus," she said. "And tahini salad and some fried eggplant."

He packed the food up for her and she put down two shekels. She shoved a piece of eggplant into her mouth before stepping out into the street. It would tide her over until she got home. At least she had settled the question of what she was going to do for dinner, but not how she would pass the time until morning.

Her mother-in-law was in the garden when she entered the compound. Rania stifled a sigh. She didn't know if Bassam had told his family he was going away, or why, but she didn't want to answer any questions about it.

"Masa il-kheir." *Evening of joy*, she said.

"Masa il warad." *Evening of flowers*, Um Bassam replied. The fragrant blossoms she was cutting must have inspired the variation on the standard response, evening of light. Rania liked the idea of an evening of flowers. She squatted next to the old woman and breathed deeply, savoring the slightly spicy scent.

"Do you want to eat with us?" her mother-in-law asked.

Rania wondered who "us" was. Maryam and Amir and their kids, she supposed. Well, she wasn't going to find out.

"Thank you," she said. "But I'm tired. I'll eat some hummus and then rest." She gestured with her bag of groceries.

"Hmmph," Um Bassam said. "That's not dinner."

"It's good enough for me," Rania said. Surely her mother-in-law would agree with that, inadequate food for an inadequate woman.

"Enough, you'll eat with us," the old woman said. She stood easily, her large frame surprisingly limber, and rubbed her hands together briskly to shake off the dirt. She left the shears where they lay in the grass and carried her basket of flowers up the stairs. Rania had no choice but to follow.

No one else was in the upper flat. A white-gowned cleric was droning away on television, gesticulating as he predicted the fall of Israel and America. Rania wondered if she could get away with saying she needed to wash up, and escape downstairs until the others arrived. She peeked into the kitchen. Um Bassam was arranging her flowers into vases, her lips moving slightly in conversation with herself. Rania watched her silently for a few seconds. The old woman always seemed so content, it had never occurred to Rania that she might be lonely. Khaled was her most constant companion; she picked him up from school every day. Perhaps inviting Rania had not been some hidden way of reproaching her with her the absence of her husband and son, but merely a thought that two women alone could keep one another company.

"Can I help you?" she asked.

The old woman handed her the two vases. Rania retreated to the living room and considered where to put them. She had never noticed flowers in her mother-in-law's apartment. In fact, she never spent enough time there to notice. When she got home from work, she was always anxious to get started cooking. If she came upstairs to let Khaled know she was home, he generally heard her at the door and came running, so she seldom walked in. More often, she just called up the stairs and went straight into her own house. When they ate together, which did not happen often, her mother-in-law normally came downstairs, rather than the other way around. She knew little about her mother-in-law's life, she realized, and she had never really wondered about it.

She placed one of the vases on the dining table and the other on the coffee table. Doubtless, Um Bassam would move them with a reproachful look.

She didn't. She entered the dining area bearing a bowl piled high with makluube—rice cooked with fried cauliflower and eggplant and threaded with silver noodles. She plunged a large spoon into the mound and set it on the table already set with two plates. Rania followed her to the kitchen. The old woman ladled two bowls of a thin white soup and handed them to Rania to put on the table. She brought out the ubiquitous cucumber and tomato salad and rounds of pita bread, and they were ready to eat.

Her mother-in-law had been waiting for her, Rania thought. That's why she had been out in the garden so late. But why had she said "us"? Was it possible that after all these years she didn't remember that her husband was dead? Did she still set two places at every meal? She couldn't ask. She would just have to wonder.

She took a sip of soup. "Delicious."

"How is your work?" the old woman asked.

"Okay," Rania said warily.

"What about the girl they found in the fields?" They found, not you found, Rania noted with irritation.

"The Israelis think a boy from Azzawiya killed her," she responded. "I am not sure."

"The newspaper said she was a prostitute in Elkana," Um Bassam said. Rania had to laugh. It was so typical of the Palestinian press to get things garbled. It didn't really matter, but it gave her something to talk about.

"She was a prostitute in Eilat, before she came to Elkana. In Elkana she took care of a rich man's children."

"They are all rich in Elkana."

"True."

"Why did my son go away?"

"He took Khaled to visit Zeina."

"You didn't want to go?"

"I have to work."

"I miss Khaled."

"So do I." Rania smiled. The one thing she had never doubted about her mother-in-law was how much she loved her grandson.

"Last week, he saw the big rooster pecking one of the little chicks. And he pointed to the rooster and said, 'That one is the Yahudi.'"

Um Bassam chuckled at the memory. Rania put her spoon down. "What did you say?"

"I said he was right."

"That's not good. 'Jew' doesn't mean a bully. It's like saying 'terrorist' means 'Palestinian.'"

"It does."

They both laughed at that. Certainly no one used the word *irhabi*, terrorist, to refer to the Israeli settlers who shot at Palestinians in the fields.

Rania was quiet, fishing in her mind for a safe subject. "Years ago," her mother-in-law interrupted her thoughts, "we were friends with the Yahud."

Rania frowned. "When? Which Jews?"

"Before the Intifada. The settlers from Elkana used to come to shop at the stores. Some of them even invited us to their houses."

"You didn't go?"

"Of course we did. Why wouldn't we? Their houses were on our land anyway."

"What happened then?"

"After the Intifada they built the big fence around the settlement. They put guards to keep us out. Some of the same children whose families we visited threw stones at our store windows."

"Bassam never mentioned it."

"He never wanted us to go. Even when he was little, he hated the Yahud."

Rania nodded. Bassam was opposed to "normalization"—building friendly relations with the occupiers. He believed the Palestinians should fight for their freedom. She did too. It was one of the things that had drawn them together in college.

"He was always stubborn," Um Bassam continued. "Like Khaled."

"It's good for Palestinian boys to be stubborn," Rania said. "If they were not, we would be gone by now."

"Not only the boys," Um Bassam said. Rania looked at her in surprise. "It's good you did not give up your work," the old woman went on.

"But... I thought you didn't want me to go back."

"True. I was lonely. I wanted you to be at home, so I would have someone to talk to."

Rania had never thought about that. Would she have stayed home to keep her mother-in-law company, if she had known? She shuddered even thinking about it, and then felt ashamed.

"I'm sorry," she murmured. The old woman waved her apology away.

"Maalesh." *Don't worry about it.* "I was also envious of you."

"Of me? But you didn't want to be a policewoman."

"No, of course not. But I wanted to be a nurse."

"So why couldn't you? That's a perfectly okay job for a woman."

"My family had no money for girls to go to school. I married into a wealthy family, to help my parents."

"But if you had no money, how could you marry into wealth? What about your dowry?"

"I was very beautiful." Rania nearly laughed. Then she looked—really looked—at her mother-in-law for the first time. She didn't exactly see beauty, but she saw what probably accounted for it—strength of character. She had Bassam's soft doe eyes.

"So you made sure your daughters could go to school," Rania said.

The old woman nodded. "They were so smart. Dunya got the highest grade on her tawjihi, boys or girls." The tawjihi was the exam that high school graduates had to pass if they wanted to go on to college. They spent an entire year studying for it.

"What about Bassam?" Rania asked.

"He only did so-so."

"Funny, he never mentioned that either." She would have to rib him about it—if he ever came back. Suddenly the reality of why she was having this tête-à-tête with Um Bassam came flooding back to her and she was no longer hungry. She gathered up the dishes quickly and piled them into the sink.

"You are tired," her mother-in-law said. "Go downstairs and rest. I will finish here."

"I don't mind," Rania said. Surprised, she realized she meant it. She would rather be here with the old woman than alone in her house.

"Go and watch television," Rania said. "I will make some tea."

"If you like."

Rania put on the kettle and finished the few dishes before it boiled. The leftovers were already in covered pots on the stove. They would be fine there. She added a tablespoon of loose tea to the kettle.

"Do you want sage or mint?" she called. No answer.

She went into the living room. Her mother-in-law was snoring in the armchair across from the television, head lolling to one side. So much for an evening of female bonding. It was just as well. She had had a hard day, and she would no doubt have another one tomorrow. Seeing Um Bassam sleep made her own eyes feel heavy. She put away the tea things and wondered if she should write a note. Not necessary, she decided. She tiptoed out, closing the door very softly behind her.

Chapter 30

Chloe wouldn't feel safe until she got out of Tel Aviv. She didn't think the SHABAK would look hard for her, but she couldn't be sure. Nir Gelenter probably knew she was staying in Azzawiya. She had better stay away from there for a few days. She caught a *sherut* to the bus station and another to Jerusalem. While she waited for the van to fill, she called Maya and told her about Avi.

"Once I get to Jerusalem, I can call a lawyer to get him out," Chloe offered.

"Never mind, I'll take care of it," came the hoped-for response.

Chloe told herself not to worry. Avi would be fine. He was an Israeli, with good connections. She resolutely put aside the nagging voice that said she should be wherever he was, taking whatever abuse he was experiencing. Probably he would be out in an hour, while in an hour, she could have been on a plane.

By early evening she was relaxing on the balcony of the Austrian Hospice, a palace-like hostel in the middle of the Old City, where the nuns let her keep some of her things in a room that wasn't usually used. She always felt a little guilty when she crossed the checkpoint into Jerusalem, knowing that her friends in the West Bank could not do so except at great risk. It was their holy city, the capital of their hoped-for country, and they couldn't set foot inside it, while she, to whom it was just another beautiful, historically rich place, could go and come as she pleased. She studiously avoided the Western, Israeli side of the divided city, but she imagined that would be small comfort to someone like Rania, with her keen sense of justice. The fact was that now and then she needed somewhere to get away from the claustrophobia of the village, to fade into a place where she didn't stand out so clearly. It gave her a chance to remember the person she was back home. She had never needed this escape so much as she did tonight.

She ordered a Taybeh beer—the only Palestinian brew, produced in a Christian town in the Ramallah area—and sat sipping it, watching the shoppers scurrying this way and that in the market down below. She scrunched up her face at the sight of the brown-shirted groups of young settlers, paramilitary groups with their guns. Had they chosen to wear brown shirts deliberately as an homage to the Nazi youth? She had never gotten up the courage to ask them.

Her reverie was broken by the sight of a familiar figure, striding through the *souq*. She first recognized the way the burgundy-tinted hair was tossed back, and then the long legs nearly galloping along the cobblestones. She was about to call out, but she felt too conspicuous screaming "TINA" through the Old City like Marlon Brando, so she grabbed her key and phone, and tore down the stairs.

Tina had stopped to finger some scarves being sold three for twenty shekels. Chloe sidled past where the other woman was engrossed in her shopping, then turned and started walking purposefully back the way she had come. She avoided looking in Tina's direction until she nearly collided with her quarry.

"Chloe!" The other woman's face lit up.

"Hey, Tina. I didn't know you were in Jerusalem."

"Yeah, I live here."

Oh, right. Staying with the aunt in Beit Sefafa. "So," said Chloe, "what are you up to?"

"Oh, I'm just doing a little shopping."

Chloe looked up and down and didn't see any bags. Tina followed her eyes and laughed.

"I'm a terrible shopper. I never buy anything the first time around, and always end up coming back to the first place I looked."

"Are you looking for something in particular, or…?"

"Well, I need some presents for my aunt and my cousins, and also for my family back home."

"Are you going home soon?" Just her luck, to fall for someone who's leaving in a few days. *Whoa, girl, you're getting ahead of yourself,* she told her id, but nonetheless she was relieved when Tina answered, "Oh, no, I just like to do my shopping a little bit at a time."

"Would you like some company?"

"Company would be great, but actually, I'm kind of tired of shopping. I thought you were in a hurry to get someplace, but if not…"

Chloe took the plunge. "How about dinner?"

"Great. Where should we go?"

Chloe was about to suggest Pappa Andrea's in the Christian Quarter, with its romantic rooftop view of Al Aqsa Mosque. But then she remembered that she had left her purse with her money in it on the balcony of the Austrian Hospice. If Tina went with her to get it, she would see that Chloe had been sitting drinking a beer, not doing errands in the souq, and her little jig would be up.

"I have to pick some things up at the place where I'm staying. Why don't we pick a place, and I'll meet you there in fifteen minutes or so?"

"Well, why don't I come with you? I'm not in a hurry."

She should have known Tina would suggest this. She would have to fudge it in another way. She led the way to the Hospice, and Tina oohed and aahed over the elegant courtyard.

"My stuff's down here," Chloe said, leading the way to the basement dorm room she had all to herself in this slow season. Tina perched on one of the cots, as Chloe stripped off her t-shirt and stood in her bra, looking for a clean shirt to wear.

"Think it'll stay warm tonight?" she asked Tina, turning to face her. She was gratified to see the jade-colored eyes assessing the bra and its contents. She was glad she'd worn the lacy red one.

"I'm always cold," said the musical voice on the other bed.

Chloe chose a filmy white cotton blouse. It was part of her Jerusalem wardrobe, too sheer to wear in the West Bank. The red bra would show through it, unless she wore a camisole. Should she or shouldn't she? She found one and held it up, silently asking Tina's opinion. Tina shook her head slightly.

"I just have to go to the bathroom, be right back," Chloe said and then dashed upstairs to retrieve the things she had left on the balcony. But wait, how was she going to hide the journal and purse? Tina was going to know she hadn't found them in the bathroom. In the end, she just walked boldly into the room. Thankfully, Tina was browsing through the books she'd left on the table, and didn't look up until she had put the things down.

"I have a great idea," Chloe said, thinking of a surefire way to impress. "Do you like Chinese food?"

"I don't go to West Jerusalem," Tina said, but Chloe shook her head.

"There's this great place in East Jerusalem. But we need to call, because they close randomly. Let's go upstairs, there's no phone service down here."

There was no answer at Dallas Chinese Restaurant. Chloe could hardly contain her disappointment. It would have been perfect; she knew the owner, and it would have been empty, *the better to seduce you with, my dear.* While she was trying to think of a suitable alternative, her phone rang.

"When do you want to come?" demanded Abu Tariq, the proprietor of Dallas.

"Fifteen minutes," Chloe told him.

"Okay, I will save a table for you," he said. Save a table? Any time she had ever been there, she and whoever she was with had been the only customers. She and Tina walked breezily out Damascus Gate and up Salah e-Din to AzZahra Street. Dallas was empty except for Abu Tariq and his two sons.

"Hello, kiif halik," he greeted her in his usual mixture of English and Arabic.

"How are you all?" Chloe said in Arabic. "This is my friend, Tina." While Abu Tariq greeted her friend, Chloe turned to his son, Tariq.

"How is the university?" she asked him in English.

"Fine, fine," answered the blind boy, turning toward her voice. "Very much work."

She ordered her usual, eggplant with garlic sauce and vegetarian chow mein, and then took Tina into the kitchen to see the Chinese recipes on the wall. She explained that there used to be Chinese workers there before the Intifada, in the days when Jerusalem teemed with tourists, and adventurous young Israelis used to cross into East Jerusalem to eat dinner. She opened the cabinet where the chopsticks were hidden, and dug out pairs in dusty paper wrappings.

When their food was served, Chloe picked up her chopsticks. She saw Tina hesitate. There were forks on the table and Tina half-reached for one, but Chloe could see she was embarrassed.

"You don't know chopsticks?" Chloe asked.

"We don't have them much in Australia."

"Here, hold them like this." Chloe demonstrated the correct positioning of three fingers, but Tina couldn't quite figure it out. "Let me help you," Chloe said.

She walked around the table and standing behind Tina, took her right hand and curled it properly around the chopsticks. For balance, she rested her left hand lightly on Tina's shoulder, bending down so that her lips were very close to the small hairs at the nape of Tina's neck. Her hair smelled vaguely lavendery. Once Tina had the hang of eating with the sticks, Chloe went back to her place. She couldn't decide if she was moving too fast or not. Tina didn't seem to object, but she also didn't exactly encourage the physical contact.

Chloe hoped that Tina wasn't a stone femme, who wouldn't take an ounce of initiative. She herself was hardly butch, and she was too insecure in romantic situations to want to be the sole aggressor. She told Tina about her afternoon, drawing it out into a wonderful adventure story. When she got to the part about Avi being arrested, she felt a twinge: she was out having a nice dinner with a beautiful woman, while he was probably sitting in some holding cell, or worse.

"I can't believe you had the nerve to run away," Tina commented. "I don't think I would've."

"Well, in the States I would never run away from the police, because it would make it worse. But here, the worst they can do is deport me, and deported is deported is deported."

"But aren't they more likely to deport you if you run away?"

"I don't think so. I don't even think the guys you run away from have much say in whether you get deported or not. They're most likely to deport us because we saw something they didn't want us to see."

"I'll try to remember that, if I'm ever arrested."

"It might be different for you, though," Chloe thought out loud. "Because they would consider you a Palestinian. Do you have a Palestinian ID card?"

"No. Just my Australian passport. But it says where I was born."

Chloe suddenly felt not so heroic. Maybe it wasn't her smarts that had saved her today, but just the fact that she was a white American. She wanted to change the subject.

"So, what kind of counseling center is it that you're working at?"

"It's for women and kids dealing with domestic violence."

"That's great. I mean, not great that they're dealing with it, but that there's a place for them to get help."

"Yeah, it's run by a really wonderful woman. She studied in the States."

"There are a lot of good DV counseling centers in the States, which is good because there's a lot of DV."

"I think there's a lot of that everywhere."

"Is that what you do at home too?"

"Oh, no. I'm a physical education teacher."

Chloe nearly choked on her tea.

"What's so funny?" Tina looked hurt.

"Nothing. It's just …" She had been about to say "a stereotype," but suddenly she caught herself. Tina had never actually said she was a lesbian. What if Chloe had read the situation all wrong?

"Just what?"

"I'm so hopeless at sports. I never thought I'd have dinner with someone who teaches them."

"Oh." Tina's expression said she wasn't quite believing that explanation, but was willing to let it pass. "No one's really hopeless at sports. You just had bad teachers."

"Well, I think I disagree about the hope, but you're sure right about the teachers."

The street was still when they left the restaurant. This midweek night at the beginning of spring, they were the only ones out. It was a little creepy, Chloe thought. Tina must have thought so too. She craned her head this way and that.

"I'd better find a cab," she said. "I don't want to wait for a service."

"What's your hurry?" said Chloe. "Come to the Jerusalem Hotel for a nightcap." Nightcap. An archaic word she'd never used before. But she didn't know if Tina drank beer, so it seemed safer to leave it open.

"I don't know," Tina said. "It's getting really late. I'm afraid there won't be transportation if I wait."

She hadn't said she was too tired, or that she needed to get home.

"Well, if you don't mind taking a cab, it seems like there are always some around late."

"Yeah, but a lot of the drivers don't like to go that far—and it can be really expensive."

"You could spend the night at the Hospice. There's no one else in my room right now."

"How much is it?"

"They give me a discount—they'll probably let you stay tonight for free." This wasn't exactly true—she would pay them something for Tina. But better sweeten the deal now, and deal with logistics later.

"Oh, right then. Why not?" Chloe almost swooned at the lovely sound of the words in Tina's musical voice.

"Wait," she said, as Tina turned them around toward the foot of Nablus Road and the elegant Jerusalem Hotel. Usually Chloe loved to sit on their patio, which was cool even on hot summer nights, sipping Taybeh and listening to the intense political conversations happening around her in five or six languages. But she didn't want to share Tina. "The J Hotel is probably really crowded. Why don't we go back to the Hospice and have a coffee or a glass of wine on the terrace?"

She held her breath as the other woman considered it. "Lovely," she said at last and Chloe nearly danced them over the cobblestones, through the gate, and up the wide stone steps.

Two glasses of wine and an hour and a half of what she hoped was scintillating conversation later, Chloe was at a loss again. She and Tina sat toe to toe, facing each other on two narrow cots in her subterranean dorm room. She couldn't figure out how to bridge the few inches between them. She had made all the moves so far, and Tina had certainly seemed willing enough, but Chloe didn't have enough confidence to take the final plunge. There was nothing else to do, she decided, but go to sleep. She arched, stretching her arms wide.

"I'm wiped," she said, standing up. She turned a little away from Tina and pulled the filmy blouse over her head. While it covered her eyes, she felt hands over hers, tugging it the rest of the way. When she could see again, Tina's lips were brushing hers, her silky curls teasing Chloe's cheek. Their tongues lapped at each other, and at whatever exposed skin they could find. Tina's found its way into Chloe's ear, drawing a little yelp. They laughed and separated.

Chloe plunged her hands into the back pockets of Tina's jeans, bracing herself so her belly touched Tina's where it poked out from under her tank top, revealing a little rhinestone-studded gold ring. For moments, they were lost in each other's mouths, tongues jamming into the depths, as if they could find each other's truest words there.

"Let's take off our clothes," Tina suggested.

Chloe had a flash of embarrassment. What would the other woman think about her jiggling curves, the heavy hair at the top of her thighs? She was no American Idol, and Tina was a goddess. But Tina could see what she was, and she obviously wanted her. She undid the button and zipper of Tina's jeans and eased them down her sturdy brown legs. Tina stepped out of them.

Chloe worked her hands into the flesh at the base of the other woman's butt, stealing into her underwear, where the wetness was already spreading. Tina's legs were trembling as Chloe lowered the panties and sank to her knees. Her tongue and finger worked in tandem, tweaking the clitoris and labia, while Tina's hands kneaded Chloe's curly mop, her nails digging into the scalp a little, reminding Chloe of the cat she had left in San Francisco.

Tina guided them onto one of the beds. She sat on Chloe's face, her hand thrusting in and out of Chloe's cunt while Chloe continued to lick and lick and lick. Chloe felt so open she was afraid she would scream, and bring the sisters running to see what was wrong. It had been so long since she had really touched anyone, been touched. She felt each push into her echoing around her body like an electric current, resonating in the little nerves in her ears and behind her neck, sending shivers down her spine. She wanted their loving to go on and on, not to crescendo too quickly. She pulled back, and Tina's hand slid out, covered with Chloe's creaminess. Chloe licked a little of it off. She couldn't remember ever doing that before, ever tasting herself. She licked Tina's fingers, slowly, one by one.

They lay face to face now, studying each other's features, arms entwined. Chloe felt the tiny hairs on her back standing on end. She thought if she really tried, she would be able to read Tina's mind. She brushed her cheek up and down the length of Tina's face, feeling Tina's smoothness against her own roughness, and knowing that the friction was fueling Tina's passion. She covered Tina's body with little kisses, from the tip of her nose to the joint of her ankles, enjoying the challenge of seeing if she could make each kiss a hair smaller than the last. "Don't let this night be a dream," she thought. "Don't let me wake up and be alone."

She worked her way back up Tina's body with her mouth, and when she reached her crotch she again buried her face deep in the salt warmth, feeling like a nursing baby who could not be satiated. Tina's hand stroked Chloe's clitoris, sending ripples so intense through her body that she bucked like someone struck by lightning. Then they were coming in rhythm, one heaving, the other pushing, over and over, rocking back and forth. Tina was starting to make too much noise. Chloe put a hand over her mouth and Tina chomped down on it; she would have a welt the next day, but it would only remind her how happy she had been in this moment, when they were melting together.

Chapter 31

When Chloe woke up she could tell it was late, even in the dim light afforded by the small window.

"I'm hungry," Tina announced.

"I know the perfect place," Chloe responded.

"Another perfect place?" Tina asked. Chloe blushed and nodded.

Showered and composed, they slipped into a booth at Amigo Emil's. Abu Emil, the owner, threw his arms wide when he saw Chloe.

"It has been so long," he said, taking her hand in both of his. "And who is this lovely lady?"

"My friend, Tina," Chloe told him. He took Tina's hand as he had hers, squeezing it. Unlike all its neighbors, Amigo Emil's was not an established business trying to hang on through the lean years. Abu Emil, a retired banker, had returned from Jordan during this Intifada and decided to open a restaurant in the tourist-starved Old City. His food was exquisite, the tiled interior stunning, but he had not yet attracted a clientele. Though it was nearly lunch time, there was only one other person eating in the large dining room.

Chloe and Tina slid into a booth, facing each other. Tina grasped Chloe's hand under the table, opening the menu with her other hand. Chloe felt herself starting to melt. The touch brought the memory of the night and morning coursing through her body.

"Ahem," said the young Armenian waiter at her elbow.

She blushed mightily. "Um, could I have a cheese omelet and cappuccino?" she said without a look at the menu. He wrote it on his pad and turned to Tina.

"I guess I'll have the same." Tina hadn't been reading her menu either, Chloe thought with satisfaction. A few minutes later, Abu Emil appeared with three cappuccinos on a tray. He slipped onto the leather bench next to her. Well, she told herself, if you wanted privacy, you shouldn't go places where you know the owners. But it was not a bad gamble. Tina had new respect for her: Chloe was no ordinary tourist. Tina and Abu Emil traded family histories while they waited for the eggs.

Chloe's phone rang. She glanced at the number.

"Thank God! It's Avi," she said and hit the answer button.

"Where are you?" she asked, but there was no answer. "Shit!" she said, then shot a guilty look at Abu Emil. She needn't have bothered; he was wrapped up in Tina. Neither of them even looked up when she walked out of the restaurant. Reception was scarce in the Old City, the cavernous thick walls frequently blocking the signal. She had to walk all the way to Jaffa Gate to call Avi back.

"What happened?" she asked.

"Not much," he replied. "They took me to the detention center in Petah Tikva. They asked me stupid questions and played loud music all night so I couldn't sleep. Then first thing this morning, they let me go."

"What did they ask you about?"

"Fareed."

"What about Fareed?"

"How I knew him… nothing much."

"What did you tell them?"

"The truth. What should I have told them?"

"I don't know… I wouldn't have told them anything."

He did her the courtesy of not saying, You have no idea what you would tell the Israeli secret police under interrogation. Instead he said, "Well, I didn't tell them anything they didn't know."

"Did they ask anything about me?" she couldn't resist asking.

"No."

She wondered what to make of that. She had been sure it was her the SHABAK was after. Yet they hadn't pursued her and hadn't asked anything about her. If Avi was to be believed, that is.

"Did you see Fareed?" she asked.

"No."

"Well, did you ask to see him?"

"Of course I did." His tone was hurt and annoyed, and she supposed hers would be too in his place.

"Sorry," she mumbled.

"They said he isn't there any more."

"Where is he?"

"They didn't know. Their job was to get the confession. Now that he's confessed and is being charged, he'll go to a regular prison."

Guilt flooded through her as his words registered. Fareed was sitting in prison for something he couldn't have done, and no one even knew where he was. His family must be desperate with worry. And she had been luxuriating in restaurants and the wonders of Tina's body.

"Try and find out where he is," she said. "I will too. If we find him, let's go see him tomorrow." She hung up quickly, before he could scuttle her plans.

Tina was alone in the booth when she walked into the restaurant. The two plates of food were there, but she wasn't eating, just staring into space. Chloe didn't dare slide into the booth, or the lure of Tina and good food and coffee would suck her in.

"I have to go to Azzawiya," she said.

Standing next to the table, she gulped a couple sips of cool coffee and several forkfuls of eggs. Then she fished in her jeans pocket for twenty shekels and left it on the table.

"Wait," Tina caught up with her near the door. "What the hell's going on?"

"I have to go home," she said shortly. "Fareed's not in the SHABAK interrogation center any more, and no one knows where he is." She didn't know that for sure, she realized. Just because Avi had been told that didn't mean it was true. She could call Ahlam and see if she had heard anything. But if Fareed's parents hadn't heard that he was moved, it would make them worry more. She didn't want to do that on the phone. She explained that to Tina. Tina was Palestinian, she would understand that when someone was in prison, romantic liaisons had to wait.

"I'll come with you," Tina said.

"You don't have to do that."

"I know I don't. I want to."

"But... don't you have to work?"

"No, I only work Monday and Tuesday."

Why didn't she want Tina to come with her? Chloe asked herself. She wasn't anxious to be separated from Tina. She wanted the chance to know her better, and she loved looking at her. She was afraid, she thought. Afraid people in the village would like Tina better than her, go to her with their problems instead of Chloe, because she was Palestinian and spoke good Arabic. And Tina would find out she was a big fake, that she couldn't really do anything for the people in Azzawiya.

Tina was behaving like it was a foregone conclusion that she was coming. Having paid their bill, she matched Chloe stride for stride on the way back to the Hospice. If Chloe wanted her to go home, she would need to say so forcefully, and she didn't have it in her. Silently, she acquiesced.

∗ ∗ ∗

Ahlam spotted them coming up the walk and waved from the kitchen window, so they went straight to the downstairs flat. Ahlam was humming to herself and scrubbing an enormous pile of grape leaves in the sink, then carefully laying them out on a cloth to dry. She dried her hands on the sides of her slacks so she could hold Chloe's shoulders and kiss her cheeks. When Chloe introduced Tina, Ahlam kissed her too, and immediately started grilling her about her family, both here in Palestine and in Australia. She settled Chloe and Tina at the kitchen table with tea, before turning back to her grape leaves.

"Can we help?" Tina asked.

Ahlam gathered the leaves onto a plate and brought them to the table along with a bowl of chopped meat and an empty dish. Tina immediately took a leaf and placed a small row of meat on it. Faster than Chloe's eyes could follow, she was placing a neat roll onto the empty dish. Chloe hesitantly reached for a leaf. Her first one looked like a misshapen cigar.

"It's too fat," Ahlam said, laughing. She opened the leaf up and took out half the stuffing. "Watch."

They made it look so simple; Chloe felt like a lumbering ignoramus. But on her fourth try, both women pronounced her effort perfect.

"Fareed says hello," Ahlam told Chloe as they rolled. "He is in Jalame, and he is able to call us almost every day." No wonder she seemed so relaxed and had the energy for a massive cooking project like stuffed grape leaves. "He says he is safer in prison than in Nablus," she said, chuckling. A friend he had made in prison told him about a lawyer who was good at getting people light sentences. Tomorrow, Jaber was going to see this lawyer and ask him what kind of sentence he could get Fareed.

"But he's innocent," Chloe protested. She knew that that wasn't really an issue. It didn't matter if you were innocent. Chloe just wanted to hear Ahlam say yes, he was innocent.

"Yes," Ahlam said emphatically.

"Don't make any deals with the lawyer yet," Chloe said. "I'll go see Fareed tomorrow." Ahlam's eyes lit up.

"He gave me a list of what he wants," she said, her hands already moving among the cupboards, picking up jars of jam and packets of spices. "You are going too?" she asked Tina.

Tina glanced at Chloe, who shook her head. "Avi," Chloe said. "I don't think I could get in without an Israeli."

"I will give you the things to take," Ahlam said.

"Why don't you want me to go to the prison with you?" Tina asked when they got upstairs.

"It's not that I don't want you to. It's just… Avi's kind of obnoxious. We'll need to hitch, and it'll be hard for three people to get rides. Plus we might go all that way and not even get to see him."

Tina didn't pursue it any further. She went through her bag and pulled out a journal, and went up on the roof to write. Chloe lay face down on her mattress. She could almost feel the weight of everyone's expectations in the small of her back. She was so far out of her depth here. She needed to just admit to everyone that she had no idea how to help them.

"Penny for them," Tina said in her ear. Chloe glanced at the clock. She must have dozed off. The sun was going down. Tina slid onto the bed next to her, gently massaging the sore place at the base of her spine. How did she know? Chloe started to dissolve under her touch.

She wriggled around to face her lover, reached up and tucked the dangling curls behind her ear. Tina brought her lips down, brushing Chloe's cheek on the way to her lips. Chloe felt her body answering the call, a deep quivering in her cervix. Her eyes strayed to the open windows. The apartment had no curtains, and she had never felt the absence of them before. She jerked away from Tina's feathery touch.

"What do you want for dinner?" she asked, already on her feet.

Tina came up behind her as she fished in the refrigerator, sorting through half-rotten vegetables for something cookable.

"Close the refrigerator," Tina commanded.

Chloe obeyed, her head pounding. She turned to see Tina standing with hands on her slim hips, jade eyes blazing. She had fallen in love with her

finally took Avi's ID and went away for quite a while, and then came back saying they were trying to get authorization for the visit.

"You can wait there," he said, pointing to a patch of grass the size of a bath mat, surrounded by cigarette butts. Chloe wondered how many visitors had spent how many hours there, and how many of them ever got inside. They waited almost two hours. Chloe shot a few pictures with her zoom lens. She doubted they would look like anything, but she didn't dare get up and focus. Finally one of the soldiers called to her "boi," come. She and Avi got up.

"Not you," the guard said to Avi in Hebrew. "Just her."

"That's ridiculous," Avi protested.

"He doesn't want to see you. He wants to see her. You can have ten minutes," he told her.

Avi stood, stunned. Chloe held her breath. She hoped he would not make so much trouble about it that they would cancel the whole visit. She started to move toward the prison. After a second's contemplation, Avi stepped back in acquiescence.

"Find out what's going on," he called as she took off with the soldier.

"I would never have thought of that," she replied over her shoulder. Did he think she was going to spend ten minutes telling Fareed what flowers were blooming in Azzawiya? Men could be so irritating.

After all that, they did not ask for her ID or to look in her backpack. They went through the bag she had brought for Fareed, removing a few things. The fresh cooked food was disallowed, and the pickles because they were in a glass jar. The fruit and vegetables were allowed, along with the dried wild zaatar and cookies. At least Fareed would be comforted for a while, with things that smelled and tasted like home.

The guards ushered her into a small wire cage, about eight by ten, with a metal table and two straight chairs. They gestured her into one of the chairs. Fareed was ushered in, flanked by soldiers but not cuffed or shackled. He looked rested and not hurt. He shook her hand and asked about his parents and little brothers and sisters.

"You look thin," Chloe said. "Is the food here so bad?"

"It is okay," he said, "but sometimes there is not enough. They are counting us all day long, every two hours we have to stand up silently on the floor for them to count, and they do it twice, and then they can't even figure out how much food to bring."

As soon as he paused for breath, she plunged in, not wanting to waste her time with small talk. "Why didn't you want to see Avi?"

"I don't trust him."

"But he's your friend."

"I thought he was my friend, but I don't know... people say he is a spy."

"Who says that?"

"Many people."

"Well, you can't believe what people say. They say that about lots of people. Plenty of people say it about me."

"I know. But this time I know it is true."

"What do you mean? How can you know that?"

"When I found Nadya dead," he said, "the little bag she had packed for running away was next to her. I didn't want the police to find it, so I took it with me."

Chloe didn't understand why he was talking about this bag, but she didn't want to interrupt. He would get around to what was causing his suspicion eventually. She just hoped she wasn't booted out by the soldiers before he did. She squirmed in her chair a little, hoping to subtly influence him to speed up the storytelling.

He and Avi had agreed, he said, that he would stay in the warehouse while Avi went back to Azzawiya to see what was happening. But he couldn't sit still. He was going crazy in the house, he needed to get out. He walked around for a while, and then he saw a bunch of shabab, young men from the West Bank, hanging out in front of the Hassan Bek Mosque. He went and sat down with them, just passing the time. There was a guy there he knew from school, whose name was Wajdi. Fareed was surprised to see him there, but he said he was working nights in a restaurant. He stayed in a house with some other guys from the West Bank and he invited Fareed to stay with them. Fareed told him he was staying with an Israeli friend on Ben Zakai and Wajdi said, "Oh, that guy."

"He knew Avi?"

"All the guys there knew who I meant. And they shook their heads and said, no, you shouldn't stay with him, he is a spy."

Wajdi had gone with him to Avi's to get his things and then they had gone to Wajdi's house and smoked argila—the flavored tobacco popular all over the Middle East.

"So that's why you trust Wajdi more than Avi, because he let you smoke his argila?"

She knew that wasn't why. But she couldn't bring herself to say, You trust Wajdi more than Avi because he is Palestinian? Why shouldn't that be true? But it made her uncomfortable.

"Did you ever think that maybe Wajdi is the spy, and he wanted you staying with him so he could keep an eye on you?"

"When I was being interrogated, the man asked me questions about the bag. He kept asking me what had happened to it. Only Wajdi and Avi knew I had the bag."

"Someone might have seen you with it."

He shook his head vigorously. "If anyone had told them they saw me, he would have said so. He would have given me their names, so I couldn't deny it. It had to be either Wajdi or the Yahudi who told them."

So Avi was now "the Jew." How quickly relationships can fall apart. "What makes you think it was Avi and not Wajdi?"

"I left the bag at Wajdi's, so if Wajdi had told them about it, they would know where it was. So it had to be Avi."

"Avi was arrested by the SHABAK," Chloe said. "They took him to the interrogation center, just like you, and played loud music so he couldn't sleep. Why would they do that, if he was working for them?"

"How do you know that happened? Were you with him there?"

He had a point. No one had seen Avi in prison, not even his lawyer. Why was she being so protective of Avi? Collaborators didn't smell bad or wear a special patented sneer. Anybody could be one. People had been turned in by members of their own families.

"Tell me about Nadya," she said.

Fareed brushed tears from his eyes. "She was the sweetest person I ever knew," he said. "She loved chocolate and Arab music. I was teaching her to dance *debka*."

"Where would you meet?" Chloe asked.

"In the fields, where she died. In the afternoons when I came home from Nablus. The older girl would come home from school and watch the children for a few hours and Nadya could go out for a little while. Sometimes I could not get through the checkpoint, and then I did not see her. She always waited for me, until the very last minute. Sometimes we would only have five minutes together."

"Why didn't you bring her to the village?" Chloe asked.

"I did once," Fareed said, "but everyone stared at her—you know how it is." He grinned at her, looking like his old self for a moment.

Chloe smiled too. He had once witnessed a spectacular meltdown of hers, when she had been so tired of people staring at her that she blurted out, "I'm not a kangaroo!" That story had been all over town by supper time.

"Nadya was Muslim, even though she wasn't very religious. When she saw Muslim men looking at her, suddenly, she felt bad about how she was dressed and... and everything. And then she saw a man who worked sometimes in the settlement, and she got really scared. She was afraid he would tell the people she worked for and they would report her to the immigration, or something worse."

"What worse?"

"She was afraid about her daughter in Uzbekistan. The man she worked for threatened that if she disobeyed him, he would tell the people who brought her here, and they would hurt her daughter."

"That bastard!" Chloe spat out. "Did you tell the SHABAK that, when they interrogated you?"

"No, I don't want to tell them anything about Nadya."

"But why not?" she argued. "If you told them the truth, they might let you go."

"They don't let me go," he said. His lips seemed to clamp shut. She supposed to him she must sound terribly naïve, thinking that the SHABAK had any interest in what really happened to Nadya. It seemed wise to back off of the subject. "What else did they ask you about, besides Nadya?" she asked.

"They ask me about Radwan. They think I am involved in the same things as him, because we are from the same village and go to the same school. They show me a picture of us together."

"What were you doing?" Chloe blurted out.

"We were just talking, at Huwwara checkpoint. You spend so much time there, you meet many other students, you talk. If you take pictures there long enough, you will find any two students together." She regretted making him defensive, and made a sign of apology, that he should continue.

The SHABAK believed he had befriended Nadya on purpose, he said, to get information from Gelenter and carry out an action against the Ministry of Defense. It was quite an elegant theory, Chloe had to admit. But no, it just couldn't be true. She looked at her watch. Her ten minutes was nearly up. She cut to the chase.

"Fareed," she said, "did you know what you were doing, when you signed the confession?"

"Yes."

"Did you sign it just so they would stop asking you questions?" His eyes narrowed. She supposed she sounded just like everyone else he had seen lately, with her nonstop questions. She hurried on. "Because if you did, your lawyer might be able to get the confession thrown out. The Israeli Supreme Court decided a few years ago that the police can't use physical or psychological torture to get confessions."

"I signed it because I am guilty," he said.

"You mean you feel guilty, because you were not there in time to save her?"

"I mean I am guilty," he said. "I killed her."

"Fareed, you don't mean that." She was almost shouting. She looked around and lowered her voice. "You just told me how much you loved her. Why would you have killed her?"

"I did not mean to," he said. The tears were rolling down his cheeks now. She started to reach out and touch him, but she remembered that he would consider it *haram* and snatched her hand back. Then the soldiers were there, telling her it was time to go.

Chapter 33

Rania was dying to call Bassam. She wanted to hear Khaled's voice, and she wanted to say they might as well come home because everyone already knew where they were. Just because Abu Ziyad knew, of course, didn't mean the Israelis did, but it also didn't mean they didn't.

She didn't call. She waited, in hopes he would call her first. It didn't seem worth making dinner just for herself, but she couldn't think of anything else to do. Without Khaled, the Human Tornado, the little house was neat as a monk's cell. She took down the lentils and put them in a big pot to soak. She turned on the radio and sang along with Fairouz and Nancy while she chopped onions. Matching her knife to the rhythm of the music, she felt relaxed for the first time in many days.

Someone was behind her. She spun around, knife ready.

Chloe stood there, backing away from the knife and Rania's fighting look.

"I'm sorry," she said. "The door was open but you didn't hear me because of the radio."

Rania took time to calm herself.

"Welcome," she said half-heartedly. Chloe hesitated. "Tfaddali," Rania said, patting the sofa. She settled herself, and Chloe finally sat on the edge of the couch.

"If you don't mind my asking," she said, "who did you think I was?"

"I don't know," Rania said. "Strange things have been happening." As her fears subsided, they seemed silly. She went to the kitchen to make tea, and Chloe followed, telling her about the visit with Fareed.

"Do you believe he did it?" Chloe asked.

"I don't know," Rania said. "You know him. I don't. I only met him briefly, and not under the best circumstances."

234

"He couldn't have done it. He's just punishing himself. He thinks he doesn't want to live without Nadya, but he'll grow out of it."

"Or maybe he doesn't want you asking any more questions," Rania suggested. "Maybe he fears that in trying to help him, you will learn something that will hurt him or others even more." She could see that Chloe didn't want to consider the possibility that Fareed was guilty of anything.

"I wish we knew what Nadya had taken from her boss's house," Chloe said.

"Wait a minute," Rania said thoughtfully. "You said that she was planning to use it to get her passport back from her employer?"

"That's right."

"That doesn't make so much sense," Rania said. "The passports—two of them—were right in his desk drawer. The drawer wasn't locked. If Nadya was so desperate for the passport that she went hunting around for something to bribe her boss with, surely she would have found the passports."

"Couldn't he have put them in the desk after she was killed, when he knew she wouldn't be looking any more?"

"If he was going to do that, why wouldn't he have disposed of them? Especially since he told us he didn't have them?"

"Why didn't he do that, before he let you in to search his house?"

"Yes," Rania said slowly. "I wondered about that too. I even wondered if for some reason he wanted us to find them. But Benny would not have searched the office, because he didn't have permission. I think Gelenter knew that, and maybe he had some reason to hold onto the passports."

"Like he was going to use them for his next illegal maid?"

"Why not? It would save him the trouble of getting new ones."

"That makes sense, I guess," Chloe said. "So why would Nadya have left the passport there on purpose?"

"I don't know. But either she lied to your friend Fareed, or he lied to his friend Avi. Or your friend Avi lied to you."

"If she lied, it could mean the DCL was right," Chloe said half to herself.

"The DCL?" Rania asked. "You talked to Abu Ziyad?"

"I didn't. Jaber did," Chloe said. "He told him Nadya was spying for the Israelis."

Rania contemplated this. It might explain why Abu Ziyad was so anxious to keep her off the case. "If she was working with her employer to trap Fareed and his friends, that could explain it. She took her suitcase and

clothes to convince Fareed she was running away with him, but left the passport because she planned to return to her employer's house."

"But the SHABAK had the opposite theory," Chloe reminded her. "That
Fareed was using Nadya to get to Gelenter. If she was working for them,
wouldn't they have known that?"

"Not necessarily. The people who recruit informers among our people are
very secretive about it. They may not even tell each other who are their spies.
And even if they did know, they may not have told your friend the truth."

So many theories were making her head spin. "How can we find out what
the truth is?" Chloe asked. "We certainly can't ask Gelenter, or the SHABAK."

"We know Wilensky met Nadya in Eilat," Rania said. "The people she was
working for there might know how she ended up here. Or her friend, the one
Gelenter told us about." She rummaged through her purse and extracted a
spiral bound notebook, flipping the pages quickly. "Vicki."

"Why don't I go down there?"

Rania shook her head. "These are dangerous people. You are not police."

"Well, someone has to talk to them. You can't go."

That was true, but Rania didn't particularly appreciate Chloe bringing it up. She almost wanted to go, to spite everyone—Chloe, Abu Ziyad,
Abdelhakim. But she couldn't really see herself traveling four hours through
Israeli territory, running around Eilat by herself, asking Israelis how to find a
woman—whose last name she didn't know—who worked in a brothel.

"I'll get Avi to come," Chloe pleaded. "He knows lots of people."

Rania doubted he knew any better than she how to find someone in Eilat.
But she did want to know how Nadya ended up in Elkana, and she wanted to
help Fareed if he could be helped.

"This woman, Alexandra Marininova," she said. "She said she had no idea
how Gelenter got her passport, but she knew Wilensky. It doesn't quite work."

"Where do I find her?" Chloe asked.

"She told us she works at a restaurant. Here it is, Chaverim. Friends."

"Did she say where in Eilat it is?"

"No. Just near the beach."

"The whole city is near the beach," Chloe grumbled.

Chloe declined Rania's offer to stay to dinner, saying a friend was staying
with her in Azzawiya and she needed to get home to her. Something about
the way she said that made Rania wonder... but she couldn't even articu-
late what she was wondering. When Chloe was gone, the house felt twice

as empty. She felt the echo of Khaled's sharp laughter in every corner. She stared at the telephone on the end table. If she stared hard enough, perhaps she could make it ring.

When it started to ring, she was so startled she dropped the receiver on the floor. When she retrieved it, there was no answer. She hung up. Maybe it had been a wrong number.

A minute later, it started to ring again. She snatched it up, holding it firmly this time.

"Yes?" she said.

No one answered.

"Hello?" she said. "Who is this?"

The response was low and hateful—the same filthy expression the settler boy had yelled at her the previous day. She couldn't remember when anyone had said it to her before that.

Chapter 34

Tina took for granted that she was accompanying Chloe to Eilat, and Chloe didn't try to dissuade her. Spending the night on the beach with her lover appealed to her. They met Avi at the Tel Aviv bus station and boarded an Egged bus to Eilat. Chloe felt uneasy as the bus rumbled down the highway. She usually tried to avoid long bus trips inside Israel.

"Wouldn't it be ironic if after everything we've done, we died in a bus bombing?" she whispered to Tina.

Tina didn't answer, just raised an eyebrow. Doubly ironic for her, Chloe reflected. She wouldn't be the first Palestinian victim of an attack against Israel, but she might be the first with an Australian passport. Not a distinction she would want, for sure.

Just before noon they reached Eilat, a completely different kind of beach city than Tel Aviv and Jaffa. It reminded Chloe of Virginia Beach, where her family had sometimes gone in the summer, with its tacky tourist places. Men were constantly pawing at her and Tina.

"I thought I was too old for that kind of attention," she said to Avi, after the third man had tried to coax her into the bushes with him.

"If you can breathe, you are not too old," Avi said.

"I guess that will help with what we're here for," Chloe observed. "Go ask one of those guys where we should go."

He obeyed. The conversation didn't take long, nor would the walk to the neighborhood the man had indicated. Chloe wanted Avi to be their pimp, trying to sell them to one of the houses, but he refused. "I'll be a client," he said. "We can split up and cover twice as much ground and maybe find this woman Vicki."

"If you have sex, I'll tell Maya," Chloe teased him.

"Don't worry," he said. "I can't afford it, anyway."

Chloe was enjoying the sibling-like banter, but she noticed Tina was being very quiet. She pushed aside the tension building in her gut and looped her arm through Tina's. "I don't think I'm going to be believable," she said.

"You will when I'm done with you." Chloe was glad to see a mischievous sparkle in Tina's eyes. They ducked into a hotel bathroom and Tina went to work with eyeliner and blush. Chloe was unexpectedly pleased with the result.

"Maybe I'll do this all the time," she said.

"I like your laugh lines better," Tina said and kissed one of the now hidden lines at the corner of her mouth. They exited the hotel arm in arm. Chloe stole a look at Avi, who had parked on a bench to wait for them. He seemed okay about hanging out with a lesbian couple. She kind of wanted to ask him about it directly, but it would be too much like talking about sex with a son.

Avi took one side of the street, and Chloe and Tina the other. They agreed to meet in two hours. They would try to find Vicki, but if they couldn't, they would try to find anyone who knew Nadya.

Tina couldn't even get through the doors. "No locals," everyone told her. Chloe wondered if that referred to Israelis as well as Palestinians. She had once seen a movie about Algerian Jewish prostitutes in Eilat, but that had been years ago. Possibly the explosion of immigrants from the former Soviet Union had put those women out of business, or pushed them up the food chain.

Chloe was an oddity. No one in these places had seen an American woman looking for work before. The bouncers did not turn her away themselves, like they did Tina. They went and checked with the owners, and the owners or managers would take her into their offices, mostly to flirt, which she didn't do well. When they asked her how she came to them, she answered that her friend Vicki told her about them, and then they all threw her out because they didn't know any Vicki.

The fourth bell they rang was answered by a Palestinian security guard. When Tina told him in Arabic what they wanted, his expression turned fatherly, though he was not much older than she was. "Arab girls do not do this work," he said. "It is not right."

"But it's okay for you?" Tina replied.

"I protect the girls from men who want to hurt them," he said. Chloe wondered if he believed that made it okay.

"Is the owner here?" she asked.

"Wait," he told her. A few minutes later, he opened an inner door for her, as all the other security guards had done. As Chloe walked through it, she saw him leading Tina back outside. She hoped Tina would be able to get some useful information from him. So far, this whole escapade had been a big waste of time.

The office was a converted dining room, big, white, and comfortable. The woman sitting behind the graceful desk of polished dark wood reminded Chloe of her grandmother. Her gray hair was pulled back in a bun and Chloe was sure an old-fashioned corset held her huge bust completely rigid. She gestured Chloe into a red velvet arm chair.

"What are you doing here, really?" she asked in heavily accented but perfectly clear English. "We have never had an American come here looking for work."

"I'm surprised. This is what I do in the States," Chloe said innocently.

"You are a Jew," the woman stated. How could she be so sure of that? Chloe wondered. It was like Israelis had a sixth sense for Jewishness. "Jews in America do not do this."

"Some do," Chloe said. She spun a tale of a feminist whorehouse in Berkeley, drawn from the true story of a woman in her writing group who got a temp receptionist job in what turned out to be a brothel. The old woman appreciated the story, though she didn't look like she necessarily believed it. She told Chloe to wait, asked her if she wanted tea. Chloe accepted.

The woman was gone for ten minutes. Then the door opened and a man came in. "At HaAmerikayit?" he asked her, and looking at his face, she felt a raw terror. He meant her harm, she was sure. Almost against her will, she nodded.

"Come with me," he ordered, taking her arm in a tight grip. For a moment, she thought he was opening the door that led to the front room, and she felt relief. But then she found herself led into an inner room, where a four-poster double bed loomed.

"Take off your clothes." The man's gesture helped her understand his Hebrew.

"I don't speak Hebrew," she said, hoping against hope that somehow this would derail his intent. She started toward the door. He wrenched both wrists behind her back and she had a moment of absolute panic, that he would have handcuffs, she would be imprisoned and raped, all the horrible stories she had heard about what happened in places like this were about to happen to her. What was she thinking, imagining she could play private eye? She wanted to scream, but she realized it wouldn't help her, no one here would come to her rescue, the people who might want to would be afraid to, and the people who could wouldn't want to. Silently, she cursed Rania, who sent her here, and Fareed, who was the reason she was involved in this case, and herself for staying in this country so long, and Tina for not being here to help her.

The man shoved her against the wall. He pressed his body against hers, one hand pinching her right nipple, the other crawling between her legs. She felt his erection against her hip, and his stubbly face was all over hers as he pressed his mouth on hers and his tongue roughly forced her mouth open. His stale cigarette-breath tripped her gag reflex. She couldn't breathe. She felt faint and then she thought, *yes, that's it*, and let herself collapse.

Maybe it was the fainting spell which convinced him she was scared enough, or perhaps he never intended it to go any further, but suddenly he was unlocking the door and shoving her out the front door, where Tina was cozily smoking and speaking Arabic with the kindly security guard.

"Don't come back," the man yelled at her. She couldn't talk. She stumbled down the sidewalk and heard Tina quickly taking leave of the security guard. Tina ran after Chloe and put her arm hesitantly around her shoulders. Chloe shrugged it off. She leaned over and retched. Tina stood close to her, one hand hovering over Chloe's shoulder, waiting for permission to touch her, which Chloe couldn't give. She felt like she could barely stand up. She wanted to curl up in a fetal position and scream and cry, she wanted to be in her house in Azzawiya right now.

She couldn't believe how filthy and violated she felt, and how terrified she was, yet she wasn't even raped. She thought about Nadya, and how many times she was raped in her two-plus years here. How did she endure it, day after day? It must have felt like a recurring nightmare. And she was pregnant. Especially when she had a daughter in Uzbekistan whom she could not see, another child surely would not seem like a blessing to her, but a curse. Chloe suddenly felt sure that Nadya's pregnancy was the key to her murder. She just had to find the lock it fit.

Amid the thoughts swirling in her brain, Chloe was vaguely aware of Tina, still waiting for her to communicate in some way what she needed. What did she need? Chloe wondered. What was there in the whole world that could make the hideous parasite she had allowed into her body shrivel up and leave her a place for herself again? She looked into the face of the woman who, fifteen hours earlier, had made her feel like the most blessed dyke in the Middle East. She tried to read in Tina's eyes if the evil she had encountered had transmogrified her own face somehow. In the other woman's expression, she read only concern, not revulsion. I'm going to keep it that way, Chloe promised herself.

"What did the security guard tell you?" she made herself ask in a normal tone of voice. Tina looked taken aback, but after a second's delay, she answered in a comfortingly conversational voice.

"He said the owner bribes the immigration police with money and sex," she said. "It's not illegal to run a brothel here, if all your workers are legal. But if they had Palestinians working there, they would have problems from the regular police, or maybe the SHABAK. He wanted to get me a job in his cousin's restaurant." She laughed a little. Chloe tried to laugh too, but it didn't come out right. Tina glanced at her, and then hurried on with her story.

"I asked him about the girls who work there. He said men always bring them in the middle of the night, usually in groups of six or eight, and the owner has sex with each one in turn. The ones who don't please him, he sends back to the man they came with."

"Can the girls who work here go out by themselves?" Chloe asked, as if Tina were the one with inside knowledge.

"He said some of them can, the ones who have been here a while. They can't go too far because the immigration police will find them, and if they run away, the people who own the house will come after them and hurt them when they bring them back."

"Hurt them how?"

"He said there are places they can press, that cause enormous pain without leaving any marks." She shuddered to tell it. "He told me he doesn't do that," she added.

"What difference does that make?" Chloe asked hotly. She found herself infuriated, that Tina only cared about whether an Arab man was participating in the abuse, rather than that the abuse was happening at all.

"It doesn't," Tina said. "I don't know why I even brought it up." She touched Chloe's arm lightly, and the touch made Chloe want to dissolve in tears. She turned away from Tina's hand.

"It's almost time to meet Avi," she said. "We probably only have time for one more house. Let's hurry."

"I don't want to go to any more brothels," Tina said. "They give me the creeps."

"They give *you* the creeps?" Chloe snapped. "You're not the one who... we can't quit now." Despite her fear, raging like Niagara Falls through her blood, she didn't want to stop looking. She had forged a stronger connection with Nadya through her experience. She *had* to find out what had happened to her now, and she knew this next place held the answer.

She marched faster, leaving Tina panting a little to keep up.

"Well, I'm not leaving you alone again," Tina said as Chloe headed up the stone stairs of the next house. "Wherever we go, we go together."

"You'll get no argument from me," Chloe said, ringing the bell.

"Vicki yesh?" she boldly asked the young woman who opened the door.

"Ken," the woman answered, opening the door wide. "Vicki!" she yelled.

Chloe's head reeled. After all that had happened, could it be so easy? But maybe it wasn't the same Vicki. She had no idea how common a name it was among Eastern Europeans.

"At makirah otam?" The woman who had answered the door was asking a woman with frizzy blonde hair if she knew them. After some quick eye contact with Tina and Chloe, Vicki gave a little nod.

"Tov." The other woman walked away. Chloe looked around the large living room. Several small groups of young women sat around, playing cards or doing each other's hair and nails. The windows were covered with heavy curtains, but one of the women was perched so she could just see through the slit from which a tiny gleam of light penetrated. A lone man sat in a corner, smoking and watching everyone. Vicki led them to a sofa across the room from him. Chloe deliberately positioned herself so she couldn't see him. Let Vicki worry about discretion.

"At hachaverah shel Nadya?" Chloe asked immediately. *Are you Nadya's friend?* She didn't want to waste time if this wasn't the right Vicki.

"Nadya?" Vicki looked startled. "Ayfo Nadya?"

"Do you speak English?" Chloe asked hopefully. Vicki shook her head. Chloe wasn't able to manage much finesse in Hebrew, but she scraped up the words for "Nadya is dead." Vicki looked sad, but not surprised.

"Nadya made big trouble," Chloe understood her to say.

"Trouble for whom?" Chloe asked.

"The man who...," but Chloe didn't understand the rest of the sentence. This wasn't going to work.

"Does anyone here speak English?" she asked Vicki. Vicki shook her head vigorously, and cast a nervous look around the room. Great move, Chloe told herself. Probably Vicki didn't want anyone else to know what they were talking about. The girl by the window called out something in Russian, and suddenly everyone was putting away their nail polish and straightening up the magazines lying all over the room.

"You must go," Vicki told them.

"Do you have a telephone?" Chloe asked breathlessly.

"No." Vicki was pushing them toward the door.

"But we have to talk more," Chloe insisted. She would not go without a way to get hold of Vicki. Tina pulled a scrap of paper from her purse, scribbled on it, and thrust it into Vicki's hands. "Bye," she said brightly in English. "Good seeing you," and she dragged Chloe out the door. Just in time, it turned out. A minute later, they watched a burly man in a leather jacket open the front door with a key.

"I need a drink," she told Avi when they met at the beachfront. They ducked into a café. Chloe ordered red wine for herself and Tina, casting a defensive look at Avi, who prided himself on being straight-edge.

"I found out one thing," he said, sipping a lemonade. "No one I met knew Vicki, but one guy knew Nadya. He wired money to Uzbekistan for her. She wired fifty dollars home every two weeks. But the week before she left Eilat, she sent a thousand."

The jingle of Tina's cellphone interrupted Chloe's musing about where Nadya would have gotten a sum like that. Tina looked at the number quizzically, then punched *talk*.

"It's Vicki," she whispered, handing Chloe the phone.

"What do I tell her?" Chloe whispered back. Tina shrugged.

"Hello?" Vicki was whispering too. In her disoriented state, Chloe could not remember one word of Hebrew.

"Talk to my friend," she said in English and thrust the phone into Avi's hand. He looked doubtful.

"Allo?" He listened for a few seconds, then told Vicki to hold on. "She wants to meet us in two hours," he reported.

"Where?" Chloe asked. He repeated the question into the phone.

"Somewhere near, but not too near," came the answer.

"How would we know?" Chloe grumbled. "What about that Friends place? Ask her if she knows where it is." After a hurried consultation, Avi said goodbye. "She'll be there," he said.

"I hope so," Chloe said. "With luck, Alexandra will be there too." And then maybe she would be too distracted to think about her near-rape. Her fragile calm might explode any minute.

Friends was a dingy waterfront diner, with six plastic booths and a Formica counter with stools. One lone customer munched a sandwich while reading a Hebrew newspaper in a corner booth. The woman lounging behind the counter more or less matched the description Rania had given of Alexandra Marininova. She looked up from a Russian-language magazine when the three settled themselves on cracked vinyl stools.

"Are you Alexandra?" Chloe asked when the woman approached.

"How do you know me?" the woman demanded in Hebrew.

"Tell her Rania sent us," Chloe instructed Avi. Alexandra's eyes scrunched up when Avi mentioned the Palestinian policewoman.

"You are police?" she asked.

"No, no," Chloe jumped in. "Our friend is in jail," she struggled in Hebrew. "We need you to help us."

"I already told the police, I don't know anything about the girl who used my passport," Alexandra said to Avi.

"Tell her we don't believe her," Chloe snapped. Fortunately, before Avi could speak, Vicki walked through the door, dark lenses covering two thirds of her face while a babushka hid her hair. They relocated to a booth near the back. Alexandra kept her eyes on her little pad when she took their orders. Chloe looked longingly at the pictures of ice cream sundaes on the menu, but she couldn't face Avi's disapproval yet again. She ordered two baskets of fries for them all to share. When Alexandra brought them, Chloe looked around the restaurant, now deserted except for them.

"Ask her if she can sit with us a few minutes," she told Avi. "Tell her we need her to translate from Hebrew to Russian." She was almost sure Alexandra would refuse, but the woman perched on the edge of the bench, even helping herself from the fries Chloe passed toward her. Everyone likes to be needed, Chloe reflected, plus she must be curious about what we're doing here.

The conversation was slow, because anything Chloe or Tina said had to be translated first into Hebrew by Avi and then into Russian by Alexandra, and then back.

"The house where you met her was not the first place Nadya worked," Alexandra translated for Vicki. "They bought her from another house."

"Bought her?" Tina blurted out.

"Yes," Vicki said matter-of-factly. "They take all the girls to a big room, naked. There are many men, and they bid on each girl, one by one. Sometimes if a man cannot afford a girl by himself, he will team up with two or three of his friends."

"Were you sold that way too?" Chloe asked.

"Yes," Vicki said. "But the man I work for is not so bad. He takes good care of us. We have enough to eat, and we don't have to work as much as some other places."

"He must have been upset when Nadya ran away," Chloe said. When Alexandra finished translating, Vicki shook her head.

"She did not run away," came the answer. "The man who sold her came and took her back."

"Took her back? Why?"

After quite a lot of animated chatter, Alexandra said only, "She doesn't know."

"She told us Nadya made trouble," Chloe said. "Who did she make trouble for?"

"The man who sold her. See, you have to pay back the expenses of your travel out of your earnings. The people who bring you here come to the house where you are working every week and take money from your employer and only give you a few shekels. The rest is to pay them back for your travel. But one time the man who brought Nadya didn't give her any money," Vicki said. "He yelled at her that she knew why. She argued with him and he hit her."

"Does she know where Nadya got a lot of money to wire home before she left Eilat?" Chloe asked. Vicki looked surprised when Alexandra translated the question.

"No," she answered, "I didn't know she did."

"Ask her to describe the guy who sold Nadya," Avi told Alexandra. He took out a notebook and created a drawing based on Vicki's description. She looked over his shoulder and corrected a few things.

"You draw well," Tina observed.

"Yes, that's him," Vicki said finally. As soon as the drawing was finished, Alexandra stood and swept up their dishes along with a half-eaten basket of fries. "I have to close now," she said.

Vicki departed quickly, not looking back. Chloe approached Alexandra, money outstretched. Alexandra waved her away, shooing them out the door. They stood on the sidewalk, wondering where to go now. It was balmy with evening just starting to fall, and throngs of young people played volleyball on the nearby beach. Several groups of young men in army green, with their guns casually swinging at their sides, passed, laughing raucously at each other's jokes.

"Well, at least we know what the guy looks like," Tina said.

"And no idea where to look for him," Chloe said. "I don't think we can hang around the brothels waiting for him to come collect his money."

"Why not?" Tina asked.

"We could show the picture around the bars," Avi suggested. "Someone is sure to know him."

"There's certainly no shortage of them," Chloe said. They started aimlessly along the beachfront, heading for the nearest set of lights.

"Wait!" Alexandra was hurrying toward them. Behind her, Chloe saw the steel grate pulled down over the restaurant's door. "I need to tell you something," she said when she caught up to them. They looked around for somewhere to sit, but nothing presented itself. They stood uncomfortably on the sidewalk.

"I didn't lie to the police," Alexandra began. "After they came to see me, I looked through my things. My old passport from Ukraine was not in my house. I never noticed, because I have my Israeli passport now, and I don't want to go back to Ukraine."

"You think someone took it, without your knowing?" Avi asked.

"I know who took it," Alexandra said. She looked around, to the right and to the left. "This man," she said, pointing to the drawing Avi carried. "He was my boyfriend. His name is Dmitri."

"Was? But now he isn't?"

"No. I have not seen him for two years."

"Did you know he was a trafficker?"

Alexandra shook her head emphatically. "I knew he went back and forth to Uzbekistan," she said. "But he told me he was importing jewelry. He even brought me things, like this bracelet," showing them a delicate silver filigree bangle on her left wrist.

"He never talked to you about Nadya or any of the other girls?"

"No. I would never have stayed with him if I knew."

"Can you call and ask him to meet us?"

"No. No, I don't want to do that. But I can tell you where to find him."

Chapter 35

The bar Alexandra directed them to was dark and had the sour smell of beer allowed to seep into the wooden floors. The bouncer sitting on a high stool in the doorway paid no attention to Chloe or Avi, but jumped up when Tina started to walk by him.

"Teudot?" he demanded, blocking her wiry frame with his bulk.

"What?"

Hearing her speak English, he relaxed a hair. "ID? Passport?"

She looked about to say something they would all regret, but stopped herself. She dug the passport out of her knapsack and flashed it at him. He glanced at it and handed it back.

"Thank you," he said in barely intelligible English. There were no other Israelis in this bar. Rapid-fire Russian engulfed them, while the other patrons, nearly all men, cast them suspicious glances.

It was Tina who recognized Dmitri. He entered flanked by two other leather-jacketed men. He had a certain rugged handsomeness, mixed with a healthy amount of sleaze. Tina caught Avi's eye and cocked her head toward Dmitri. Avi maneuvered until he stood next to Dmitri at the bar.

"You have something I want to buy," Avi said in Hebrew.

"I'm not selling anything," Dmitri answered.

"I hope you will change your mind," Avi said. He motioned to the bartender to pour Dmitri another drink—vodka straight up. He ordered a beer for himself and clinked Dmitri's glass with it.

"Skol," he said. Dmitri didn't answer, but tossed back the vodka. Avi turned the tall glass in his hands without drinking from it.

"So what is it you want?" Dmitri asked, impatiently tapping his empty glass on the table.

"An Uzbek girl called Nadya. This tall, long hair, pretty."

"Nadya? She's trouble, that one," Dmitri said. "I give you another girl, for a good price, who won't make so much trouble."

"What kind of trouble?" Avi asked.

"She's a liar and a thief. Forget her, I get you a real good girl."

"What do you mean? Did she steal from you?"

"She tried. I taught her a lesson."

"I heard you beat her up."

Dmitri laughed. "You want to see beat up, I show you beat up. The girl played with fire, she got a little burned."

"What did she try to steal?"

"Money."

"Are you sure she gave it all back?"

Dmitri looked him up and down, as if wondering if he was all there. "I *got* it all back. I'm sure."

"When was that?"

"All these questions. What are you, a cop?"

"If I'm going to shell out money for this girl, I want to know what I'm getting."

"I'm telling you, you'll just be getting a no-good whore. I thought about turning her in to the immigration, letting them ship her ass back to Uzbekistan. I should've done it."

"Why didn't you?"

Dmitri cocked his head. "She was good, you know?" He made a poking gesture with his fingers, a universal sign for intercourse. "Men were crazy for her. Just like you."

Avi laughed. "Yeah, I get it." She *was* good, Dmitri had said. But that could just be a slip of the tongue from a non-native Hebrew speaker.

"Thanks for the warning. So if you didn't beat her, how did you teach her a lesson?"

Dmitri seemed to be weighing options, some of which Avi was certain he would not like at all. He opted to answer, though the sneer accompanying the answer suggested it might bear scrutinizing.

"I sold her to two big military guys."

"Two guys?"

"Yeah, they were going to share her, half, half."

"Well, what was wrong with that? Seems like it would be better than working in a brothel."

"You don't know these guys. They like to do things…" Dmitri shook one hand vigorously toward the floor.

"How do you know?"

"From my girls."

"They were clients?"

"Yeah, asshole, they were clients."

"And they hurt your girls?"

"One of them, he was okay. Just a little, you know, kinky. But the other one, he's got a nickname. They call him the Butcher."

Chapter 36

Rania called Captain Mustafa in the morning to say she was heading to Ariel before coming to work.

The made-up watchdolls at the front desk tried to stop her, but she brushed them aside and took the steps two at a time to Benny's office.

"Gelenter lied to us," she stated without preamble.

He was sitting with another policeman, going over some files. The other man let himself out, clearly wondering who on earth this hijab-wearing madwoman was who could barge in and talk to the boss like this and not end up in cuffs. Of course, she could end up in cuffs yet. Benny tipped his chair back, two legs perilously off the floor, and gave her that infuriating, slightly amused smile she remembered well.

"What's so important, you couldn't even knock first?" he asked.

She told him what she had learned from Chloe, but not how she'd learned it. Fortunately, he didn't ask.

"Doesn't mean anything," he said.

"It means he's a pig and a liar."

"Well, okay, if that's how you want to put it, but that doesn't change the fact that someone else confessed to killing the girl."

"That confession is worthless, you know that."

"I have my opinion about that, and you're entitled to yours, but it'll be good enough for a judge. As far as my bosses are concerned, the case is closed."

It was the first time he had ever mentioned bosses. She had never thought about who he might have to answer to, but she supposed that in a case like this, he must be subject to pressure too. Maybe she should lighten up on him a little. She didn't feel like it. But she made an effort to sound less belligerent.

"What about the woman at the employment agency, Galit? Why do you think she told us that whole story about Nadya coming to her in desperation, and Gelenter finding her there?"

She had caught his interest. He humphed and hawed as he flipped through his rolodex. Then he made a long phone call. Whoever was on the other end did most of the talking, but what Benny said, she couldn't understand. He hung up and turned back to her.

"I have a friend in the immigration police," he explained. "He recognized the trick. A man in Nir's position cannot risk anyone finding out he bought a woman from a trafficker. So the seller arranges for the woman to go to an agency, and the client happens to go to that same agency and poof, the deal is legitimate."

"Would Galit have known what was going on?"

"My friend doesn't think so. Dmitri probably gave Nadya the name of someone who really was placed through that agency, to say she was referred by."

She had to admit it was clever. She was halfway to the door when he said, "I was going to call you today."

"Really? What for?"

"I had a blood test run on Fareed. He wasn't the father of Nadya's baby."

"Why did you do that?" asked Rania. "You said the case is closed."

"I'm thorough at my job," he said.

"So why are you telling me? What can I do with it?"

"I just thought you'd want to know."

She did, but she wasn't even sure how it helped. He voiced her thought.

"You know, it doesn't prove your kid didn't kill her. It gives him an even stronger motive."

"It also proves someone else has one. Are you going to get a blood sample from Nir?"

"I can't do that."

"Why not?"

"We've been through this."

She picked up a Gumby doll from his desk and squeezed it into a nonhuman shape. "You're just protecting these guys because they're big military honchos."

"What do you think they pay me for?" He was laughing at her. How could he be so cavalier about an innocent boy going to prison? She knew, intellectually, that he couldn't care about Fareed the way she did. Even though she only met Fareed that once, when she hadn't been particularly nice to him, she thought of him as a nephew. To Benny, he was just another unlucky kid who was probably a terrorist.

While she was arguing with herself, he had opened one of the hundreds of manila files littering his desk. He was rifling through it, and now he handed her a piece of paper.

"What's this?" she asked. It was some kind of lab report, she could tell because some of the letters were in English, but most of it was in Hebrew. She didn't want to say she couldn't read Hebrew, but damn it, he must know that. Most Palestinians could not read Hebrew, even if they spoke it.

"It's from Nir Gelenter's service records," he said. "It proves he couldn't be the father of the baby either."

Her heart sank. Why did he have to make everything a game? Couldn't he ever just come out with what he knew straight away?

"But if not him, then who?"

"Who knows?" he was waving another, identical slip of paper at her now. "But this one says that Colonel Wilensky could be."

She gaped at him. As far as she knew, he hadn't even known Wilensky had any connection to the case until today. But wait… a terrible thought hit her like an ice storm. "You knew all along it was him in that picture!" she choked out. He didn't confirm it, but he didn't need to.

"You have to get them in here!" she shouted.

"On what grounds? You can't prove anything."

"They bought a slave from a sex trafficker."

"We only have the word of the sex trafficker about that."

She tossed the flattened Gumby on his desk. "Except we know Nir had the passport and lied about it."

"No offense," he said, "but you're a Palestinian policewoman. The men you're trying to take down are two of the most beloved heroes in our country. Who do you think we are going to believe?"

"No offense," she threw at him, "but you're a son of a bitch."

She tore out of the office and out of the station. It was a long walk down to the settlement gate, and it was hot. She wasn't going to walk it, so she defiantly stood at the bus stop, daring the drivers to pass her by. Two did, but the third one didn't blink to see a lone woman in jilbab and sneakers climbing aboard and asking how much in English.

★ ★ ★

Back in the office, she called Chloe. "As long as Fareed stands by his confession, there's nothing I can do," she said. "And there's something else. Nadya wired the thousand dollars home a couple days before the Azzawiya boy was arrested for planning an attack."

"But Nadya had never been near Azzawiya then," Chloe objected.

"No. But she knew Wilensky, and maybe also Gelenter." The timing suggested two possibilities: Palestinians hired Dmitri and Nadya to help them gain access to the Ministry of Defense through Gelenter, or someone in Israeli intelligence paid them to set up Fareed and his friends. Either scenario increased the chances that Fareed's confession was genuine.

"I don't believe it," Chloe said. "Please, you've got to convince Fareed to take back his confession."

"How can I do that? I don't even know him, and I have no way to talk to him."

"He calls his parents nearly every day. Maybe they could get him to call you."

Rania considered that. "I suppose it's worth a try," she said. "But I doubt I could convince him of anything in a few minutes on the phone."

"When I went to Jalame, they didn't even ask me for ID," Chloe said. "You sound like a native English speaker. If you dress like an international, I bet they would let you in."

Rania's heartbeat quickened. She loved the idea, she had to admit. Sneaking into Israel, masquerading as an international, with the freedom and privilege they possessed, breezing into an Israeli military prison. But if she were caught, it would not be like it was for Chloe. For her, it could be the end of everything. They could even shoot her, pretend she had been coming to bomb them. Who would know otherwise?

"It would have to be on Friday," she said. "I can't miss any more work. But how would I get there?"

"You have to go with an Israeli. We can ask Maya to take you, she's Avi's girlfriend. I'm sure she can borrow a car from someone. I'll call you back in a few minutes."

"I have no ID," Rania said.

"That's just as well," Chloe replied. "This way, when you tell them you lost it, you'll be telling the truth."

Chapter 37

Rania was light-hearted as she walked purposefully through the fields. In all this time since Israel had been off limits, she had never thought to sneak across the Green Line. With one part of her brain, she thought she must be nuts to rely on a young Israeli woman she had never met to keep her out of trouble. But Chloe had told her Maya was coolheaded and would know how to charm the soldiers. In the last olive grove before the road, she took off her hijab and jilbab. She started to fold them into her enormous purse, but then she thought that wasn't such a good idea. Just because the soldiers hadn't searched Chloe's things didn't mean they would not search hers. Of course, if they searched her very well, she would be in trouble, but at least she didn't need to have traditional Muslim clothes in plain sight.

She remembered the tree where Fatima had kept her things. It had been easy to find, because it was the tallest one in the area. She looked around at the trees where she stood. They all looked alike to her. She placed her things next to the low stone terrace, and quickly covered them with leaves and branches. She fished a handkerchief out of her purse and tied it to one of the nearest trees, to mark the spot. She prayed no one would be using the rest day to come and prune these trees. She reached the road and carefully peeked over the last ridge in case there were border police in the area. When she saw none, she climbed the rest of the way up and stopped just inside the guardrail, while the cars whizzed by.

Fortunately, she didn't have to wait long. The girl who picked her up in a late-model Subaru was even younger than she expected, and wore the spaghetti straps and short skirt that most Israeli girls would wear on a hot day. The blue slacks and off-white turtleneck she had chosen for this trip were likely to make her stick out almost as much as the jilbab would have. Hopefully the soldiers at the prison wouldn't know any American women.

The black-haired girl looked very glamorous, with her wide dark eyes outlined in kohl. She seemed as uncomfortable as Rania, and they mostly listened to music on the long drive to the prison.

"Whose car is this?" Rania asked once.

"Avi's parents," Maya responded. Chloe had mentioned that Avi's family was a long time in Palestine and very wealthy. They must like his girlfriend a lot, to let her drive their new car.

"Who is this singing?" she asked.

"Me, myself."

"Really? You sing very well." The girl looked pleased. It wasn't an empty compliment. Rania didn't think much of the music, which was loud and grating, but the voice was strong and rich. She wouldn't have thought such a powerful sound could come out of such a thin body.

"Would you rather hear the radio?" Maya asked. Rania hesitated. She really would, but she didn't want to hurt Maya's feelings.

"Perhaps make it a little softer," she said, but Maya laughed and changed back to the radio. She even fiddled with the dial until she found an Arabic station from Nazareth.

"Thank you," Rania said.

"No problem. Punk isn't everyone's thing."

They both sang along with Fairouz. Maya flirted with the soldiers at the checkpoint on the Green Line, and they sailed through in one minute. At the prison, she flirted some more, while Rania stood uneasily in the shadows, trying to be unnoticeable.

"But what if he won't see us?" Rania had asked Chloe on the phone. "He refused to see your friend Avi, and he doesn't even know me. Plus if I tell them my name, they'll know I'm Palestinian."

"They probably won't even ask your name," Chloe assured her. "Just say you're his American friend from the village. He'll assume you're me. The guys who are there probably won't be the same ones who were there when I came."

It worked. After ten minutes of giggling and eyelash-batting from Maya, one of the soldiers beckoned to Rania in that annoying way that they told people to come, crooking a finger. For an instant, she thought his eyes narrowed with something like recognition. *Don't, don't ask for my ID,* she subvocalized. A few seconds dragged out to eternity, until he said, "Come with me."

"You're not going?" he asked Maya.

"No, I don't know him," she replied. "I just brought my friend."

He almost looked like he was going to reconsider. But his buddies were happy to have the beautiful Israeli girl to themselves and motioned to him to go, go. Five minutes later, Fareed entered the small cage room. When he saw her, he looked confused and almost turned to say, there's some mistake.

"Fareed, you look good," she said hurriedly in English.

"Oh, thank you," he replied, sitting down opposite her at the small table. The soldier was too near for them to speak Arabic. He probably couldn't hear exactly what they were saying, but he would certainly be able to hear what language they were speaking. She would have to do this in English.

"Do you remember me?" she asked softly. "I was at Ariel the day you were arrested."

He shook his head slightly, then his eyes widened. "The police?" he asked. "From Mas'ha?"

"That's right. Chloe asked me to come talk to you. She thinks you are making a terrible mistake."

"I made a terrible mistake," he said, and immediately the tears were there.

"Which mistake? Loving Nadya? Or killing her?"

"I don't know... both."

"Chloe does not believe you killed her. Neither does your friend Avi."

"He is not my friend."

"I think you are wrong about that," she said. What did she say that for? she asked herself. She didn't even know Avi. Why did she care if Fareed misjudged him, and how could she know the truth? But somehow, from all Chloe had said, she didn't think Avi had betrayed Fareed. Never mind, she was not here to talk about Avi.

"Your parents," she said, playing the one card she knew would work. "They deserve to know why you are going to prison. Do you want them to think they raised a boy who could kill a girl for no reason? Do you want them to think they raised a boy who will confess falsely, just to stop the interrogation? Tell me what happened."

At the mention of his parents, his face crumbled and he really began to sob. The soldier looked over at them.

"Pull yourself together," she whispered to him in Arabic. "We don't have much time." Then in English, "What happened that day?"

"Every day we meet at six o'clock in the fields," he said. "Three days before, she tell me she find something in her employer's office that she think will help her get her passport from him. She tell me bring Avi to translate it for her. I talk to him that day and he say he cannot come until Sunday. The next day, I tell her and she say fine. But then on Saturday, she say she know what the document is, and say tell Avi to come the next day with the car and take her to Tel Aviv. And she say come at six-thirty. I ask her why not six o'clock as usual. She would not say, she just say come at six-thirty."

"Did she have the passport then?" If she did, Rania thought, she must have had yet a third one. This was possible, but it was not found on her body, so if she had it, the killer must have taken it for some reason.

"She did not say, but I think so."

"And what was she going to do in Tel Aviv?"

"She say with the passport she can work in Tel Aviv until she make enough money to live on her own. Then she can move to Ramallah and we will get married."

"But if you were going to marry, why couldn't you do so right away, and live in Azzawiya?"

"She was afraid to be near her employer. And she did not want me to leave school."

She guessed that made sense. It also made sense that Nadya didn't want to live covered up like a good Muslim village wife. And there was the baby, which would be early even if they married right away.

"Did you know she was *hamel*?" she asked him, turning her face from the soldier as she used the Arabic word. She didn't know if he would know the English. His face gave her the answer even before he spoke.

"Hamel? No, no, she was not. She could not have been."

"She was. Almost six weeks."

He started to cry again. "She was a liar," he said flatly. "I thought she loved me, but she lied."

"Continue with what happened," she said coldly. If she indulged his emotion, she would never get the information she came for. He could cry when he was back in his cell.

"I could not sleep, so I thought, I will go early and just wait for her, surely she will also be anxious and maybe she will come early. I got near the place where we always met, and I saw her. She was with a man."

"What man? Did you know him?"

"No."

"What did he look like?"

"Young. Not so tall. Dark hair." Not Wilensky or Gelenter. It could have been Dmitri. Chloe had not described him, but even if she had, it probably wouldn't have helped, Fareed's observation had been so nonspecific.

"What were Nadya and this man doing?" she asked before he could start crying again.

"They were talking. He had his hand on her arm. She was laughing."

"Did you speak to them?"

"No. I went away. I was angry and I decided to go home and not meet her. But then I change my mind. I went back, and first I did not see her. Then I walk a little and I find her lying in the groves. She is bleeding from her head."

"Bleeding? Not dead?"

"No. She is breathing, but she does not wake up. I think I will carry her to the village and find a doctor. But she is heavy. I think, I will go back to the village and get a doctor to come look at her. So I put her body in the dirt, where the trash is, and cover her with some grass so no one will see her."

"But you did not go back," Rania said.

"No, because when I get to the mafraq," the crossroads, "the army is there. And they are there a long time. So I go back to where I left her and she is not breathing. She is dead. And I take her bag with me, because I think maybe there is something in it about me, and if someone find her, they think I am the one who kill her."

Telling the story had calmed him. He seemed spent, listless. Rania leaned toward him across the table.

"Is this the truth you have told me?" she asked.

"I swear, it is."

"It was not your fault," she said. "You did not kill her."

"It is my fault," he said. "If I did not leave her, she might be alive." She had no time to find out whether he meant if he hadn't left her with the man she was talking to, who presumably caused her head wound, or if he hadn't left her body in the groves. The soldier was at her elbow, telling her her time was up.

"Fareed," she said. "Do not give up. We will get you out of here."

* * *

Maya seemed to be having a cozy chat with the soldiers, but she jumped up when she saw Rania.

"L'hitraot." *See you later*, one of the soldiers said to her.

"I hope not," Maya said so only Rania could hear.

The fastest way back to Mas'ha would have been to take Road 60 south past Jenin and Nablus, turning west at Zatara. But that road was littered with checkpoints, and she had no ID. Anyway, Maya said she didn't want to drive through the West Bank—Palestinians might mistake them for settlers and throw stones at the car. She turned north, toward Afula and Hadera. As they sped down the highway, Rania found herself wishing she could prolong the trip. Israel was a small country, but it felt limitless to her. As she thought of crossing the Green Line, she felt the world contracting around her, like an oppressive blanket. It occurred to her that since she had lost her ID, she felt freer, as if she had removed herself from the rigid system of permits and checkpoints. It was an illusion, but a happy one.

"Could we go to the beach?" she asked Maya.

"Oh, of course," Maya said. "I should have thought of that." When they reached Hadera junction, instead of turning south on Highway 4, she continued to the coast road, Highway 2, and Rania read the signs, in English, Arabic and Hebrew, for Zebulun Beach, Olga Beach, Beit Yanai, Ets Or, Netanya. Most of them she had never heard of, but Netanya was the beach city outside of Tulkarem, where she had been many times before the closure came in the nineties. Ets Or sounded familiar, but she couldn't think why. It nagged at her as they sped closer.

Just before they passed it, it dawned on her. "Turn here," she said to Maya.

Maya started to object, but seeing that Rania was on the verge of grabbing the steering wheel, she jerked it to the right.

"I need to do something," Rania told her.

Kibbutz Ets Or was a small enclave of maybe one hundred fifty families. They passed fields of corn and broccoli, orange groves and greenhouses, just like the ones that had thrived in Tulkarem before the Wall came and separated so many of the people from their land. At a small grocery, the shopkeeper gave Maya directions to the Shabtai home.

Luckily, Yuri Shabtai's mother did not work. Even luckier, she was not skeptical about an American journalist and her Israeli translator showing up to ask questions about her son's death two years ago. She was an attractive woman in her early forties, with brown skin and golden hair. She ushered them into a pleasant living room, shaded by a huge fig tree. She even served them coffee with biscuits and figs from the tree.

"I'm very sorry about your son," Rania began. Maya dutifully translated for Mrs. Shabtai, who told them to call her Miri.

"Thank you," Miri said.

"Were you surprised when he… took his life?"

Miri seemed to give the question a lot of thought. "Surprised, yes, of course," she said. "If I had thought my son would kill himself, I would not have let him go back to the army."

"Did he think about not going back?"

"Yes. He planned to testify to the Knesset, and he said after that, he would not be able to go back to the army. He asked his father and me if that would be a problem for us, and we told him he should do what he needed to do."

"But he did go back after he testified," Rania said.

Miri shook her head vehemently. "Not that time. There was going to be another hearing, right about the time that Yuri… died."

"But there was not," Rania said. "Did they cancel it because of his death?"

"I don't know," Miri said. "You would need to ask Mr. Kalman."

"Who is Mr. Kalman?"

"The man from the Knesset. Gil Kalman."

Miri had nothing more to tell them. They finished their coffee, thanked her for her time, and accepted a bag of figs each to take home.

Chapter 38

Rania's phone call yanked Chloe out of a fast-moving funk. She had returned to Azzawiya without Tina, who had to teach in Ramallah the next day. When Rania told her what Fareed had said, Chloe knew what she needed to do. She took the bus into Elkana, and waited behind the house for Malkah to come home from school. Malkah's face lit up when she saw her, but instantly clouded over.

"I am forbidden to talk to you," she said. "You must go before someone sees us and tells my father."

"Where can we meet? I have to ask you something," Chloe insisted.

"I need to tell you something, too," Malkah said. "Meet me on Wednesday, in Tel Aviv. I can meet you instead of going to my skating lesson."

"Won't your dad find out if you miss your lesson?"

"I'll call my teacher and say I am sick."

"Where can we meet?"

"Anywhere not near the Kirya."

* * *

They met at a small café Avi had recommended on Sderot Yerushalayim in Jaffa. Chloe bought them coffee and they sat down. Chloe was practically jumping out of her skin to know what Malkah had to tell her, but she knew she needed to let the girl spill it at her own tempo.

"How long have you been ice skating?" she asked.

"Since I was ten," Malkah said proudly.

"Are you good?" Chloe bit her tongue too late. Why had she asked that? She didn't want Malkah to think she cared if she was a good skater.

264

"Not really," Malkah said. "I can do a single axel."

"But that's the hardest jump," Chloe exclaimed. "I'm impressed."

Malkah looked pleased at the praise, and her body relaxed a little. She put a cellphone down on the table while she sipped her coffee.

"That's the same phone I have," Chloe said, placing hers on the table next to Malkah's.

"My father's," Malkah explained. "He gives it to me when I come to Tel Aviv, in case something happens and I need to call him."

"I'm sorry you got into trouble because of the pamphlets I brought you," Chloe said.

"Bseder." *It's okay*, Malkah said. "The girls in my class whisper about me, but they never liked me anyway. Some girls I did not know before talk to me now. They think it's funny, what I said to the principal."

"So you have some new friends?" Chloe asked.

"I don't know if I want them for friends. They are kind of bad kids," Malkah commented.

"Sometimes 'good' and 'bad' aren't what you think they are," Chloe said. She had an uneasy feeling, like someone was watching her. She glanced around the coffee shop. There were only a few patrons, and the young man behind the counter, who was flirting with a pretty young woman. She didn't see anyone suspicious. She was nervous, though, and didn't want to make any more small talk.

"Malkah," she said, "Nadya took something from your dad, didn't she? Something that could have gotten him into trouble?"

Malkah's eyes widened, and she nodded slowly. "I came from school and she was in the office," the girl said. "She told me she was looking for her passport and she didn't find it. Instead, she found this envelope inside a book of Talmud," Malkah said.

"Then what happened?" Chloe prompted.

"Nadya looked in the envelope, and there was a letter. She could not read Hebrew. She asked me to tell her what it said."

Chloe waited. Malkah's speech was getting more forced, the English words not coming as easily as when they had talked about skating and school. She was breathing a little hard.

"And did you read the letter?" Chloe asked.

Another nod, this one even fainter. Chloe was afraid to breathe, lest she say or do something to send Malkah flying out of the café. She drank her coffee and reminded herself patience was a virtue.

Suddenly Malkah jumped up, her hands covering her mouth. Chloe was sitting with her back to the door. She twisted in her chair just in time to see Nir Gelenter point her out to a guy with a snake tattoo crawling out of a short-sleeved white shirt. There were two other men with them, in identical white shirts and dark slacks. Malkah was crying as they bundled Chloe outside, pinching her hands together behind her back.

"How did you find me?" Chloe heard her ask.

"I thought I could trust you," was her father's reply.

* * *

Every Palestinian office had a book called the *PASSIA Journal*. It was published by an organization in Jerusalem, and contained addresses and telephone numbers for all the governmental and nongovernmental agencies in the Occupied Territories. It also had numbers for some Israeli officials, and one of them was Gil Kalman, Member of Knesset. Rania dialed the number.

"Mr. Kalman is not available," said the curt woman who answered the phone.

"I need to speak with him," Rania said in Hebrew. "I am from the police." She prayed, *don't ask me which police*. The woman didn't. She put Rania on hold, and a loud Hebrew radio station played in her ear for a few minutes. Then a man's voice said, "Ken?"

There was no point pretending to be an Israeli; her Hebrew wasn't good enough. She had better hope the fact that he was listed in *PASSIA* meant he was sympathetic to Palestinians. She explained in English what she wanted to know.

"Ah, yes," he said, and she said a quick silent thanks to Allah. "Yuri came to me and said that he wanted to change his testimony. I started reinterviewing witnesses and found that there was enough doubt for new hearings. But before we could schedule them, all the Palestinian witnesses pulled out."

"What do you mean, pulled out?"

"They all refused to testify."

"At the same time?"

"More or less."

"Was one of them a young man named Mohammed Omar?" she asked.

"Yes, he and his mother."

"One more question," she said. "When was this?"

"Just before Yuri died," he said. Funny, she thought, how everyone said "died" rather than "killed himself." Perhaps in Israel "suicide" was reserved for Palestinian bombers. But his answer confirmed her suspicions. The Palestinians who planned to testify had been paid for their silence just before the young Israeli had killed himself. It all fit together, but what did it have to do with Nadya?

Maybe Chloe had gotten information from Malkah which would supply the missing piece. She tried the American's number, but only got her voice-mail. It was hours before the return call came.

"Chloe, what happened?" she said as soon as she punched the talk button.

"Hello? Who is this?" someone whispered.

"Chloe? I can't hear you. Where are you?"

"I'm not Chloe—the police took her."

"Police? What police? Who is this, please?"

"I'm Malkah."

"Malkah?" Rania was baffled. What was Malkah doing with Chloe's phone, and what did she mean about police? "It's me, Rania, the Palestinian police-woman who came to your house. Where are you?"

"In the bathroom," came the whispered reply.

"If you are in the bathroom, why do you have to whisper?"

"If my father hears me, he will take the phone."

"How did you get Chloe's mobile?" Rania asked.

"I put my father's telephone on the table. Hers looks just the same. When the police came for her, she took my father's phone instead of hers." Good move on Chloe's part, Rania thought, but it would be a problem when Malkah's father asked her for the phone. She told Malkah to say she left the phone on the bus, and reminded her to turn off the ringer.

"You will help her, yes?" Malkah asked. "My father says he will make them send her back to America. I do not want her to be in trouble because she talked to me."

"It isn't your fault," Rania told her. "If it's anyone's, it's mine. I will not let them send her away." She hoped she could deliver on that promise.

Chapter 39

Chloe was in a dark concrete cell. She thought she had been there for hours, though she couldn't be sure, since every minute seemed eternal. From a distant hallway, she periodically heard thuds and screaming. She still had all her things with her, including, thankfully, a book, *Scheherazade Goes West* by Fatema Mernissi. She would like to call someone but she didn't know anyone's phone number; she always relied on the ones in her phone. Hopefully Malkah would figure out how to get a message to someone, and they would call her, if she could manage to hold onto Gelenter's phone. She had to figure out somewhere to hide it before anyone came to search her. She tried tucking it into her underwear. Besides the discomfort, and the likelihood that it would come plopping out when she least expected it to, she thought she would look like she was packing a major dildo.

"Not really my style," she said to herself, turning again to contemplate the scarce contents of her backpack. Crumpled up pamphlets, a few aged raisins, a bandana, a sanitary napkin—got it! If only... Yes, there it was, a seldom-used lipstick. She made a few red marks on the sanitary napkin, pried open the cotton layers, tucked the phone between them, and then shoved the whole thing into place between her legs. Now she was ready. If anyone asked why she had a charger and no phone, she would just say she had forgotten the phone at home.

Soon a woman cop came and ushered her into another slightly larger dark concrete room, containing a table and two chairs. The cop dumped everything out of the backpack onto the table, inspected it cursorily, set aside everything with Arabic writing on it and put the rest back, including the charger, which she had not even touched.

"Get undressed," she said. Chloe removed her shirt and jeans and then stood facing her in bra and underpants.

"Take off everything," the policewoman ordered.

"This is enough," Chloe said. The woman seemed like she couldn't quite decide what to do. She hadn't even glanced at the clothes she had taken off, so it certainly didn't seem like she was too worried about what she might have hidden in or on them. She was more interested in humiliating her, Chloe decided. Well, she was pretty humiliated standing here in her underwear.

"Wait here," the woman said.

She went out and came back a minute later with the snake tattooed guy. His nonchalance suggested he talked to middle-aged women in their underwear every day.

"Why you will not take off your clothes?" he asked in heavily accented English.

"I did take off my clothes," she said, indicating the pile sitting on the table.

"Why you not take off the rest?"

"I don't like people looking at me naked—unless I know them really well."

To her surprise, he nodded and told the woman "Zeh bseder." *That's fine.* He left and the woman told her to get dressed. Then she opened the door and Snake Tattoo returned. He fingered the Arabic brochures the woman had taken from Chloe's backpack and the scrap of bag from a bakery in East Jerusalem. Then he sat down and let out a big sigh.

"Chloe, Chloe, Chloe," he said, as if she were a malfeasant grade schooler. "What am I going to do with you?"

She hoped that was a rhetorical question.

"How do you know Nir Gelenter?" he asked.

"I don't. I met him once at his office." That, she figured, was safe enough to say. He knew she had been there; he had tried to arrest her there.

"Why did you lure his daughter to that café?"

"Lure her?"

"Why did you get her to meet you there?"

"I didn't. I just ran into her."

She was prepared for many more questions, but they didn't come. The man made one call after another, some on a land line and some on his mobile. At times he was talking on both of them at once. Many hours later, three policemen led her into a waiting van.

It was nearly two a.m. when she saw the big metal sign proclaiming that they had reached the city of Hadera, halfway between Tel Aviv and Haifa. She knew there was a prison there with a special section for deportees. At least she would get to sleep now, she thought. Not yet. None of the police knew how to find the prison. They drove up and back, around and down. They made calls on their mobile phones and got very agitated. Of course they would not stop to ask anyone. Forty-five minutes passed before they turned into a massive complex with bars and curls of razor wire all around. She had never been so glad to see the inside of a prison.

A policewoman showed her into a little sitting room, where four or five women were watching *Who Wants to Be a Millionaire* in Russian. Apparently this prison had no lights-out policy. Next to the window she saw a few open bags of white bread and bricks of margarine, with little packets of jelly and tea bags. She was very hungry. She had not eaten since she left Azzawiya. The policewoman was impatiently indicating for her to continue into an inner room, where she found three sets of bunk beds. She had to climb up onto the top one and arrange the scant bedding she found there, trying not to waken the woman snoring beneath her or the three who occupied other bunks.

She lay still, wondering what would happen. She couldn't do anything to help herself right now. She would get some sleep, and in the morning presumably she would get to eat, and then she would figure something out. She turned onto her side and let Tina's face creep into her mind's eye. Would she ever get to see her again, or would this be the last stop before she ended up on a plane?

The door to the little room opened and a small figure crept over to where she lay.

"At yeshenah?" the woman asked.

"Hmm? No, I'm not sleeping."

"You are hungry."

The woman thrust a margarine and jelly sandwich into her hand and set a cup of tea on the ledge next to Chloe's head. She was gone before Chloe could thank her. Chloe ate and drank and let sleep overtake her.

✷ ✷ ✷

"Boker tov, banot!" *Good morning, girls!* The false cheer of prison guards was the same in every language. Chloe had been in jail several times after protests in the States, and it was always the same. They woke you up at the crack of dawn and you had all day to do nothing. She didn't imagine there would be any work shifts in this jail.

She was right. After the morning count, one woman mopped the floors with a squeegee, which took only a few minutes in a space so small, and then most people went back to sleep until almost lunch time.

After some initial inquiries about where she was from and why she was here, her roommates showed no interest in her. She managed to ask in Hebrew where they were from, how long they had been here, and whether they wanted to go home. They answered with a few words, and went back to watching television and talking on their mobile phones.

Only the dainty girl who had brought her supper the night before was friendly. She had big chocolate fondue eyes and her face exploded in dimples when she smiled, which was often. Her name was Ursula, she was from Uzbekistan, and she had appointed herself Chloe's protector. That morning, as the women crowded around the breakfast table, grabbing cartons of cottage cheese and slices of bread, Ursula plowed into the throng and emerged, thrusting a plate containing two hard-boiled eggs and two slices of bread into Chloe's hands. She had fought so hard for them that Chloe couldn't tell her she didn't like eggs.

"Where were you living?" she asked Ursula.

"Eilat."

Eilat! And she was Uzbek. But Ursula shook her head when Chloe asked if she knew a Nadya or a Vicki. She had heard of Dmitri, but not met him. There were lots of men like him, she said. Reluctantly, Chloe abandoned the subject. Instead, she asked Ursula general questions about her life in Eilat. She had liked it, Ursula said. She had an Israeli boyfriend, who was going to come get her out of jail and marry her. Chloe asked what his work was.

Ursula shrugged. "He's rich."

Pretty Woman syndrome, Chloe thought. Ursula didn't seem that naïve. Well, who was she to judge? Maybe Ursula really did have a rich boyfriend who would come bail her out and take her home as his bride. She was certainly beautiful enough for a trophy wife.

"How did you get here?" Chloe asked.

"From Egypt," Ursula said. "It took many days. We were thirty or more women, and we had to walk very fast." She mimed being beaten. Then she was done talking. She wandered off, leaving Chloe to worry about how she was going to get out of there. She had all her things, including Gelenter's mobile, but the only number she knew by heart was her own and she was

afraid to call it, because who knew where Malkah was? She could only wait
and hope that someone was doing something to help her.

* * *

Just after lunch a tiny, waif-like policewoman with a sleek black ponytail
came to get her. According to the badge she wore, her name was Diana.
Chloe heard one of the prisoners ask her in Hebrew if she had a good trip.

"Where did you go?" she asked in English, as Diana led her downstairs
and out into the courtyard.

"My country."

"Where are you from?"

"Romania."

"When did you come here?"

"Five years ago, at fifteen."

Physically, she could be the sister of many of the women locked up here.
If she were not Jewish, she might well have been one of them. Not long ago,
Chloe reflected, being born Jewish in Romania would have been no one's
idea of good fortune.

Diana escorted her into a room where a man and a woman sat. The
woman sat behind a desk, and the man to her right.

"I'm Elisheva, and this is Yoav. We're from the United States Embassy."

They asked if she was being treated okay, and if she had been beaten.
When she said no, Yoav leaned forward and asked, "Are you sure?" She wondered, was it so rare that a US citizen was arrested and not beaten? She hated
to disappoint them, but she had to confess that she had not been beaten.

That settled, Elisheva handed her a stack of papers, and then told her what
each of them said. One said that they weren't going to help her get out of jail,
regardless of whether she had done what the Israeli authorities accused her
of. It told her what would happen when she was deported, making it all
sound quite grim and inevitable. The second was a list of lawyers. At the
top of the list was a disclaimer, saying that the embassy didn't know if any of
these lawyers were good.

Chloe decided that even the diversion of speaking English wasn't worth
prolonging this encounter. She took the papers, thanked them for coming,
and called Diana to take her back to her room.

At least the papers were blank on one side, so now she had some scratch paper. She was here because of Nadya's death. If she wanted to get out, she would have to figure out who had killed her and why. She started making a list of everyone who knew Nadya. "Fareed," she wrote and drew a circle around his name. "Radwan," and she drew a line to Fareed's circle. "Gelenter" in another circle. "Wilensky," linked to Gelenter. "Dmitri," down below, for "Eilat," which was down below. "Vicki." "Malkah," she added, with a short line connecting her to Gelenter, who kept her on such a short leash. "Avi," she threw in. After all, he had been part of the events that had led to Nadya's getting killed.

When Diana came to get her a second time, she was absorbed in the chart. Whatever Diana wanted this time, she wasn't interested. But there was no point in refusing. Police didn't go away because you told them you weren't in the mood. She put on her shoes and followed her to the administration building again.

In the same desk room where she had met Elisheva and Yoav, Avi and Tina were pacing. Tina was as beautiful as she had been in Chloe's fantasies. Seeing Avi standing there grinning felt like having a brother show up. She hugged them and hung on, hoping their scents would penetrate her body, so she could still smell them when they were gone.

"How'd you know I was here?" she asked.

"Rania called me," Avi answered. "The kid from Elkana called her." Chloe cheered for Malkah in her heart. The girl must have thought to redial the last person Chloe had called.

"Rachel, the lawyer, is working on getting you bail," Avi said.

"Why bail? I haven't done anything."

"As a foreigner you don't have too many rights. They've canceled your visa and issued a deportation order against you. You only have three days to challenge it, and then they can deport you, unless you can get out on bail."

"I don't know how I could pay any bail. I don't have any money."

"Don't worry about it," Tina said firmly.

How could she not worry about it? She didn't like the idea of Tina hitting up her family members for money, if they had any. But she wasn't going to tell Tina not to do whatever she was doing. She was too afraid she wouldn't ever hold her again. She reached for Tina's hand. Their fingers felt like they belonged laced together.

The phone in Chloe's pocket jingled. She hastily hit the "reject call" button. When she had been brought in the night before, they asked if she had a phone and she said no because she thought they would take it from her. Now, she feared that they would take it away because she had lied. But Diana didn't seem to have noticed anything. She wasn't even looking at them; she was smoking and gossiping with another woman cop.

"Who was it?" Avi asked. "I gave Rachel your number."

Chloe clicked the "recent calls" button. The last number began with 00.

"It's from out of the country," she told Avi.

"Let me see it."

Normally, she would have balked at his bossiness, but after two days of nonstop worrying, it felt nice to have someone else taking charge. She handed him the phone.

"It's Wilensky," he said. "He can use his Israeli phone from Italy."

"Maybe I should have answered it," Chloe joked. "I haven't been answering any calls 'cause I figured no one knew I had this phone."

"I think Rania tried to call you, but you didn't answer," Tina said. "Oh, I brought you some stuff." She went behind the desk and emerged with a small rucksack and a bouquet of flowers.

"Oh, they're beautiful," Chloe effused. She opened the bag. Three shirts, some new pairs of underwear. She couldn't restrain herself. "No chocolate? Or books?"

Tina looked apologetic. "They told us we couldn't bring any food." She held out one lone book. "We had some others, but they said the captain had to approve them, because they're 'political,' and he's not here today."

Chloe held out her hand for the one book. Raymond Carver short stories. She didn't even like short stories, but hey, they had tried.

"This is great," she said. She hoped Tina couldn't hear her half-heartedness.

"Time to go," Diana said. Chloe put their numbers in her phone. Then she hugged Avi and kissed Tina long and hard.

"See you soon," Tina whispered.

"Inshalla," Chloe whispered back.

As she followed Diana back to her cage, she felt lonelier than before they came. She tried to read Raymond Carver, but he was as dour as she remembered. She turned back to her chart. "Rania," she wrote in one corner, even though Rania was not a player in the case, any more than she was herself. That reminded her, Tina said Rania had tried to call her. If she could figure out which number was hers, she could save it in the phone so next time, she would know to pick up. She took out the phone and punched up the call list. There was only one call from this morning, at about ten o'clock. The number looked somewhat familiar. She couldn't be sure, but probably it was Rania's. Nir Gelenter must not use his cell phone very much, or maybe he had more than one. There were calls on this one going back three weeks. She scrolled through them. One caught her eye. She checked it, then checked again. It didn't make sense. Avi had said Wilensky was out of the country when Nadya was killed. He had gotten a postcard from him, he had told her. But here was his number, on that very Monday, in Nir Gelenter's mobile phone without the 00 for out of the country.

Had Avi lied to her or had Wilensky snuck back into Israel that day? Someone would need to find out.

"Call me. C.," she spelled out, then sent the message to the number she fervently hoped was Rania's.

Chapter 40

Rania was in the village of Marda, interviewing a farmer who said his sheep were being stolen. Of course, he suspected the settlers from Ariel, which sits on the hill above Marda. Rania doubted she could do anything to help him, especially if it was settlers. His sons, it seemed, had been charged with keeping track of the sheep. She tried to tactfully suggest that it was possible one of them had sold some of the sheep, but he was adamant. No, no, it had to be the settlers.

"I will talk to the Israeli police and see what they can do," she told him, confident that the answer would be absolutely nothing. "Meanwhile, you may want to spend more time with the sheep yourself." He muttered something about being too old to herd sheep, but thanked her, and his wife produced the obligatory cup of coffee.

She took out her phone to call Benny and saw a message from Chloe.

"Excuse me," she said to the farmer. "I will be right back."

She walked outside and called Chloe back. As soon as they were done, she called Benny, who said he would come meet her. The farmer seemed impressed at her clout with the Israeli authorities and pleased at the opportunity to rail against the settlers to one of their own officials. Benny saved her the trouble of working the conversation around to the Nadya murder.

"How is your boy Fareed?" he asked as they walked away from the field where the sheep were grazing.

"What makes you think I know?" she asked. He simply gave her that look that said, I know what I know.

"He is tired of being in jail," she said. "And he should not be." She told him what Chloe had found out. "I need to know if Wilensky was really in Italy at all, and if so, how he came back," she said.

She had prepared elaborate arguments that stopped short of begging. She was almost disappointed that for once, he wasn't in the mood to make her jump through hoops. It took him only a few phone calls to tell her that the colonel had flown to Italy on Air Italia on Friday night, and had not returned on any commercial flight.

"Commercial flight? What other kind—oh! You mean he came in a military plane?"

"It seems possible," he said. "You'd better call Mustafa and tell him we're going to be a while."

"I warn you," Benny said as he started the car. "You are making some very powerful enemies."

"I'm a Palestinian," she said. "I'm accustomed to having powerful enemies."

They drove for a long time, deep into the Nakab desert. As they plunged deeper into the scorching heat, Benny loosened his tie and opened the neck of his blue policeman's shirt. After nearly three hours, they drove through a series of gates. Benny got out of the car and shook hands with a blond young man who must have been nearly seven feet tall, wearing the special light-colored fatigues of the air force. Nearby, a group of similarly dressed young men kicked around a soccer ball. A tiny slip of a dog was playing goalie.

While Benny spoke to the airman, Rania took in the scene in the distance. Military aircraft sat in neat rows, like toys or sheep, looking so harmless. Yet she recognized the F-16s that terrorized her childhood in Aida, with the huge Stars of David painted on them in bright white paint. After a long conversation with the blond giant, Benny climbed back into the car and revved the engine on the way into the bowels of the base.

"Where are we?" Rania asked.

"Hatzerim," he answered. She knew the name Hatzerim mainly because of one incident, years ago, that had been widely reported in the Arab press. Two planes had crashed in a training flight, a number of Israeli soldiers had been killed, and the Israeli prime minister had become ill when he came to look at the damage. The Palestinians had loved the image of the head of Israel emptying his guts all over the wreckage.

They were ushered into the captain's office and served weak tea without enough sugar in it. After the pleasantries, the captain called in two young men who stood before her with sullen condescension in their faces. The captain introduced them as Uriel and Gadi. They were draft age, but they were not just serving out their time until they could go to India and climb mountains. They were Israel's finest, the Baraks and Sharons and Wilenskys of the future. They were the ones she had nightmares about.

Benny did all the talking. It irritated her, but there was nothing she could do about it. She barely understood what they were doing here. And even if she knew what to ask, her chances of getting any information out of these arrogant officers was nonexistent. So she sat in her chair and fidgeted as loudly as she dared.

"Tell me what happened the night of seven May," Benny said.

"A reserve officer needed to take a plane out and return in a few hours," said Uriel.

"Does this happen often?" Benny asked.

"Not often, no."

"But sometimes."

"Sure."

"So when it does, what is the procedure?"

"We check their ID, we check the plane, and they have to sign the log."

"So this man, who came here that night, signed the log?"

Uriel and Gadi exchanged glances. "Of course," Uriel said.

Rania could not contain herself any longer. Finally, she was going to get her proof. "May we see the log?" she asked.

"I don't know," the captain answered. "We have to call the commander of the base to get permission to show it to you."

"Oh, come on," she blurted out, "stop stalling."

Benny flinched. She saw he was about to touch her shoulder, but stopped his hand in mid-air, brushing his own head instead.

"Did you know the man?" he asked Uriel.

"I knew who he was."

"What do you mean? You knew him or you didn't know him."

Gadi said, "We had never met him, but when he came in, we knew who he was."

"Well?" Rania thanked Allah that Benny had asked the question, because she couldn't have contained herself. Even he seemed to be tiring of dragging information out of these soldiers' mouths two words at a time.

They said the name. It wasn't Wilensky and it wasn't Gelenter. It was impossible.

"Let me see the log book," she demanded. All of them stared at her in astonishment, but apparently now that they'd said the name, they didn't see the need to call anyone for authorization. Gadi rummaged in a tall metal filing cabinet, which had a lock with a key hanging from it, and drew out a thick clothbound book. He flipped the pages and found the one he was looking for and handed it to her open. Of course, after all that, she couldn't read the Hebrew words. She showed it to Benny, who confirmed the name for her without drawing unnecessary attention.

"The name sounds familiar," she said softly in English. "Who is he?"

"Perhaps you have heard of him," Benny said. "He gives the news every evening on Israeli Channel 2." She supposed she might have heard of a popular Israeli newscaster. She never really watched Israeli news programs, but you couldn't avoid Channel 2. But she still didn't want to accept, couldn't accept, that they hadn't given her anything on Wilensky or Gelenter.

"You say he left and returned the same night?" she asked Uriel.

He nodded.

"And he didn't say where he was going?"

"No." He was looking like she was more or less an idiot. Obviously, conscripts, even air force ones, didn't ask important older men where they were going or why.

"Did anyone come back with him?"

"Not that I saw," Uriel answered.

"Not that you saw?" Benny said. "Did you have some other reason to think..."

"No one was with him as far as we know," Gadi amended.

Rania accepted it, because they obviously weren't going to get anything else. She was nearly silent on the long drive back. It was fully dark when Benny dropped her at the Qarawa blocks. She dialed Chloe's number while she waited for a cab. The phone rang and rang and then Nir's voicemail came on.

When she opened the gate to the family compound, she saw lights on in her house. Her first thought was the army. But there were no jeeps, no sentries, no spotlights. When the army came to your house, they didn't come in secret. She recalled the settler youths with their eggs and the dirty phone call a few days ago. Was she being stalked? She mentally flipped through the people who were angry with her—Nir Gelenter, Abu Ziyad, Abdelhakim. Would any of them have been able to get someone into her own house?

She fished her phone out of her purse, wondering whom she could call. If it turned out to be nothing, who would not remind her of her foolishness for the next ten years? The only person she could think of was miles away in Jericho. She stole up to the front door and threw it open. She could hear voices.

"Hello?" Her voice came out as a little choking sound. She was shaking. She couldn't be this scared, standing in her own doorway. "Who's here?" she managed to get out in a fairly authoritative voice.

"Rania?" Her mother-in-law called from the kitchen. Great, now that they were so chummy, Um Bassam was going to be breaking into her flat whenever she felt like it? That wouldn't do. She would tell the old woman, kindly but firmly, to wait until she was invited to come downstairs. Steeling herself, she took a few steps inside.

"Mama!" A little ball of flesh flew through the air and then she was burying her face in Khaled's woolly hair. When she looked up, Bassam was standing in the living room doorway, smiling the lopsided smile that had made her love him that first day in college.

"Mama called," he said. "And Mustafa did too. They said you seemed very lonely."

Chapter 41

Chloe had never been so bored. Whenever she had been arrested at home, she had been with busloads of other people like herself. It had been like summer camp, groups of women giving each other massages and having workshops and talent shows. She had thought going to jail for real would be scary, like those B-movies about Babes Behind Bars. She had never thought about how *dull* it would be, just to be left with nothing to do and no one to talk to.

She wandered over to where Ursula was playing cards with a willowy blonde named Yelena and a brassy-haired older woman Chloe thought was called Katya. She tried to make sense of their card game, or think of something to say in her few words of Russian, but couldn't quite manage either. She went back to her cot, wondering if she would start getting bed sores soon.

"America!" a man's voice bellowed from the outer room. "Boi!"

Well, let them bellow. Her name wasn't America, and she didn't answer to commands. If they wanted something from her, they could come ask nicely. She huddled under the blanket, pretending to sleep. Soon Diana was pulling the blanket aside, her pixie face a study in irritation.

"Didn't you hear us calling you?" Diana asked.

"No, I heard someone say 'America,' but that's not my name."

"Here, it is. Come."

She supposed she might as well find out what they wanted. Maybe it was something good—maybe Rachel had found a way to get her out. She followed Diana into the sitting room.

Two men stood there, chatting with some of the other women. One was round and dark and balding. His eyes darted from one person to another, and his face seemed to twitch with barely controlled hostility. He reminded

Chloe of a terrier. The other man was tall and slim, with a gentle, amused expression. He was the one who brought their food in the morning.

"HaAmerikait," said Diana.

"Boi, tishvi." *Come here, sit down,* said the shorter man, pointing to one of the plastic chairs next to the table where they ate. She squinted to read his name tag, which read "Shaul Gabi" in Hebrew. She had heard people say that Shaul was the captain here. He didn't introduce himself.

"Hello, how are you?" he began, in the slightly menacing tone guys like him are so good at.

She answered, "Fine."

"Hakol bseder? Ein b'ayot?" *No problems?*

"No," Chloe answered, "everything's okay. I mean, I'd rather not be here …"

"Why not? You have a problem here?"

"No, it's just, this isn't what I planned on doing."

He shoved a paper and a pen across the table at her.

"Sign this."

"What is it?"

"Your deportation order."

"No, I would rather not sign it."

"You have no choice. You are in prison."

"I do have a choice, and I'm exercising it."

"Mah he omeret?" Shaul looked at the other man, who was apparently the translator, though his English was not that great either. His name tag read "David." He said something in Hebrew. Chloe couldn't tell if he got it right or not.

"You're a prisoner. If I tell you to sign something, you sign."

The other women had turned off the television and gathered around. Live entertainment, she supposed, was better than soap operas.

"I don't know that much about Israeli law," Chloe said, "but I know I don't have to sign anything. And I want to see a lawyer. Are we done?" She stood up and walked back toward her room.

"You are in my place," Shaul said with carefully controlled violence. "You can't do whatever you want. You can stand up when I say so."

Chloe turned around. Shaul was gripping the edge of the table so hard that his knuckles whitened. The tension in the room was thicker than ketchup that won't come out of the bottle. She looked around at the twenty female eyes fixed on her and wondered whom they were rooting for.

She walked back and sat down, directly under Shaul's nose. He glared down at her. What about her had aroused so much instant hatred in this guy? It made no difference if she signed the paper or not. If not signing a deportation order could stop anyone from being deported, few people ever would be.

"Do you think of yourself as a control freak?" she asked.

"What did she say?" Shaul asked David.

"I didn't understand," David admitted.

"What did you say?" Shaul demanded of Chloe.

"I wondered if you need to get your way all the time."

"Mah?" to David. David translated for him. Shaul's neck turned dark red and his Adam's apple bobbed up and down. His tie seemed to be choking him. Chloe was afraid he was about to have a heart attack right in front of them.

"You're not better than the others," Shaul suddenly said in English.

"Which others?"

"The other prisoners here."

Had she given the other women that impression? Was that why they didn't like her? "I know I'm not."

"When I tell them to do something, they do it."

Oh, that. "Maybe they're afraid of you, but I'm not."

The competition was suddenly over. He asked her once more, "You won't sign?"

"No."

"Ein b'ayah," he said after a final long stare.

If it was no problem, then why all the drama? She didn't ask. She also didn't walk back into her room. She stood, along with the other women who still watched silently as he took the massive set of keys from his belt loop, unlocked the cell door, and ushered his entourage out. When he was gone, the room exploded like a popped balloon.

"Kol hakavod, Chloe," said Yelena. *Good for you*, that meant. Everyone was laughing with each other and smiling at her. Ursula kissed her hard on both cheeks. Katya appeared with a chocolate bar and sectioned it out to celebrate. She was one of them now. But she still had no language to ask them what she wanted to know. She smiled at them and turned the television set back on. Soon enough, they were fixated on the screen instead of her.

Her phone was beeping at regular intervals, telling her there was a message. Thankfully, she could get into Nir Gelenter's voicemail without a password. She listened to the message and texted Rania that she was available. A minute later, her phone rang.

"Meron Levav?" Chloe gasped when Rania finished her story. "You're sure?"

"That's what Benny said was written in the log book. Do you know him?"

"Not him," Chloe said. "His son."

Chapter 41

Rania woke at dawn, to the familiar blend of rooster's crow and call to prayer. She rubbed her cheek softly against Bassam's hairy chest. He murmured but did not wake. She heard the faint sound of Khaled's light snoring next door. She climbed out of bed soundlessly, wrapped herself in a light robe, and went out to gather eggs for breakfast.

The door to the chicken coop was open. She must have failed to close it firmly behind her the day before. It had been dark when she got home, and her mind was occupied by seeing the light in her house, but her mother-in-law had been home all day. Every day in the summer, she spent hours out in the garden. Rania couldn't imagine how she could have failed to notice the gate swinging wide open. Could the old woman have opened the coop for some reason, and then gone to answer the phone or something? There was no way to know.

She gathered the eggs and checked on all the chickens. None of them seemed disturbed. They wandered around clucking just as they always did. Two of them were quietly perched together on a mound of straw in the corner. She went to peer at them. They seemed fine, just licking each other's feathers. She headed back to the house, but something made her go back and look more closely at the mound where the two lovebirds sat.

"Shoo," she ordered, snapping her fingers. They obligingly waddled off, only a little indignant at having been rousted so early. Reaching into the straw, her fingers touched fabric. She tore away the layers of straw. There was a small canvas tote bag with leather top and handles. What on earth was it doing in her chicken coop, and who had left it there?

She cradled the eggs carefully in one hand and carried the bag in the other. Leaving the eggs on the counter, she opened the bag and dumped the contents out on the kitchen table. Four thin blouses and two pairs of slacks, a pair of high-heeled sandals similar to the ones Nadya had been wearing. A gilt double picture frame, one side holding a picture of Fareed, the other a chubby-cheeked girl, about three years old with dark hair. A delicate golden filigree *hamsa* on a small chain, the right size for a child.

There were no papers, no name inside, but she didn't need any to know whose things these were. But who had left them in her chicken coop, and why? She would worry about that at the office. As much as she wanted to delve into the mystery right away, she would not squander this morning with her son. For at least one day, she would act like someone who had learned something. She fried the eggs with lots of olive oil and salt and put flat bread spread with zaatar, in the oven to bake. The smells brought her boys to the table just as she was pouring sweet tea into glasses with springs of mint.

She carried the heavy bag with her to the bus stop.

"Going on a trip?" said a voice behind her. She spun around.

Abdelhakim. What was he doing here? He lived in Kufr Yunus, on the other side of Hares. There was no reason for him to be at Qarawa this time of the morning.

"I spent the night at my aunt's house, in Biddia," he said, as if reading her mind. Her eyes went to his shoes, vainly searching for fragments of straw. Of course, if she had found any, it would have meant nothing. Doubtless his aunt had chickens as well. But as far as she could tell, his shiny dress loafers were spotless.

The bus pulled up and they boarded. She took a seat next to Um Raad, and Abdelhakim moved toward the back where she heard him greeting several of the younger men heartily.

"I heard Bassam got back," Um Raad said as the bus pulled away from the blocks.

It was six in the morning. How could word have spread so quickly? People two towns away must have known her husband was home before she did.

"Yes," she said. "He had a nice visit with his sister, but now he is home. I am very happy."

When she got to the office she went straight to Captain Mustafa's office. He was on the phone, but he hung up quickly when she entered.

"I found this in my chicken coop," she said, placing the bag on top of his desk. "It is the bag that Nadya was carrying the morning she was killed, the one Fareed took with him."

He extracted a cigarette from his breast pocket and took his time lighting it.

"How did it get in with chickens?" he asked.

"I have no idea. Someone obviously put it there."

"Who would do such a thing?"

"I told you, I don't know. But the point is, what do I do with it?"

"Did you tell Benny?"

"No. I wanted to talk to you first. Do you think I should tell him?"

"What is in it?"

"Clothes. A little jewelry. Pictures. I don't think there is anything that helps or hurts Fareed."

"Leave it here."

"What are you going to do with it?"

"I am not sure. If I give it to the Israelis, they might believe that you found it the first day and kept it all this time. If the boy is going to plead guilty, perhaps they do not need it."

"Do you think someone was trying to get me in trouble with the army?"

"I do not know. It is possible."

Who would do such a thing? She looked out the glass window into the office. Abdelhakim was at his desk, diligently going over files.

"Go back to your work," the captain said. "I will think about this."

As she walked toward her desk, the phone started to ring. She rushed to answer it.

"Meet me outside," said a low voice. It sounded vaguely familiar.

"Who is this, please?"

"At the fruit stand on the corner." He hung up. At least she thought it was a man. The person had spoken so low, she couldn't be sure.

She saw Abdelhakim watching her as she took her purse and walked outside. She looked around her carefully to make sure no one was following. Of course, she couldn't know who was watching from what windows. Her conversation with Um Raad on the bus had reminded her how few secrets there were in this area. But she had to know what was going on.

The little fruit shop was empty except for Abu Mahmoud, the shopkeeper. She wondered where she should wait. Why had the caller picked this little stand? A bigger place would have given them more cover. She picked up a handful of cherries, as if inspecting them.

"Come this way." The young man had not come from outside, but from a doorway in the back. He indicated she should follow him back that way.

They mounted the stairs and she followed him through an open door into a pleasant apartment. A woman a little older than her was peeling okra at the sink.

"Who are you?" she asked the boy. With his wavy black hair and thick lips, he reminded her of a Lebanese fashion model.

"My name is Wajdi. This is my aunt, Um Mahmoud."

Um Mahmoud turned one shoulder in her direction. "Assalaamu aleikum," they murmured in unison.

"You are Fareed's friend. The one he left the bag with."

"Yes."

"Why did you put it in my yard?"

"Someone told me to."

"Who?"

"I cannot say."

"So why are you telling me now?"

"The person who told me, he said to leave it where you would not find it. But when I saw you come with it this morning, I did not want you to worry."

"I am not sure I believe you."

"It is the truth."

"Did you tell the Israelis Fareed had left the bag with you?"

"No. The Yahudi must have told them."

The response was practiced and too fast. Wajdi had no way to know that the Israelis knew about the bag at all, unless he had told them. But she couldn't be sure, and even if she were, what would she do? To accuse a young man as a collaborator was a very serious, even deadly thing to do. She was not ready to do that to Wajdi. Time would tell what he was.

"You called me before," she said.

"No, only this morning."

"At home. You called my house a few nights ago. Who told you to?"

"No one. I don't know what you are talking about."

He was lying. She was not going to waste more time with him. Probably she would never know why he had done any of it. Someone must have intended to tip off the Israelis so they would search her yard and find the bag. Someone wanted her to be afraid. She didn't know who and she didn't know why. She suspected some combination of Abu Ziyad and Abdelhakim, but she would not give them the satisfaction of accusing them, since they would only deny it. She didn't think Wajdi would be making any more problems for her. Hopefully he would also not make any for himself or Fareed.

Chapter 42

Chloe went back over everything that had happened since Fareed was arrested. She thought about Fareed's friends saying Avi was a spy, and Avi acting like he thought Fareed was guilty. That day at the Kirya, she had wondered why Gelenter let Avi be arrested. Maybe it was all a set-up—they had come for her, and only pretended to be taking him. Maybe his job had been to stay with her and let Wilensky and his father know if she was getting too close to the truth. She couldn't stand to follow where her train of thought was going, but she couldn't afford not to. If what she was working out was true, then she was really, truly alone and no one would help her. She started to cry, only a little bit at first, but the hot tears felt somehow comforting on her skin. She lay face down, hiding her face in her pillow so no one would see or hear, and let the tears flow.

Her phone rang. Startled, she nearly answered it before she remembered that it was not really her phone. She looked at the number. It was Wilensky's out of country number. Her finger was pressing down on the connect button even as her mind was still considering whether it was a good idea.

"Hello?" she said.

There was silence on the other end. She would have thought that he had hung up, except she could hear him breathing. He didn't breathe easily, there was a little wheeze; he must be or have been a smoker.

"Hello?" she said again.

"Malkah?" he guessed.

"No."

"Mi at? Ayfo Nir?" In the midst of recovering his balance and asserting his accustomed authority, he must not have registered that she had spoken English.

"Hu lo po," she said, he's not here, before realizing that it didn't make sense to start a conversation in Hebrew, since she would almost certainly not understand whatever he said next. In English, "I'm a friend of his daughter's."

"What are you doing with his Pelephone?"

"Um, he kind of lent it to me. How is Italy?"

"How do you know who I am?"

"Nadya told me."

He was silent for so long that she thought for a second he had hung up. Then he said, "Nadya is there with you?"

She tried to parse his expression and the various possible meanings of his question. He was shocked, but that in itself did not prove anything. Was he trying to get her to confirm that Nadya was dead, fearing perhaps that he had not actually killed her? Or did he really mean, Is Nadya there with you? And if she said, Oh, yes, she's right here, would he say, Let me talk to her?

"Allo?" she heard from the phone, and realized she herself had now been quiet a disconcertingly long time. At least, she hoped it was disconcerting for him, and not simply annoying enough to make him hang up.

"I'm here," she said.

"What do you know about Nadya?" he asked.

That was more what she expected to hear. He wanted to know what she knew. But what should she say? Should she confront him directly with her knowledge of Nadya's murder, or should she try to make him say it? She tried for a middle ground.

"You're the only one who really knows what happened to Nadya," she said. "Why don't *you* tell *me*?"

"Look, whoever you are, I am going to tell Nir that you stole his phone."

"If I had stolen his phone, don't you think he would have figured that out by now? You don't know who I am. What are you going to say, 'Someone I don't know took your phone, I don't know how or when or why?' That's going to be very convincing. It'll probably get you another medal or two. And you won't even have to murder any more people for it."

"Who do you think you are talking to?"

"I know who I'm talking to. The Butcher of Jenin."

"Whore!" he spat out the Hebrew word, *zonah*. "Shut up! I'm going to have you arrested!"

"Well, it might comfort you to know that I'm already arrested."

He hung up on her, leaving her wondering if it was a good idea to tell him that. In that case, obviously she was not with Malkah, or Nadya, or any other member of the Gelenter household, and moreover, it would probably make it easy for him to figure out who she was. On the other hand, she was not the one with anything to hide. She was trying to smoke him out, and if he decided to come after her, maybe she could set a trap for him—not that she had many resources to call on right now.

"Mishehu rotzeh hachutza?" Diana's voice called. *Does anyone want to go outside?*

Chloe jumped up and put on her shoes. Half an hour wandering around a caged-in blacktop would not normally qualify as a major treat, but then, she wasn't normally in prison. She glanced outside and saw that it was a double treat—the canteen truck was here. She made sure she had money in her pocket. Now she could buy chocolate and instant coffee and milk. Life was getting better by the second.

When they came back inside, she made coffee with milk for everyone, and they had it with the cookies she had bought. It was like a little party.

"Where's Ursula?" she asked, suddenly noticing that the one person who had been kind to her all along wasn't here to share her paltry largesse.

On cue, Ursula appeared at her side. There was another woman with her, and they were speaking a language Chloe didn't recognize. Uzbek, she assumed, though this woman looked nothing like either Ursula or Nadya. With bright copper hair, hazel eyes, and almond complexion, she could have been Irish or Hungarian. Uzbekistan must be as much a melting pot as the US, Chloe thought. She had barely heard of Uzbekistan before this. When she got out of here, she would have to look it up on Wikipedia.

"This is Lydia," Ursula told her. "She knows English."

"Are you new?" Chloe asked Lydia. Lydia shook her head, then patted her shining mane back into place, not that it needed it.

"I sleep in the other building." She pointed out the barred window, to another barracks barely visible across the courtyard.

"She is not supposed to be here," Ursula giggled in Hebrew.

"After bachutz, when they call for Building 1, she whisper to me come," Lydia explained. "She say, there is girl here, speak only English."

Chloe wondered why Lydia would take such a risk just to talk to her. "What will they do if they find you?" she asked idly.

Lydia lifted one delectable shoulder. "Nothing. What can they do?"

What, indeed? Chloe thought. Unlike sentenced prisoners, the inmates here had little to lose.

"Why did you want to talk to me?" she wasn't sure whether the question should be directed to Ursula or Lydia.

"They want to know about you," Lydia said, opening her hands toward the assembled women. "Why you are here?"

What should she answer? I'm here because a military man thought I was trying to corrupt his daughter? Or, I'm here because a friend of mine confessed to a murder, and I'm trying to prove he didn't do it? The latter route would be more likely to elicit useful information from them. She told Lydia a compressed version of Nadya's story. It took her a long time to translate, but when she did, the others were spellbound.

"Did you know this Nadya?" they asked each other.

"I think... which one? What did she look like? No, that was another Nadya. No, no, I don't know her."

"I know Dmitri," Yelena announced.

Now they were getting somewhere. Chloe mentally kissed Lydia's feet.

"What do you know about him?"

"He sells women secrets about the men they work for. A friend of mine, her boss stole money from his company. Dmitri sold her a paper for five thousand shekels, and the man paid her ten thousand for it. She sent that money home to Georgia, so her mother can build them a big house on the Black Sea."

Chloe thought about whatever Nadya had taken from Gelenter's office. Could that have been why Dmitri sent her to work there in the first place?

"Where would a woman get five thousand shekels?" she wondered aloud.

Lydia translated for the others. They were full of suggestions.

"You can save," Maria said.

"Not if you don't get paid," Ursula interjected.

They all nodded vigorously at that.

"A Chinese girl in my building," Lydia pointed. "She didn't get paid for two years. Then when she asked for her money, her boss called the immigration. The police beat her so bad, she was in the hospital two weeks."

"Can't she do anything?" Chloe asked.

Lydia shrugged. "The human rights hotline, they say they will send a lawyer to take her story. But until now, no one comes."

"A Moldovan girl in Eilat," Katya said, "She is pregnant. She call the hotline but they don't answer the phone. She leave a message. Her boss hear her leave message and he take her down to a basement. He chain her to a bed and keep her there seven months, until the baby born."

Chloe stared at her. The others did not look shocked at all. They were nodding, like they had heard such things before.

"But that's a horrible story," she burst out. "What happened to her then?"

"He take the baby," Katya said. "And sell it to another man from Moldova."

"He sold the baby?" Chloe couldn't get her head around this. It occurred to her that if Nadya knew this story, or another like it, she must have been terrified when she found out she was pregnant. It seemed unlikely that Gelenter, evil as he was in his way, would chain her in a basement and sell her baby to a trafficker. But what did she really know about what he would do? Certainly he would not have wanted her bringing her baby into his house, especially if it looked like him. He had no way of knowing he wasn't the father.

"A lot of girls must get pregnant," she speculated out loud. "Do most of them have the babies?"

The others discussed it among themselves, in Russian. Then Lydia delivered the consensus.

"No, most get rid of them."

She had heard that abortion was easy to get in Israel, at least for citizens. For illegal foreign workers, she didn't know. "Is it easy to get rid of them?"

"It is not hard," Lydia said. "You go to a doctor and he takes six hundred dollars."

"But if you are more than three months, it is nine hundred," Yelena added.

That explained why Nadya needed to get money right away. It would also explain why she didn't tell Fareed she was pregnant. Perhaps she really was in love with Fareed, Chloe thought. Maybe once she got rid of the unwanted pregnancy she meant to live with him, eventually marry and start their own family, just as he hoped. It comforted her to believe that.

She thanked Lydia for her translation and went back to sit on her bed and think about all they had told her. Dmitri had told Avi he got back whatever money Nadya stole from him. But somewhere she had gotten a thousand dollars to send home. Could she have held out on him in a previous blackmail scheme? Or had he meant for her to find him something to use against Gelenter or Wilensky, and she double-crossed him? Either way, he would have had a good motive for murder.

She needed to talk to Wilensky some more and get him to tell her what the precious document was. She didn't know how much credit was left on her phone. She couldn't waste any on a long distance call. How could she get him to call her?

She typed out a text message. "Did u know N gave someone copy of doc b4 u killed her?"

She pressed send, and went back to the road map she had been making. With a felt pen she drew lines from Nadya to Gelenter, Wilensky, and Fareed and wrote "sex" and "pregnancy." On the lines leading to Gelenter and Wilensky, she wrote "blackmail," and on Dmitri's, she added, "theft?" She drew a line to nowhere and wrote "abortion?" On the short line between Fareed and Radwan, she reluctantly wrote, "bombs." Okay, so she had all the possible reasons for someone or someones to kill Nadya, but how did it help?

"Efshar l'kanes?" She recognized Shaul's boom, asking if it was okay to come in—not that he waited for an answer. He strode over to her bunk, jabbing his index finger at her.

"Pack your things," he ordered. "You're leaving."

"Where am I going?"

"I don't have to tell you. Yalla. Kadima." *Come on*, in two languages.

"If you won't tell me where you're taking me, I won't go."

His steely eyes flashed. "I'll take you by force."

He would enjoy that, she thought. She got up, started to gather her few possessions.

"You have five minutes," he growled and left, triple locking the door behind him.

She packed slowly. Several of the others were crying.

"He will hurt you," Yelena wailed from her bunk.

Funny, Chloe thought, *yesterday you weren't even speaking to me. Now, the thought of someone hurting me makes you cry.* Aloud she said, "No, I'll be okay."

She hoped she was not lying.

She contemplated the telephone. If she put it in her pocket, there was a good chance someone would search her and take it away. If she hid it among her things, maybe they wouldn't find it, but would she be able to get to it when she needed it? She got an idea. With the tip of a pen, she made a small hole in her jacket pocket. It wasn't jacket weather, but she would just have to *schvitz* a little. She typed out a text message, and without hitting send,

pushed the phone through the little hole, and felt it settle in the hem just as
the clacking of bolts announced it was time.

"America. Yalla," Shaul barked.

Chloe went to each roommate and hugged and kissed her. Katya's cheeks
were wet as she covered Chloe's face with kisses, yet they had barely said
five words to each other. Ursula held her the longest, until Shaul began to
grumble.

"What's your hurry?" Chloe asked him. Just to annoy him, she walked
around once more, asking each woman to write her home country address
and telephone number in her book. She wondered if she would ever write
or call any of them.

"Your flowers," Ursula said, bringing them.

Chloe smiled and reached for the flowers. Seeing them brought Tina's
face into her mind, made her relax a little. But then she thought, wherever
she was headed, she probably would not be able to take flowers.

"You keep them," she said to Ursula, bending once more to kiss her sweet
face.

"Boi," Shaul said, tugging on her arm. He led the way to a white van and
ushered her into the back. David climbed in next to him and they took off
at a roar. The two policemen played the radio and chatted with each other,
ignoring her. Good. She slipped her hand into her jacket pocket and felt for
the phone, keeping two fingers touching it. They were traveling south, but
that didn't tell her much. Nearly the whole country was south of them.

After an hour or so, her worst fears were confirmed. Shaul merged into
the lane marked in Hebrew and English "Ben Gurion Airport." She wouldn't
wait to be absolutely sure. She cast a studious look to the men in the front
seat. They seemed to be paying her no attention, but no doubt they could see
her in the mirrors. If they heard her moving around, they would surely look
to see what she was doing. She worked the phone into her hand and slowly,
slowly eased it just out of the pocket, holding it in her palm and glancing
down only quickly enough to find the address and hit the send key. So far,
so good.

Chapter 43

Rania was putting Khaled to bed. She heard the distinctive peal of her mobile phone in the other room, but she ignored it. She was so happy to have her family back, she wasn't going to interrupt their time together. She would call whoever it was when Khaled was asleep, if it was important. If not, she was looking forward to some private time with Bassam.

"Another story," Khaled pleaded.

She didn't bother resisting, because they both knew she would give in. "A short one."

"The Flying Duck."

"No, that's a long one. The Little Red Train."

"I want to go on a train."

"We don't have them in Palestine. A long time ago, we did, but no more. They have them in Jordan. Some day soon, maybe we can go there on a holiday."

She found the book, and he settled back into his pillow to listen. When he looked up at her like that, her heart felt in danger of bursting. She looked down at the book quickly, so she wouldn't start to cry in his face. Her phone's song began for the third time. Whoever it was, was persistent.

"I'll be right back," she told Khaled.

Book still in hand, she yanked the phone from the charger. Chloe.

"What's the matter?" she answered.

"They're taking me to the airport. We're almost there. I have to hurry. If they see me on the phone, they'll take it away." Chloe was whispering.

"You think they will try to put you on an airplane against your will?"

"I'm sure of it."

"I don't know what I can do to stop them," Rania said.

"Do whatever you can," Chloe said. "I'm glad I met you." She hung up before Rania could even say, "I'm glad I met you, too." Maybe she was afraid I wouldn't say it, Rania thought.

What should she do? What could she do? Really, Chloe should have found someone better than her to turn to for help in a crisis. Rania dialed Avi's number. He knew, he said. He sounded breathless. He had gotten a text message from Chloe. He had called Rachel, the lawyer, who was on the phone with the police at the airport, trying to stop her flight. He himself was already on his way to Ben Gurion.

"On the train?"

"No, I borrowed my parents' car."

Why had Chloe texted him and called her? Because she believed he would act right away but figured Rania would have to be prodded? Or because she didn't know if he would help, but trusted Rania to do something? Or maybe she *didn't* believe Rania could help her, and just called to say goodbye.

She didn't dare leave Chloe's fate in Avi's hands, not with all the questions they had about him. She needed to think of a plan and fast. Maybe she could call Benny. She looked at the clock. Surely he would still be up.

No. She was sick of asking Israelis for favors. If she called Benny, she would have to play some stupid word game for five or ten minutes before he would even say if he was or wasn't going to help.

"Pick me up on the road," she told Avi.

"No, it will take too long. It's better I go by myself."

"I will meet you at Yarkon Junction in half an hour." She hung up before he could say anything else.

She took a scarf from her closet and wrapped it tightly over her hair, tying it in front and then tucking the knot under the rim, as the settler women did. She rummaged among the hangers and came up with a long blue skirt and a white long-sleeved peasant blouse. She felt guiltily happy, wearing her old Bethlehem clothes out in public.

Her hand stretched into the depths of the closet until it closed on something steel. She took out the pistol and looked at it. It had been Bassam's father's, and Bassam refused to give it up when the call came for all Palestinians to turn in their weapons. "Let the Israelis turn in their weapons first," he had said.

Rania was entitled to carry a gun because she was police, but she had never done so. Her job was about talking to people, not about guns. She didn't even know how to shoot a pistol. She wondered if she could. If she were caught carrying a gun into Israel, she would go to prison. No question. Khaled would grow up without his mother.

This is *majnoon*, said a voice in her head. She didn't know what she imagined doing with the gun. She just knew that she was going to meet someone she couldn't trust, who was connected with some dangerous people. Those people were trying to get rid of Chloe, and if Rania got in their way, they wouldn't hesitate to get rid of her. They couldn't put her on a plane. They could only shoot her. If they were going to shoot her, she would shoot them first, if she had the chance.

They can get away with shooting you much more easily if you have a gun, her practical side objected. Shooting an armed Palestinian is no crime in Israel. She tucked the gun into the waistband of her skirt, well hidden by the loose blouse.

Bassam was outside, smoking argila with his brothers. Should she tell him where she was going? He would never allow it. Well, it wasn't his to allow or not. But she had no time to fight with him. Guiltily, she looked at the little train book, still sitting on the nightstand next to the telephone charger. She had completely forgotten about Khaled, waiting for her to return. She peeked into his room and found him conked out, his head flopped over. She pulled the quilt over him, though it was not chilly in the room. Probably he would throw the covers off. She kissed her fingers and laid them ever so softly against his cheek, afraid to wake him with a real kiss. She prayed this would not be the last kiss she would give her son. She switched off his light and went back to her room. She buttoned a jilbab over her clothes and covered the settler scarf with a hijab.

"We are out of milk," she told Bassam breezily. "I am just going up to Abu Kushri's."

"Do you want me to go?" he asked between lazy rings of cherry-scented smoke.

"No, I can use the air. Just listen for Khaled, in case he wakes up." She left the door slightly ajar, so he could hear.

When she reached the corner, he would still be able to see her from the porch, so she needed to turn left toward the main road, where Abu Kushri's store was, and go another block before turning right toward the fields that led to Highway 5. When she reached the fields, she broke into a trot. She was not going fast enough. She would never make it in time to help Chloe. She kicked off her shoes and clutched them, momentarily thinking of Nadya's loose shoe which had started her on this entire adventure. She ran faster than she had run in twenty years. She couldn't sustain it. Soon she doubled over, panting and clutching a stitch in her side. She hid her clothes where she had left them when she went to Jalame with Maya, the last grove before the road.

Though it was late, there was plenty of traffic on the road. A steady stream of yellow-plated cars zoomed past in both directions, filled with young people going and coming from the night life in Tel Aviv. She saw a few service taxis, what the Israelis called *sherut*, white vans with Hebrew writing on the sides. She held out her hand, palm down, not sure if they would stop along this road, even for a settler woman. They didn't.

Finally a car pulled up, its brakes squealing as it slowed quickly. A woman, her head covered just like Rania's, leaned out of the passenger's window.

"L'an?" she asked

"Ramle."

"We are going to Herzliya, but we can drop you at the Yarkon Junction, where you can get a bus."

"Maayfo atem?" she asked immediately upon settling into the back seat. She needed to know where they were from, before they asked her.

"Anachnu? Me-Itamar." They were from Itamar, the most violent settlement in the north. Recently, a young man from near Nablus had been killed in cold blood in front of many witnesses by a man from Itamar. Yet here were these ordinary-looking people, picking up a strange woman late at night, smiling at her.

"You shouldn't be tramping on this road so late," the woman said. "It is very dangerous."

"My car broke down about a mile back."

"Yes," the man said, "we saw a car." Did they, she wondered? Or were they just suggestible?

"Do you want to go back and let Chaim look at it?" the woman asked.

"No, I am going to my cousins in Ramle and they will drive me back tomorrow. My cousin Nimrod is a mechanic."

"Oh, that's good," said the woman, who said her name was Ainat.

When Ainat asked where Rania was from, she said Elkana. At least she knew a few streets, in case they asked where exactly. They didn't.

"Where did you grow up?" Ainat asked her instead. They could tell from her poor Hebrew she was not Israeli. What should she say? Yemen? Syria? She knew a lot of Jews had moved to Israel from those countries more recently than from Iraq or Libya, but she didn't know exactly when.

"Artzot Habrit," she said finally. The US. At least she spoke English, and she was sure they had every kind of Jew in the States. "I've only been in Israel a little over a year," she added.

"Which state?" Chaim asked in English.

Her and her great ideas. What should she say? Chicago. No, that wasn't a state, it was a city.

"California," she said, thinking of Chloe.

"Los Angeles?" the man asked, just as she had.

"No, San Francisco," feeling like she was reading from a script.

"Oh," he sounded disappointed. "I have family in Los Angeles."

She had reached the end of her script, and they had reached the checkpoint. One agony became another.

The soldier gave her a long, long look. She made herself gaze back at him without blinking. Oh, God, she recognized him. He was there under the bridge the day she found Nadya's body. He was the one who had been about to shoot at the kids when Chloe appeared. Please, she prayed, don't let him remember my face. How could he? Palestinians looked alike to Israelis. In this garb he would never recognize her.

"Mi zot?" he asked Chaim, pointing at her with his chin. Not a very polite way to ask someone who is in his back seat. What if she was Chaim's sister or cousin? But she supposed some subtle difference in clothing or demeanor told him that she wasn't.

"She lives in Elkana," Chaim told the young soldier.

"You know her?"

"No," Chaim admitted. "Her car broke down and she is going to her cousins in Ramle."

The soldier motioned to her to roll her window down. She obeyed.

"You are going to Ramle?"

"Yes."

"To visit?"

"To visit my cousins, yes." Did he think she would contradict what Chaim had told him? Even if she was a liar, she wasn't deaf.

"Where do they live in Ramle?"

Damn. She had never been in Ramle in her life.

"Herzl Street," she said, looking directly into his eyes. "Near Weizmann." Every town in Israel has streets named Herzl and Weizmann, for the founders of their state. Briefly, she wondered if Ainat and Chaim could have named even one man her people would name streets after.

"Nsiyah tovah." *Good trip*, the soldier said to Chaim, and seconds later, they were clear of the checkpoint.

Chapter 44

Chloe figured her phone had done her as much good as it was going to do. She punched in Tina's number and waited impatiently through one, two, three rings. When she realized Tina wasn't going to answer, she felt salt burning her eyes. Five, six, seven. At least, let her voicemail come on, so she could hear the melodious voice once more. Click. Shit, it was going to cut off, no voicemail even.

"Hello?" Tina's voice was faint against a background of loud music.

"I love you," Chloe said at once. There, at least she wouldn't go home without having said it.

"Sorry? I can't hear well. Who is this?"

Chloe couldn't remember being so crushed. "Chloe," she said.

"What? Wait, I have to go outside. The reception here is terrible."

Chloe heard crackling, and the line went dead. Shit! They were almost at the airport now. She saw the high-rise hotels on her right, and cargo terminals loomed just ahead.

Her phone rang. Shit, she had forgotten to turn off the ringer. She quickly pressed the answer key and pushed it to her face. It was too late. David was turning around, and yelling to Shaul, "Yesh la pelephone." *She has a phone.*

"I love you," she said again into the phone.

"—too," she heard just as the phone was torn out of her hand.

The van stopped next to a beige sandstone building that looked like a prison. Shaul left David and her in the van and went inside, the motor still running. A few minutes later, he returned and opened her door.

"Get out."

She sat.

"Come on!"

It wasn't going to take much to get him to use violence. Chloe ordered her heart to stop racing and her breath to stop coming short and quick. She stared straight ahead, resolutely not looking at Shaul or David. She scooted over until she was square in the middle of the wide seat, so that in order to pull her out, one of them would have to lie halfway across the seat. Not a dignified position from which to exercise authority.

"If you do not come now, I will use force," Shaul said in the ritual words that so often preceded an ugly episode.

Chloe counted the wrinkles on her hands: one, two, three.

Her head smashed against the door frame as he hauled her from the van like a sack of potatoes. Each policeman took an arm and they dragged her unceremoniously up the stone steps, depositing her smack in the middle of a big room full of men, women, armed guards, and luggage. Shaul delivered a kick for good measure before stomping out.

The eyes of forty or more people from every continent made her self-conscious. She doubted she made an attractive picture, sprawled there on the floor. With as much dignity as she could muster, she stood up, straightened her t-shirt, combed her hair with her fingers, and looked around for a place to sit. There was not a vacant chair in the room. In fact, people were standing three deep, smoking, chatting in fifty languages, drinking from small plastic cups that came out of the coffee machine in the corner. A clump of Africans over here, a cluster of Filipinas there, Russian speakers occupying the center. On one wall was a small barred window, behind which a uniformed woman exchanged Israeli money for the currencies people would need back home.

Chloe picked a path through the luggage to the corner farthest from the door and hunkered down, squatting on her haunches. The room cleared mercifully quickly. One group of ten or twenty names after another was called, and the people moved out with their suitcases, presumably to be searched and get on their flights. Soon enough there were plenty of chairs.

Her name was called after she had fidgeted for an hour and a half. What should she do? Sit still, keep silent, and hope to delay long enough to miss her flight? Or go and argue with the people that she wasn't supposed to be deported yet, and hope that one of the officials was reasonable? When in doubt, do nothing, she decided. She ignored the voices calling her name again and again, and it seemed to work. Another hour passed. Who knew? Maybe she would pass years in this room. There was a guy she had heard about, a Palestinian, who had been living in the Paris airport for five years because no country would accept him.

She heard her name again. Trying to be surreptitious, she glanced up and saw Shaul standing in the doorway with two armed guards, whose uniforms were different from his. He saw her and pointed, and the three of them marched over to her, menace in their gait. Had he driven back to Hadera, then turned around and come back in order to identify her? If so, she was sure it had done nothing to improve his temper. Hadn't she missed whatever flight they were planning to get her on?

The two khaki-clad men with rifles slung over their chests yanked her out of her chair. One twisted her arm crazily behind her back. She gritted her teeth, unwilling to give him the satisfaction of crying out. When they started to walk, she could not resist walking with them; the pain was too intense. She was not cut out for torture. Well, who was? Maybe, if what you had to protect was worth it. Most people who withstood torture, she had heard, did so because they didn't know anything they could use to stop the pain.

They half-carried, half-dragged her out of the building to the El Al terminal, where the contents of her backpack were placed methodically in bins and run through X-ray machines batch by batch. A woman ran a black wand over her clothes, then set up a screen around Chloe and yanked her pants down to her ankles. They separated everything with Arabic writing on it and super X-rayed it again. Chloe wondered, did they imagine that you could hide a bomb in the little pamphlet she had gotten from Addameer about Palestinian prisoners?

Then Shaul was grabbing her arm and trying to make her run.

"Hurry, hurry," he urged. "We don't have time."

"We have plenty of time because I'm not going anywhere," Chloe told him for the fifteenth time.

They carried/dragged her back through the terminal and piled with her into the van. They drove in what seemed like smaller and smaller concentric circles until they were sitting on the tarmac, next to a Continental jet with its engine running. Its light was whirling on top and she could see the coolant discharging to eat away at the ozone layer. A flight attendant stood on the top step, waving to them frantically.

"We have been waiting for you," she said to the police accusingly. "We are late."

"She is a problem," Shaul said briefly.

Chloe called on every reserve of fight and contrariness she had been saving up for the last ten months. She curled into a tight ball on the seat, squirming out of their grasp when they tried to grab her. She rolled off the seat and onto the floor, smacking her head on the floor of the van.

Once they succeeded in hauling her out, she lay on the ground, screaming at the top of her lungs.

"I am being deported illegally," she yelled in the general direction of the chagrined stewardess.

The neatly pressed woman reached up and rubbed her temple. What ever happened to simple problems, like not enough champagne glasses for first class?

"I REFUSE TO GET ON THIS AIRPLANE!" Chloe shouted. "IF I AM FORCED TO, I WILL NOT OBEY ANY OF YOUR RULES. I WILL NOT BUCKLE MY SEAT BELT. I WILL SING LOUDLY DURING THE SAFETY PRESENTATION. I WILL DISABLE THE SMOKE DETECTORS IN THE BATHROOM."

"If you do not shut up," Shaul hissed, "I will sedate you and take you in chains." At least that's what she thought he was saying. She didn't understand the Hebrew words, except for "shut up" and "take you," but his gestures spoke volumes.

She continued screaming. Two of the armed guards went to talk with the flight attendant. Then they were ushered into the plane, presumably to talk to the captain. She saw passengers staring out the window, trying to get a view of whatever the commotion was. She had no idea if they could hear or see her or not. Now someone else was running toward them, from the direction of the terminal, waving his hands. She hoped it was not the vet with a hypodermic.

The man who ran up was wearing fatigues and had a rifle over his shoulder. He came straight to Shaul. "Mah koreh," he demanded. *What's going on?*

Shaul looked surprised, but answered at length, with expansive gestures.

"No, no, no," the man said. "We do not do this."

Was this for real? Was the untimely end to her sojourn here about to be averted by a deus ex machina in enemy's clothing? It looked that way. The man was showing Shaul a sheet of paper, and Shaul was taking out his cellphone.

Rachel's fax! Chloe thought. Avi had come through for her after all. He had called the lawyer and she had sent a fax showing that Chloe's three-day hold was still in effect. She started to breathe a little easier.

Shaul didn't reach whomever he was calling. He disconnected and tried another number. The stewardess kept waving at him, wanting to know what was going on. He made the wait signal with his hand. She pointed at her watch—the flight was very late already, come on, we have to get going. After ten minutes that felt to Chloe like ten hours, Shaul gave a bye-bye wave, and the doors of the jet slowly slid shut. Not until the wheels started to move back did Chloe's heart stop playing the *William Tell Overture*. She was suddenly exhausted. She could fall asleep right here on the tarmac. She supposed she would be going back to Hadera tonight. If so, it would be hours before she got to a bed.

Shaul was arguing with the soldier. Whatever the argument was about, Shaul lost. The olive-garbed man came over to where she sat and stretched out a hand to help her up.

"Come with me," he said in a pleasant but commanding tone. "I have a few questions to ask you."

"What kind of questions?" she asked, suddenly wary. She was in no mood to answer any questions.

"Don't worry, they won't be difficult questions. Just a formality," he said.

"Fifteen minutes," he said to Shaul over his shoulder as he led her away. They walked past the van in which Shaul had driven her here, past several other planes waiting for clearance to take off. The man did not keep his hand on her. He didn't seem worried that she would run away, but indeed, where would she go?

"Who are you?" she asked him.

"I'm the army."

Thanks for nothing. "Well yes, I can see that, but what are you doing here? I mean, the army doesn't usually get involved in deportation cases, right?"

"This is a special case."

Fear tugged at the edges of her brain. To whom was her case special? Wilensky? Gelenter? But why would either of them want to stop her from being put on the plane? Presumably, it was one of them who had arranged this eleventh hour flight in the first place.

"What's your name?" she asked.

"Adam," he answered.

He walked her all the way around the terminal, to the front of the line of cars dropping off passengers, and helped her into the front seat of a dark blue sedan. That seemed odd too; army guys usually came in jeeps. She figured it wouldn't do any good to ask about the car, so she did as she was told. He drove fast, following the signs pointing to "Exit Airport". While he drove, she memorized his face, for whatever good it might do her if there was something to complain about later. He looked to be about forty-five, stocky and muscular. Although it was pitch dark out, he wore shades. He was also wearing a crocheted kippa over his thinning hair. His most distinguishing feature was a nose that closely resembled a squashed potato.

"Where are we going?" she shouted over the radio and the noise of the engine.

"My office," he shouted back.

"Is it far?"

"No, very near."

Just before the exit to the terminal, he hooked a sharp right. Now they were on some kind of private access road. Adam opened a gate with a magnetic card and pulled to a stop in front of a long, low building made of olive-colored prefab slabs. It was surrounded by short brown grass, and behind it she could see a chain link fence sporting white signs with red hands, the danger sign, every few feet.

Adam was examining his keys, hunting for the right one. The metal door had three locks, a deadbolt, a regular door lock, and a padlock. Whatever this building was, it couldn't be used that much. It certainly wasn't Adam's office, because he wasn't sure which keys to use. He tried one in the padlock, but it didn't budge. He attacked the deadbolt next, and coaxed it open. It didn't sound like it had been opened in a long time. He finally found the right keys, and the door swung open. Adam indicated that Chloe should precede him inside.

Her eyes could make out nothing at first. The building was one long room, nearly empty, with walls made of concrete. It looked like a warehouse of some kind. It had no windows, just a tiny slatted opening near the ceiling. Adam didn't turn on any lights, if there were any to turn on. Instead, he walked halfway across the cement floor and came back dragging something beside him. He set two chairs down facing one another.

"Sit," he said.

Not a gracious invitation, but she took it. The sooner she did, the sooner she would find out what this was all about, and the sooner she would get back to—well, where? Somewhere she wanted to be, which included Hadera at this point.

He took the gun off his chest and sat down opposite her. He gave her a smile, which didn't reach his watery eyes. "All right, Chloe," he said in a tired voice. "Who has the document?"

She went cold all over. "What document?"

"Do not play games with me." Icicles would not have melted in his mouth.

"How do you know about that? Who are you, anyway?"

"Do you need to ask?"

"It's you!" she breathed. How could she have been so stupid? She had just been so relieved not to be on the plane. Adam, he had called himself. The generic Hebrew word for "man." She squinted across at him, trying to make out his face in the darkness.

"But you're in Italy," she said.

"I was in Italy. Now I am here."

"How did you get here so fast?"

"Wonderful things, airplanes. Now where is the document?"

"I don't know—there isn't one."

Wait, that wasn't right. He needed to believe there was a document. He would have killed her already, except he wanted to know who had it. If she could keep him believing she knew, maybe he would leave her alive, but for how long? Not long enough for anyone to find her here. Not long enough to escape. If he left her alive in here and locked the door, she would starve to death unless he let her out. This wasn't Hollywood, where the heroes always found a way out of every iron trap. In real life, the odds were against you when you were up against someone like this, who had killed with impunity for years. She needed to distract him, give herself time to think.

"So what's in the document?" she asked.

"That is none of your concern."

"Maybe not, but what would it hurt you to satisfy my curiosity? You're going to kill me anyway."

He pushed his head toward her and the whites of his eyes swelled, glowing in the darkness. "You think I am going to kill you?"

"Aren't you?"

"Chlooooeeeee, Chloooooeeeee. How can you say this about me? I am not a killer."

It was her turn to gape at him. The man was both a professional killer and an amateur. Slowly, it dawned on her what he meant. Sure, he had killed Palestinians, an Uzbek prostitute, but these were not people. She was another story. As despicable as she was, as big a threat to his reputation, she was a Jew.

"If you're not planning to kill me, why did you bring me here?"

"I brought you here so we could talk undisturbed."

He looped the gun over his shoulder once more and stood up. He crossed to her chair, and reached out a hand. She screamed. She wasn't sure where the pain had come from, but her entire body rattled with it. She thought about what Avi had reported from his conversation with Dmitri. One of the men was a little kinky, but the other was called the Butcher.

He had returned to his seat and was contemplating her with faint amusement around his lips. He enjoyed hurting people, that was clear. That tiny encounter had been an espresso bean for his libido. He wasn't going to get any more out of her. She would make him shoot her before she would be his play toy.

"Are you ready to tell me who has the document?" he asked placidly. Like he had all night, which presumably he did.

Who could she name? Not Fareed, not Malkah. Avi? Would he believe that? But if Avi was on his side, he wouldn't care.

"Dmitri," she said at last. He leaned toward her, as if he found what she said fascinating. She sat on her hands, to keep them from shaking.

"Dmitri who sold Nadya to us?" She nodded. "You lie. He told me he did not take it from her." Wilensky was moving toward her again. She bolted for the door. A shot nearly burst her eardrums. The bullet flew past her shoulder and smashed against the concrete wall. She whirled.

"You said you wouldn't kill me."

"Bullets can do a lot of things besides kill."

She didn't doubt it. What was she going to do? She couldn't leave, and she couldn't stay.

"I lied," she said finally. "There's no copy. At least not that I know of."

"Why did you tell me there is a copy?"

Why indeed? It had seemed like a good move in a theoretical chess game.

"To see what you would do, to find out if you really killed her."

"That was clever," he said, lifting the gun and aiming it straight at her. Her knees were foam rubber. Her face was a thousand degrees. She thought she was having a stroke.

"Khara!" echoed from outside. *Shit*. A stream of Arabic curses followed. Wilensky swung toward the sound, away from Chloe. She took steps toward the door, then stopped. She was pretty sure who was out there, but if she made it to them, Wilensky might kill them all.

Someone was shaking the door now. "It's locked," Avi said in English.

"Get back," a woman's voice responded. Chloe was between Wilensky and the door. She turned to face him. His gun was pointed directly at her, and at whoever was about to come through the door.

"We might as well let them in," she said conversationally.

He hesitated. Before he could move one way or the other, the deadbolt exploded and the door swung open wide. Chloe almost didn't recognize the settler woman in the peasant blouse with the gun in her hand.

Chapter 45

Rania was looking directly into the barrel of the machine gun. Wilensky's finger was on the trigger and he would have pulled it, but he stopped short when he saw who was with her.

"Avi, what is going on?"

"That's what I was going to ask you." Avi said.

He moved slowly but deliberately, coming to stand right next to Chloe. Rania remained a little bit behind them, her gun pointed down at the floor.

"Who is that?" Wilensky demanded, pointing at her with his chin.

"No one you need to worry about," Avi answered.

"You should not be here," Wilensky said to Avi. "You don't know what you are dealing with."

"I know enough," Avi said, maintaining direct eye contact. He moved to stand in front of Chloe, blocking her with his body. His chest was less than a foot from the barrel of the gun.

"Go ahead," he said. "Kill me, like you killed Nadya."

This kid had guts, Rania had to concede. She had never thought she would see an Israeli show that kind of courage, to stand unarmed facing a loaded gun. They were so used to having weapons at their disposal.

The gesture moved Wilensky too. Incongruously, his cheek muscles slackened, his eyes softened. He relaxed his death grip on the weapon, let it fall to his side.

"I couldn't kill you, Avi," he said. "You're like my own son. Besides, it doesn't matter if you accuse me of killing Nadya. No one will believe you."

"They'll believe me," Nir Gelenter said.

None of them had heard the car, but when Rania looked outside the dim hangar, there it was, next to Avi's.

"Shaul Gabi called and said Chloe didn't get on the plane," Nir said to Wilensky. "He said a colonel came and stopped her flight."

"I never thought I'd be glad to see him," Chloe whispered to Rania.

"Are you sure he's here to help?" Rania cautioned.

The two men were focused on each other now, completely ignoring the rest of them. The other three moved back, until they were nearly in the doorway.

"How did you know where to find me?" Chloe whispered to Rania.

"We found that captain, Shaul, and he told us an air force colonel took you away. Avi said he knew where you would be. He came here as a child, with his father and his uncle."

"How could you do it, Israel?" Nir was asking Wilensky.

"She said someone had a copy of the letter," Wilensky explained, gesturing toward Chloe. "I needed to find out…"

"I meant Nadya," Gelenter clarified. "How could you kill her? I loved her!"

"She didn't love you," Wilensky said. "She betrayed you."

"I know," Gelenter said. Rania almost felt sympathy for him. "You told me you were going to pay her."

"I did pay her," Wilensky said. "But she would not give me the paper."

They were speaking in Hebrew. Avi translated in a soft voice for Chloe and Rania.

"He says he didn't mean to kill her. The day before he left for Italy, she told him she had something that would destroy him. She said if he didn't give her ten thousand dollars, she would go to the police. He told her to forget it. But then after he was gone, he thought about it and decided the risk was too great. He called her at the house and said he would pay. But she said it was too late, she was selling it to someone else. She said, 'Tomorrow I destroy your life.' So he came back to stop her. He knew she met Fareed in the fields; he had followed her there once. He waited there for her. He saw her talking to Dmitri, and then he saw Dmitri walking away. He intercepted him and demanded the document. Dmitri said he didn't buy it, her price was too high.

"He went after Nadya. They sat in his car and argued. He demanded she give him the document, but she wouldn't. He tried to grab her bag from her, and she ran from the car. They struggled, and she fell down the embankment and hit her head on a rock."

Nir was wavering, Rania could tell. He wanted to believe it.

"Why did you steal the car?" Rania stepped out of the shadows. She could see Gelenter's steely eyes glinting in the dark.

"What are you doing here?" he asked through clenched teeth.

"Trying to learn the truth," she said. "And what you just heard is not the truth."

"How do you know?"

"We found fragments of Nadya's clothes scattered over the land in a lateral pattern. There was blood on the grass from her head wound, but no rock with blood on it. Someone dragged her along the creek bed."

"We already know that the Palestinian kid moved her," Gelenter objected.

How had he gotten access to the kid's confession? How could she imagine that he wouldn't have? It wasn't that important, but it galled her.

"If you know that much, you know that he didn't drag her, he carried her."

"So he says."

"The physical evidence confirmed it." She turned back to Wilensky. "If you paid her, what happened to the money? She had no money when we found her."

"So the Palestinian kid took it."

Once again, Fareed was proving a convenient scapegoat. "If she had fallen down the embankment, she would have dropped her bag and it would not have been next to her when Fareed found her. I think she ran away, and you followed her, because you could not allow her to live with what she knew."

"No. It wasn't that way. It happened just as I said."

"Did it?" she turned to Gelenter. "Think about my question. If he did not plan to kill her, why did he go in a stolen car, instead of his own?"

Logic, she could see, told him she was right. Everything he believed told him not to take the word of a Palestinian woman over his oldest friend's.

"Nir," Wilensky said.

Gelenter cut him off with a wave of his hand. He turned away from them all, wrestling with his own demons for a long few minutes. When he turned back, he was in command again.

"Avi," he said, "You cannot tell anyone about this."

"Fareed is my friend," Avi said. "I won't let him sit in jail for a crime he didn't commit."

"You don't know all the facts," Gelenter insisted. "Tell him," to Wilensky.

"Tell me what? What are you talking about?"

Chloe and Rania glanced at each other.

"How do you think I got back into Israel and back to Italy, with no one knowing?" Wilensky asked Avi.

Confusion played on the young man's face. "I don't understand what you're trying to say," he said. His eyes scanned one face, then another, finally locking on Rania's.

"It was your father," she said. "He took a plane from Hatzerim."

"My father?" He looked around for confirmation from the others, and received it.

"You knew too?" he asked Chloe.

"She told me."

"Why didn't you tell me?"

"We weren't sure you didn't know."

He sank to the floor, sitting cross-legged, head in his hands. Chloe stooped next to him, awkwardly patting his shoulder.

"We just didn't know what to think," she said softly. "This country, it screws with your mind."

"Yeah, well, unfortunately it's my country." He sat a few minutes longer, his fingers making designs in the dust.

"My father didn't know what you were going to do," he said weakly.

"Who can be sure?" Gelenter asked. "In your father's line of work, a person must be completely free from scandal. Don't you think this might cause difficulties for him?"

For a long moment, no one and nothing in the old hangar stirred. Rania thought she could hear blades of grass blowing in the breeze outside.

"What about Fareed?" Avi said.

"If I get him out, will you let this go?" Gelenter asked.

"You will get him out?"

"I promise."

Rania exhaled. She was disappointed, but she shouldn't have been. People were who they were. In his place, she would probably have done the same. Gelenter seemed relaxed now that he had Avi's agreement. He wasn't worried about her or Chloe at all, Rania thought. It was like they didn't even count. But of course, in his world, they didn't.

She and Chloe headed for the door and no one stopped them. Avi followed, saying nothing to the two men who were huddled together, Gelenter with one arm across his friend's shoulder. They climbed back over the fence where she had cut her hand on the razor wire in the rush to save Chloe. It took them ten minutes to walk to the place where Avi had stashed his parents' car. An hour earlier, they had run the distance in under half the time.

Avi wanted to go through Deir Balut checkpoint, or Azzun gate, to take her all the way to Mas'ha. She insisted he drop her on the road.

"The checkpoints are closed," she said.

"Not for a yellow-plated car," he objected.

"I don't want anyone asking where I've been."

"Give me the gun," he said as he stopped the car above Azzawiya bridge.

"Why? It was my husband's."

"Because soldiers are going to be searching your house for it sometime soon. It can't be there when they do."

She handed him the gun. And thanked him, though it rankled to do it. Then she ran down the embankment, praying she could find the place where she had left her clothes. She wasn't looking forward to explaining to Bassam how her trip to the store had worked out.

Chapter 46

The smell of fried cauliflower and fresh bread greeted Chloe before she reached Ahlam's door. She could hear lots of happy chatter inside.

It was a double party—Fareed's homecoming and Chloe's leaving. Rachel, the lawyer, had been able to recover her passport, but she had to agree that Chloe would leave Israel within ten days. The good news was that supposedly the Ministry of Interior would not stop her from returning at another time. Rachel didn't know how good her chances actually were of getting in again, but she emphasized that they would be much better if Chloe left now as agreed.

The living room was full of children and young men, Fareed's friends from school. Chloe studied Fareed's face. He had already started to lose his prison pallor and gained back a little of the weight he had lost. He looked older, too. He was telling prison stories now, surrounded by his friends and younger brothers. Avi sat next to him, listening, not saying anything. Everything seemed normal again, but Chloe suspected there would never be quite the same easy trust between them. Well, nothing would ever be quite the same for Fareed. He had been through a rite of passage.

Avi would be spending more time in the village in the coming days, so they would have plenty of time to work out their relationship. The injunction against the construction on Abu Shaadi's land had been lifted. Avi had met with Jaber and Abu Shaadi and the mayor that afternoon to plan strategy. Fareed had gone too. Before his arrest, he had not had much interest in activism; he had been too busy with school. The Israeli authorities had created one more radical, Chloe reflected.

Alaa ran to Chloe to be swept up in a hug.

"Imi fi matbach," the little girl said, and obediently, Chloe followed her into the kitchen. Ahlam kissed her twice on each cheek, murmuring "Hamdilila assalam."

"Allah ysalmik," Chloe gave the ritual response, her eyes drifting to the figure peeling cucumbers at the sink. She didn't think she could stay in here. She wanted to wrap her arms around those slender hips and plunge her hands places that she couldn't see. If she was going to kiss Tina, she didn't want it to be on the cheeks. She hoped her face didn't show her "flustration," but she wouldn't have wanted to take bets.

She put a soft hand on Tina's shoulder. Even that little contact made her crazy. "I'm going outside for a while."

She made her way back through the mob and stood on the porch, breathing hard. Shit, she needed to stop acting like a horny teenager. She needed to stop *feeling* like a horny teenager. How was this happening to her, and could the timing be any worse? Hopefully she would stop being obsessed with Tina when she was back in the States. Otherwise, she was going to be buying a lot of batteries for her vibrator.

"Chloe!" Dilal, the grocer, was walking toward the house with a young girl. The girl was strangely dressed, in a long denim skirt and a long-sleeved turtleneck. As they got nearer, Chloe realized it was Malkah. She walked out into the road to intercept them.

"Shuftha fi tariq," Dilal explained. *I saw her on the road.*

"Shukran," she thanked Dilal and quickly ushered the girl up to her apartment.

"Malkah, it's nice to see you, but you should have called first."

"I brought your phone." Of course. Gelenter's phone had been taken from Chloe at the airport. She had gotten a new one, but Malkah didn't know the number. Malkah produced Chloe's old phone from her pocket and held it out.

"Thank you," she told the girl. "Why don't you keep it? I have a new one now."

"Really?"

"Sure. You don't have to tell your dad. It can be our secret."

"Will you give me your new phone number?" Malkah was already pressing the button to add a contact to her address book.

"Um, Malkah, I have to go back to the States for a while. But I tell you what. When I get home, I'll send you a text message, and then you can text me back sometimes. Okay?"

Beaming, Malkah carefully put the phone into the front pocket of her backpack.

"Is that the reason you came?" Chloe asked her. "It was really nice of you, but you know, it's not so safe for someone who looks like a settler to just walk into a village, with no one knowing they are coming."

She swallowed her feelings of disloyalty. Malkah was thirteen and on a learning curve—not so different from her own a few years back. The girl wasn't quite ready to understand that international law guarantees the right to resist occupation by force of arms. She did need to understand that the daughter of a high Israeli military official could not go walking into Palestinian villages on her own. She would be perfectly safe in Jaber's house, but on the street, someone might see an opportunity.

"I know," Malkah said, "but I needed to see you. Since I met you in Tel Aviv, my father watches me all the time. The only place he won't find me is a Palestinian place."

"You must have something very important to tell me," Chloe said.

Malkah opened her backpack and pulled out an envelope.

"After I told Nadya what the letter said, she used my father's fax machine to make a copy," she said. "She asked me to keep for her."

Chloe pulled out the letter. "It's in Hebrew," she stated the obvious. She had forgotten that she, like Nadya, wouldn't be able to read it.

"It is from a soldier named Yuri Shabtai," Malkah told her. "It says, 'I cannot live with what I did. I killed Arabs in… Jenaan'?" She looked at Chloe for confirmation.

"Jenin," Chloe corrected. "Killed them how?"

"'I killed women and children, not terrorists,'" Malkah translated. "'I did it on Colonel Wilensky's orders. Then I lied to the Knesset and said the Arabs shot the women and babies.'"

Malkah's voice was wobbly. Chloe thought maybe it would be good for her to cry, but she didn't want her to be embarrassed.

"Thank you, Malkah. It was right for you to give me this. Is there something else?" she asked. Malkah still seemed close to tears.

"If Nadya died because of this letter," Malkah struggled, "my father must have killed her because Uncle Israel was in Italy."

Chloe mentally smacked herself. She'd forgotten what it was like to be a thirteen-year-old girl.

"Malkah," she said. "Your father did not kill Nadya."

"You know that for sure?"

"I'm absolutely positive." The girl's face broke into a happy, toothy smile. Chloe put an arm around her shoulder.

"Chloe?" Someone was banging on her door. She opened it to Tina and Rania.

"Dinner's ready," Tina said. "Everyone's waiting for you."

"Tina, this is my friend Malkah. Malkah, Tina's phone number is in my phone, and if you need something sometime, something important, you can call her. Right?"

Tina didn't look too happy. An Israeli settler girl wasn't her idea of a suitable protégée. But Chloe was confident that when Tina learned what Malkah had done, she would be happy to be her friend. As it was, she was too polite to hurt a kid's feelings.

"Of course," she answered.

"Hello, Malkah. It's nice to see you." Rania held out a hand for Malkah to shake.

"We'd better find Malkah some transportation," Chloe said.

Avi drove Malkah home in his parents' car, and returned just in time to drive Chloe to the airport. Rania walked to the car with her and Tina. Rania's handsome, serious husband watched from the porch while their son ran constantly back and forth from one to the other. Chloe tried to gauge if Rania understood her relationship to Tina, and if so, what she thought about it.

"I wish I could have gotten to know you better," Chloe said.

"Inshalla, when you return," Rania said. She kissed Chloe twice on each cheek. The one extra kiss meant they were really friends, Chloe decided.

✶ ✶ ✶

Rania entered the police station and headed straight for the coffee pot. Cup in hand, she strolled to her desk. Abdelhakim's chair was empty, his desk devoid of any traces of occupancy.

"Where is Abdelhakim?" she asked the men who sat nearby.

"Don't know," one answered.

"Haven't seen him today," said the other.

Captain Mustafa emerged from his office and joined them. "I suggested to Abu Ziyad that Abdelhakim might be happier working in his office," he said.

She tried not to look too happy. She could gloat later, at home with Bassam. The captain handed her a manila envelope.

"Benny asked me to give you this."

She waited for him to walk away before she opened it. She withdrew a folded sheet of paper containing two newspaper clippings. "Thought you would be interested," the note read.

The first article was several columns long, from the English edition of the left-wing Israeli newspaper *Haaretz*. It said that an anonymous source had uncovered a letter written by the soldier, Yuri Shabtai, before he committed suicide in April, 2003. The letter, the article continued, charged that Col. Israel Wilensky (ret.) of the air force had ordered his unit to fire on unarmed civilians during the Battle of Jenin. Wilensky denied the allegations.

"These are very serious charges. The Ministry of Defense will investigate them thoroughly," said Deputy Minister Nir Gelenter.

The other clipping was barely one inch high, cut from a bottom corner of the *Jerusalem Post*.

The murder of Uzbek national Nadya Kim remains unsolved, three weeks after her body was discovered in an abandoned olive grove near Elkana. According to police spokesman Benny Lazar, there are no suspects and no clues as to why the young woman was killed. "Kim was one of thousands of Uzbek and Moldovan women who fall prey to criminal consortiums in their home countries which bring women to Israel against their will," said Lazar. Israel's immigration police have vowed to increase their efforts to locate and repatriate trafficked women.

Glossary

Abbreviations:
Ar. = Arabic
Heb. = Hebrew
fem. = feminine   m. = masculine

ajnabiya *(Ar.)* foreigner (fem.)

Al Jazeera Arabic television network based in Qatar

Aleikum Salaam *(Ar.)* Peace to you all (said in greeting).

Allah maakum *(Ar.)* God be with you all (said in parting).

Allah yirhamha *(Ar.)* God's mercy on her (said when a woman has died).

Allah ysalmak (ysalmik *fem.*) *(Ar.)* response to "Hamdililah asalaam"

allo *(Heb., Ar.)* hello

Ana maak *(Ar.)* I am with you (m.)

Ana mush kanghara *(Ar.)* I'm not a kangaroo.

anachnu *(Heb.)* we

Anglit *(Heb.)* English

Aravim Hachutzah *(Heb.)* Arabs get out!

argila/nargila *(Ar./Heb.)* flavored tobacco

Artzot Habrit *(Heb.)* United States

Asfi *(Ar.)* I'm sorry.

Assalaamu aleikum. *(Ar.)* Peace be unto you. (Arabic greeting)

323

at *(Heb.)* you (fem.)

At makirah otam? *(Heb.)* Do you know them?

At po? *(Heb.)* Are you here? (fem.)

At yeshenah? *(Heb.)* Are you sleeping? (fem.)

Atah kevar yodea et zeh. *(Heb.)* You already know this.

Atah tamut hayom. *(Heb.)* You are going to die today.

Atini shantatik *(Ar.)* Give me your handbag.

Atzri *(Heb.)* Stop! (to a woman)

ayfo *(Heb.)* where

ba'id *(Ar.)* far

babayit *(Heb.)* at home; in the house

bachutz *(Heb.)* outside

baladiya *(Ar.)* city hall

banot *(Heb.)* girls

baregel *(Heb.)* on foot

barra *(Ar.)* outside

beemet *(Heb.)* really; in truth

beit hawwiya *(Ar.)* ID card container

belagan *(Heb.)* mess

boi *(Heb.)* come (to a woman)

Boker tov *(Heb.)* Good morning.

bseder *(Heb.)* okay; fine

Btihki Arabi *(Ar.)* Do you speak Arabic?

Btselem Israeli human rights organization

caffe shachor *(Heb.)* black coffee

chaverim *(Heb.)* friends

chayalim *(Heb.)* soldiers

Chiif halach *(Ar.)* How are you? (rural form of "Kiif halak")

da *(Russian)* Yes

debka Palestinian dance

Diiri baalik a la haalik *(Ar.)* Take care of yourself.

Diiri baalik, fii jesh honak. *(Ar.)* Be careful, the Army is there.

deportatsia *(Heb.)* deportation

doorna *(Ar.)* our role

Efshar l'kanes *(Heb.)* May I come in?

eid *(Ar.)* holiday

Ein b'ayah. *(Heb.)* No problem.

Ein b'ayot? *(Heb.)* There are no problems?

eser dakot *(Heb.)* ten minutes

etzim *(Heb.)* trees

Falastinait *(Heb.)* Palestinian (fem.)

fii *(Ar.)* there is ...

fok *(Ar.)* up; upstairs

haAmerikayit *(Heb.)* the American

Haaretz an Israeli newspaper

habibi/habibti *(Ar.)* my dear

hachaverah shel ... *(Heb.)* the friend of ...

haajes *(Ar.)* roadblock

Hai mushkele kbiire. *(Ar.)* This is a big problem.

haj/haji *(Ar.)* An elder; one who has made pilgrimage to Mecca.

Hakol bseder? *(Heb.)* Is everything all right?

hamdilila assalam *(Ar.)* Good wish for a person who has returned from a journey, recovered from an illness, or been released from prison (response: "Alla ysalmak/ysalmik").

hamdililah *(Ar.)* Thank God (response to "Kiif halak?")

hamel *(Ar.)* pregnant (literally, carrying)

haram *(Ar.)* shame

hawiyya *(Ar.)* ID card

he *(Heb.)* she

hijab headscarf worn by many Muslim women

Hinei hu *(Heb.)* Here he is.

hitnachlut *(Heb.)* colony; settlement

hon *(Ar.)* here

Hu lo po. *(Heb.)* He is not here.

Huwwa hon. *(Ar.)* He is here.

Il banat ajau. *(Ar.)* The girls have arrived.

imi *(Ar.)* my mother

Imi fi matbach. *(Ar.)* My mother is in the kitchen.

Inglizi *(Ar.)* English

Inshalla *(Ar.)* God willing; hopefully.

Inta qawi. *(Ar.)* You are strong.

irhabi *(Ar.)* terrorist

Jamiyat Ittadamon Iddawliya fi Falastin International Organization in Solidarity with Palestine (fictional group)

jasoosia *(Ar.)* traitor

jesh *(Ar.)* army

Jesh bifattash ala Fareed. *(Ar.)* The army is looking for Fareed.

jilbab traditional long coat worn by many Palestinian women

Kadima *(Heb.)* Let's go; come on.

ken *(Heb.)* yes

ketubah Jewish marriage contract

Khaife min jesh *(Ar.)* I'm afraid of the Army.

khalas *(Ar.)* enough; stop

khara *(Ar.)* shit

Kiif halik?/Kiif halak? *(Ar.)* How are you?

kippa headcovering worn by Jewish men (Yiddish: yamulke)

Kol hakavod *(Heb.)* Good for you.

Kul ishi tamam hon? *(Ar.)* Is everything okay here?

kum *(Heb.)* get up

L'an *(Heb.)* Where to?

L'hitraot *(Heb.)* See you later.

laa *(Ar.)* no

labneh *(Ar.)* cheese made from yogurt

lo *(Heb.)* no

lo po *(Heb.)* not here

maalesh *(Ar.)* never mind

Maamoul Date cookie

Maayfo atem *(Heb.)* Where are you all from?

mafraq *(Ar.)* crossroads

mah *(Heb.)* what

Mah at rotzah? *(Heb.)* What do you want? (fem.)

Mah he omeret *(Heb.)* What is she saying?

Mah kara/mah koreh? *(Heb.)* What happened?/What's going on?

Mah zeh *(Heb.)* What is this?

majnoon *(Ar.)* crazy

mMakluube Palestinian dish made from rice, vegetables, nuts, and normally chicken

marhaba Arabic greeting

marhabteen Arabic greeting in response to *marhaba* (literally "two marhabas")

masa il warad *(Ar.)* evening of flowers (possible response to "masa il-kheir")

masa il-kheir *(Ar.)* good evening (literally "evening of joy")

matai *(Heb.)* when?

mawjood *(Ar.)* present; here

Mi at? *(Heb.)* Who are you?

Mi zot? *(Heb.)* Who is this? (fem.)

Miin inti? *(Ar.)* Who are you?

miit shekel *(Ar.)* one hundred shekels (shekel = Israeli currency, also used in the Occupied Territories)

Min Azzawiya, inta? *(Ar.)* You are from Azzawiya?

mish shughlik *(Ar.)* not your business

Mishehu rotzeh hachutza? *(Heb.)* Does anyone want to go outside?

mishmar hagvul *(Heb.)* border police

mishtara *(Heb.)* police

mitnachlim *(Heb.)* settlers; colonists

mjaddara Palestinian dish made from lentils and rice

mlochia Egyptian spinach, usually used to make a creamy soup

muhabarat *(Ar.)* secret police (normally referring to Palestinian secret police)

mumkin *(Ar.)* possible; perhaps

Mush khaif *(Ar.)* Don't be afraid.

mush mawjood *(Ar.)* not here

mush tawbaane *(Ar.)* not tired

mustahil *(Ar.)* impossible

Njarrab bil Arabi. *(Ar.)* We'll try to speak Arabic.

nos hilwe *(Ar.)* half sweet (in ref. to coffee)

Nsiyah tovah. *(Heb.)* Have a good trip.

Pelephone *(Heb.)* mobile phone

politsia *(Russian)* police

Qaddesh? *(Ar.)* How much?

ruhi *(Ar.)* Go (command) (fem.)

Sabah al-kheir, ya banat. *(Ar.)* Good morning, girls. (literally, "morning of joy")

Sabah an-noor. *(Ar.)* Morning of light. (response to "sabah al-kheir")

sayara *(Ar.)* car

schvitz *(Yiddish)* sweat, be sweltering

schwei *(Ar.)* a little

sea *(Ar.)* one hour

sea w nos *(Ar.)* an hour and a half

seateen *(Ar.)* two hours

shabab *(Ar.)* young men

shalom *(Heb.)* hello; peace

sheesha flavored tobacco; also knows as *argila* (*Heb. nargila*)

sherut *(Heb.)* shared taxi

shetach sagur *(Heb.)* closed zone

shnia *(Heb.)* second

shorta *(Ar.)* police

shu *(Ar.)* what

Shu biddo? *(Ar.)* What does he want?

Shu bisir? *(Ar.)* What is happening?

Shu sar? *(Ar.)* What happened?

Shuftha fi tariq. *(Ar.)* I saw her on the road.

shukran *(Ar.)* thank you

Sinit *(Heb.)* Chinese

skol Russian toast

Sobbi shai. *(Ar.)* Pour the tea.

souq *(Ar.)* market (*Heb.* shook)

taboun *(Ar.)* clay oven built into the earth for baking bread

taht *(Ar.)* down; downstairs

tamam *(Ar.)* okay

Tanach Jewish religious book comprising the Torah, Prophets, and Writings

Tawjihi Exams taken by Palestinian youth after high school; a full year of study is required and college acceptance is based on it

tayeret *(Heb.)* tourist

teudot *(Heb.)* identification

tfaddali *(Ar.)* Welcome; please join us.

tik alaafia *(Ar.)* A version of "Allah ya tik alafia," God grant you health, said to one who is working

tishvi *(Heb.)* sit down (to a woman)

todah *(Heb.)* thank you

todah rabah *(Heb.)* thank you very much

tov *(Heb.)* good

tsilum *(Heb.)* copy

ulpan an Israeli school for intensive Hebrew instruction

ulpena an Israeli religious girls' high school

Um aysh? *(Ar.)* Mother of whom? (a way of asking a woman how she wants to be addressed)

usquti *(Ar.)* shut up

w ideek(i) *(Ar.)* response to "yslamu ideek"

wahad *(Ar.)* someone

Wallah! *(Ar.)* Oh my God!

walla kilme *(Ar.)* not a word

walla wahad *(Ar.)* no one

Weyn rayha? *(Ar.)* Where are you going? (fem.)

ya *(Ar.)* often used for emphasis, as in "ya haram," or an indication of friendship, as in "ya shabab."

Yahud *(Ar.)* Jews (usually meaning Israelis)

Yahudia *(Ar.)* Jew (fem.)

yalla *(Ar.)* let's go; come on

yesh *(Heb.)* there is

Yesh Gvul Israeli war resisters' organization (There Is a Limit)

yesh la *(Heb.)* she has

yishuv *(Heb.)* settlement; community

Yslamu ideek(i). *(Ar.)* Bless your hands (said to someone who serves you something).

zaatar wild thyme grown in Palestine, a condiment usually dried with sesame seeds

zaki *(Ar.)* delicious

zeh *(Heb.)* this

zonah *(Heb.)* whore

zuruf *(Ar.)* circumstances

Acknowledgments

This is a work of fiction. It is the product of my imagination and experience—the experience and imagination of a white, Jewish American who spent around eighteen months in Palestine, with brief forays into Israel. It is not a book that a Palestinian or an Israeli would write. During my time in Palestine, I was privileged to get to know many impressive and caring people. They took me, and other international visitors, into their homes, shared their food, warmth, space, and lives with us, asking only one thing in return: that we go home and tell the world their stories. Bits and pieces of those stories have found their way into this book in some form, but no Palestinian character is based in whole or in part on any real person. A few people to whom I owe particular thanks are Intisar, Hanan, Fatima, Shams, Mayisa, Um Rabia, Abu Rabia, Issa, Iltezam, Abu Ahmed, Um Ahmed, Fareed, Riziq, Tayseer, Abed, Fares, Naima, Um Fadi, Munira, Asia and Amal.

I am deeply grateful to Naomi Azriel and Jonathan Pollack for their stories about growing up in Israel and help with geography and Hebrew, as well as their thoughtful reading.

So many people read and gave feedback on all or parts of this book over so many years, I will never be able to remember and thank them all. It takes a village, or several, to produce a book. I could not have gotten through this process without the support of Arla Ertz, Arlene Eisen, Blue Murov, Chaya Gordon, Daniel Ward, Deeg Gold, Deni Asnis, Dmitri Iglitzin, Elaine Beale, Erica Marcus, Erica Raphael, Hannah Mermelstein, Huwaida Arraf, Janet Reid, Jean Tepperman, Jen Angel, Judy Betts, Judith Mirkinson, Julie Starobin, Laura Petracek, Laurie Van Gelder, Lloyda French, Lisa Manning, Lorrie Sheets, Michelle Byrd, Nancy Ferreyra, Radhika Sainath, Ralowe Ti Ampu, Sasha Wright, Steve Masover, Steve Susoyev, Ted Nace, and Tory

Becker. Thanks also to the members of Virtual Muse for their helpful critiques and endless efforts to demystify the changing worlds of authorship and publishing. Dunya Alwan always reminds me of the power of art.

I could not have had a better editor/coach than Elana Dykewomon, who is also a role model and inspiration. Finally, thanks to Mary DeDanan for her painstaking copy edit, mapmaker Mike Morgenfeld, Lorna Garano Publicity, and to Brooke Warner and the team at SheWrites for believing in this book and bringing it to birth.

About the Author

Kate Raphael is a San Francisco Bay Area writer, activist, journalist, and clerical worker. She spent eighteen months as a peace worker in Palestine and spent six weeks in Israeli immigration prison because of her activism. She has won a residency at Hedgebrook writer's colony and was once elected grand marshal of the San Francisco LGBT Freedom Day Parade. She produces a weekly feminist radio show that is heard throughout Northern and Central California.

SELECTED TITLES FROM SHE WRITES PRESS

She Writes Press is an independent publishing company
founded to serve women writers everywhere.
Visit us at www.shewritespress.com.

Watchdogs by Patricia Watts
$16.95, 978-1-938314-34-6
When journalist Julia Wilkes returns to the town where her career got its
start, she is forced to face some old ghosts—and some new enemies.

In the Shadow of Lies: An Oliver Wright Mystery Novel by M. A. Adler
$16.95, 978-1-938314-82-7
As World War II comes to a close, homicide detective Oliver Wright returns
home—only to find himself caught up in the investigation of a complicated
murder case rife with racial tensions.

Faint Promise of Rain by Anjali Mitter Duva
$16.95, 978-1-938314-97-1
Adhira, a young girl born to a family of Hindu temple dancers, is raised to
be dutiful—but ultimately, as the world around her changes, it is her own
bold choice that will determine the fate of her family and of their tradition.

Fire & Water by Betsy Graziani Fasbinder
$16.95, 978-1-938314-14-8
Kate Murphy has always played by the rules—but when she meets charis-
matic artist Jake Bloom, she's forced to navigate the treacherous territory of
passionate love, friendship, and family devotion.

Clear Lake by Nan Fink Gefen
$16.95, 978-1-938314-40-7
When psychotherapist Rebecca Lev's father dies under suspicious circumstances, she becomes obsessed with discovering what happened to him.

Trinity Stones by LG O'Connor
$18.95, 978-1-938314-84-1
On her 27th birthday, New York investment banker Cara Collins learns that
she is one of twelve chosen ones prophesied to lead a final battle between the
forces of good and evil.